"THERE CA[N]
ANYTHING OUT THERE!"

"But there is, Laciel," the demon Inthig contradicted her with a low, chill-making growl. "Something *is* out there, but what and where, I can't quite—"

Inthig's voice broke off and hen it was racing toward one sectino of the ruins, a black streak of coldly calm destruction. Then the demon attacked, and *nothing* happened. There appeared to be nothing there for Inthig to catch.

"Laciel, I can't *reach* it," Inthig called, trying one last slashing strike, then backing up. "I'm positive it's there, but I can't affect it in any way."

"Maybe it's one of those ghosts we've heard about," Laciel suggested.

"Look out!" Inthig shouted suddenly. But the warning came too late, as sudden unbearable agony gripped Lacile's left shoulder and arm. . . .

SHARON GREEN
has written:

Far Side of Forever Series
THE FAR SIDE OF FOREVER
HELLHOUND MAGIC

The Terrilian Series
THE WARRIOR WITHIN
THE WARRIOR ENCHAINED
THE WARRIOR REARMED
THE WARRIOR CHALLENGED
THE WARRIOR VICTORIOUS

The Jalav: Amazon Warrior Series
THE CRYSTALS OF MIDA
AN OATH TO MIDA
CHOSEN OF MIDA
THE WILL OF THE GODS
TO BATTLE THE GODS

The Diana Santee Series
MIND GUEST
GATEWAY TO XANADU

Other Novels
LADY BLADE, LORD FIGHTER
MISTS OF THE AGES
THE REBEL PRINCE

THE FAR SIDE OF FOREVER #2

SHARON GREEN
HELLHOUND MAGIC

DAW BOOKS, INC.

DONALD A. WOLLHEIM, PUBLISHER

1633 Broadway, New York, NY 10019

For Klon, Uncle Timmy, and
all the rest of the matchless
Libertycon crew.

Cover art by Iain McCaig.

DAW Book Collectors No. 799.

First Printing, November 1989

1 2 3 4 5 6 7 8 9

PRINTED IN THE U.S.A.

CHAPTER 1

It was very early afternoon when I led my horse through the gate, but I didn't pause to admire the pretty day before mounting. I felt really good after what I had just accomplished, but I also felt tired. What I needed was to get home, give Morgiana a big hug, then sit down for a while with my feet up. I felt safe in believing I'd earned that, and Su and Kadrim had agreed with me.

I smiled as I touched my horse with a heel, urging him into a gentle canter through the woods we'd emerged into. The woods were green and lovely, just the way they were supposed to be, happily different from what had greeted me the last time I'd come home through a gate. The time hadn't been all that long ago, but it had been before the stolen Balance Stone had been returned to the Tears of the Mist, and my world had been in the grip of the first upheavals that would have taken very little time before destroying it. Seven of us had ridden to recover the Balance Stone, and we had done it; it hadn't been easy, but we had all come through it more or less in one piece.

"And most of us even got to collect our rewards," I muttered to a small red bird fluttering happily through the leaves of the trees. "We all reclaimed lives that had come close to being lost, and Zail and Dranna were even happier than you with the rest of what they were given. They went home a good deal wealthier than they'd been when they'd arrived, Dranna with coin and Zail with a work of art he'd thought had been destroyed centuries ago. He was so delighted, he didn't even look for me to say a final good-bye."

The small red bird I'd been talking to came winging over to inspect me, then decided to settle on the finger

I held up. It hadn't understood what I'd been saying, but it cocked its head to one side once it was riding my finger, one bright black eye urging me to go on.

"It's not that I was really disappointed, you understand," I obliged with a small laugh, enjoying the feel of tiny talons holding gently but firmly to my finger. "I couldn't have been happier that Zail was no longer interested in me, but at least he and Dranna could have said good-bye. Graythor would have given them the extra minute or two before sending them home."

The bird bobbed its head up and down before turning it so that it might look at me with its other eye, obviously agreeing with what I'd said. It, too, seemed to believe that quest companions should have some pretty close ties once the quest is over, but Zail and Dranna had apparently seen the matter differently. And come to think of it, Su and Kadrim hadn't been especially surprised or bothered. It was almost as though they had expected Zail and Dranna to behave like that.

"Su and Kadrim were much better about it," I continued to the bird, stroking its soft breast with the side of a free left finger. "Those two decided to stay together now that the quest is over, and we all went back to Su's home. There were some people there Su wanted to have me meet, people called the Wolf tribe. They were the ones responsible for almost wiping out Su's tribe, and I had decided they should meet my magic as well as me. I'm not a wizard like Graythor, but I didn't think a sorceress of my ability would have much trouble with those people, and I wasn't wrong. It took a little effort, but we made them see reason."

The bird opened its beak and trilled happily at that, giving its full approval to such a pleasant outcome. My companions had been just as pleased, especially Kadrim when he found out he could stay with Su and still keep the restored youth that had been part of his own reward. Su's world had some nonaware elementals I was able to use to maintain the youth spell once I went home, which meant Kadrim could stay behind without worrying. He had done a lot to help me impress the

Wolf tribe, and when I'd left he'd been staring off in the general direction of the nearest city, murmuring something about how easily it could be conquered.

"Probably with what's left of the Wolf tribe," I told the bird with a shake of my head. "They were already taking orders from him by then, and they didn't strike me as the sort of people who would be happy to settle down in peace and tranquillity. Su doesn't like cities, so I think the idea of knocking down walls appealed even to her."

I shook my head a second time, wondering how some people could so enjoy going out *looking* for trouble, then noticed that the bird was staring at me with its head to the side again. It seemed to be waiting for something more to be said, which meant all I could do was sigh.

"All right, so I *haven't* mentioned our last two quest companions," I grudged, wishing it was just as easy not to think about them. "Rikkan Addis and InThig, who were gone even before I woke up from that last fight. Rik hadn't wanted to wait until Graythor had recovered enough strength to *send* him home, so InThig volunteered to open a gate for him. InThig's a demon, and demons have no trouble with gates, so they left together."

But probably with less quest-companion feelings than even Zail and Dranna had shown, I admitted to myself, looking away from the bird. Rik and InThig had started out being really close, but then Rik had said he loved me, and I'd thought he was under a spell and actually hated me, so I'd told InThig a bunch of half-truths that got the demon very angry with Rik. . . . I'd meant to use InThig's anger to keep Rik away from me until the quest was over and then tell the demon the truth, but they'd left before I got the chance.

And then I'd found out Rik hadn't been under a spell after all.

"Will you please stop looking at me with all that accusation?" I said to the bird, not quite able to meet its eye. "Sure I let Rik think I'd chosen Zail over him, but I didn't do it to *hurt* him! I was trying to make it easier on him for the time when he found out he really hated me. How was I supposed to know there *was* no spell to remove . . . ?"

I'd felt rather—relieved—when I'd learned Rik didn't hate me, and I'd wanted to go after him and tell him that I didn't hate him either. After all, Rik had saved my life during the quest after I'd all but thrown it away, so I did owe him *some* kind of explanation. I'd also wanted to smooth things over between him and InThig, and Su and Kadrim had volunteered to go with me before we tackled the Wolf tribe—but then I'd learned something that had kept me from going after all.

"It wouldn't have been fair to him," I explained to the bird, trying to keep the pleading tone out of my voice. "I mean, how could I have gone after him, just to tell him I couldn't see him again? I can't plan on seeing *anybody*, not when it's black magic I'll be working with."

The bird gave a sudden squawk of alarm, then left my finger with a lot more flurry and haste than it had used in arriving. I watched it disappear behind the nearest tree, then sighed with a silent admission that I couldn't blame it. When Graythor told me it was black magic I was going to be working with, that I'd been born with a talent for handling it, I'd felt just like the bird. Black magic is so dangerous and unpredictable, and there I was, not even a wizard yet, but all set to start studying and experimenting. . . .

I sighed for the twentieth time as I stirred in my saddle and looked around, happy to see that it would be only another few minutes before I was home. I hadn't stayed long at Graythor's house after deciding I'd be going with Kadrim and Su directly to Su's world, so I hadn't had the chance to find out exactly when my new studies would start, or what they would consist of. Graythor wanted me to start immediately, but Morgiana tended to take things at a slower, more realistic pace. I'd talk to her about it, and then we would see.

I spent the rest of the ride looking at the countryside and thinking about Morgiana, mostly in an effort to forget about black magic. I'd been living with Morgiana for ten or eleven years, ever since she'd caught me trying to steal from her purse. She'd been a full wizard for many years by then, which meant she hadn't had any trouble recognizing me as one of the Sighted, one of those who had the potential to do magic. The only home I'd known was the streets of Geddenburg; I was one of those who roamed in packs and lived as they could, and once she'd caught me she hadn't let me go again. She'd taken me home with her, given me fresh food to eat and a clean, warm room to sleep in, and after that had worked very hard to get me to trust her.

I smiled a bit ruefully at how long it had taken Morgiana to get me to trust her, but that hadn't been *her* fault. Growing up on the streets of a city isn't the sort of life that develops trusting souls, and I knew I'd probably be doubting people for the rest of my life. I trusted Morgiana and I trusted Graythor, but there weren't many others I felt the same about.

Except for InThig. I may have sighed again as I watched Morgiana's house grow larger as I neared where it stood, ahead and off to the left of the road I moved along. It was a big house and some people said it should really be called a castle, but Morgiana and I always called it her house, and we were the ones who lived in it. Along with InThig.

That time I was too upset to sigh, the feeling caused by the realization that I couldn't simply forget about InThig. The big black demon had been my companion for half my life, the half I'd spent with Morgiana, and trying to forget about it had never worked. Now that I owed it an explanation I would not find very easy to come up with, forgetting about it was practically impossible. I would have to tell it what I'd done and why I'd done it, and then I'd have to hope it would find it possible to forgive me.

I was really getting very tired of sighing, which meant I was happier than ever to pay attention to turning off the road onto the side road that led directly to Morgiana's house. If it had been really early in the morning, there would have been more people around, the people who took care of the house for Morgiana and me. Neither one of us actually needed servants, not with magic so readily on tap, so to speak, but having people around makes a big, cold house into a large, warm one. It also gave jobs to people who needed to support themselves and maybe their families, and it wasn't as if Morgiana couldn't afford to pay them. We both had all the gold we needed, so it would have been silly—and selfish—not to spend some of it in a way that helped everyone.

I was almost to the front of the house before I was spotted, and then a small flurry of activity began. Ferim came loping out of the house with a big grin to take my horse, showing that he'd probably been flirting with one of the girl servants instead of doing whatever he was supposed to be doing in the stables, which was usual for him. Despite his long, horsey face and habitual slowness of movement, Ferim considered himself irresistible to women, an idea no amount of female refusal seemed able to shake. If he hadn't been so good with animals of all sorts, he wouldn't have gotten away with half of what he did.

"Afternoon, Honorable," he greeted me as he held my bridle, watching me dismount. "It's good seein' you back after you been away so long."

"It's good to *be* back, Ferim," I answered, completing the trite exchange in a very mild way as I gave my horse a final pat. "Make sure you take very good care of him. He's earned a lot of pampering and rest."

"Sure will, Honorable," was all Ferim said, even though his dark eyes showed he wished he could turn what *I'd* said into an encouraging comment. A couple of years earlier Ferim had tried cozying up to me the way he did with the serving girls, and had gotten something he hadn't been expecting. I'd never liked having people decide to put their hands on me without asking, and Ferim had learned how stupid a move that was with a sorceress. After two days of not being able to touch anything at all including food and clothing, he found the apology he hadn't been able to locate sooner and delivered it to me as fast as he could get it out. It was the *only* time he'd ever apologized for the advantage he took, and every girl in the house had enjoyed the occasion.

When Ferim moved off with my gray, I started for the house, and only then noticed that Yallah stood beside the opened door, her hands held in front of her, a very small smile on her face. She was a big woman, within half a head of me, in fact, and there was no telling from looking at her just how old she was. Her gray-streaked hair was pulled back in a severe bun, her dark-eyed face was ageless, and her sturdy body was always in a dark-colored, long-skirted dress. She'd been making sure Morgiana's house ran right for more years than *I'd* been there, and I'd never been able to decide whether or not she liked me.

"I trust you had a pleasant time on your travels," she said as I came up to her, her dark eyes only on my face, her voice the cool neutrality it always was. "Is there anything I can get or do for you?"

"Thank you, no," I answered as I stopped, wondering for the millionth time why she never called me by name. Laciel was the use name Morgiana had chosen for me, but Yallah never spoke it. In more than ten years, she had never called me anything at all. "Is Morgiana busy? If not, I'd like to tell her I'm back."

"The mistress is not at home," she informed me, stepping aside to give me access to the open door. "There is, however, a guest in the house, one who is here awaiting your arrival. He would like to have you join him as soon as you've refreshed yourself from your journey."

"He?" I echoed, briefly wondering who it could be, and then the obvious answer worked its way through my tiredness. There was only one "he" Yallah would describe as a guest rather than a visitor, something I'd never quite understood but had had no trouble noticing. "Uncle Graythor is here? Why?"

"I'm sure I don't know," she said, following me into the house and pausing only to close the door behind us. "The master has gone to his usual apartment, and told me he'll most likely be here for dinner as well. I'll have two of the girls prepare a bath for you."

"I don't want a bath," I said as I turned away from her, for once not caring how quietly shocked she was. I'd had a very long day and I *needed* a bath, but more than that I needed to know why Graythor was there. If he intended insisting that I start studying immediately, *I* intended demanding to know what the rush was.

I began moving across the large, tiled entrance hall at a brisk pace, which means I left Yallah and her cool distance behind. The woman *never* hurried, not under any circumstances, but there are times when a dignified, ladylike floating just doesn't suit my needs.

I realized that had to be the first time I'd ever refused to do something Yallah thought needed doing, and probably the first time I'd ever walked away from her like that. I'd always had the feeling I'd be failing in some way if I didn't do exactly what Yallah wanted me to, but suddenly I didn't see it like that any longer. I had too many disturbances of my own to concern me, which meant Yallah's would have to wait their turn. If she didn't like it, she'd have to learn to live with it.

I was so involved with everything I had to think about, I barely saw the warm, rich surroundings of the place I called home. I went up the wide, thickly carpeted staircase to the half-floor landing, then turned right and continued up in the direction of the apartment Graythor usually used when he stayed with us. He seemed to like the plain stone walls and broad hallway, the occasional hanging or painting, the several delicate stands with vases or busts on them, the elegant simplicity of it all. I usually enjoyed it even more myself, but that time was an exception.

I reached the door to Graythor's apartment and raised my arm to knock hard on the beautifully carved wood, then deliberately calmed the effort down to no more than a brisk rap. The man who had helped train my talent didn't deserve to have my flying emotions explode in his direction, even if the reason for some of the way I felt *was* his fault. It wouldn't have been right treating him that way, and his being the most powerful wizard of our time had nothing to do with it.

"Come in, Laciel, come in," his voice said out of the air in front of the door, showing he'd looked to see who it was before giving his permission to enter. It was handy being able to do that, and I usually did it myself.

"Uncle Graythor, Yallah said you were waiting to see me," I told him as soon as I was inside the sitting room, stopping just past the opened door. "Is anything wrong?"

"Nothing that required your immediate presence," he answered with a frown from the chair he sat in, an open book in his hands, his dark, piercing eyes examining me closely. "I distinctly told Yallah I expected you to rest and refresh yourself before joining me, even if you weren't ready until after dinner. Didn't she tell you there was no rush?"

"She said something about a bath, but I wasn't in the mood for a bath," I replied, relieved to know there was no crisis, but still too upset to feel soothed. "Since I'm already here, why don't you tell me what you wanted to see me about."

"There's something of a personal nature I need to discuss with you, but it really would be best if you rested first," he said, his narrow, sallow face taking on the twisted smile I knew and liked so well. "You must be rather tired from the days you spent with Kadrim Harra and Targa Emmen Su Daylath, and personal discussions should never be indulged in when people are tired. Did your visit turn out satisfying?"

"In a manner of speaking," I allowed with a nod. "Su, Kadrim, and I were satisfied, but for some reason the Wolf tribe didn't feel the same. Uncle Graythor, what *sort* of personal discussion are you expecting to have? Does it have anything to do with black magic?"

"Only tangentially," he said, his smile now an odd mixture of amusement and wryness. "Some people firmly believe that unSeen magic is *always* involved in situations of this sort, but that's only a belief, not a proven fact. You might like to look into the matter once you begin your studies, but that's for another time. Right now you look as though rest is what you need most, so why don't we speak again later, hmm?"

He'd put a finger in his book to save his place, and even though he was still looking at me, I could almost feel the way he was ready to get back to his reading once I'd accepted being dismissed. Possibly under other circumstances I would have simply smiled, then left to do as he'd said, but right then I was a little too tired to be sent along to take my nap like a good girl. He had to have been keeping track of me with magic to know so accurately when I was due back, and then he'd made sure to arrive first and be waiting. After all that effort, I was now supposed to believe what he wanted to talk about wasn't very important and could wait? Somehow, I didn't think so.

"Uncle Graythor, I've already managed to shock Yallah, so I might as well add you to the list," I said, folding my arms to show I wasn't as ready to leave as he thought I should be. "If you want to talk to me, I'm afraid you'll have to do it now. Later I might not be here."

"Not be here?" he echoed, his expression trying to decide between surprise and annoyance. "My dear girl, you just got back. Your leaving again so soon is quite out of the question."

"The last time I looked I was fully grown and not a slave," I said very softly, beginning to feel the first hint of outrage. "Are you trying to say I'm not free to come and go as I please?"

"I said nothing of the kind and you know it," he returned as he put his book down, most of him tipping over onto the side of annoyance. "All I meant was that it was unreasonable of you to consider leaving again *so soon*. Where in the worlds do you intend going?"

"Oh, I don't know," I said with a slight shrug as I looked casually around his sitting room. "I've been working rather hard the last few days, so now I'm due a little fun. I've been thinking about visiting that dimension I heard the witch-apprentice Nedra raving about, the one where everything is perfectly sedate and prim—unless you happen to be Sighted. She says the men are even friendlier than the women, so . . ."

"Men?" Graythor interrupted with what was almost a shout, sounding as though he'd never heard the word in polite company before. When I looked back to him in surprise, he was on his feet, and his expression couldn't be called anything but thunderous.

"How can you talk about going to a place like that at a time like this?" he demanded as he walked closer to me, so wrapped in outrage that his eyes were just about crackling. "Earlier you had the excuse of believing what wasn't so, but that no longer holds true. I never would have thought you weren't a better person than that, young lady."

"Uncle Graythor, was I supposed to have understood what you just said?" I asked, blinking down at him with surprise and confusion both. "It almost sounded like the language of spells, but if it *was* a spell, I don't think it worked. Unless it was supposed to make *this* language unintelligible. And what's so special about this particular time?"

His expression went peculiar as he stared up at me, consternation taking the place of outrage, and someone who didn't know him would probably have had trouble believing how powerful a wizard he was. Right then he looked more like a little boy caught doing something than a small, pleasantly ugly man who was usually too wise to make mistakes. He seemed to be trying to find words that would fit whatever the situation was, but after another moment he just shook his head.

"Laciel, child, if I hadn't lived so many years, I never would have been able to understand how a basically simple situation like this could grow to such complexity," he said with a sigh, and this time I had the feeling he *knew* I wasn't following him. "It would have been much better if we could have discussed this when you weren't tired and irritable, but you've left me no choice at all so I'd like to ask you a question or two. When the quest for the Balance Stone was over and I assured you Rikkan Addis had *not* been under a spell during that time, you immediately left your room to look for him. Why did you do that?"

"Why?" I echoed, suddenly inheriting Graythor's previous problem with finding the right words. "I'd— thought he *was* under a spell and because of that there had been a—misunderstanding between us, and I'd wanted to—straighten it out. What has that got to do with . . ."

"After you discovered he was no longer in my house, you seemed to be prepared to follow after him," Graythor plowed on, his tone gentle but his manner implacable. "You were going to do that even before you saw to the Wolf tribe, but something made you change your mind. What was it?"

"It was the realization that I didn't have much time to waste, not with studying unSeen magic still ahead of me," I answered, this time having no trouble finding what to say. "And unless I'm mistaken, that's the second of your 'question or two.' Was there anything else you wanted to talk about?"

"If you insist on putting it that way, yes," he said, a firm nod doing nothing to take his dark eyes from my face. "Going from eager to follow after someone to not wanting to waste the time, isn't usually done in one single and easy step. What were you going to tell the man, that it became such a waste of time?"

"That's a third question, Graythor," I remarked, folding my arms as I returned his stare. "If you have even more than that, why don't you ask them all at once and get them all off your chest? You'll feel a lot better after that."

"So I'm no longer 'Uncle' Graythor," he remarked back, his annoyance beginning to grow heavy. "Have I ever told you, Laciel, that your stubbornness is the envy of every stone wall I know? Rikkan Addis fell in love with you during the quest journey, and Soffan Dra told me that at one point she thought you felt the same about him. You very carefully showed him nothing of how *you* felt, however, because you were certain he was under a spell and that he didn't really feel what he thought he did. He left here thinking you wanted to have nothing to do with him, and once you knew the truth you started to go after him. Why don't you take up the narrative from that point."

"I already have," I *pointed* out, not in the mood to let him bully me. "That was when I found out I'd be studying for a career experimenting with unSeen magic, which meant my spare time would be strictly limited. I'd already promised to help Su out against the Wolf tribe, so I went ahead and kept that promise. I considered the effort slightly more necessary than catching up to someone I'll never see again, just to explain about a silly misunderstanding, but obviously you don't agree. If you thought explanations were all that necessary, you should have gone yourself."

"But I didn't *have* to go myself," he answered, an equal blandness in both the words and the look he sent me before turning away. He walked a few steps toward the room's unlit fireplace, his hands clasped behind his back as though he were wrapped in thought, then he abruptly stopped to turn partway back to me. His physical pose may have made him look as though he were thinking, but the sharpened look in his eyes said he'd already done all the thinking he needed to.

"If Rikkan Addis had left alone, no explanations could have been given him unless one of us did go after him," Graythor said, now looking grimly satisfied. "What you seem to be forgetting, though, child, is that the man *didn't* leave alone. InThig went with him, to open the gates leading back to his world."

"Which couldn't have been very pleasant for him," I said, not quite as satisfied as Graythor seemed to be. "InThig knew even less about the misunderstanding than I did, and on top of that had developed some—misimpressions about Rik. I don't think InThig would have hurt him, not after everything we'd all been through together, but it must have been a very—silent—trip to and through the gates."

"Silent because of InThig's usual habit of refusing to

speak to people it disapproves of," Graythor said with a nod just before I looked away from him. My arms were no longer folded in front of me, but he probably hadn't noticed. "But what do you think would have happened if it *didn't* refuse to speak to the man? What sort of information would they have been able to exchange?"

"I think I understand now," I said with a sigh, even more unable to look at him than I had been. "InThig found out that I'd lied, grew furious with me for using it like that, and now won't be coming back. Well, I can't really say I blame it; if I were in its place, I'd probably do the same. I know it won't make any difference, Uncle Graythor, but if you see InThig again, please tell it I'm sorry."

I stood there for a moment, staring at a patch of carpeting I wasn't really seeing, wondering if that was the true beginning of the loneliness I was destined to live with for the rest of my life. Wizards who worked with unSeen magic usually did so alone, not about to make innocent people share what could become a very sudden, very final fate. Rik was gone and now InThig was also gone, and I hadn't even reached wizard level yet. It looked like I really did have a gift for associating with the unSeen, even when magic *wasn't* involved. Very suddenly I didn't want to think about that any more and began to turn away to leave the room, but Graythor's hand was unexpectedly on my arm.

"Laciel, child, InThig hasn't left for good and always," he said, his voice having taken on the gentleness I remembered so well from my years of growing up. "It returned to my house after you and the others had gone, and after it had mastered its annoyance over your not being there, it told me what it had learned. I, in turn, contributed what *I* knew, which leads me to ask you yet another time: why did you change your mind about going after Rikkan Addis? What were you going to tell him?"

"Uncle Graythor, I'm really very tired," I said, my voice sounding lifeless even to me. "None of it matters any more, not even if InThig *hasn't* left yet. All I would have told Rik was that I—didn't dislike him, which makes no difference to anyone. Now I'd like to go to my apartment, and I'll see you . . ."

"It makes a difference to *me*," another voice interrupted from behind me, freezing me in place with shock. "Considering the way you treated me just about every time we were together, finding out that you don't dislike me after all is more than I ever thought I'd hear. Will you say it again, just to convince me that I'm not imagining things?"

Graythor was smiling a wide, crooked smile, the satisfaction in his eyes saying everything was going just the way it was supposed to, but I couldn't find it in me to agree. I turned slowly, really hoping *I* was hearing things, but no such luck. Rik stood there not five feet away, his bronze eyes glowing with warmth and happiness, his broad, masculine face creased into a grin, and I just didn't know what to do. I'd never had trouble making decisions in my whole life, but right then I couldn't even remember what my options were.

"When InThig returned to my house, it didn't return alone," Graythor said from behind me, his voice sounding the way his face had looked. "The three of us spoke and came to certain conclusions, then InThig went off on an errand while Rik and I made arrangements to come here. I'm afraid Yallah considers him one of my retainers, but that doesn't matter. What does matter is that you two are together again, and now your quest journey can have a completely happy ending. Call me a romantic if you will, but I do so enjoy happy endings."

"So do I," Rik said, his grin having faded from what it had been, faint worry now lurking in his eyes. "The only problem is, Graythor, Laciel doesn't look like she agrees with us. Are you all right, Laciel?"

"I'll find out and let you know," I said, beginning to be aware of a very unexpected feeling. The upset I'd been in the grip of was giving way to the start of anger, and outrage, and indignation, and any number of other emotions I couldn't quite put a name to. The only thing I knew for sure was they had no relation to

romance and happy endings—or even to a partially
good mood. I turned away from Rik to see that
Graythor was considerably less satisfied than he had
been, and once my eyes were on him the man I called
"uncle" very nearly flinched.

"My dear girl, what's wrong?" he blurted, more
distressed than I could remember seeing him in quite a
while—except for after the successful conclusion of the
quest. "You look positively irate."

"What I feel is positively murderous," I answered
from between teeth that wanted to clench, my hands
rolled to fists at my sides. "How dare you do something like this, how dare you?"

"But, child, what have I done?" he asked in bewilderment, honestly understanding nothing of what was
getting me so wild. "I was trying to help you erase
an episode that should never have been, to rebuild
bridges burned in error. Why should that . . ."

"*Help* me?" I demanded, for the first time in my life
interrupting a wizard without thinking about consequences. "I make a firm decision for reasons of my
own, you completely negate that decision, and that's
what you call *help?* Without my having even asked for
your help? How dare you intrude in my life like that?"

"I knew it was unwise beginning this when you were
too tired to be reasonable," he said with a sigh that
was actually very faintly annoyed, his dark gaze calm
again. "Calling the efforts of someone close to you an
intrusion isn't how you were taught to behave, young
lady, and once you've had a chance to rest and think,
I'll expect an apology. If Morgiana were back, I think
she would be very disappointed."

"And I think Laciel needs more than a minute or
two to get used to the idea that I'm back and won't be
leaving for a while," Rik said before I could answer
Graythor, coming over to stand to the wizard's right.
"Laciel, now that I know there's a chance for us to
have again what we once had very briefly, I'm going to
do my damnedest to make it happen. And once you
relax and stop fighting it, you might even find you
enjoy it."

He was looking at me with bright bronze eyes, a faint smile on his face, his expression as a whole softer than Graythor's. I let my gaze rest on each one of them briefly, saw nothing that didn't match to what they'd said, then gave it up by turning and walking out of there. The door to the apartment across the hall from Graythor's was open, which was probably where Rik had come from, but there was nothing there that I wanted to see. I turned left up the hall and just kept going, intent on nothing but reaching my own apartment.

I felt enough like a fugitive trying to outrun pursuit that I expected to be stopped before reaching my door, but it didn't happen. I made it to my apartment and then inside, closed the door and leaned on it for a moment, then roused myself to go to the chair farther back against the right-hand wall and sit. The room was its usual bright and cheerful self, yellows and reds and pinks with strong touches of blue, but I was so tired it might as well have been gray for all the good it did against my mood.

"How could he have done that to me?" I whispered to the sitting room, really needing an answer. "How could both of them?"

I had been working so hard trying to adjust to the fact that my future was not going to be as bright as I'd hoped it would be, that it would be horribly unfair to Rik for me to try seeing him again, and then Graythor goes and—*interferes* to the point of bringing Rik right to me. He'd known well enough that if I'd wanted to see the man again I could have gone after him, but I'd chosen instead *not* to go. It shouldn't have mattered *why* I'd made the decision I had, only that I'd made it.

But Graythor didn't agree with the decision, so he'd gone ahead and changed it to suit his own preferences.

Tired or not, the anger rose up in me again, the sort of anger I hadn't felt in many years. As a child living on the streets of Geddenburg I'd been the leader of a pack of other kids, a position I'd worked hard to win and keep. Every once in a while someone, usually a boy, had come along to try taking that leadership away from me, and the first thing they'd done toward that end was argue my decisions. I was half a lifetime and a lot of love and caring away from those days, but there were certain things that could still jerk me right back to the feelings I'd had then—like someone insisting that *their* ideas were better than mine. Whether or not it was true made no difference; it was the attempt itself that got to me, that set off the stubbornness Graythor liked so well.

The stubbornness he was scheduled to see a lot more of.

I thought about getting up to pace around the room, but even with anger poking at me from the inside I couldn't work up any enthusiasm for pacing. It was so unfair of Graythor to have done what he had, so disappointing to find him doing something I'd never thought he would, but that wasn't the worst of it. The worst of it was Rik himself.

I kicked my short boots off and folded my legs in front of me in the chair, then leaned down to rest my elbows on my thighs. I owed my life to Rik more times than once and I'd never forget what being with him had been like on the blind world, but I really wished he'd never come back. He was looking for something he'd never find with me, and the sooner he understood that, the better off we'd both be. It would have been nice if he'd been right about the two of us having a chance, but he was wrong and had to be shown that. By me. And all because he was here.

I felt furious with Graythor all over again, most especially over the pain Rik would be given because of him. It would be painful for me as well, but I took things like that better than other people, and Rik *needed* to be shown how wrong he was. He and I had no future together, and once he was made to see that he would leave and not come back again.

I leaned back in the very comfortable chair again to close my eyes, remembering in spite of myself how good it felt to be held in Rik's strong arms, to press up against the hardness of his body, to know the touch and warmth of his lips. His kiss had always been something new, something that made me feel very complete, but he and his kiss were meant for someone other than me. For Rik's sake I had to stay well away from him, never cause him to smile that beautiful smile, never encourage him to reach for me with that look in his eyes—

"Bring it in here and stop complaining," a cool voice suddenly broke into my distraction, the words coming right after the door to my sitting room was opened. "The kitchen men are all busy right now, but that tub still needs to be brought. It won't hurt either of you lazy girls to work for a change, to make up for all the time you spend gossiping and flirting with—oh."

By that time Yallah had turned to see me sitting in my chair, and the abrupt stop she came to also stopped the two serving girls who were trying to fight one of the large wooden bathing tubs through the doorway. The tubs were usually kept in the storage room near the kitchen, and were brought out if and when somebody asked for one.

"I hadn't realized your conversation with the master was already over," Yallah said just about at once, her surprise quickly dying. "I had the impression you would be with him for some time, but it's just as well you weren't. As soon as the tub is where it belongs, the girls will bring you hot water, and then you can bathe and change into proper clothing. In the interim you might care to remember the way a young lady is expected to sit in a chair, which never includes her feet being up in the air. I'm sure we won't need to discuss the point with the mistress when she returns. Girls, bring the tub now."

She turned back to the two serving girls with the last of her commands, but her casual dismissal of me wasn't the breaking straw. That final sliver of hay had come the minute I'd seen the tub being brought in despite my previously voiced refusal, a declaration of war I wasn't about to ignore ever again. Yallah had spent a lot of years doing everything *her* way and nothing mine, but that was about to change.

Without saying a single word I gestured with my left hand, and the big tub the two girls had been rolling

along on its side came to a complete and utter stop.
The girls made sounds of surprise and confusion, tried
again and harder to get the tub rolling, then looked at
each other with bewilderment and dismay. The two
big girls had been having a little trouble handling the
bulky tub, but the trouble they were having right then
was more than that.

"Well, why aren't you bringing it in?" Yallah demanded of them in very cold tones, having turned
back to look at the girls after crossing half the room.
"Do you think it can be filled while standing on its
side in the middle of the doorway?"

"No, ma'am," and "Of course not, ma'am," the
two girls answered at the same time, clearly becoming
frightened. Yallah ran the house with a very tight
hand, but I hadn't done what I had to get two innocent serving girls in trouble.

"But of course the tub can be filled while standing
on its side in the middle of the doorway," I said,
putting my feet to the floor and then rising. Yallah
turned farther around to tell me I wasn't being
amusing—as she had on any number of other occasions
—but this time the words designed to end the discussion on her terms were never said. Instead it was my
words that got spoken, in the language of spells, and a
moment later the two girls were trying very hard not
to laugh.

"How clever," Yallah said with an ice-tinged smile,
one that said she saw nothing funny in my having filled
the tub with water that wasn't spilling out of it despite
the tub's being on its side. "When you're quite through
with practicing your lessons, we'll appreciate being
allowed to get on with what we came here to do. A
task, I might add, that's being done for *your* benefit,
even while other chores remain unseen to."

"Other, more important chores?" I asked pleasantly, knowing well enough that was exactly what she'd
been suggesting. Doing things for me had always been
a favor Yallah granted, never something that was due
me, and if there was ever a day I was tired of being
done favors, that one was it. "You've always been so

good to me, Yallah, much better than I deserved, and now it's time I did the same for you. You must be tired from working hard all day, so I insist you take the time to relax and refresh yourself. I know, what you need is a nice bath."

The woman finally thawed enough to begin looking slightly worried, but that was all she had the time for. I spoke my spell with more relish than I thought I'd be feeling, and the next thing Yallah did was howl as she was dumped into the tub I'd brought into the middle of the room. She flapped around, getting water all over my carpeting while sputtering incoherently, and then the two girls were hurrying over to help her out of her predicament.

It took more doing than I, at least, would have guessed, but after a not-so-brief and rather confusing struggle a very bedraggled Yallah was back on her feet. Her dark dress was pasted to her body and her hair had come half undone, but rather than looking shaken she was absolutely furious. She pulled out of the grips of the two girls without giving them a word of thanks, then turned to send imaginary spheres of hellfire at me with her eyes.

"You!" she spat, sounding as though she had spoken the foulest word she knew, her face twisted with what she was feeling. "You think you're so much, so high and mighty a sorceress, but you can't *begin* to match the mistress! You just wait until she gets back, she'll see to *you!* Years ago she promised me she would, and now that promise will be kept! When it happens, it will be *my* turn to laugh, and I certainly will!"

Having said her piece she tossed her head to put her nose in the air, then turned and squished out of my apartment. The serving girls hesitated very briefly before hurrying out after her, and they hadn't quite been able to look at me before they did. When Morgiana got back, I would be in for it, and they wanted nothing to do with a situation like that.

I stared for a minute at the door they'd closed, then I sighed before gesturing away bath tub and water together. It hadn't been enough that I had Graythor and Rik to contend with; I'd had to pick just that time to get offended over Yallah's abrasiveness and drag Morgiana into the mess. It made everything even more perfect than it had been, so perfect that I was seriously wishing I'd never come home. If I'd stayed a little longer with Su and Kadrim, or maybe even gone looking for a place to put a home of my own—

The idea startled me with its abrupt appearance, but once it was there to be looked at I had to admit it made sense. I didn't *want* to leave Morgiana and head out on my own, but I would have had to do it at some time or another, and what better time than right then? Walking away from Rik and Graythor would be easier than trying to make *them* do the walking, and I could always come back later to say a proper good-bye to Morgiana. I'd be on my own again, the way I'd been as a child, but this time I'd be a little better equipped for it.

I looked around my sitting room in the light coming through the balcony windows, memorizing as much of it as I could, then I headed for my bedroom. What I needed most was sleep, and once I had it I'd be on my way. The thought of climbing into my very comfortable bed was one I wouldn't be able to resist for long, but what needed to be done wouldn't *take* very long. Before I put myself between clean, fresh sheets, I first had to take a bath.

CHAPTER 2

When I awoke, it was full dark. I stretched comfortably, then lay still for a minute or two before convincing myself that I really did have to get up. I'd slept away most of the tiredness I'd been feeling, but I would have simply turned over and gone back to sleep if I hadn't had things to do. The spell I'd used to create a bathtub in my bedroom before I'd slept had included the description of a small but tasty meal, all I'd been interested in or needed at the time.

But I did have things to do, so I yawned once, spoke a spell to create a small, private candle that would follow me with its light, then threw the covers aside and got up. Under normal circumstances I would have lit all the candles in my room with a gesture, but I didn't want anyone knowing I was up and around until the house was a long way behind me. It would be hard enough leaving the best part of my life behind me; having to talk to people before I did it would make it that much worse.

The small candle flame didn't do much to show the various hues my bedroom was decorated in, but I didn't need to see the colors to find the clothes I'd laid out before going to bed. Pale yellow leather trousers to make the riding I'd be doing easier, a silken tunic in cobalt blue belted with pale gold links, and dark blue, mid-calf boots. I'd wondered at first if I might be overdressing for the occasion, but running away from home in the middle of the night wasn't something I did on a regular basis, at least not since I'd been very young. It deserved to be marked in some way, and dressing in one of my best outfits was all I could think of.

I caught myself in the middle of a sigh, muttered a brief but very descriptive estimate of my intelligence, then got down to dressing. I was willing to admit I didn't *want* to leave Morgiana's house, but with all the problems surrounding me there I had no choice at all. If I stayed, Morgiana would find herself coming home to a riot, and she hadn't done anything to deserve something like that. I would get in touch with her once I was settled and explain my decision, and might even be lucky enough to have her understand.

Getting into my clothes didn't take very long, and by then I was deep into considering exactly where I would go first. I couldn't very well stay on that world when Graythor would be looking for me, but I didn't much feel like traveling aimlessly just to see what other worlds had to show. I took a brush and my candle to a mirror as I thought, and sight of my long, pale yellow hair and violet eyes faded behind consideration of what there was to do during time that had to be killed. Maybe I *should* take a look at that dimension the witch-apprentice Nedra had raved about. . . .

I shook my head hard and finished brushing my hair, then left the mirror with a snort of scorn and a firm resolve. I'd gotten into enough trouble once by deciding I had to go where Nedra had gone, and if I was stupid enough to try it a second time, I was hardly likely to find Graythor there and ready to pull me out of it again. Besides, the thought of meeting men, especially very friendly ones, wasn't as attractive as I once would have considered it. Probably because of how depressed I felt—over leaving home, of course.

I looked up from my hands to find I'd been standing in one place doing nothing, which annoyed me enough to get me moving. I glanced around my bedroom one last time, saw nothing I'd forgotten to do or take, then headed for the door. I'd leave the house, ride to the nearest gate and go through it, and then I could spend all the time I liked figuring out where to go next.

I banished my private candle flame before stepping out into the lamplit hall, closed the door to my apartment quietly behind me, then headed for the stairs through the nighttime silence filling the house. I fleetingly wondered just how late it really was, then dismissed the question with a shrug. Once night settled in, most of the household staff went to their own quarters or homes, which meant I wasn't likely to run into anyone who would ask where I was going. Not that I'd have to tell them even if they did. When I'd been twelve, Morgiana had made me account for my comings and goings; when I reached twenty-two, even she was no longer bothering to ask.

The heels of my boots clicked faintly as I crossed the tiles of the entrance hall, but I was moving at a brisk enough pace for the noise to last only a couple of minutes before I reached the front door. I had the urge to stop and say some sort of good-bye rather than simply walking out without a backward look, but there was no one to say good-bye to and I really didn't have the time. Instead of being maudlin I reached for the door bar, pulled on it firmly—

And accomplished nothing at all. I frowned at the door as I tried again, but despite the fact that it hadn't yet been locked for the night, it refused to budge. I tugged at it another couple of times, annoyed enough not to understand, and then a very nasty thought occurred to me. I stopped fighting with the door and moved three paces back from it, looked at it with the Sight, then softly used some of those words Morgiana disliked so much.

The door wasn't stuck or simply being obstinate on its own; it had been spelled into refusing to open.

"Graythor!" I muttered under my breath, putting my fists to my hips as I sent my Sight to the nearest set of windows in another part of the house. They showed the same glitter as the door did, the unmistakable indication of a spell designed to keep someone from going through them. I spoke a brief spell of my own, trying to force a way through Graythor's spell, but the effort was just as successful as you would expect. Graythor was the most powerful wizard of our time, and I was just a sorceress who hadn't even *lived* half as long as he'd been practicing magic. My spell touched his and immediately melted away, and that was the end of that.

"Did I hear you calling me, child?" a very satisfied voice said from a short distance behind me. "I thought I heard you speak my name."

"If you were listening, you sure as Hellfire heard a lot more than your name," I growled, turning around to glare at the small spark of bright red light that Graythor had sent into the hall to speak to me through. "I'm not going to pretend you accidentally sealed this house against my leaving it, I'm not in the mood to play childish games of phony courtesy. Cancel the warding and let me out of here."

"Laciel, child, why must you always be in such a

hurry?" the fiery red spark asked with a sigh. "Rikkan Addis and I have been holding dinner, waiting for you to join us, and we'd like you to do just that. We're in the small dining hall, looking forward to the pleasure of your company."

"If you two expect any pleasure from *my* company, you must be suffering from delusions caused by hunger pangs," I stated, looking directly at the red spark. "If you won't let me out of here, I'm going back to my apartment."

To find my own way out, I added silently as I began stalking back across the hall, so furious I should have been glowing as red as the spark I passed in three strides. The *nerve* of that man, trying to keep me penned up like a prisoner or a backward child, and then expecting that I'd actually take a meal with him! Well, if they were waiting for me before they'd eat, they were scheduled to become really close acquaintances of starvation.

My thoughts were still raging wildly as I approached the foot of the stairs, and then I ran into something that made it even better. It would have helped if the phrase "ran into" didn't turn out to be literally true, but that's exactly what it was. I strode right into an invisible wall that kept me from getting anywhere near the stairs, but it wasn't like the wall I'd once put in Rik's path. This one was as soft to run into as a cloud bank, undoubtedly due to Graythor's not wanting to see me hurt, and wasn't *that* considerate of him!

"Now, Laciel, it isn't polite to keep people waiting, especially when they're here for no other reason than to visit with *you*," Graythor's voice came again, and I knew that damned red spark had followed after me. "Come to the dining hall, and then the three of us can discuss our common problem over a good meal. If we talk about it, I'm sure everything will work out just fine."

I spun around to tell him I'd rather spend the rest of my life in that entrance hall than even five minutes in *their* company, but apparently he'd not only expected the reaction, he'd prepared for it. Before I could do more than splutter out a couple of disjointed syllables I felt that very soft invisible wall at my back, and then I was being gently but inexorably pushed toward what was now the right of the stairs and the door that stood in that wall. Behind that door would be a short hallway, and at the other end of the hallway, behind a second door, would be the small dining hall.

"There now, do you see how much more pleasant cooperation and agreement are?" the red spark asked as it paced my forced progress, pretending I was going along with that underhanded coercion of my own free will. "Stubbornness never accomplishes anything but adding to already existing difficulties, so we're going to dispense with it for a while."

"Are we," I muttered as I fumed, no longer bothering to look at the red spark. It was abruptly Graythor I wanted to look at instead, and face to face rather than through a surrogate. If he wanted to talk, I suddenly had something to talk about. That was the point I stopped fighting the wall and moved ahead on my own, which means a minute later I was throwing open the door to the small dining hall.

"Ah, how nice of you to join us, my dear," Graythor said when he saw me, rising with a smile from the table. The room was a good deal smaller than the formal dining hall, which made the table large enough to seat no more than fourteen people. Graythor had taken the end seat to the right; when he stood I saw that he'd dressed himself in the silk and ruffled finery that was the usual accompaniment to the expensive rugs and detailed wall hangings and pure linen and silver and crystal of that room. The golden glitter of his surroundings made Graythor's slate blue and pale gray look even richer than it normally would, but he wasn't alone in his radiant beauty.

Rik stood up from his place to Graythor's right more slowly, but not because he seemed to need prompting or was feeling ill at ease. Clothing-wise he was at least as magnificent as the wizard, his rust-colored leathers having been replaced with trousers and a short, waist-tight jacket of dark green matched to a ruffled shirt of pale silver. The swordbelt I was so used to seeing belted around him was probably wherever his leathers had been left, and instead he wore a wide silver belt with a filigreed buckle. His longish black hair also seemed neater than usual, but the picture of casual opulence was spoiled by the not-quite-happy expression he wore. Rik was feeling bothered by something, but he didn't know half of what being bothered really meant.

"Come and sit beside me, Laciel, and we'll be able to begin our meal," Graythor said, gesturing to the empty chair at his left hand, his warm smile suggesting there was no difference between that time and all the hundreds of other times we'd broken bread together. "I've arranged for privacy for us without denying us the comfort of being served, so please don't hesitate. But possibly you'd like a moment to change your clothing into something more appropriate. Please do, my dear, and then we can really begin."

"I'm not hesitating, and my clothes are just fine the way they are," I told him flatly from where I stood in the doorway, ignoring the memory of my own earlier thoughts about my clothing. "You wanted to talk, so why don't we make the first topic something really relevant, like what you referred to as 'our' problem. None of this is any of your business, so how can you have the colossal nerve to butt in anyway? Have you finally started believing all those ego-inflating things the unSighted keep saying about you?"

"This is meant to be a discussion, not an exchange of insults," Graythor said stiffly, and I suddenly felt that soft but undeniable wall at my back again. "Come and sit down, Laciel, and please don't make me repeat myself again. If you cause me to lose my temper with you, Morgiana may never again speak to either of us."

Meaning, of course, that if he got mad at me he would use as much of his strength as he had to in order to reach me. Considering what my personal defenses were like these days it would take quite a *lot* of his strength, which definitely wouldn't have done the furnishings in that room much good. Morgiana hadn't produced *any* of it with magic, something she considered a point of great pride, and if any of it got damaged because of Graythor and me, recreating it afterward would not do *us* any good either.

"Now, then, just make yourself comfortable while the food is being served," Graythor said as I was pushed at and into my chair, the invisible wall behind me curving around to accomplish my seating. "There's enough for three or four times our number, so take as much as you like."

He gestured in a way I recognized before he and Rik took their own chairs again, but the glittering table settings and sudden handless flurry among the serving platters and wine decanters didn't distract me the way he obviously hoped they would. I did my own gesturing at whatever came near me, which left my plate and goblet as empty as I wanted them to be.

"Laciel, you're really beginning to exasperate me," Graythor said after a moment, his left hand tightening on the cup of wine he held, his dark eyes directly on me. "Have you lost all vestiges of common courtesy?"

"What I've lost is the answer to the question I asked," I said at once, meeting his gaze. "None of this is any of your business, so what gives you the right to meddle?"

"The fact that I caused you two to come together makes this my business," he answered, the way he shifted in his chair ruining the tailored lines of his finery. "You both want to be together, but something is standing in the way of that happening. Since you obviously need *someone* to help, I've volunteered myself as the one to do it. Does that answer your question?"

"Maybe—we would be better off working this out alone," Rik said before I could reply to Graythor, his expression showing he was still bothered about something. "She may be insisting that she doesn't care to listen, but I've been known to be rather—persuasive."

He gave me a very faint smile at that, those beautiful bronze eyes glowing, and all I could do was look down at my hands. For his sake I couldn't let myself be persuaded about anything, but being near him made that harder to remember.

"My dear friend, persuasion of any sort only works on someone who is there to be persuaded," Graythor answered, his tone gentle and filled with understanding. "I know it disturbs you to see her forced into our presence like this, but if I were to free her she would be gone instantly. You do realize we only just kept it from happening a few moments ago?"

"Yes, I realize that," Rik said with a sigh, still sounding unhappy but also sounding resigned. "After twice coming so close to losing her for good, I'm not fool enough to want to chance a third time before we talk this out. What I was suggesting was the possibility of the two of us being alone, preferably in a room she couldn't simply walk out of. She and I tend to do better when we're alone."

"Rik, I'm afraid you keep forgetting what she is," Graythor said with a sigh that matched what the bigger man had produced, also sounding just as unhappy. "I've taken the precaution of warding you against accidents, but Laciel seems to look at magic the way no Sighted has for centuries. You've had experience with her unusual ability; if she decides she doesn't care to listen to you, how successful is she likely to be in her decision?"

"Too successful," Rik answered with the faintest growl in his voice, the bronze gaze on me now showing a hint of impatience and annoyance. "She's an absolute master when it comes to avoiding things she doesn't want to talk about, but this time I get to have *my* way. And my say—unless she's too *afraid* to listen."

I immediately bristled up at that, well on the way toward outrage at the suggestion. He didn't understand anything about it, and had no right pretending he did.

"Not wanting to listen to something doesn't happen to be the same as being afraid," I told him with the stiffness I was beginning to find very familiar. "Just because Graythor refuses to listen to what *I'm* saying doesn't mean he's afraid, only that he isn't interested in my feelings. And I suppose you can't really blame him for that. It's natural for a person to consider his own feelings first."

"Laciel, that's an extremely narrow-minded view of what I'm trying to accomplish!" Graythor objected with agitation, obviously stung by the truth of what I'd said. His response interrupted Rik, who also seemed interested in commenting, but I still had lots more to say. I began listing all the ways Graythor was being unfair while he tried refuting the bits and snatches making it through his own arguments, but the shouting didn't get the chance to be as loud as it might have. After no more than a couple of minutes, the side of a heavy fist hit the table.

"That's enough out of both of you!" Rik shouted, the volume he produced overriding both Graythor and me. "For a supposedly adult wizard and sorceress, you sound like a couple of very small children. Graythor, you've said you're doing all this for *my* benefit. If you really feel like that, I'd like you to let *me* make the effort to straighten things out. Are you willing to do that?"

"If you think you see a way of accomplishing it, by all means," Graythor answered, his tone and expression very faintly shadowed with the stiffness that was supposed to be mine. He wasn't used to being shouted at, but he seemed to think he owed it to Rik not to come down all insulted. He waved one hand in dismissal and permission, and Rik took the gesture as a cue to move those bronze-colored eyes to me.

"Laciel, you and I and the others went through quite a lot together before we recovered the Balance Stone," he said, the words as sober as his expression. "No matter what happens I'll never forget the time, and I'd like to know if you feel the same way."

His question was as odd as it was unexpected, and I couldn't understand what he thought it would accomplish. I hesitated very briefly, looking for traps that didn't seem to be there, then told the truth.

"I don't think any of us will ever forget it entirely," I answered, making no effort to avoid his gaze. "What has that got to do with holding me a prisoner against my will?"

"It has everything to do with it," Rik plowed on, running right over the automatic protest Graythor began making. "People who go through something like that quest together owe each other more than a quick wave good-bye and a cheerful wish for good luck. I didn't let anyone hold you prisoner against your will then, so I can't see doing it now. As soon as this meal is over, I'm going to ask the wizard to release you completely."

"You are?" was all I was able to find to say, too deep in remembering the way he'd gotten me loose on the blind world to even meet his stare any longer. I felt absolutely terrible, and more than a little like that small child he'd mentioned.

"Yes, I am," he confirmed, his deep voice now softer and more gentle. "But what I'd also like to do is ask you for a favor, from one quest companion to another. Will you give me two days that we can spend together, two days during which we can talk? If at the end of that time you still want me to leave, I'll go without a single argument. You have my word on that, and I think you know how I feel about keeping my word. Will you grant me the favor?"

I had to look up at him again at that, wishing I could simply refuse, but of course I couldn't. That was the trap I hadn't been able to see sooner, the pit he'd been digging under my feet without my knowing it. He was taking advantage of my feelings concerning the quest, but it struck me suddenly that he just might have outsmarted himself.

"You want two days to talk, and after that you'll leave," I said, stating his request in the clearest terms possible. "You won't try extending the time, or making excuses as to why you can't go through with the agreement. You'll simply leave."

"If you still want me to, there won't be any arguments or excuses," he agreed, the faint gleam in his bronze eyes showing he had other plans that didn't involve time extension. Well, I had plans of my own, ones that were firming up more with every minute that passed, and we'd see whose turned out to be more effective.

"All right, starting tomorrow morning you can have your two days," I said, then moved my eyes to Graythor. "Right now I'd like to go back to my apartment. Since I won't be leaving for those two days, I have the time to catch up on more of the sleep I'm missing. After that I should have a normal appetite again."

"Which will let you join your guests for meals during those two days," Graythor said with a nod, a calculating satisfaction now shining in his dark eyes. "I knew things would go much more smoothly once you were adequately rested, and I do hope you'll excuse Rikkan Addis and myself for insisting on your company before you were ready to give it properly. By all means do return to your apartment, and take with you our wishes for a good night's rest."

He gestured with his left hand as he gave me one of those familiar crooked smiles, and although Rik looked faintly disappointed, he didn't try objecting. I nodded to each of them before rising from my chair, then left the room to return to my apartment.

Once I had closed the door to my bedchamber, I spoke a short spell to produce a meal of my own, then sat down to it while I thought about what the next two days would bring. I'd agreed to stay and let Rik talk to me, but in spite of knowing exactly how effective a talker he was, I felt very little regret over having had to give him a chance at me. Those two days would be the last association I ever had with Rik, and I intended getting what I could out of them—while Rik learned something our quest and even Graythor's lecturing hadn't taught him.

That I was a sorceress, and not a very usual one. That no matter how well he was protected, he'd never feel absolutely safe around me. That as far as bright futures went, he would have one only with someone else, never with me. Two days would be more than long enough to teach him all that, and afterward he'd find the idea of leaving a lot more attractive than he did at the moment. And he'd never come back a second time.

I finished the meal I'd made for myself, but only because I knew I'd need all the strength I could gather in preparation for the upcoming days. Once I banished the remnants and got into bed, though, I couldn't even remember what I'd eaten.

It was very early when I awoke the next morning, but going back to sleep was out of the question. I was all slept out and feeling really good, which meant the day was about to start whether I wanted it to or not. I stirred under my covers and tried to decide whether or not I did want that new day to be beginning, then gave it up. There were better ways to waste time, and I had some preparations to make.

I sat up and rubbed at my eyes while I thought, then constructed and spoke the various spells I'd decided I'd need. I know most spells aren't spoken until and unless they *are* needed, but I was involved in the sort of situation that couldn't in any way be considered usual. It went without saying that Graythor would be watching me closely, which meant my opportunities for on-the-spot speaking of spells would be severely limited. I had to make do with a if-this-happens-then-this-spell-is-activated kind of preparation, and simply hope I'd covered it all.

Once I was out of bed and washed, my next decision had to be what to wear. I couldn't remember ever worrying about that before, no matter where I was going or who I would meet once I got there. This time I wasn't even going anywhere, but I was having more trouble deciding on clothes than I'd had with constructing those spells. I took a deep breath and let it out slowly, wishing I understood more about my own feelings and reactions, wishing even harder that Morgiana would get back. There were a lot of questions I wanted to ask, and she was the only one who could answer them.

But Morgiana wasn't there, and I couldn't very well

wander about the house and grounds naked. The outfit nearest my hand in the wardrobe consisted of gray riding pants and a yellow tunic, so I grabbed that and a pair of gray, calf-high boots, got dressed, then went for a walk.

This time I had no trouble leaving the house, and outside it was the start of a bright, fresh day. Inside I'd passed the sounds of clattering in the kitchens, showing the servants were up and starting their own day, but I wasn't yet interested in food. I needed to walk around in the peace and quiet of trees and grass for a while first, getting my thoughts in order before it became necessary to talk to—and be reasonably civil to—other human beings.

I'd left the house by the side door that led to the gardens, one of my favorite places in all the worlds, and it didn't take long before the beauty all around began relaxing me the way it always did. The flowers were all the colors of beauty, their scents turning the air to perfume, and the bushes were as neatly clipped as the grass. A wide flagstone path wandered around the flowers and beyond to the trees, encouraging whoever walked it to continue wandering on their own, which was what I did. Into the trees and then among them, the fresh, early-morning smell making me feel more than at home.

I kept to a slow and easy pace as I wandered, my thoughts trailing away to other times and situations, the memories bringing a faint shadow to the loveliness of the morning. There had been so many times in my life when things hadn't gone at all well, when the people who associated with me were made to regret their having put themselves so near. I didn't need any more memories of that sort, memories of disillusionment and disappointment and loss and pain, but above that I knew I couldn't handle any more. The only one who seemed to have escaped getting spilled on was Morgiana, but she was a very powerful wizard. Those without the Sight had no chance at all, not even if they were big and strong and brave . . .

"Well, good morning," a voice suddenly came, an

unexpected voice that pulled me out of my thoughts. "I didn't expect to find you up and around this early."

That made two unexpecteds, which usually equals an awkward. I stood where I'd abruptly stopped, staring at Rik where *he* stood leaning against a tree, my mind trying to come up with something for me to say. I'd expected to have a little more time before it began, but it looked like the old saying was right: three unexpecteds and you're out.

"I'll bet you're out for a pre-breakfast walk," Rik said into the awkward silence caused by my lack of response, his voice now a shade too hearty. "Since I'm out for the same thing, why don't we do our walking together?"

He came away from the tree a few steps to stop again and look down at me, the smile on his face trying for encouragement. I'd told him I'd spend two days listening to him, and apparently he had no intentions of wasting any of the time.

"I see you're back to wearing your leathers," I observed, plunging in with an inner shrug of resignation. "But you really didn't need to bring your sword. The squirrels are trained not to attack our guests, and they're the most dangerous life-forms you'll find around here."

"I'd hate to tell you how many times I trusted trained squirrels, then just managed to live to regret it," he answered very solemnly, only his bronze eyes bright with amusement. "To this day, the sight of a fluffy tail makes me reach automatically for my hilt. I'll try to control myself during our walk, but I can't really promise not to panic. These things tend to affect you deeply."

"Yes, I noticed how prone you are to panicking during the quest," I said, the words dryer than I'd intended them to be. "And our quest could be one of the reasons I'm out here this morning. I'd like to get back to being used to walking through vegetation that isn't trying for my blood. What brings *you* out at this early an hour?"

"There wasn't anything to do last night besides going

to bed, so that's what I did," he answered with a shrug, left hand resting on his sword hilt. "When I woke up feeling completely rested, I decided to get some exercise before the first battle of the day started. Now that I see you looking just as well-rested, we can get right to it. Laciel, tell me *why* you refuse to have anything to do with me beyond these two days that were forced out of you. I know you felt what I did when we were together in that barn, so tell me why everything has suddenly changed."

"That's the biggest part of the problem," I said, wishing I could look away from the now-sober bronze eyes staring down at me. "You see things as having changed, but in reality they're just the same as they were. I'm a sorceress, Rik, and anyone who doesn't have magic of his own can never be completely safe near me—most especially now. Did you enjoy that time I accidentally hurt you? Was it so much fun you're now eager to spend the rest of your life falling into more of the same?"

"Your hurting me was more my fault than yours," he retorted immediately, the start of stubbornness now showing in his eyes. "I didn't understand as much about magic as I thought I did, so I ended up learning the hard way. That misunderstanding has nothing to do with what we can have together, now or at any time in the future. I've never needed magic to keep myself safe, and I don't expect that to change."

"How often have you associated with magic users, that you can make such a blanket statement so calmly?" I asked, beginning to feel annoyance of my own over how stubborn he was. "You're running toward a bottomless pit with your eyes closed tight, and you have the nerve to say you don't see any danger? Try opening your eyes, and *then* make that statement."

"If you see things so clearly, why don't you *help* me open my eyes," he countered, folding his arms across his chest. "The only danger I find myself in right now is being argued to death by the most stubborn woman I ever met. If you see more than that, tell me about it."

"You stand around *letting* yourself be argued to death, and you call *me* stubborn?" I returned with a snort, then waved away the beginnings of a new argument from him. "No, you asked a question, so I'm going to respond to it. Would you like to tell me how you intend keeping yourself safe from black magic, when I'm not even sure *I* can keep *my*self safe? If you have something all figured out, I'd love to hear it."

"What's there to figure out?" he asked with dark brows slightly raised, honestly at a loss. "The wizard said something about you having a gift for advanced study in magic, and he was looking forward to what you came up with once you got into the study. What has that got to do with black magic?"

"That advanced study he was talking about is in unSeen magic, which *is* black magic," I said with a sigh, finally understanding that Rik didn't know what he was up against. All I had to do was explain, and then he would be on his way. I should have been happy about settling the problem so quickly and easily and I *was* happy, but only for Rik's sake. As far as my own feelings went, I was—happy for Rik.

"Let's sit down, and I'll explain," I said, gesturing toward the pretty stone bench that stood under a nearby tree. Rik nodded and walked over to it with me, and once we were sitting his eyes were directly on me again. Very briefly I found myself wishing the explanation could have been put off at least until the following day, but that was too silly a thought to do more with than ignore.

"I think you already know how magic works," I said with another sigh, looking down at my hands where they rested in my lap. "You have to be born Sighted; if you are, you can learn to do magic. The Sight lets you See down into the very core of things, and if you describe what you See in the language of spells, you have power over the object you're describing. The more detail you describe the more power you have, and the longer you study magic, the more detail you learn to See. It's a self-increasing progression, and the language of spells lets you describe something in minute detail without the spell taking all day."

"Because it's a verbal shorthand of some sort," Rik interrupted, sounding faintly impatient. "I do already know that, but knowing it isn't helping me understand the problem."

"Jumping around interrupting is going to help even less," I said, raising my eyes to look at him with a touch of annoyance. "What I just described is considered Seen magic, and you can't do much accidental harm with it unless you're a real bungler. If you speak a spell based on what you See, you can't go too far wrong.

"That doesn't happen to hold true for unSeen magic, simply because it *is* unSeen. There's nothing for you to See and describe, so whatever spell you speak is based on nothing but guesswork. Some of the spells covering the unSeen were developed many many years ago, and they've long since proven themselves safe to work with. Others work on a sometimes-yes, sometimes-no basis, meaning there are situations where they *should* work, but don't. No one has yet figured out *why* they don't always work, so using that kind of spell is risky."

I paused very briefly, wondering if I would be interrupted again, but Rik was too busy frowning and thinking about what I'd just told him. It was clear he *didn't* know as much about magic as he thought he did, but his higher education wasn't over with yet.

"And then we have the out-and-out killers," I said, seeing how quickly his attention came back to me. "There are some spells that look perfectly safe and harmless to use, but if a Sighted speaks one of them, that's the end of the Sighted. Spells like that are kept in black grimoires, to make sure anyone seeing them knows exactly how dangerous they are. All the unreliable spells and the killer spells—as well as the so-far-safe spells—are considered black magic, basically for the amount of specific knowledge we have of them. But the black part also stands for the probable future of anyone who fools around with them, not to mention the futures of any unSighteds who happen to be silly enough to expose themselves right along with the Sighted. How are we doing *now* with figuring out easy solutions?"

"I think I'm more confused now than I was before you started," he muttered, running a hand through his hair before bringing his eyes back to me. "What has all of that got to do with simply studying the subject? The wizard didn't say you'd be *working* with unSeen magic, only studying it."

"Rik, I've been studying Seen magic ever since Morgiana found me," I pointed out, trying to be gentle. "Does that mean I haven't been working with it at the same time? And didn't Graythor say he was looking forward to what I came up with once I was into the studying? He was talking about new spells for the unSeen, or maybe taming some of the ones that don't yet work right. He tells me it's what I was born to do."

"Then he and I don't happen to agree," Rik said very flatly, a near growl in his voice and hardness staring out of his eyes. "No one is born for what amounts to throwing her life away, messing with things that should probably be left strictly alone. You asked if I had a solution to the problem? Well, the answer is yes, it so happens I do. You just won't study unSeen magic."

"That's your idea of a solution?" I asked with a laugh of incredulity at his innocence, turning more fully toward him on the bench. "If I didn't know you were serious, I'd compliment you on the great joke. Rik, when Graythor said I was born to work with black magic, he meant it was part of my nature to become involved with it. I'll admit I've been thinking twice about starting the studies, but that's only something to kid myself with. I've already started with black magic, by using it during the quest, and I can't begin to tell you how natural it felt. It also happened to work right, which is a horrible sort of encouragement. That kind of luck won't hold forever."

He continued to stare at me with that same frown on his face, heavy disturbance in his eyes, and then he rose abruptly to pace around among the trees. Rik was a man with a link-form, a great bronze beast he changed into when he needed or wanted to, and right then his pacing reminded me more of the beast than the man. The disturbance I'd seen in his eyes was echoed in his movements, but none of it lasted more than another couple of minutes. His pacing stopped as abruptly as it had started, and then he came back to the bench to look down at me.

"All right, we do have something of a small problem," he grudged, but his eyes were filled with determination. "I know trying to force someone to go against his or her own nature doesn't work, so I won't try talking you out of getting involved with unSeen magic. We'll discuss the situation in detail, and figure out some way of working around it."

"What's all this 'we' business?" I demanded, disbelief bringing me up onto my feet to glare at him. "You sound as if you didn't hear a word I said. Studying black magic isn't only dangerous for *me,* it can and has spilled over onto innocent bystanders. I refuse to be responsible for the death of the helpless."

"I don't blame you," he said with a shrug as he folded his arms, hard sobriety looking down at me despite the easy tone he'd used. "I feel the same way about dragging noncombatants into battle. The only thing that changes my mind is finding out the person I considered helpless is no such thing. Once I understand that thoroughly, the rule no longer applies."

"But if it does apply, you stick with it," I countered, understanding only too well the point he was trying to sell me. "You stick with it to save a life that would otherwise be lost through not really understanding what it would have to face. Even if the owner of the life isn't bright enough to admit he can't handle it."

"I usually give the owner of that life a chance to *prove* whether or not he can handle it," Rik returned, his calm undisturbed as he unfolded his arms again. "That's the only way of finding out for certain, you know. You simply give the man a chance to prove you wrong."

He began putting his arms around me then, obviously intending to draw me close, giving me no time to think about using magic to stop him. His plan was a good one and probably would have worked—if I hadn't already prepared against that exact possibility. Those big arms moved fast to sweep me into them—but sometimes sweeping turns up the unexpected.

"What the hell?" Rik exclaimed, suddenly finding himself trying to cuddle up to the invisible, square-cornered block of not-quite ice my spell had embedded me in. "What is this?"

"It's the new sort of warding I thought up this morning," I told him, folding my arms as I watched him step back and rub at his arms where the sharp corners had caught him. "Did you think you could get through or ignore my defenses because Graythor warded *you?* That might have happened if I hadn't known what Graythor had done, or if I was only so-so at using magic. But I'm not only so-so, I'm damned good, and no one without magic can hold his own against me. Realizing that gives a nice boost to the ego, doesn't it."

His head rose as the last of my words touched him the way they were supposed to, and the look in his eyes hardened more than it had up until then. At that point he should have been disgusted enough to turn and walk away for good, but cooperating with me had never been something he went out of his way to do.

"My ego is fine, thanks, so you don't have to bother trying to boost it," he said, the words sounding not very happy, but also not terribly final. "And I've met people before who thought I couldn't do something, but their thinking it didn't make it true. As long as *I* think I can do something, it usually turns out that I can. Would you like to go for that walk now, or are you ready for some breakfast?"

"You intend going on with this?" I demanded in disbelief, a good deal less than happy myself. "Can't you see what a waste of time it is? You can't . . ."

"I can and will have the two days I was promised," he interrupted, his bronze eyes now glowing with stubbornness. "Unless, of course, your word isn't worth what it's supposed to be. If it isn't just say so, and then I *will* leave."

He stood there almost daring me to go back on what I'd said, and at that point I really did wish it was possible for me to break a promise like that. That was one of the few things I'd never learned how to do well, and when you fail to learn that necessary a skill, you end up regretting it.

"I suppose I shouldn't be surprised that you have nothing better to do with your time," I said, deciding I'd just have to work a little harder at getting him to accept what would prove best for him. "For some reason I'm not in the mood for walking in the garden any longer, so I think I *will* go in to breakfast."

I gave him a brief, distant smile and then gestured with my left hand, but not to freeze him in place the way I had once before. Since the end of the quest I'd figured out that Graythor hadn't protected Rik with *any* spells or warding during our previous time together, the wizard had only pretended he had. This time I was sure there was no pretense involved though, so I hadn't bothered putting together spells that would never reach the man I wanted them to reach. Instead I'd circumvented him—or at least I hoped I had.

As soon as I gestured, I stepped quickly back away from Rik, then moved another few steps to one side. The movement was necessary because as far as Rik was concerned, my gesture had made me disappear from under his very nose. The dark-haired shapeshifter was very briefly startled and then he was reaching out fast with his hands, trying to find out if I really was gone. He knew I could make myself invisible, he'd once seen me—or not seen me—do it, and I didn't want him to know I'd simply done it again. What I wanted him to think was that I'd transported myself back to the house, even though a trick like that took someone with Graythor's level of power to pull it off.

Rik began feeling around in slightly widening circles, so I turned around on the invisible platform-path my spell had also created and ran slowly toward the house. I wanted to get back to the house as fast as possible but didn't want to be out of breath when I got there, not when there was a chance Rik would move fast enough to arrive right behind me. My square-cornered warding kept him from knowing of my where-abouts by scent, the platform-path kept him from hearing me or seeing any footprints, and the invisib-ility kept him from seeing me. As long as there was nothing like heavy breathing to give me away, my plan ought to work.

I got to the house and slipped inside, made sure no one was around to notice, then gestured away the invisibility. I remembered well enough how Zail and Kadrim had reacted when I'd rubbed their noses in the fact that I was a sorceress, which was why I was playing those little games with Rik. The black-haired man would obviously require more nose-rubbing than our former quest companions had, but sooner or later he would understand what I was just as clearly as they had. I straightened my tunic as I headed for the small dining hall, deliberately pushing away the memory of a question I'd once had on just how persistent some men could be. Even though I'd never really gotten an answer, I didn't expect the question to come up again.

Graythor was already in the small dining hall, help-ing himself to the various dishes that had been and still were being put on the table in front of him. This time the food was being handled by members of the house-hold staff, and Graythor turned from thanking them to smile at me.

"Well, good morning, my dear," he said with warm welcome, gesturing toward the chair I'd used the night before. "Come and sit and have breakfast with me. Did you sleep well?"

"I slept very well," I answered, reaching the chair and sitting down in it, at the same time ignoring a coldly silent Yallah, who set the table around me before following the other servants out. "I've been sleeping for years now, so I should know how to do it right. Practice does make perfect, you know."

"Is that witticism supposed to mean you're still an-

gry with me?" he asked, faint annoyance glinting in
the dark eyes examining me. "If you weren't so stubbornly set on seeing things in no way but your own,
you'd know I was acting for nothing but your own
good."

"*Your* definition of my own good," I corrected,
reaching for the platter of scrambled eggs. "The one
question I still have for you is, what comes next? *You*
decide I need a man, *you* decide who that man should
be, and *you* force me into his company. Do I next get
married off to him, with a wedding gift of having my
ability suppressed so my new husband can be safe
from me? Just exactly how far does doing things for
my own good go?"

When I moved my eyes to him, he was staring at
me, but the frown on his face had nothing to do with
insult. It was more closely related to the deep disturbance in his stare, and I knew I'd finally reached him.
At one point in his life people had tried to do something very terrible to Graythor, something they'd insisted
was in his own best interests. When Morgiana had told
me the story, I'd shuddered over what people did in
the name of help, but I'd never thought I'd one day
have to use that story against the man who was almost
its victim.

The lack of a verbal answer to my question meant I
was free to continue filling my plate, which I did even
when I heard the sound of someone else entering the
room. The someone else was wearing boots, and even
the thick carpeting couldn't muffle the sound of his
slow and heavy stride around the table to the chair on
Graythor's right. The chair was pulled out and a big
body was settled into it, and then Graythor stirred just
a little.

"I bid you a good morning, Rik," the wizard said,
the words warm but on the subdued side. "Please help
yourself to whatever appeals to you."

"I already tried that out in the garden," the dark-
haired man answered, his tone a dry growl. "The try
wasn't exactly a success, but that's between Laciel and
me. What's more to the point is the fact that she

violated the agreement we made last night, and I'm right now lodging a formal protest to the witness of that agreement."

"I did no such thing!" I immediately denied in outrage, finally looking up to see hard bronze eyes resting on me. "I agreed to stay here for two days and listen to what you had to say, and anyone with the brains of a flea can see that's exactly what I'm doing. If you look around for someone like that to help you out, you might just be able to understand it yourself."

"And I say she broke the agreement," he maintained with carefully controlled calm, ignoring the way I'd tried to insult him. "She may be going along with the part about staying here, but she's turning up a little short on the listening. I've never learned the knack of carrying on a conversation with someone who disappears from in front of me."

"Laciel, is this true?" Graythor asked, looking faintly perplexed. "Are you using magic to avoid listening to Rik?"

"I most certainly am not," I answered emphatically, looking back to the hard bronze stare. "I was asked if I wanted to take a walk or go in to breakfast, and I chose to come to breakfast. It's not my fault if your friend over there can't keep up with my means of traveling. If he could have kept up, I would have continued listening."

"You can't agree to listen, then do things that guarantee you won't *have* to listen," Graythor said before Rik could do more than part his lips, the wizard's tone even but final. "Either you keep to the agreement in its entirety, or you take your word back and end it altogether. Fair is fair, Laciel, and what you're doing doesn't fit the definition."

"You mean he can't handle it if I don't give him every break and then some," I said with a put-upon sigh, then shrugged in resignation. "I still think this is a complete waste of time, but I agreed to go along with it so I will. If it makes you feel any better, I promise to take it easy on him."

I gave all my attention to my breakfast after that,

finding it very easy to do in the ringing silence supplied by my two meal companions. Rik and Graythor were bending some teeth on my last speech, both of them so deeply involved in their own thoughts that they apparently missed how little I was eating. I had no appetite left at all by then, not after what I'd deliberately said to hurt Rik, and I wished I could go back to my apartment to be alone for a while. But if I went back to my apartment, Rik would know I'd been playing obnoxious on purpose, saying the sort of thing I knew he hated.

I took a forkful of eggs and chewed them without really noticing, paying more attention to keeping my expression bored and uncaring. All I could remember was how hurt Rik had been during the quest, when he'd thought I was using my ability with magic to take over leadership of our group. It hadn't been the idea of losing the place of leader that had bothered him, it had been the idea that I would play that unfair and come at him from behind. Playing unfair was the key to sending Rik on his way, and if it hadn't been the only way to save his life—

"I think I'll have to ask to be excused for a while, Graythor," Rik said abruptly, his voice horribly even and calm. "There's something I forgot to do in my apartment. I'll see you later."

He rose from the table and left the room with even more deliberation than he'd shown coming in, and I hadn't needed to look up to know he hadn't even glanced in my direction. There was quiet for a moment after he was gone, and then I could feel Graythor's eyes on me.

"Are you proud of yourself, Laciel?" he asked very softly, a definite weariness tingeing the words. "You've gone quite a distance toward proving how good you are, and the cost of that proof is nothing more than the pride of the man who loves you. That's a rather cheap price, after all, so you must be very pleased."

"As a matter of fact, I am," I responded, still pretending to be absorbed in my breakfast, but the pretense didn't have to go on much longer. When I didn't

add anything or show any signs of the remorse he must
have been searching for, Graythor threw his napkin on
the table and got to his feet, then left the way Rik
had. At that point I wanted to slump in my chair and
cover my eyes with my palms, but I didn't dare. Just in
case Graythor was watching from a distance, I finished
my breakfast and strolled back to my apartment. Once
there, I spent quite a long time hating myself, but that
didn't do any good at all.

CHAPTER 3

I wasn't feeling very well, but after a couple of hours I
had to leave my apartment. The meal I'd stuffed down
felt completely undigested and I would have enjoyed
lying down for a while longer, but as far as I knew the
game I'd been playing wasn't over yet. I was very glad
I'd started out by telling Rik I didn't really dislike
him; the way things were going, it was fairly safe to
assume I'd have no chance to say something like that
before he left.

Outside the house the sun was glarey and hot, but at
least I could breathe a little more easily than I'd been
able to inside. I thought about walking in the garden
again, decided I wasn't feeling well enough to appreciate it, then turned toward the stables. I'd visit with my
horse for a while to make sure he was comfortable,
and then I'd try to think of something else to do.

Reaching the stables was a definite effort, but at
least it was cool and dim inside the big building. It also
smelled worse than it ever had before, and that despite the clean straw I could see already spread in the
stalls. I could feel my stomach turning as I walked
toward the stall my mounts were usually kept in, but I
clamped my teeth and just kept going. It was nothing
more than guilt making me feel that way, I knew,

which meant there was nothing I could do about stopping it. Once I was finished with having to do stomach-turning things, it would stop by itself.

When I finally got to my horse's stall I looked inside, but for some reason the stall was empty. I leaned against the wooden end brace and stared at the emptiness, but that didn't produce my horse. He was completely gone, without a single trace, and I just couldn't understand why.

"Somethin' I c'n do fer ya, Honorable?" a voice said from behind me, a smooth and easy voice I seemed to recognize. "You lookin' fer a mount so's you c'n go ridin'?"

"My horse is gone," I said to the face that appeared in front of me, a face I was finally able to recognize as Ferim. He took care of the stables and the animals, I remembered that almost clearly. "Ferim, my horse is gone. How can I go riding if my horse is gone?"

"Horses'r out in th' pasture this time a day," Ferim said, a sly smile on his long face as he moved a little nearer to me. "You couldn' a forgot thet, Honorable, we been doin' it too long. Strikes me you come here lookin' fer somethin' else."

"I did?" I asked, wondering what that something else could be. "How do you know that?"

"I knowed fer a long time you'd be comin' 'round," Ferim said, looking and sounding very satisfied. "They all come 'round sooner 'r later, some by theyselves, some with a tad a help. I been wantin' t'help ya fer a long time, Honorable, an' now I c'n."

"What kind of help do I need?" I asked as his arm went around me, really curious to know. "I'm not feeling very well, but I didn't know I needed help."

"I'd say you been swallowin' too much a the mistress' wine," Ferim chuckled, the arm he had around me pulling me closer to him. "Shouldn't oughta be drinkin' this early in th' day, but you don't need t'worry I'll be tellin'."

"I didn't have any wine," I said, knowing that for certain even though many other things were blurry. "I'd never have wine with breakfast. . . ."

My attempted explanation was cut short when two lips pressed themselves to mine, at the same time cutting short my air. I was having enough trouble breathing without that, and on top of it all Ferim smelled worse than the stables. I found the strength somewhere to push hard enough to free my face, but when I tried to step back, I discovered there were two arms around me rather than one.

"What are you doing?" I asked, panting a little and feeling even dizzier than I had. "Ferim, let go of me, I need to go back to the house."

"If'n you wanted t'go back fer real, you'da used magic t'get loose," he answered, doing some panting of his own as he buried his face in my neck. "I know how bad y'want me, an' ya don't got t'worry none. I ain't gonna play hard t'git."

I really wasn't understanding anything he was saying, and especially not about magic. I knew I was a magic user and a pretty good one, but somehow I couldn't seem to remember how it worked. I was also supposed to have certain automatic defenses, but they must have gotten turned off. I almost remembered how to get loose without using magic, but for that I couldn't find the strength. I struggled as hard as I could, the sickness inside me getting worse, and then—

"Having fun?" a very cold growl of a voice asked, and then Ferim was yanked away from me so quickly that I nearly fell. Once I had most of my balance back, I looked up and saw that Rik had Ferim by the shirt front and had lifted him off the ground. Ferim squirmed and choked in the merciless grip he couldn't free himself from, and he looked absolutely terrified.

"Where I come from, real men don't force themselves on women," Rik said in that same growl, his bronze eyes blazing. "Only clods and losers refuse to give the choice to those weaker than themselves, and I think it's time you learned how that works. Since you're so interested in matching strength with someone, why don't you try *me.*"

Ferim wasn't a small man, but being held like that seemed to have reduced him in size. He stuttered and shook his head violently, obviously rejecting Rik's offer, obviously desperate to get loose and run. I thought I saw Rik's lip curl, and then he pulled the terrified man even closer.

"If I ever find you trying this with another woman, if I hear even a hint that you *thought* about it, I'll make the choice *for* you," Rik told him. "That will make it just you and me, and trying to run then won't help you even a little. Right now you'd better get out of my sight fast."

Rik finally let him go with something of a push, but Ferim didn't let almost falling keep him there any longer than absolutely necessary. The stableman stumbled down to one knee and a hand, but was up again in a second, running so fast he would have outdistanced any of the horses he usually took care of. Rik watched him skid through a small side door and disappear, and then he turned his attention to me.

"I apologize for interfering, but I find it hard controlling myself when I see something like that," he said, his words and the look in his eyes somewhat distant. "I know you don't need the help of an inferior being, but— Laciel!"

His shout might have startled me if I hadn't been in such deep pain, the way it suddenly hit sending me down to my knees in the scattered straw. I wanted to double over or curl up on the ground, but the arms abruptly circling me and holding me up didn't let it happen.

"Laciel, what is it?" Rik demanded, one big hand gently brushing the hair out of my eyes. "What's wrong with you?"

"It's only what I get for hurting you like that," I whispered, very glad I was able to look at his beautiful but too-worried face. "We both know I did it for your sake, but I still hurt you so I deserve to be hurt back. I'm sorry, Rik, and I—don't dislike you—very much."

I was really too dizzy to say anything else just then, not to mention hurting too badly, but it didn't seem to matter. Rik lifted me in his arms and began hurrying somewhere, and just as he started shouting something, everything just sort of melted away.

*   *   *

Waking up took more effort than it should have, and my store of strength seemed horribly depleted. I slitted my eyes open to find that I was in my own bed, but I couldn't remember getting into it. As a matter of fact I couldn't remember much of anything, and that was annoying enough to make me stir where I lay.

"Are you awake, Laciel child?" Graythor's voice came, and then he was standing at the side of the bed and looking down at me in a worried way. "How are you feeling now? Is there any pain left?"

"I feel achy, but I'm not in pain," I answered, starting to roll myself into the first stages of sitting up. "What happened?"

"You were poisoned," Graythor answered, reaching down to put his right hand on my left shoulder. "Don't try to sit up yet, not until you get the rest of your strength back. You had a hard fight keeping yourself alive, and even though I helped all I could it was still a draining struggle. Right now what you need most is rest."

"How could I have been poisoned?" I demanded, even more annoyed that Graythor was having no trouble making me lie still. "Even if someone managed to get poison into me, as soon as it began working my defenses would have neutralized it. Only a half-wit would try hurting someone at my level like that."

"I suppose narrow-minded could be defined as having only enough head space for half the normal amount of wit," Graythor said with a faint smile and something of a nod, the attempt at lightheartedness apparently done for my sake. "From what I've been able to find out, the one so eager to send you out of this life was Yallah."

"Yallah?" I echoed in disbelieving shock, even while part of my mind nodded with grim acceptance. "Just because of one stupid argument? Uncle Graythor, I never said *anything* to her before, not anything! How could she have hated me so deeply that she tried to kill me?"

"Jealousy drives people to many things," the wizard

said gently, sitting down still facing me on the side of my bed. "When Yallah first came to work for Morgiana, she seemed to believe that if she spent enough time around a wizard, the Sight would begin developing in her. Quite a few of the unSighted believe much the same thing, and no matter how many times Morgiana tried telling her differently, Yallah refused to listen or understand. And then Morgiana brought *you* here to live with her."

"And I was born with the Sight, but Yallah didn't believe that," I said with a sigh, draping one arm over my eyes. "She probably thought I stole what was rightfully hers, because of how much closer to Morgiana I was. No wonder she treated me the way she did, like something she would have preferred stepping on."

"Over the years, she got a good deal of pleasure out of intimidating you into doing things her way," Graythor said, patting my shoulder in commiseration. "Or at least *she* thought she was intimidating you. Morgiana and I knew you were only trying to keep from starting trouble, but one day you would reach the end of your patience. From what the girls in the kitchen tell me, you reached that point yesterday."

"I sure did, but that's what makes this all so difficult to understand," I said, lowering my arm so that I could look at him again. "Yallah told me Morgiana would be on *her* side in the argument, and would punish me when she got back. I had no reason to disbelieve her, so why would she try poisoning me?"

"For the reason that she was lying," Graythor said, now looking somewhat grim himself. "Morgiana would never have sided with Yallah against you, and Yallah knew that. Most likely she said what she did in an effort to force you into apologizing, which would have fed her ego and increased her status tremendously in the house. I'm sure she realized you did believe her— and when you still failed to apologize, she grew desperate. When Morgiana got back, she would find out how Yallah had lied—and why—but only if you were still alive."

"So she tried to kill me," I summed up, shaking my

head as best I could while still lying down. "After the quest I thought I was used to that sort of thing, but maybe it isn't possible to get used to it. I'd still like to know how she got around my defenses, though."

"She had an accomplice," a new voice put in, flatly and with definite tones of continuing anger. "She didn't *know* she had one, but he did his bit to help right after she did hers."

I twisted my head around to see Rik sitting in the chair to the far right of my bed, his face expressionless but his eyes two pools of sullenly glowing metal. I realized then that it was just about dark, and a lamp had been lit on my bedroom wall.

"He's quite right, Laciel child," Graythor said, his voice sounding so dead I immediately looked back at him. "I became Yallah's accomplice, and you nearly lost your life because of it."

"But—now I really don't understand," I stumbled, trying to sit up no matter how much effort it took. "Uncle Graythor, you don't expect me to believe that? If you ever wanted my life I'd give it to you, and not just because I already owe it to you. The only problem is, I can't imagine your ever wanting it—no matter how much trouble I give you."

"You were told not to try sitting up yet," Rik said as he got out of his chair, his voice so filled with inarguable command that I found it impossible to ignore him. "This entire mess has the same central core, which I was finally able to see once you were out of danger. The way you were acting with me, and the things you said—it was all deliberate, aimed at causing me to *want* to leave."

It wasn't a question he was asking, it was a statement he was making, and I honestly didn't know what to say. I also didn't know how such a good plan had gotten so badly messed up, but certain answers were just waiting to be given to me.

"The main problem was I didn't know you were acting snobbish like that on purpose, and neither did Graythor," Rik said from where he stood next to the bed, looking down at me. "I was having a lot of second thoughts, so I left the dining hall to give myself a chance to think them in private. From what he tells me, you two had words after I left, and that's what made him do what he did."

"It was pure outrage that made me remember what you had said about having your abilities suppressed," Graythor took over the explanation with a sigh. "Once I left the dining hall I used an invisible eye to look at you where you sat at the table, and you seemed so unconcerned over the deep hurt you had given an innocent man that I couldn't keep from speaking a suppression spell. I had no idea that Yallah had coated your fork and plate with a poison of her own devising, I merely wanted to teach you a lesson. If the poison had been one that killed quickly rather than slowly . . ."

He shuddered and shook his head, a sentiment I more than shared. Yallah had done something to hurt me that shouldn't have worked and I had done something to hurt Rik that should have, and none of it had come out right.

"I was in the stables, thinking about asking for my horse so that I could ride around for a while, when I overheard the trouble you were having," Rik said, taking up the story again. "You sounded more than a little strange, but I was too involved in planning to scare the hell out of that stinking little coward to notice there was a real problem. When you started to collapse, I knew I'd made a bad mistake dismissing what I'd only half noticed, and it was almost too late. I picked you up and ran back toward the house while shouting for the wizard . . ."

"And then it was my turn to understand about bad mistakes," Graythor picked it up, his dark eyes still troubled. "I canceled the suppression spell, but that poison had spread too far for your automatic defenses to handle alone. I joined my strength to yours and guided the effort while our talents worked in tandem, and that way it was possible to neutralize the poison. When it was finally done, Rik told me what you had said."

"What did I say?" I couldn't help asking, feeling at the same time that I was about to learn why my plans had failed. I couldn't remember much about the barn incident beyond a vague recollection connected with Ferim, but I still made sure to look at no one but Graythor.

"You apologized to me," Rik said with that horribly flat tone returned to his voice, making me glad I wasn't looking at him. "You told me we both knew you were only doing it for my sake, but you'd hurt *me* so you were being hurt back. Then you told me you—very much didn't dislike me."

I closed my eyes to block out sight of the sympathetic pity on Graythor's face, too weary to try thinking of something to say in response. I'd made a real mess of that whole thing, and whatever I had to contend with next was no one's fault but my own.

"So now that we all know the truth, I'll be leaving as soon as I see you back on your feet," Rik went on, just as though he were announcing the time of day. "You can forget about that agreement I forced out of you, there's nothing more I want you to listen to. It finally occurred to me that I was doing exactly what that piece of trash in the barn tried to do, force myself on you despite your clearly-stated wishes to the contrary. It doesn't matter *why* you don't want me around, all that matters is that you almost died because I refused to take no for an answer. If you care enough about me that you'll live freer of mind with me elsewhere, I have no way of showing I care just as much except by doing what you want me to. I—wish it could have worked out differently, Laciel."

By then I *was* looking at him, but all I saw was him turning away from staring into midair and then striding out of my bedroom. He didn't even glance in my direction again before disappearing into the sitting room and then out of the apartment altogether, which meant he didn't see me struggling to cope with sudden success. He'd be leaving just the way I'd wanted him to, taking himself to the safety I so much wanted him to have. I was very relieved and happy that everything was going to work out after all, more relieved and happy than I'd thought it was possible to be.

"If you love him so much you feel you must give him up at any cost, I can do nothing more to help you than stand aside and let it happen," Graythor said very gently, his fingers lightly touching my hand. "I see now I should never have interfered, but I did so want you to be happy. Perhaps some day you'll see matters differently, and then you *will* find happiness. Right now you'll do best for yourself by sleeping. If you need anything, I'll know."

He patted my hand again before getting up and leaving, never realizing how wrong he was. I was *very* happy right then, just the way you're supposed to be when all your plans work out right, and would even have a little extra time with Rik before he left. But the one thing Graythor had been most wrong about was saying I loved Rik. I didn't love him, of course, I merely didn't dislike him. No one sends away someone they love; you only send away someone you don't love, the way my parents, whoever and wherever they were, had sent *me* away.

I cared about Rik and wanted to see him safe, and now he would be, which would make me happy. For the rest of my life I would be as happy as I was right then, very happy, very, very happy . . . and all I needed was a little sleep . . .

I lost all the rest of that day and half the next morning to eyelids that refused to open, but at least the time brought back part of my strength. It may be harder to hurt a Sighted than an unSighted, but it's also harder to heal one. As I moved around uncomfortably in my bed, I realized Graythor had done all he could, and the rest was up to me. The one point I was disagreeing with was the part about staying in bed, even if Graythor did think it was necessary. Staying in bed is boring, especially when you're only a little weak rather than sick.

"If you keep throwing yourself around like that, I'll have to remake your bed," Tissi scolded mildly over her shoulder while she ran a dust rag around the room. "If I didn't know better, I'd think there was a small child abed rather than a grown woman."

I felt the urge to stick my tongue out at her back just to prove the point, but Tissi didn't deserve being the butt of my shortened temper. Dusting my apartment wasn't in any way her job, but she was refusing to let any of the rest of the staff near me until I was completely recovered. She'd been horrified to find out what Yallah had done before disappearing completely, and since Yallah's position in the house was now hers, her first decision had been that I needed looking after and protecting. Tissi was a number of years older than me, but we had always been friends.

"As long as I'm not sleeping, staying in bed is a waste," I grumbled, this time moving my feet around. "Another couple of nights' sleep and my inner strength will be back to where it was, just the way my physical strength already is. I'm going to get up for a while."

"Without knowing who, if anyone, was working with Yallah?" Tissi said, this time turning to look at me. "She *seems* to have left for good, and good riddance *I* say, but what if she hasn't? What if she's still around, terrorizing one of the kitchen girls and making the poor thing do her dirty work? How could you protect yourself? You're not even *physically* strong enough yet, and you know it."

She stood there with one fist on her hip, dark-haired and dark-eyed, shorter than me and chunkier, but almost sharing some personal background. Tissi had also spent her childhood in Geddenburg, and although she'd had a family to live with she'd passed part of her time on the city's streets. She'd run with a pack made up of poorer kids who just roved the streets during daylight hours, the kind of pack my sort ignored as being beneath our notice, and then her mother had finally gotten work out of the city and they'd moved. She'd grown up in Morgiana's house and then had gotten her own job there, but she'd never forgotten what street-running was like.

"Do you expect me to get a bodyguard just to walk down the hall?" I asked with a snort of ridicule. "Especially when I *don't* need one? Most of the girls in the kitchens are at least as afraid of me as they are of Yallah, with magic or without. They'd never work up the nerve to come after me, so why worry about it? I have better things to do."

"Like what?" she asked very flatly, folding her arms as a match to the frown she wore. "You're specifically betting your life on just how afraid of you people are, but I happen to know more about that than you do. The people in this house think of you as just as much a victim of Yallah's as they were, which takes care of which of you they're more afraid of. With that in mind, what can you have to do that's so important you're ready to risk your life to do it?"

"Tissi, I won't be risking my life," I said in exasperation, tired of being lectured. "I'm sure Uncle Graythor has me warded until I'm back to being able to do it myself, so what's the big deal? Would *you* like to try getting through his warding?"

"At this particular moment, that's the wrong question to ask me," she answered, her tone on the dry side. "If you're all that eager to get up, a better question would be, why not ask the wizard? If *he* gives his approval, you won't hear another word of argument out of me."

I tried not to glare at her as I searched for an effective counter to that suggestion, but I missed out all the way around. She must have known Graythor wanted me in bed, and didn't care that his reasoning was more whim than logic. She was assuming he had a good reason for insisting I stay put, which closed her off against any ideas to the contrary.

"I thought so," she said with satisfaction after a minute or so of getting nothing but silence from me. "You may be eager to get up, but you're not at all eager to talk to the wizard about it. When you are, just let me know."

She turned away from me again to finish the dusting, then waved briefly with a very bright smile before leaving the room and then the apartment. I waited a few minutes to be sure she really was gone, then I got up and went toward my wardrobe. The floor length nightgown I had on was high-collared, long-sleeved, and completely opaque, but I preferred doing my walking around in *real* clothing.

Which, it turned out, I couldn't get to. My wardrobe had no lock on it and had never been known to stick shut in all the years I'd used it, so it took no more than a matter of seconds before I realized Graythor had anticipated my getting up. He knew me well enough to know I wasn't about to go trotting around naked, and also knew *I* knew I could not in any way afford to waste strength speaking a spell to make myself clothing. Inner strength flows into an empty reservoir slowly, speeding up only as the reservoir fills more and more to the top. If I'd used up my strength on outer doings that didn't concern me personally, I'd have had it back after one good night's sleep. Using it to fight so close to myself, though, much like the confrontation I'd had with the thief who had stolen the Balance Stone, meant it would be a while before I had anything extra to use on nonessentials.

Like clothing. I thought about giving in gracefully, grimaced at the idea of going back to that bed, then looked down at the nightgown again. When I traveled, I usually preferred sleeping in nothing, but at home Morgiana had gotten me used to wearing nightgowns. It wasn't the best sort of outfit for sneaking around in, but it was certainly better than nothing. I gave a small shrug, and then I headed for the door.

I opened the hall door just a crack and peered out, but as far as I could tell the hall was empty. The main stairs leading down were to the right, the easy direction for the way my door opened, but that wasn't the way I intended going. The rarely used back stairs were to the left, and they should get me downstairs and out without anybody knowing about it.

I eased the door open a little more, stuck my head out to make sure Tissi had kept going, and when I saw she had I slid the rest of me out after my head. I closed my door very quietly while watching toward the main stairs, then turned fast to hurry along the other way. That was when I crashed into the big body standing no more than a step away, and would have gone down backward if two arms hadn't circled me quickly to keep me upright. I was so startled I almost lashed out with magic, which made it a damned good thing my strength was too low to support automatic reflexes.

"I think you took a wrong turn," Rik said, making sure I was steady on my feet before letting me go. "Your bedroom is back through that door you just came out of."

"You almost gave me a heart attack," I gasped with one hand against my chest, trying to convince the pounding to ease up. "What are you doing skulking around the hall near my apartment?"

"I wasn't skulking, I was waiting the way Graythor asked me to do," he answered, those bronze eyes still nowhere but on me. "Now that your question's been answered, you can turn around and go back to your apartment."

"I'm too hungry to go back to my apartment," I said, an inspiration that saved me from having to argue with a man who would soon be gone forever. "Graythor doesn't want me to just lie there and starve to death, does he? I was on my way down to the kitchens to see what I could scrounge. If you like, you can go with me."

I was already beginning to circle around him with that, intending to start walking and let him follow or not as he pleased, but he didn't seem to care for that idea. His left arm came up, blocking my path to freedom and pushing me backward just a little, and then he was lifting me off the floor.

"I think a much better idea is letting the wizard make you something to eat," the miserable wretch said, already heading up the hall toward the other side of the house. "That woman Tissi had a good point when she said we don't yet know who in the house can be trusted, so there's no sense in tempting them by putting you right in their hands. And besides, you're not supposed to be wandering all over the place until more of your strength comes back."

"How do *you* know how much of my strength is back?" I demanded, trying to squirm out of his hold on me. It was upsetting to be held by him like that, so close and so gently. I'd wanted to see him for a while before he left, but not in that particular way. "And put me down! I'm perfectly capable of doing my own walking."

"And a very fine job you do of it, too," he said in a ridiculously agreeable way, a faint smile on his face. "I usually enjoy watching you doing your own walking, you've obviously had a lot of practice at it. I'm glad girls walk the way they do, instead of walking like men. A man's walk is dull and boring to watch, but a girl's walk, now there's something . . ."

"Rik, put me down!" I interrupted furiously, disgusted with myself for having actually been lulled into listening to that nonsense. "Put me down this minute!"

"Laciel, if you keep kicking like that, you'll tire yourself out," he said very mildly, a faintly concerned look now pasted on his face. "Besides, acting like that isn't very ladylike, and I happen to know you *are* a lady, in the finest sense of the word. How would you feel if people started thinking you *weren't* a lady, just because . . ."

"I'll get even for this," I interrupted for the last time, glaring at him with all the fuming fury burning inside me. By then we were only a few steps away from Graythor's door, and the way it was already swinging open told me it was far too late to get loose and go elsewhere. "Even if it takes me three hundred years I'll get even, you wait and see if I don't."

"In three hundred years I'll be on my way to becoming an old man," Rik said as he moved sideways through the doorway into Graythor's sitting room. "Do you mean to say you'd take vengeance on an old man, not caring that he was losing the ability to defend himself? You're not that heartless, I know you're not, and no one can convince me you are."

"Put her down on that lounge," Graythor directed, the faintest trace of annoyance in the way he looked at me as I was carried past him. "If we're going to have to guard her from everyone else and herself as well, we might as well do it by being in the same room with her. Later, when Tissi's schedule allows it, she'll stay in her own bedroom with her. Thank the powers that be we'll only have to do this for another day or so."

"And then she can go back to guarding herself," Rik said as he put me down against the fluffed pillows softening the back of the lounge between its two arms, then took the cover Graythor held and dropped it over me. "That would be a good time for me to do a little hunting, to see if I can pick up that woman's trail. If she's hiding somewhere in this area, we should find it out."

"That's a project I intended getting involved with myself," Graythor said, nodding in approval. "If we cooperate, we can make short work of it. And now, Laciel, what would you like to eat? If you're all that hungry, you should have no trouble deciding."

He'd moved his dark eyes to me with the question, letting me know he'd heard everything I'd said, but I was too disgusted with that entire situation to care about what he *or* his good friend thought. I hated being taken care of and I hated being treated as though I were helpless, and I didn't care if they *were* doing all that to protect me. I still felt like a prisoner or a captive, and the day would never come that I cooperated with captivity.

"Laciel, child, your expression suggests you're not hearing a word I say," Graythor pointed out after a moment, doing a good job of interpreting the air I was trying to project. "If you don't give me some idea of what you'd like to eat, you'll have to take whatever *I* decide on."

"Laciel, we're only trying to help you," Rik said, crouching down to my left with sobriety in those eyes. "If we'd let you run around barefoot in a night gown and without being able to use magic to protect yourself, there's no telling what would have happened to you. Did you expect Graythor and me to simply stand by while you risked your life for no reason?"

He sounded so seriously concerned I was tempted to

smile and tell him I understood and it was all right, but it *wasn't* all right. As far as we all knew for certain, the only thing I was risking by leaving my room like that was dirty feet; having a suspicion was no reason for keeping me locked up like a criminal. I might not have the strength to get the better of Rik, but with most other people self-protection, even without magic, was not much of a problem at all. Despite the odd urge I was feeling nothing had changed, which means I paid as much attention to Rik as he had paid to me earlier.

"Most human beings are made out of flesh and bone," Graythor said, the words dry to the point of sharp annoyance. "Laciel, however, is carved from a single block of pure stubbornness, and the proof of it is the fact that she can resist your talent of Persuasion even when it reaches her. I'm sorry your victory turned out to be less than you had hoped for, Rik."

"I'm not defeated yet," Rik said as he straightened to his full height, sharing Graythor's annoyance while I kept confusion all to myself. "I can feel it when my talent reaches through to someone, and I felt it reach *her* while her abilities were suppressed. I expected the link to break once she was out from under your spell, but it hasn't broken yet and now I don't think it will. I don't understand why she isn't responding the way other people do, but even if it turns out that the link will grow stronger the stronger *she* grows, it doesn't matter. If she tries taking off on her own again before you say she's ready, I'll sit on her."

If I was simply keeping quiet before, right then I was speechless. Rik's talent of Persuasion was one of the reasons Graythor had named him leader of our quest group. If Rik really believed something or wanted others to believe something, his talent usually made it happen. I'd never felt the effects of it because those who were Sighted had a natural immunity to that kind of thing, but if what Rik had said was true, Graythor's meddling had changed that for me. I couldn't imagine what would happen because of it—didn't *want* to imagine any happenings—but at least one point was on my side. In a very short time Rik would be leaving, and after that I'd never see him again.

"While you're sitting on her, I might as well make something for all of us to eat," Graythor said with a chuckle. "I have a feeling she wasn't telling the truth when she said she was hungry, not after what that poison did to her before it was neutralized. If she really is hungry, she can join us; if she isn't, we can let it go for now. What would you like, my friend?"

Rik was just about to answer the question, when a movement in the air to his left and Graythor's right distracted him. I watched with them as the air turned darker and darker, then thickened to black as a cloud of vapor appeared. The black, thickened cloud had two burning red eyes, and as it settled to the floor and took on the shape of a big cat, Rik grinned.

"InThig, you got back just in time," the big man said to the demon, obviously glad to see it. "You can help me with a job I just volunteered for, and with *this* job I'll need all the help I can get."

"My help will always be yours for the asking, Rik," InThig answered while Graythor chuckled again, but the demon wasn't as amused as the two men. "At the moment, however, I've come looking for the help of all of *you,* and the matter is rather urgent. I've finally succeeded in locating Morgiana."

"Why are you making it sound like a tragedy?" I demanded, throwing that stupid cover aside so that I could begin getting off the lounge. "InThig, Morgiana has only been traveling and vacationing—hasn't she?"

"At first," InThig grudged, sympathy in the burning red eyes holding to me. "Since she had no particular destination or itinerary in mind, I first assumed my difficulty in locating her lay in my being in the wrong place at the wrong time. After returning Rik to Graythor's house I became determined to find her, and so went about it in a properly methodical manner. I traced her to a world-dimension I'd never visited before, an odd place I've never even heard discussion of, and that's where she is."

"And?" I prodded, dreading to hear the rest but

frantic to know just how bad it was. "Is it a blind world, where she's become trapped?"

"Whatever that place is, it certainly isn't blind," InThig denied with a headshake, its tail moving in agitation behind it where it sat, catlike, on the carpeting. "Magic is as natural there as it is here, despite the fact that very few people practice it. She—seems to have become associated with the High King of that part of the world, a man who does indeed practice magic. She even lives with him in his palace."

"Then what's the problem?" Rik asked before I could, his tone trying very hard to soothe me. "If she's decided to stay there for a while, isn't that her right? From what I hear she isn't a child, after all, so what can we . . ."

"Rik, that's where the difficulty comes in," InThig interrupted, uncomfortable but determined. "I waited until she was alone and then I tried speaking to her, but she didn't know me. In fact, she insisted she didn't even know Laciel and Graythor, and then she called for guards and ordered them to destroy me. Something has been done to her, Rik, and if we don't succeed in freeing her, I'm afraid she'll be lost to us forever."

CHAPTER 4

"I'll be ready to leave in ten minutes," I said to InThig, then glanced at Graythor where he stood frowning with worry. "Take the spell off my wardrobe *now*, or I'll break it open with an ax. There's no time to waste on silly games."

"Time is the one thing we *have* to take," Rik said as he quickly moved himself into my path, blocking the way out of the room. "InThig has to tell us everything it knows about that world, and then we have to decide on a plan of action. Racing out without stopping to think won't do anything but make a bad situation worse."

"I've learned how to think while I'm traveling," I informed him, pushing away the strong urge to take his advice without arguing. "Doing it that way means I'm right on the spot by the time I have a plan developed, and then I can put it into effect without any delays. Get out of my way."

"And if the traveling doesn't leave you in any condition to make plans or put them into effect?" he demanded, still planted directly in front of me. "You'll have thrown away any chance of giving Morgiana the help she needs, and all because you refused to listen to reason. Does she deserve that kind of treatment?"

"Laciel, child, you *must* take the time to recover first," Graythor said from behind me, his tone remorseless. "If someone—or something—was powerful enough to overcome Morgiana's defenses, what possible hope will *you* have against them, especially as you now are? How will it benefit her to have you accomplish no more than joining her in captivity?"

"What's been happening here while I was gone?" InThig asked with a growl when I hesitated, trying to think of a slant that would poke holes in Rik's and Graythor's arguments. "What's wrong with Laciel that she needs to 'recover'?"

Graythor quickly told the demon the highlights of the fun we'd been having while I stood with one hand over my eyes, trying to think lucidly instead of with frantic worry for Morgiana's well-being. Morgiana was a wizard, almost as strong as Graythor—who was one of the best ever—and if *she* had been overcome face-to-face, *I'd* end up a smear on the cobblestones. Graythor was absolutely right about that, but how was I supposed to just sit back and relax while the woman I owed everything to was being—being—

"Laciel, Rik and Graythor are correct in saying haste is unwise, nor is it necessary," InThig broke into my thoughts, its voice sounding growlier than it had a couple of minutes ago. "As far as I could see, Morgiana was being treated extremely well, and those guardsmen came very quickly when she called. Whatever danger she may be in most certainly has to do with the loss of her memory, and *that* has already been inflicted on her. If her rescue is possible today, it will be possible two days from now. If two days from now is too late, she's already lost to us."

"I won't ever accept the idea of her being lost," I said, dropping my hand from my eyes as I took a deep breath. "I'll get her free of whatever's holding her even if it's literally the last thing I ever do. But what about *you*, InThig? Did those guardsmen manage to cause you any harm?"

"You must be joking, Laciel," InThig said with a snort, finally wrapping its long cat-tail around the front of its feet. "They wore swords and carried spears, and there weren't even any *untrained* Sighted among them. How could they possibly have harmed me?"

"After the last couple of days, I'm beginning to believe *anything* is possible if enough people do the wrong thing often enough," I said, not quite up to matching InThig's level of disdain. "Once Morgiana is safely back where she belongs, I think I'm going to find a world that's totally empty, and then spend a year or two enjoying the peace and quiet. Maybe even more than a year or two."

"A desire inspired, no doubt, by that woman Yallah," InThig said, a very chill tone matching coldly blazing red eyes. "You needn't worry about her any more, Laciel, now that *I've* come back. Finding where she's gone will take no more than moments, and then the problem she poses will be no more."

"Sorry, InThig, but you won't be going after her any more than those other two will," I said, gesturing toward Rik and Graythor. "Settling accounts with Yallah is something for me and Morgiana to do; after all, we're the ones who made it possible for this situation to develop in the first place. Morgiana should have gotten rid of her as soon as she understood why the woman was really here—not to be secure in a good job, but to gain something special for herself. And

I—I should have had it out with her years ago, letting her know she couldn't get away with treating me like a resented house pet. Morgiana and I will take care of it—and hopefully learn better for next time."

"I dislike the idea of leaving her free to continue her mischief while we're gone," InThig answered, the dissatisfaction in its voice matching the expressions Rik and Graythor wore. "You should, at the very least, bind her in some way so as to neutralize her."

"I'll worry about that when I'm back to being *able* to bind someone," I said, beginning to feel impatient again. "Right now I need to hear everything you can tell me about that world-dimension where Morgiana's being held. If I have to waste good travel time, I should at least be able to use it for planning."

"Just a minute," Rik said, interrupting InThig as it was about to answer me. "I think it would be a good idea if you listened while lying down, and then we can all do the planning together. That way we'll *all* know what we're doing when we get there."

"The only 'we' involved here is InThig and me," I responded, disliking the sound of everything he'd said. "Graythor has more responsibilities than any ten people, which means he can't simply pick up and rush off to other worlds. You have a life and a military career to get on with, and now that InThig is back you don't have to put off leaving. That settles the job of freeing Morgiana right where it belongs, on the two individuals closest to her. If InThig and I find we can't handle it—which I seriously doubt will be the case— we'll send back word asking for help."

"Before or after the situation becomes critical?" Graythor demanded, his annoyance so strong his black eyes crackled with it. "You, young lady, have enough arrogance in you for *twenty* people, and I've had more than enough of it! Morgiana and I have been close friends for longer than you've *lived,* and you dare to stand there loftily proclaiming that I'm much too busy to help her in her need? Perhaps you'll be kind enough to allow me a proclamation of my own, which is that I *will* be there to assist in her rescue! Unless, of course, you feel you've grown to sufficient size in your abilities to keep me from it."

He had begun walking toward me slowly, and even if I'd been at full strength, I wouldn't have been able to keep from backing away. Until you've seen an angry wizard coming toward you you haven't seen *anything*, and it wasn't hard remembering what had happened the last time Graythor had been that angry with me. His final words had been a good deal softer than the rest of his speech, but that made it worse rather than better. Since I wasn't watching where I was going, I managed to back into Rik, whose hands came gently to my upper arms from behind. For some reason that stopped Graythor's advance, so I quickly grabbed the opportunity to backtrack.

"I'm sorry, Uncle Graythor, I didn't mean to try shutting you out of something you want to be a part of," I said, wishing he would stop looking at me like that. "I know Morgiana would be just as furious with me if it was *you* needing the rescuing and I tried to go alone, so . . ."

"So we'll say no more about it," he finished for me, still angry but willing to let the disagreement blow over. "You'll have to learn, child, that there are few things more objectionable in this universe than an arrogant magic user. And even fewer things more dangerous than *being* arrogant. If you believe you can handle anything that comes along and therefore refuse to listen to the opinions of others, sooner or later you find yourself in a situation you haven't anticipated and therefore aren't prepared to cope with. Are you all that eager to throw your life away to no purpose?"

"No, sir," I muttered, recognizing lecture number 73, "The Responsibilities of Being a Magic User." There was a lot more to it than the excerpt Graythor had just gone through, and I didn't know if I'd be smarter bracing myself for the rest, or trying to head it off. If Graythor was lecturing me he wasn't likely to be doing anything else, but if I said the wrong thing a second time he'd probably switch to something a lot more unpleasant than lecturing. Physically I was much larger than Graythor, but once his anger grew beyond a certain point his body usually began doing the same. . . .

"Speaking of throwing things away to no purpose," Rik suddenly put in from behind me, "Laciel belongs back on that lounge before whatever strength she's regained disappears again. After that we can all get comfortable for listening to what InThig has to tell us."

Graythor's expression said he agreed with that completely, which killed the idea of any sort of protest from *me*. I had no choice but to let Rik guide me back to that stupid lounge by the hands he had on my arms, then sit and shift myself against those pillows again. I wasn't feeling as angry as I might have at Rik, not when it seemed very likely he'd gotten me out of that lecture, but then I wondered how much of my calm gratitude stemmed from his talent of Persuasion. I was so—bothered—by that thought, I missed seeing Graythor and Rik settle into chairs before InThig cleared its throat.

"There is, unfortunately, very little I can tell you about the world Morgiana is on," the demon began, letting its gaze touch each of us in turn. "It seemed a rather backward place, and that despite the fact of its being almost to the same level as this world. The people apparently live in awe of magic and those who perform it, and as I said earlier there aren't many who *can* perform it. Most of the Sighted of that world live beside and with the unSighted, and not as equals. Untrained Sighteds are apparently neither well treated nor accepted."

"What sort of military setup do they have?" Rik asked, his full attention on InThig. "Do they have a casual Guard structure and small standing army like here, or do you see uniforms everywhere you look?"

"You're asking if the High King of that place is conquest oriented," Inthig said to Rik, approval in both voice and eyes. "The answer is yes, and as you were undoubtedly speculating, that's very likely the reason Morgiana was taken captive. Or at least one of the reasons. The High King's army is large and surely filled with any number of those who would not be soldiers had they been given the choice, but there seemed to be little fear of press gangs among the populace. Those observations led me to theorize that magic plays at least as great a part in war as the size of one's army."

"Which would make Morgiana very valuable indeed," Graythor said, one hand stroking his chin, his gaze distracted. "A trained magic user of wizard strength, in a place where magic users of any sort are rare and/or unknowing. There's no doubt this High King will be absolutely ruthless in his attempt to retain possession of her, therefore must we brace ourselves to be equally as ruthless. Your experiences on the quest will stand you in good stead, Laciel child."

"I don't think coming up with enough ruthlessness will be our major problem, Uncle Graythor," I said, disturbed over what InThig had told us—and hadn't told us. "We still haven't answered the question of how Morgiana was taken, and if there's as little magic use as InThig says, there's something very wrong with the general picture. InThig—just exactly how much stronger than Morgiana *is* that High King?"

"I had no opportunity to find out, Laciel," InThig answered, its long black tail swishing again. "Magic isn't used casually there, only very deliberately and under very special circumstances. I wasn't even there long enough to find out what those special circumstances are, not to mention see them. The High King's strength would be an important point for us to keep in mind, of course, but other than that I see nothing significant in the matter."

"I believe the point Laciel is trying to make is a good one," Graythor said, his dark eyes worried. "If the High King is so much stronger than Morgiana that he was able to subdue her without hurting her, what possible need could he have for *her* power? And on a world where magic is rare and as rarely practiced, how did he get to *be* that powerful?"

"And if he isn't that powerful, how did he trap

Morgiana?" I added to the list, bringing the circle back to the place I felt it had to be. "We've agreed that he probably took her because he needs her strength, but why would he need it that badly if he's stronger? I'm sure he knows what a risk he's taking, the risk that Morgiana's friends will find out what he's done and come after him, but apparently he doesn't care. He isn't even bothering to hide her in a back room somewhere."

"Which means one of two things," Rik said slowly while his mind raced through possibilities, his body low in the chair with his legs out straight in front of him. "Either his trap is good enough to take *anyone* who comes to the rescue, or he's convinced he has nothing to worry about for some other reason. Considering the fact that he knows his situation while we don't, that other reason could be just about anything."

"And we must bear in mind the fact that he undoubtedly knows all about Graythor, Laciel, and myself," InThig put in, its tail moving in sharp, jerking arcs. "Morgiana's memory has certainly been taken, but surely not before the High King was given access to it. My having been seen at the palace will be taken as a clear warning that others will soon follow, attempting to free Morgiana. I believe your words concerning the foolishness of arrogance should have been addressed to me, Graythor."

"Stop blaming yourself, InThig," Rik said before Graythor could, complete dismissal in his tone. "You couldn't possibly have known what the situation was before walking into it, and if Morgiana's memory hadn't been gone you probably could have freed her simply by doing what you usually do. At least we know they'll be looking for and expecting you three, so you'll have to disguise yourselves. I'll be the wild card they *aren't* expecting, which should give us something of an advantage."

"I thought you were leaving," I said very quietly, a definite contrast to the way I felt inside. "As a matter of fact, I thought you gave your word."

"I did give my word, and I'll keep it," he said, those

bronze eyes serious and not trying to avoid the point.
"As soon as Morgiana is safe I'll be on my way, and I
won't need to be reminded. Right now I think you all
need my help in this."

"Rik is correct, Laciel," Graythor assured me, his
tone calm and sure rather than coaxing. "I'm convinced we *will* need help, and specifically nonmagical
help. There's something about all this . . ."

He shook his head in frustration, a wordlessness I
understood completely. There *was* something about
that situation that touched me on a level below a
conscious knowledge, but there was no denying the
conviction of the feeling. There would be trouble for
us in what we were about to do, unanticipated trouble
and therefore unprepared for.

"How do you anticipate the unanticipated?" I muttered to myself, a question I'd once asked InThig. The
demon hadn't been able to come up with an answer
any more than I had, but it was an easier question
than the one that revolved around how I felt about
Rik's coming with us. Part of me was glad I'd be
having more time with him before he left forever, but
another part wanted the time of separation already
over with and behind me. I couldn't decide which way
I should feel, but that doesn't mean I wasn't feeling
anything. Confused was the way I was feeling, and
very upset, and bothered more than I would have
cared to admit.

"You anticipate the unanticipated by making general plans as well as specific ones," Graythor said,
surprising me with an answer to a quesion I hadn't
thought he'd heard. "You also make the effort to be
as flexible as possible in that planning, so that an
unexpected turn of events won't leave you floundering
for a reply. I think we'll have that meal now, and then
I'll leave you all briefly to see to my affairs before we
begin this rescue mission. I'll provide dinner for us
tonight, and after dinner we'll begin planning in
earnest."

He got out of his chair to walk to the side of the
room, thought for a moment, then raised his arms and

spoke his spell. A long table appeared with a large number of covered dishes, as well as at least three pitchers and half a dozen empty cups. Since I had to get my strength back as fast as possible I'd decided to force myself to eat, but when I began getting off the lounge a big hand came to my left arm to hold me where I was.

"The specialty of this brand new roadhouse is waiting hand and foot on all customers who happen to be weakened blonde sorceresses," Rik said, back to crouching beside my lounge. "I'll see what there is to be had and tell you about it, and then you can decide what you want."

"But I already know what's there," I said to his smile, working to keep myself from being annoyed. "Since I heard Graythor speak his spell, how could I not know? And didn't anyone ever tell you that sitting around *increases* weakness? If you want to build up your strength you have to work for it, not rest for it."

"When you're wounded, you first have to rest until you're healed, and then you can get somewhere with activity and effort," he countered, a shade too patiently for the emotion to be anything but forced. "You were wounded on the inside by that poison so you can't see what it did to you, but that doesn't mean you weren't hurt. The wizard has helped to heal you most of the way, but he couldn't do it all. The rest is for you to do, now with resting, later with your power. Do you understand?"

"As a matter of fact, I don't," I said with a frown for the thought that suddenly came to me, a thought that helped me push aside the strong urge to listen to Rik and do as he said. "Uncle Graythor, why didn't the efforts of the two of us heal me *all* the way? And why isn't it possible to recover magical strength faster than a crawl? Is the—opening—where the strength enters too small? Is the source it comes from too thin and weak to develop a decent rate of flow? And what *is* the source?"

"Laciel, child, you *were* healed all the way," Graythor said in a strange voice, staring at me in a very peculiar way. "The only problem is that the healing must be considered on a par with growing a patch of new skin on one's body after losing the original patch. The new skin is strong and healthy, but needs a short time of toughening before it grows beyond its beginning oversensitivity. As for the rest of what you asked—my dear child, I haven't the faintest idea. Questions like those are meant to be answered by the ones who can think of them in the first place, not people who did no more than dismiss them even if the concept *did* occur to them. Perhaps one day you'll be able to answer them for *me*."

He turned back to the table to reach for a pitcher and a cup, but not before I saw the pride shining in his eyes. It wasn't the first time I'd seen that look in Graythor's eyes, but the other times had been when I'd *answered* questions, not simply asked them. It annoyed me that there weren't any ready answers to satisfy my curiosity, and I could see I'd have some thinking to do once we got back with Morgiana. It shouldn't be *too* hard to figure out what I wanted to know, and once I had the time . . .

"Well, if you already know what's there, then tell me what you want," Rik said, the words reminding me that he still crouched to my left. When I looked at him, I saw that his smile and patience were gone together, but hadn't been replaced by anger or anything like that. Mostly it seemed to be sadness and resignation which held him, and that was something else I didn't understand.

"I'll have some chicken salad, a slice of potato pie, a cup of broth, and tea," I answered, feeling as if I *was* in a roadhouse or inn. "The only thing that isn't over there is the tea, but Graythor won't mind making some."

Rik nodded and straightened up, but once he headed for the table I wasn't all alone. InThig padded into the place Rik had vacated, and then sat down to inspect me closely.

"It disturbs me that I was elsewhere during your time of difficulty," it said, blazing red eyes looking a good deal more than disturbed. "I had also supposed that matters between you and Rik would have been settled by now. From what I've gathered of the conversation and exchanges I've overheard, matters are settled between you in a way I hadn't anticipated. You've asked him to leave and he's agreed?"

"He and I know it's the best thing for both of us," I said with a shrug, leaning back against the pillows again. "He didn't understand that at first, but now he does. How long will it take us to travel to the world where Morgiana is?"

"Not as long as our last journey took, nor will the way be nearly as difficult," InThig answered, those red eyes unblinkingly on me. "Morgiana was, after all, vacationing and taking her ease, as least for the most part. I wonder if you would take the trouble to explain to me how the separation of you and Rik would be of benefit to anyone at all, least of all to the two of you."

"What do you mean, Morgiana was vacationing and taking her ease 'for the most part'?" I asked, knowing the demon far too well to let a comment like that slide by. "Did she accidentally walk into something that we'll have trouble with, or do you think she went looking for whatever it is?"

"Laciel, Morgiana's—enjoyment of the unusual—is on a par with yours," the demon answered with a sigh. "That she indulges the humor only when on vacation, indicates her level of maturity. Knowing her final destination will allow us to avoid a good part of her itinerary, but certainly not all of it. Am I to understand that you don't care to discuss the matter of you and Rik at this time?"

"I think I would enjoy your understanding that I don't care to discuss that—matter—at all," I said, looking straight at the demon. "If the most I can get is a reprieve for right now I'll take it, specifically for Morgiana's sake. I have a feeling we're all going to need everything we have before this is over."

"And since some of us don't have as much as we're supposed to, it's time to eat," Rik announced from my right, coming back with the food I'd asked for. "Conversation can wait for another time."

"Preferably five or six hundred years," I muttered very low, smiling my thanks to Rik as I took the plate of food. I knew InThig was concerned about me and I appreciated that concern, but just then I couldn't spare the attention. Once Morgiana was safe, I'd have time for a lot of things including idle conversation, but hopefully by then InThig would be beyond needing to ask. Rik was a problem that had already been solved, and even a demon can't make a new problem out of something like that.

CHAPTER 5

The next morning I was awake early and dressed quickly in the butter-yellow leather pants and blue tunic I'd put on to run away from home in, but my speed didn't mean I had to wait for anybody. InThig doesn't sleep so it couldn't very well oversleep, and it was always ready to go somewhere at an instant's notice. One step out into the hall showed me Rik waiting at my door, his rust-colored leathers fresh and fitting as well as they always did, his sword belted firmly around his hips. InThig was amused to see Rik there, but all I did was nod a greeting and head for Graythor's apartment. It was too early to start any arguments, not to mention the fact that Graythor was also ready and waiting. We all went out to the stables to get horses for Graythor, Rik, and me, and then we were finally on our way. Behind us we left the wizard Aggan, one of Graythor's friends who owed him a favor. If Yallah waited until we were gone and then tried to make trouble, Aggan would see to it that she never troubled anyone ever again.

Graythor had had to use a minor spell to calm his

horse and Rik's against InThig's presence, but my horse was still under the original spell from the beginning of the quest for the Balance Stone of the Tears of the Mist. Rik's horse had originally been covered by the same spell, but my having left that world while Rik and his horse stayed in it had canceled the spell. That, of course, was the major reason for Aggan's assistance. Graythor needed someone to maintain his spells while he was gone, and Aggan had the necessary strength. He was also going to maintain Morgiana's spells and the few that I had rattling around, but the matter couldn't have been left in more capable hands. As soon as we got back, Aggan would take over for Graythor as the new Guardian of the Tears of the Mist.

The early morning was a little on the gray side as we rode along the road to the gate we would use, but it should have been blazing red to match the impatience I was feeling. The previous day had been more frustrating than fruitful, at least as far as regaining my strength went. Trying it for a while showed me that sitting still in one place did nothing to hurry the process of refilling my empty reservoir, but that didn't mean Graythor or Rik—or InThig—were ready to be reasonable about the conclusion. When Graythor left to take care of his personal business, Rik and InThig took turns watching and bullying me, which meant I wasn't speaking to either of them when Graythor got back for dinner. The wizard had ignored my silence in the same way Rik and InThig were doing, and after dinner we had made plans.

Or, *they* had made plans. I had sat on that stupid lounge and listened without commenting, mainly because very little of the planning had specifically concerned me. Once we got where we were going, Graythor would disguise and protect us, Rik would begin looking around and asking questions, and InThig would sneak into the palace and try to shake loose whatever secrets the place held. I, apparently, was just going along for the ride, or would be there to keep Graythor company while the other two found out what we needed to know and he watched over and directed us. I'd sat and listened to all that for quite a while, and then I'd left the lounge and gone back to my apartment. All three of my—"companions"—had tried questioning me on my way out, but I'd ignored them and had just kept going.

My gray was feeling really good and was having no trouble keeping up with Rik's roan and Graythor's chestnut, and I fidgetted with the wish that I could feel the same. The only reason I was there to begin with was Morgiana; if it hadn't been her safety at stake, I would have been gone no matter how many wardings Graythor had erected around me. They had made it very plain that I wasn't needed for that rescue effort, that I was being allowed to come along only because they were too kindhearted to try telling me I might as well stay behind. And after the fuss Graythor had made when I'd tried suggesting I didn't need *him* . . .

"We'll stop for breakfast at that inn a short way ahead," Graythor suddenly announced into the silence, his voice calm and confident and serene. "Now that we're on our way, we won't begrudge the time as a delay, and I think we can all use the nourishment."

"I know I can," Rik said from where he rode to Graythor's left, both of them just a little ahead of me. "My stomach's been thinking I forgot about it, so it's taken to reminding me it's there in the usual way. I've been trying to ignore it, but when I'm not under attack I find that difficult to do."

"Yes, there are definite times when trouble is of more use than peace and quiet," Graythor said with a chuckle, glancing at Rik in amusement. "That's not to say, of course, that trouble will be welcome in the days ahead. We'll take regular meals at regular times, and see to the matter that way."

They lapsed back into a companionable silence then, but I had the distinct feeling they'd been trying to rope *me* into the conversation. That comment Graythor had made about "all" of us needing nourishment, and the fact that neither he nor Rik had insisted we stop for breakfast before we left. He and Rik were being so terribly solicitous of my feelings of impatience, useless addition though I was. How sweet of them to make me feel warmly wanted and so carefully cared about.

I shifted in my saddle as I clenched my teeth, needing that clenching to keep from joining their conversation in a way they weren't expecting. InThig was running slightly behind us to the right rather than ranging ahead as it usually did, undoubtedly keeping more of an eye on me than on where we were going. I didn't think I was supposed to have noticed that, though, not with the way Rik and Graythor had very ostentatiously stopped fussing over me, just as though they believed I was completely recovered and back to my old self. But we would be riding only for a short while before we stopped for a rest disguised as a meal, a rest during which it should be possible to see whether or not I was pushing myself too far too fast. . . .

I had a lot of trouble swallowing down the growl that tried forcing its way out of my throat, but I finally managed to do it by distracting myself with a question. What would happen, I wondered, if I felt so terrible during breakfast that I was forced to turn back while the others went on without me? They would be devastated over losing my invaluable presence, of course, and might be so upset about being on their own that they'd miss noticing they were being followed. Going after Morgiana by myself was an idea I still found appealing, almost as much as the idea of separating myself from those who were sure they didn't need me. I've always had a thing about not staying where I wasn't wanted, even if those who didn't want me were as wrong as my three current companions.

As wrong as I *knew* they were. Graythor was more powerful than me, Rik stronger, and InThig more resilient and adaptable, but there was still no doubt to the feeling I had. Without me, they would have no chance of rescuing Morgiana, no matter how effective a team they were. In order to succeed *I* would have to be there, and I *would* be there. Without their knowing about it, but still there.

Making that decision finally let me relax a little, and

in fact cheered me up to the point of beginning to feel
as good as my mount. I hadn't been on my own in too
long a time, and I was starting to think more and more
about finding a place with lots of elbow room. The
short time I'd spent alone coming back from the world-
dimension where I'd left Su and Kadrim didn't count
for much, not when I'd gotten used to being alone for
most of my life, and I was really looking forward to
parting company with those I traveled with. They could
spend their time bothering each other, and I would be
well out of it.

It took less than an hour to reach the inn, and by
then my plans had been sketched in a little more
thoroughly. It had occurred to me that I couldn't
afford to seem too weakly or sick, or I would end up
with an escort back to Morgiana's house where I would
be left in the care of Aggan. The wizard Aggan was a
man who never raised his voice, but only because he
didn't have to. If he told someone to do something
and they did it, all fine and good; if he told someone
to do something and they *didn't* do it, rather than
argue he simply took steps to see that they did what he
wanted whether they cared to or not. He was the
stern, no-nonsense sort that Graythor was only at certain times, and if I was left in his care he'd put me
under his thumb and keep me there until Graythor got
back.

Which meant I couldn't afford to be taken back to
Aggan. If I tried hard enough I might find it possible
to get away from him, but I also might not. With
Morgiana's well-being at stake I couldn't take the
chance, so I had to make escape unnecessary. If
Graythor, Rik and InThig were convinced that something like pinched pride rather than lack of health was
responsible for separating me from them, they would
continue on with small sighs but no backward looks,
leaving me free to do what I had to.

The inn was different from other inns only in color,
the one way innkeepers could assert their individuality
without sacrificing the size and layout that proved best
for inns. Roadhouses were another story, of course,

primarily because they had no need to put up guests. Roadhouses provided food and drink only, and if you happened to reach one late at night, more drink than food. Inns provided everything including stabling for animals, and when we pulled up in front of the big, two-storied red and brown house one of the half-dozen stable boys came trotting over to take our horses.

"We'll only be here for breakfast, young man, so simply tie them somewhere out of the way," Graythor directed as he dismounted, having seen the two or three knots of people trying to get their mounts so they might be on their way. The boy seemed happy to hear our horses would not be needing attention, and was even happier when Rik threw him a copper coin. The young stablehand snagged the coin out of the air, gathered up our three sets of reins, then led our horses off to be tied somewhere out of the way.

"I must compliment InThig on its decision not to accompany us into the inn for breakfast," Graythor said in a low voice to Rik as we began walking toward the house. "With all these people about, the sudden appearance of a demon would be likely to cause any number of disturbances."

" 'Likely' is too indefinite a word," Rik answered, probably remembering the time InThig *did* include itself in on a breakfast taken at an inn. "We'd end up trampled in the rush of everyone trying to get clear, or having to revive the ones who fainted. It would be easier passing on the meal ourselves."

"Easier, but not particularly wise," Graythor said, opening the inn door and stepping through to hold it for me. "You haven't said much this morning, Laciel. How are you feeling?"

"I'm just wonderful, Graythor," I answered without looking at him as I walked past him, making the words very cool and distant. "And how are *you*?"

"My question wasn't an attempt to exchange amenities," he came back with the beginnings of annoyance, leaving the door so that he could move along with me to my right. "Would you prefer my having the house doctor look you over?"

"Since I'm not a child, he can't look me over without my permission," I said with comfortable satisfaction, paying more attention to the table of food I walked toward than to the man who spoke to me. "It looks like you're stuck with taking my unreliable, unsubstantiated word for it."

I could almost feel the huffing annoyance grow stronger inside the wizard, but he didn't come up with any immediate words. I was willing to bet he was fighting to control his temper, telling himself that that wasn't the time or the place to start a brawl. Graythor was strong enough to knock me flat and then force a responsive answer out of me, but people tend to react to the presence of a wizard almost as badly as they do to the presence of a demon. Add to that the fact that he would also never be so dishonorable as to fight with someone who wasn't in peak condition, and you have one smallish wizard with a very tall problem.

"I think if Graythor and I, each in our own way, insisted, that doctor would examine you without your permission," another voice chimed in from my left, the body producing the voice stepping forward after that to hand a silver coin to the woman who stood behind the food table. "For three breakfasts, ma'am, the largest you offer."

The woman simpered at Rik's smile as she took the silver and began to count out his change in copper, but simpering wasn't what *I* felt like doing to him. That miserable beast had just threatened me, and not for the first time, either. Other people made very sure not to even *appear* as though they were threatening a sorceress of my strength, but Rik had never seemed to understand how dangerous it was. Or, which was much more likely, he dismissed the idea that he might be putting his foot in it. After all, wasn't he protected by a very powerful wizard, and wasn't the sorceress in question still much too weak to do anything about feelings of insult?

"If you would make the effort to understand we are concerned about you, young lady, *we* would find it possible to be a good deal more polite," Graythor said, probably in reaction to the expression on my face. "I seriously doubt if Morgiana would be pleased to find herself rescued at the expense of your health and ability. Choose your breakfast, now, and we'll continue this discussion once we're seated at a table."

Graythor's gesture directed me ahead of him and behind Rik, who was already telling one of the inn girls what he wanted from the array of food on the table. The girl held a large platter and moved along the table with him, scooping up mounds of food at his direction and depositing them on the platter. If we'd stayed at the inn we would have been served at a table, but as walk-in meal customers we were only entitled to decide on what we wanted, not have it served. Of course, we could have paid to have it served, but apparently Graythor had decided against being too ostentatious.

Another of the inn girls stood there waiting for me to make my own selections, so I took Graythor's advice and left the argument for later. It so happened I felt one step away from absolute starvation, and part of my plan was to walk off with offended dignity *after* I'd eaten, not before. I began pointing things out to the girl as though I didn't really care *what* I chose, and by pure accident ended up with lots of eggs and fried potatoes and steaks and bacon and sliced fruit and a thick wedge of bread. Graythor's annoyance came back briefly when I chose a large mug of coffee instead of milk, but he stuck by his own injunction and didn't make an issue of it.

Rik had already chosen a small, round table near the wall beyond the food table, so I carried my platter and mug and a fork over and claimed one of the three chairs standing around it. A moment or so later Graythor joined us, and then the three of us were digging in. The food wasn't bad at all; if not pure works of art, then tasty and hot. I'd eaten better in my life, but I'd also eaten a lot worse, not to mention going hungry altogether. Everything comes in degrees, and how good the degree you're up to is depends on where you started and how far you've come.

The first one to finish was Rik, but I wasn't far behind him. I'd needed that meal even more than I'd thought, and as I sat back with my coffee I could feel eyes on me. One pair would have been understandable, but what I felt was two pairs.

"You certainly did that meal justice, child," Graythor observed, still working on what his own plate held. "Perhaps your strength *has* advanced from yesterday's ebb."

"My strength has done more than just advance a little," I answered, trying for unostentatious obnoxiousness. "I think it would be safe to say I'm practically back to where I started from, so let's take a few minutes to discuss what I'll be doing once we get where we're going. I think it would be a good idea if I tried to find that High King's opposition, the person or group most against him. If someone has a weakness, his enemies usually know about it even if they can't take advantage of it."

"That's very true," Graythor said, the words a good deal more neutral than the look he exchanged with Rik. "It's also an excellent line of attack we hadn't thought of, and I must commend you for suggesting it. However . . ."

"However," Rik picked up the dropped thread Graythor had dangled, the wizard apparently finding it too difficult to go on, "it may not be the best of ideas for you to start work on that as soon as we get there. InThig and I will do some preliminary scouting, just to give us an idea of what's going on, and then the four of us will be able to sit down and discuss our first move. Depending on what we find, that move may very well be the rooting out of the High King's chief enemy."

"May very well be," I echoed flatly, ignoring the urge to be reasonable and agreeable that I was right then feeling. "Whether it is or not, what do you picture *me* doing while you and InThig scout and Graythor maintains our protection? Sitting and counting my thumbs? And once we have that discussion and make our decision, do you three get to sit around while *I* do all the work?"

"Laciel, why must you make this so much more difficult for us?" Graythor asked with a sigh, the fork he held more drooping over his food than poised. "When your strength proves itself sufficiently returned, you may do your share in assisting us, but first you must recover and at least be able to defend yourself if the need arises. Are you able to argue the fact that at this moment, despite the hearty breakfast you so conspicuously devoured, even self-protection is beyond you?"

"You think I'm only pretending to be recovered?" I countered with all the stiffness I could muster, trying to bring a flush to my cheeks as I put my coffee mug down with a slam. "You see me as nothing but a burden on this journey, and an unreasonable burden at that? Well, do you?"

"Laciel, you're not a burden," Rik said with a sigh to match Graythor's, drawing the heat to himself as the wizard struggled to find the words to deny what he so obviously believed was true. "You may be unreasonable, but where you're concerned that's nothing new. Right now you're not up to your usual ability, and the worst part about that is our not knowing how soon you *will* be up to it. Since we don't want to give you things to do before you're able to handle them— and thereby make things worse—we'll just wait to see how everything goes before making definite plans. It's the only reasonable way to handle it."

"Reasonable," I repeated flatly and bitterly, trying to project as much unhappiness as he was projecting compassion and concern. I moved my eyes to Graythor long enough to see the complete agreement he showed with Rik's words, then nodded my head and got stiffly to my feet.

"Since you're both so interested in reason, it isn't reasonable to drag a useless burden along on a rescue mission," I told them, still speaking flatly and bitterly. "That being the case, when you get back with Morgiana you can send a message to Rencie Arram's house in Geddenburg, announcing your success. I wish you three all the luck you need and some to spare."

I offered them the sentiment of the old saying with a touch of irony, then turned and marched away toward the door out of the inn. Truthfully, I really was the least bit annoyed, but the longer I stayed in Graythor and Rik's company, the more used to it I was getting. It would be hard to find two more annoying men, even if you went searching through every world-dimension ever explored.

I strode angrily out of the inn without looking back, and immediately headed for the stables to find where they'd put my horse. I wanted to be well on my way before they could decide to apologize and insist that I go with them anyway, and I was glad I wouldn't have to wait until one of the frenzied stable boys could get around to bringing out my horse. There seemed to be just as many people trying to leave as there had been when we'd first arrived, which didn't seem very— reasonable.

Walking into the stable showed me another wide door like the one at the front, only that one was all the way down to the left and almost to the end of the immense building. The aisle of stalls were to the right, and bales of hay stood piled high down the wide left-hand aisle, stacked against the outermost stall walls on the right. If the horses of transients were any-where, logic said they had to be there to the left, where they would be both handy and out of the way. I couldn't see any horses from where I stood, but there was probably a gap in the hay bales where they could be left without tempting a casual passerby with a ca-sual sense of who owned what.

If I could have asked one of the stable boys, I would have done it, but without the use of a net it didn't seem possible to catch one of them. They flew back and forth, going in empty-handed and coming out with one or more horses, and the noise of the people who still didn't believe they were moving fast enough was just short of deafening. I shook my head as I moved off to the left, wondering why people had to be so unreasonable, but there was no easy answer. Some people rushed others because others rushed them, but you can always find those who rush just for the sake of rushing.

The more distance I put between me and the front of the stable, the dimmer and quieter it got. I moved up the wide aisle quickly, anxious to be mounted and away, remembering that I had to be on the lookout for InThig once I left the inn. If I stayed alert, I should be able to avoid the demon, but first I had to find my blasted horse. There was no gap in the bales piled to the right, which meant there were also no horses.

Since I was already just about down there, I decided I might as well look through the wide door on the left before going back and trying to net a stable boy. The door was just a short distance ahead, beyond a separate, lonely-standing stack of hay bales, and as I got a little closer I silently patted myself on the back for not giving up. Just outside the door, beyond the edge of bales, I caught sight of a horse's tail swishing. The horse might turn out to be someone else's, but it could just as easily prove to be mine.

I was more interested in trying to look out the door than in watching all around me, so the abrupt appearance of four men, two in front of me, two behind, was something of a surprise. I realized at once that the single stack of bales now blocked off sight of me from the front of the stables, and the dirty grins the men wore confirmed that supposedly disconcerting truth.

"Well, now, will you look at what we got," one of the men drawled, a big man who wasn't dressed any better than his three friends. All of them were dirty as well as shabby, and their beards were more stubble than deliberate beards. "This one's gonna be the best yet."

"I do like it," the one standing next to him agreed, his mean, narrow eyes glinting as they moved up and down the length of me. "Whatever silver or gold she's got, and her throwed in on top. Yes, sir, I do like it."

"And it don't matter how loud she yells," a third, one of those behind me, put in gleefully. "With all the noise them yahoos is makin' up front, ain't nobody gonna hear her. We got her fer as long as we want."

The one who had spoken first was studying my face with amusement, most probably searching for the first signs of panicked helplessness. That would be one of the things he liked best, he and his sort, the screaming fear of those they victimized. When everything around you in your world convinces you you're useless, the sole source of power and self-importance you have is the fear of the people you can victimize. They were sick, all four of them, sick with the disease known as being an outcast, but I didn't have the time to mess with them.

"Go away!" I hissed impatiently at the two in front of me, idiotically trying to keep my voice down even though I knew I wouldn't be heard by anyone but them. "I'm in a hurry to get out of here, and you're wasting my time!"

"Pretty girl, we're gonna be spendin' a lot of time together, but ain't none of it gonna be wasted," the second said with a leer, not noticing the way the first man was now frowning. "I got a real weakness fer blondes, so you treat me real good and mebbe I'll keep you fer a while. But I said *real* good."

"You can't begin to understand what I'll treat you to if you don't get out of my way!" I snapped, beginning to be really angry. Leaving them there would be no big thing—after all, the next victims they would try for would be Rik and Graythor—but they insisted on standing there and babbling at me. "This is the last time I'm going to say it: step back and do it *now!*"

"You got some reason we oughta get outta your way?" the first man began to ask, suspicion and faint uneasiness now appearing with his frown. The fact that I wasn't showing the expected fear bothered him, but the second man wasn't as observant. Rage filled him over what I'd said, and his roar drowned out the first man's question.

"You think you're gonna tell *us* what t' do?" he demanded, his skin under the stubble darkening. "You rich ones think you own th' world, but you don't own *us* th' way you do everthin' else! Right now *we* got the ownin', an' I'm gonna be the first t' prove it."

His grab for my arms was so fast and vicious, I didn't have the time to do what I'd intended. I'd wanted to scare them a little—a *very* little!—but before I could override the reaction my automatic defenses flared into being. As the second man touched me, he was suddenly bathed in furiously flaring blue, and his scream was followed by the screams of the others as the blue sparks jumped to every one of them. Intention controlled that spreading, their own intention to do me harm, and in seconds all four of them were rolling on the ground as they screamed. I cut the projection off with a curse, but it was far too late to keep the damage from being done.

"Laciel, are you all right?" Rik demanded as he came racing around the bales of hay, his bronze eyes blazing. His hand was also wrapped around his sword hilt, but it was fairly obvious weapons weren't necessary.

"I'm perfectly fine," I answered stiffly, silently cursing the fact that he must have left the inn only moments behind me. "I don't know how many times I have to say that, but I hope this will be the last. I'm leaving now, so you won't . . ."

"Just a moment, young woman!" another, heavily angry voice interrupted, the voice of someone I'd been hoping was still finishing breakfast. "There are explanations to be made here, and you'd best get to them this very instant!"

"Why are you asking for explanations?" Rik said in a puzzled voice to Graythor as I closed my eyes in pain. "She was obviously attacked by those four, and her personal defenses were able to handle it. Are you afraid she's now back to being as empty as she was?"

"Empty!" Graythor echoed with a growl, furious and not trying to hide it. "Don't you see—? No, of course you don't, so let me explain. Rik, the strength behind that flaming curtain of defense wasn't minimal, it was as full as it's ever been, maybe even more so! You often have a choice as to how much power to put into a spell, but automatic defenses use everything that's there, everything you have. That girl isn't empty, she's probably stronger now than she was before the trouble!"

"But—how is that possible?" Rik groped, trying to understand what he'd been told. "You said it would be days and days before she was back to normal, and even *she* said . . ."

"Yes, even *she* said," Graythor interrupted, still too angry to be polite. "Now I will hear *why* she said, and also how this little—surprise—was made possible. Until just a moment ago, I was prepared to swear it wasn't."

Rik's silence was fraught with all sorts of overtones and undertones that were clear even though I wasn't looking at him, but in spite of that it was definitely time to counterattack. I opened my eyes and turned my head to Graythor, and even managed not to flinch anywhere but on the inside.

"I do beg your pardon, sir, but I think you're accusing me of lying," I said in the coldest tones I was capable of, pretending I didn't see the way he was glaring at me. "If you believe that's true, you shouldn't have any trouble quoting what I said that *was* a lie."

"Young woman, you know very well what you said that was a lie," he came back at once in that same growl, his dark eyes just short of glowing. "When I asked how you were, you said you were—that is, you led me to believe you were— Confound it, child, you let me believe you weren't yet recovered!"

"I *told* you I was fine," I corrected, refusing to back away from the frustrated anger bubbling at me. "I *said* I was just about back to where I should be, and I said it more than once. Was it my fault that you refused to believe me? That you were so unyielding in your disbelief that you drove me away with insults? Now you stand there accusing me of lying, and that's supposed to be my fault, too? I think I've had all of this I care to take, so you'll have to excuse me. There are lots of places I can go to be insulted and accused, and I'd prefer any of them to this one here."

I turned my back on Graythor with my nose in the air, happily aware of the expression of appalled upset on his face, beginning to believe I'd pulled it off after all. Graythor was too fair-minded a person not to be bothered by the fact that I *hadn't* lied, but I was counting my golden eggs before the hen laid them. Two big hands coming to my arms from behind kept me from taking even the first step toward escape, hands that didn't activate my defenses because they were warded, and then Rik proved he was no longer confused about what had happened.

"I think there are still one or two questions to be answered before you go stalking off in high dudgeon," he said, sounding more annoyed than embarrassed. "If everything you did was so honest and aboveboard, why didn't we find out first thing this morning that you had gained back everything you'd lost? Why did you wait until the question was brought up to you, and then make it sound as if you were indulging in wishful thinking rather than discussing fact? And if you managed to do something even Graythor didn't know was possible, why weren't you right there telling him all about it?"

The questions he'd thrown at me were one step away from being demands, and the moans of the men still on the ground weren't keeping him—or Graythor—from listening closely for my answers. He sounded as though he thought he had me cornered, but the job couldn't be done quite as easily as that.

"You're wondering why you weren't given the details of my recovery this morning," I commented, keeping the words as cold as the ones I'd addressed to Graythor. "I'd thought the bunch of you had noticed I wasn't talking to any of you this morning, but I suppose one has to be important for people to notice something like that. When I was finally asked how I was, I again expected to be treated like an adult human and again I was disappointed. Rather than a polite inquiry as to how I could be as recovered as I claimed, I was chided for not answering responsively and then threatened with a forced physical examination. If that's your idea of encouragement designed to foster shared confidences, I suggest you rethink your battle plan."

By then his hands were gone from my arms and for

the second time I thought I'd won free, but no such luck. I got to take half a step toward the doors that meant escape, and then Graythor took another of his turns in the conversation.

"Forgive me, Laciel, but I'm afraid your going off on your own right now is out of the question," he said, sounding as apologetic as his words suggested, but also sounding determined. "You and I must speak about this—discovery of yours, and since you've proven you'll be anything but a burden on our journey, there's no longer a reason for you to consider remaining behind. We can be on our way again and have an opportunity to talk once the matter of these miscreants is settled with the inn people and authorities."

At that point I heard the babble of demanding voices drawing nearer through the stable, and realized that the screaming of all four men together—and, probably, sight of my defenses flaring into action—had gotten the attention of both travelers and inn people. They'd all show up demanding to know what had happened, but however much of a delay they caused made no overall difference. My clean escape was done for, and if I simply walked away it wouldn't take long for Graythor and Rik to figure out exactly what I was doing.

I had the time to move a couple of steps to one side with a sigh before the legions of the demand descended on us, but the mess was handled faster and more intelligently than I'd been expecting. One of the inn men was a district court surrogate who had been appointed to handle trouble at the inn, and he had the older stablehands tie the four men and then look around. The wide-eyed travelers gasped in horror when five bodies were found, the bodies of one group and a single traveler who had stopped at the inn for breakfast. The four men had killed and robbed all of them, and because of the chaos surrounding early morning rush, no one had noticed.

We stayed long enough to hear one of the four confess that he and his friends had gotten the idea when they'd seen where their horses had been put when they'd finished their own breakfast, and then we'd left. The four had almost been ready to leave with the stolen coins and the horses the dead would no longer need, and then I had come along. Only one of the four had spoken because the other three had been shaking too hard, their pain and panic-filled eyes staring at me with desperate fear. I usually disliked the terror some people showed when they found out I was a sorceress, but just then I didn't mind it a bit. Those four deserved to be terrorized for what they'd done, and the only thing I regretted was that I hadn't the time to stay around and continue the treatment.

Once we were mounted and back on the road, we rode toward the gate we were going to use in unexpected silence. Both Graythor and Rik seemed wrapped up in their own thoughts, and I had something to think about as well. My plan to go off on my own hadn't worked out, but since my companions didn't know about it, I wasn't in any sort of trouble. As a matter of fact my position might have improved quite a bit, as there was now no longer a reason for them to exclude me from any of the rescue plans. If they tried to exclude me anyway, I could always pick up and walk away, but they probably wouldn't do that. No, things were definitely looking up, and that despite the way the skies were turning even darker.

InThig came out of the woods to rejoin us a few minutes before we reached the gate, and we made it just in time. The glowing slit positioned between two trees some distance off the road responded to the presence of those with the Sight, and spread into the coruscating curtain that was a gate between worlds. Our demon companion, being the one who knew the way, went first, and I followed behind it, leading my horse. Rik held to the tail of my horse and Graythor brought up the rear, and Rik, at least, got a little wet before he was able to enter the gate. Big, fat raindrops began spattering down as we formed up in front of the gate, but a gesture and a word kept Graythor from getting wet. I didn't know why he didn't include Rik in

his umbrella spell, but I knew that the oversight bothered me.

Once we stepped through the gate into the next
world, umbrellas of any sort became unnecessary. A
red sun was shining brightly, blue clouds floated lazily
in a clear pink sky, and multicolored birds chirped
happily or sang from the surrounding vivid yellow
trees. The bushes and grass were also vivid yellow,
and I couldn't help wincing at all the enthusiastic
color.

"This dimension is very popular as a change-of-pace
area," InThig said, looking around as it waited for the
rest of us to clear the gate and get mounted again.
"After you've spent a little time here, ordinary world-
dimensions come as a vast relief rather than as boring
sameness."

"I don't know whether to worry more about my
hearing or my sight," Rik muttered as he swung into
his saddle, waterdrops glistening in his dark hair. "These
colors are so loud they're nearly deafening, but my
eyes are sending me the impression they're about to
shift out of desperation into seeing nothing but shades
of gray. How long do we have to stay in this place?"

"Morgiana chose a gate that's hours away, so I'm
afraid we're in for something of a stay," Graythor said
as he led his horse forward, then shook his head at our
demon. "InThig traveled a good deal faster when it
first followed her trail this way, but we're not equipped
to use that particular mode of travel. I wish we were."

"Humans are, unfortunately, rather restricted,"
InThig commiserated, unbothered by the fact that
Graythor had answered Rik's question rather than
allowing the demon to do so. "I will, of course, keep
to your speed this time, which should give me more of
an idea about what you're all going through. I won't
suffer as much as you do, but I will get something of
an idea of it."

"From our moans and groans, if no other way," I
commented as Graythor got himself mounted, absolutely certain InThig wasn't bothered by the color
scheme at all. "Sometimes I get jealous enough to

wish I could find a world-dimension that bothered demons but not people."

"Ah, but there *is* a world-dimension like that," InThig answered, hiding its grin as it shifted from sitting to walking. With the three of us mounted, there was no reason not to continue on our way. "Should I ever wish to give you a gift, Laciel, I may perhaps tell you where it is."

"Well, you know how safe the knowledge would be with *me,* InThig," I answered very virtuously, moving my gray after the demon. "I would never ever even *consider* visiting a world like *that.*"

The only response InThig gave me was a deep-throated chuckle of amusement at what I'd said, Graythor and Rik briefly joining in the reaction. For some reason I didn't think any of them believed me, which was really very wise of them.

We rode on through the horribly garish landscape, and I, for one, was glad I'd never been to that world-dimension before. It wasn't just that everything around us was the wrong color; it doesn't much matter *what* color something comes in, as long as that color gets along with the other colors around it. The shades and hues of that place didn't even have a nodding acquaintance with the ones nearest them, and clashing is too mild a word for the way they impinged on my senses. I felt very much shaken out of the everyday, but not into a more invigorating frame of reference. It was very clear that whoever designed that world had to have been colorblind.

The one thing that world didn't seem to have was danger, but after drawing that conclusion I found out I was only partially right. We were approaching a small wooded area consisting of yellow and purple trees when the pack of whatever-they-were jumped out at us, all bristling green hides and pointed pink fangs and claws. Rik immediately reached for his sword and Graythor and I raised our right hands, but none of us got to do anything in the way of defense.

As soon as Graythor and I moved a sickly orange glow surrounded the two of us, and the attacking animals drew to a screeching halt so fast I thought they'd run into an invisible wall. They were already angling their approach to avoid InThig, and as soon as they saw the glow they gave it up altogether. More than one of the pack looked like it was muttering to itself in disgust as they turned and trotted back toward the trees, and if they weren't shaking their heads and glaring at us over their shoulders, it was only because they weren't built right to do those things.

"Was it something we said?" I wondered aloud, noticing at the same time that InThig had made no defensive movements at all, and was right then simply standing and watching the beasts trot away. "And are you supposed to feel insulted when the predators of a world turn their noses up at the idea of considering you prey?"

"They're well known to have had prior experience with magic users," InThig said in answer, grinning out its amusement as it looked at me. "When you and Graythor began drawing this world's power to you, they immediately knew they would be much happier elsewhere. They seem to have more than rudimentary intelligence, and may well develop into this world's most advanced life form."

"I'd thought that was what the orange glow was," Graythor said in satisfaction, watching the beasts disappear into those woods. "On most other worlds it isn't possible to see the power being gathered, not unless someone has spoken a spell to arrange the phenomenon."

"They also seem to have had prior experience with demons," Rik put in, apparently as amused as InThig. "But then, if I remember correctly, most life-forms seem to feel the same. I can't recall a single one from the quest that was willing to tangle with you, my friend."

"My kind not only gets around, it tends to be remembered," InThig replied, surprisingly trying not to sound too smug. "When humans have been in existence as long as demons, Rik, they'll find themselves being given the same sort of respect."

"Respect," Rik echoed, swallowing most of a laugh. "That's not exactly the word *I* would have used, but maybe you're right. One day humans will be respected, but right now some of them are judiciously avoided. I think I'm going to enjoy this journey a lot more than the last one you and Laciel and I shared. I may even let myself get fat and lazy."

I looked at him quickly to see if he was serious, and the well-satisfied expression on his face seemed to indicate he certainly was. I would have thought he would have disliked the idea of not having anyone to protect, of not even needing to protect himself, but apparently that wasn't so. Rik wasn't bothered by being in the company of two strong magic users and a life-form that didn't need to use magic, and somehow the idea of that was bothering to *me*.

We rode on in peace after that, time and distance slipping away behind us but not entirely unnoticed. Graythor eventually stirred in his saddle, and then pulled his chestnut to a halt.

"I think we would do well to stop now for a meal and a short rest," he announced, looking around at the bright yellow meadow we rode through. "From what InThig has told me, we still have something of a way to go before reaching the gate Morgiana used to leave this world."

I looked up at the clear pink sky to see that the bright red sun had lowered to the point of mid-afternoon, then began to dismount with a sigh. It would probably be after dark before we reached the gate we wanted, but maybe that would be for the best. Once darkness falls, individual colors can't be distinguished any longer.

"But wait a minute," I muttered almost to myself, suddenly realizing something important. "If that's a *red* sun up there, why aren't the colors down here affected by it? Should there be bright yellow grass and trees when there's a red sun in the sky?"

"An excellent point," Graythor said, and I looked up to see him studying the landscape in a way different from the one he'd been using. "Truthfully it's a rather obvious point, but the sort of obvious that becomes clear only after someone notices it. A conclusion to match would be that we're not seeing the *actual* colors of this world, only approximations that our human senses can accept and handle. How do you perceive them, InThig?"

"As extremely garish," InThig answered, a shrug in its voice as it sat itself in the grass. "It's possible for me to shift them out of my vision entirely, just as I shift darkness out of my way, but other than that I see nothing different."

"When I have the time and attention to spare, I fully intend returning here to look into the question," Graythor decided, reluctantly turning away from our surroundings. "At the moment, unfortunately, we have more serious concerns than curiosity to occupy us, but we may as well be comfortable for our meal."

That sickly orange glow returned as he raised both arms and began speaking a spell, and I discovered that trying to See the glow was as much of a waste of time as trying to See a difference in the landscape. Whatever laws governed that world, they couldn't be Seen any more than they could be seen. Poking and prying would be needed to get to the bottom of them, and we didn't have the time for that.

Graythor produced a table covered with food and drink as well as indecently comfortable chairs for us to sit in, and he didn't forget about InThig or the horses. InThig got a large, plush section of bright red carpeting to stretch out on, and the horses found lush green grass under their feet. Rik immediately began bending over the table to see what was available, but Graythor moved his eyes to me as we both settled into our chairs.

"You may be wondering why I haven't yet asked you for details concerning your accomplishment, Laciel," he said, his expression and tone no more than politely neutral. "The truth of the matter is I've spent our ride thinking, and now I believe I'm ready to hear facts that may be compared with speculative conclusions. Would you prefer eating before getting into the discussion?"

"I don't think I'll find it too hard doing both together," I said, reaching for one of the chicken sandwiches he'd created. "To tell the truth, there aren't many details I can give you about what I did. I needed a particular effect, so I designed a spell and tried it out. I didn't know if I had enough strength to make it work, but apparently I did. Would you like to see the spell?"

He nodded without saying anything, so I wiped my right hand on a napkin before gesturing into existence a piece of paper and a lead-filled marking rod. You don't speak a spell unless you intend activating it, and I didn't think it would be wise activating my spell a second time. In theory it shouldn't have done any harm if it *was* called into play again, but theory without experimentation to back it has a habit of turning around and biting.

It took only a moment to write down the spell and then pass the paper to Graythor, but that ended our conversation for a while. Rather than simply look the spell over he began studying it, which meant I had the time to finish my sandwich, take another and finish that as well, and in the interim help myself to some ale. Graythor ate distractedly while he studied, Rik simply enjoyed the meal, and InThig let its eyes move from one to the other of us, its tail swishing sharply. The demon was curious about what was going on, but apparently didn't care to distract Graythor from what he was doing. Only when I saw that did I remember InThig hadn't been with us at the inn, and therefore didn't know I was back to the way I was supposed to be. I toyed with the idea of filling it in, then decided to wait. Explanations could be taken care of when Graythor's questions were answered.

The wizard in question finished the hot roast beef sandwich he was eating, drank half the ale I'd poured for him, then leaned back in his chair. His dark eyes were distracted and stayed that way for another moment or two, and then he was entirely returned from the realms of thought.

"This spell," he said to me without preamble, his hand gesturing to the piece of paper. "How long did it take you to design it?"

"Not long once I decided how to phrase what I wanted," I answered with a shrug, wondering why he was asking. "It was the phrasing I had to spend some time on, to make sure I came as close as possible to what I was trying to accomplish. I don't think I have to tell you how hard it is to describe something without fully defining it."

"No, on the contrary, please do tell me how hard that is," he said, and I suddenly noticed the heavy anger lurking in the dark of his eyes. His voice had come very close to being a rasp, and his hand had turned to a fist on the arm of his chair.

"What's wrong?" Rik asked at once, putting the question before I could. "Did she make a mistake?"

"No, no mistake," Graythor denied, the anger still smoldering away. "If she'd made a mistake the way you mean it, either the spell would have failed to do anything at all, or conversely she would have been hurt or killed. No, the spell worked properly and did as it was supposed to, but that isn't the issue here. What I'm concerned with is the fact that she actually went so far as to describe something no one has ever seen, or is even certain exists! Have you any idea how dangerous that is?"

Rik frowned as he tried to imagine the danger, but InThig, who knew considerably more about magic, didn't have to try. The demon hissed as it rose into a sitting position, and those blazing red eyes were directly on me.

"Really, Laciel, I'm beginning to believe you need to be put under guard," my half-lifetime long companion growled, more than simply annoyed. "I'm sure Morgiana didn't fail to mention how disreputable a hobby suicide is, but possibly it's time to repeat the observation. What in the worlds could you have been thinking of?"

"I was *thinking* about helping to rescue Morgiana," I answered, deliberately borrowing some of InThig's growl as I straightened in my chair. "I needed the strength to flow back into me faster than it was doing, so I created a spell to make it happen. Do you realize how foolish you sound, yelling at me for succeeding with what I wanted to do?"

"That isn't what's angering us, and I believe you know it," Graythor took over while InThig blinked at me with the beginnings of doubt, the wizard's eyes having narrowed. "In order to have the strength flow into you more quickly, you used what strength you did have to create more—openings—for the power to flow in by. As I recall, we discussed the matter of what sort of opening there might be inside us for that purpose, and we also agreed we had no idea what its exact nature and shape was. This spell you designed details an *unSeen* phenomenon, and could just as easily have caused you to burst apart! That you regained your strength instead was purely a matter of fortune, and that terrible danger was risked simply because you hadn't the patience to wait for an outcome that would have eventuated in its own good time!"

"You're bent out of shape because I used black magic?" I demanded, letting a laugh of incredulity escape. "Uncle Graythor, you were the one who said I was *born* to use black magic. What's the difference between risking myself for something *I* need now, and risking myself for the needs of others later?"

"My dear child, the difference is in the matter of training," he came back, leaning forward to emphasize the very serious words he spoke. "Right now you're simply groping in the dark with your talent, when you should be using it to guide you. The studies waiting for your attention will teach you the safest possible use of your talent, and will also detail the fatal errors made by others. What possible use can there be in your blundering into their mistakes through the courting of danger without first preparing yourself to withstand it? If working with unSeen magic was certain death under all conditions, do you imagine I would have suggested your involvement with it under any circumstances whatsoever?"

I opened my mouth to answer his questions, but he seemed to have used up all the readily available words. Of course, I knew he would never throw my life away without a thought, but how prepared can you make yourself against something that can—and does—bite your head off without warning or reason? The only way to keep yourself safe under *those* circumstances is to find something else to occupy your study time, but something else wasn't what he and Morgiana wanted me to do.

"I have the feeling Laciel didn't think she was risking herself unnecessarily," Rik suddenly spoke up, surprising me with the calm attempt at defense on my behalf. "I know she got used to thinking on her feet during the quest, doing what had to be done quickly and efficiently, and once you've picked up a habit like that, it's hard to break. I think we ought to be glad she's as good as she is, and simply leave it at that. Considering what's ahead of us, we'll probably all end up being put at risk."

"Those are excellent points, Rik," InThig said, its voice sliding easily into a near-purr as it grinned. "We're fortunate to have someone with us who feels more than simple affection for Laciel. It takes someone with a very close bond to really understand her, I think."

"Oh, that isn't entirely true, InThig," Rik protested, but in a warm, friendly way. "Laciel and I are former quest companions, just as you are, and we don't need anything else to understand each other. You'll find I'm right once we have Morgiana back, and we each go our own separate ways. We'll be able to meet again years and years from now, and we'll still understand each other."

This time it was InThig's turn to have trouble finding something to say, and its grin was abruptly no longer in evidence. Rik, however, didn't seem to notice any of that; he finished the ale in his cup, then stood up to stretch.

"Yes, I think it would be best if we continued on

now," Graythor said as though someone else had made the suggestion, picking up the paper with my spell before getting to his feet. "We'll most likely have a delay to face once we go through the next gate, so it behooves us to make the best possible time now. Are you ready, Laciel?"

I nodded wordlessly as I stood, giving him the chance to wave away the table, chairs, and food he'd created, then joined the general movement toward the horses. InThig and Graythor seemed marginally upset, possibly because of what Rik had said, but I, of course, didn't feel anything like the same. He had promised to leave once Morgiana was rescued, and now had confirmed the fact that he intended doing just that. I meant nothing more to him than any former quest companion would, and that was just the way I wanted it.

Just the way I wanted it.

I mounted up with the others, and we headed again in the direction of the next gate.

CHAPTER 6

It was as dark as an unborn world-dimension by the time we reached the gate, but only there under the trees where the gate was. Out in the open the sky was a dark pink with brilliantly glowing mint green stars, a combination that had to be seen to be believed. No moons had made an appearance as yet, and we were all hoping to be gone before one or more could.

The gate flared open in brilliant color as we approached it, and as soon as we were all dismounted we followed InThig through. I thought I detected the least hesitation before the demon trotted ahead, and once I exited on the other side I knew I was right. I recognized the staid dark-wood paneling and leather furniture surrounding the gate on that side, the entrance setting for a place InThig, for some reason, really disapproved of. The flagstoned floor didn't mind our leading horses onto it, and the area was more than large enough to take our party without crowding. I knew that place, all right, and that was why I was confused.

"Uncle Graythor, I have to be imagining things," I said, turning to him as he led his chestnut farther away from the gate. "I'm ready to swear this is the Realm of Dreams, but it can't be. The last time I came it took weeks to get here, and Morgiana and I used the shortest route she knew."

"Apparently Morgiana just discovered a shorter route," Graythor answered, looking around with InThig's level of enthusiasm. "I would venture to guess that the gate we just used is virtually unknown in this direction, and known about but shunned from the other worlds it leads to. Most of the Sighted I know would not have been able to complete the journey we just made. The less strength you have, the more painful that oddly-colored world is."

"Now isn't that strange," I said, not having known that about the garish world. "I have the feeling it's another clue to the truth of that world, but where it fits in is anyone's guess. You know, when you go back to study it, I just may go with you."

"If you do, you'll be as welcome as always," he said in partial distraction, his frown for the neat emptiness around us. "Just this moment, however, I would welcome the appearance of one of the gate attendants. Our first concern is how long a cycle we must wait through here, before we can continue on."

"What makes you think we'll have to wait?" Rik asked in curiosity, still held by the surprise of finding a gate leading into a building like that. "And even if we do have to wait, why are you making it sound like a hardship? If the rest of this place is as posh as what we're now standing in, it should be nothing short of pure pleasure."

"It so happens this entrance area is bare bones compared to the rest of the resort," Graythor grudged, turning an unhappy gaze on Rik. "This is the Realm of Dreams, a place created for and catering to the Sighted and their guests. What's done here is possible only because its location is so far out of our own sector that it's all but on the Far Side of Forever. When you travel to a world that far away, any gates dipping back in are invariably timed."

"And the world we're going to does indeed dip back in," InThig said, sitting on the flagstones and wrapping its tail around its feet. "Most of the gates out of here can be used at any time, but that one opens only in specific cycles. It must have made Morgiana curious, and since she was in the midst of vacationing, there was no reason for her not to try it."

"It must be the reverse of the one on the world that tried to eat us alive," Rik said with a nod, remembering our quest experience with a timed gate. "We couldn't leave that world until the gate cycled open, but that white beast was able to come through the other way. Okay, I can see why we may be stuck here for a while, but I still don't understand why you're so unhappy about it, Graythor. Is the resort that badly run?"

"This resort has some of the best food and services ever created," Graythor told him with a sigh, groping to put his dissatisfaction into words. "It isn't the resort itself, it's the—games and practices those who come here indulge in. Most of them would never dream of behaving like that elsewhere, but here it seems to be the next thing to required. I detest being imposed upon, but I've never had a visit here yet when I haven't been."

I could see Rik was ready to pursue his line of questioning until he got some concrete examples of what Graythor had been talking around, but he wasn't given the chance. A group of four conservatively dressed men and six boys stepped through an entry into the area, and as soon as we were spotted, one of the men began hurrying in our direction with his fingers snapping to draw a boy along with him.

"Oh, I do beg your pardon for having made you wait, Honorables," he burbled, letting the words flow free as he looked carefully at each of us in turn. "The boy will take your horses this instant, and in another moment we'll have you settled into your accommodations. The last party arriving just before you was absolutely enormous, and it took all of us to see to them."

"Accommodations can wait until we know how long we'll be here," Graythor answered, looking up at the man with a forced and somewhat chilly politeness. "The gate we intend going through is closed now, but we mean to take it as soon as it cycles open. Is there someone here who can tell us when that will be?"

"I'll have to check, but it certainly won't be for hours and hours," the gate attendant said, looking faintly surprised. "That gate opened not long ago, and as usual no one cared. Forgive me for asking, but why in the worlds would anyone use it? It leads nowhere but to a dead world, and beyond it is nothing but more of the same."

"Not entirely," InThig answered, drawing the man's gaze. "One of its farther gates leads to a populated world, and it's extremely important that we get there as soon as possible. Will you check on the timing for us now?"

"If it's that important, of course I will," the man said, looking and sounding seriously concerned. "Excuse me for just a moment."

He turned and hurried back toward the place the other attendants stood, apparently heading for a spot to the left of the faint entry outline, and Rik shook his head.

"That has to be the first stranger I've ever seen who didn't panic over your being there, InThig," he said. "The people here must be *very* used to magic users and their companions."

"There are four other demons here at this very moment," InThig answered, idly flexing its claws against the flagstones. "They don't happen to be in cat shape and they certainly aren't involving themselves in the goings-on, but everyone knows they're around. If an employee of the Realm was prone to panicking, he or she would have an extremely unpleasant time working here."

"About all these goings-on," Rik began, still trying

to satisfy a curiosity that seemed destined to be around for a while; the words were no sooner out than the gate attendant was back with the information he'd gathered.

"The gate you need won't cycle open again for quite some time," he reported, dividing his attention between InThig and Graythor. "Just how much time isn't precisely known, but I now have one of our sorcerer-apprentices keeping an eye on it. As soon as its cycle downswings far enough, he'll find you wherever you happen to be and alert you. May I see to your accommodations now?"

"I suppose you might as well," Graythor grudged, finally holding his reins out to the boy who was still waiting patiently to take our horses. "Give us a triple suite with dining facilities, and make sure your people know we intend taking most if not all of our meals in private. If at any time we have to provide for ourselves, the effort will be charged against our final accounting."

"Which would be perfectly understandable, of course," the gate attendant agreed, gesturing us all with him as soon as the boy had our horses. "If any part of our service isn't exactly as it should be, we fully expect to be told about it. We specialize in giving our guests delight rather than excuses. My name is Nigor, and our first destination is this way."

Graythor grumbled a little under his breath rather than say any more out loud as he followed, but the attendant Nigor ignored his rather clear intention to be anything but delighted. If it made Graythor happy to be miserable, no one at the resort would dream of arguing. Some people loved being miserable, and chances were most of that group made regular visits to the Realm of Dreams.

Nigor led us to the entry and through it, bringing us to one of the resort's main transfer points. The big round room was all of glass, and the golden sunshine pouring in from one section of it was enough to warm the coldest of hearts. Through the glass it was possible to see naked and almost-naked people frolicking in beautiful green water beyond crashing white surf, their laughter and enjoyment just short of tangible. Rik's attention was immediately captured, and when Nigor saw the reaction he smiled with understanding.

"I believe, sir, we've never had the honor of serving you before," he said, moving to Rik's side. "While the transfers are being prepared for your party, allow me to show you a small number of the diversions available in our Realm. That beach is for those who joy in that kind of relaxation, and they find that the sunshine and warmth never fail. There is nothing of night in that glorious area, only golden, glowing day."

If Rik was looking at anything it certainly wasn't the beautiful weather, but Nigor very carefully failed to notice that. He waited a discreet moment or two, then gestured toward the next few sections of window.

"The area displayed beside the beach scene isn't physically located next to it, but with the system of entries used here in the Realm it truly isn't more than a few steps away. The rain you see is just as perpetual as the beach's sunshine, and rain outdoors can be just the thing you'd want most if you happened to come across a congenial new acquaintance. If isolation even on a temporary basis doesn't attract you, there's dining and dancing under the stars, sporting events to watch or participate in, entertainment of all sorts, gaming and daring . . ."

He went on and on with his list of attractions, but when he got to being snowed in, I stopped listening. I remembered a time of being almost snowed in, but there was really no point in remembering it. I walked a few steps forward to stare sightlessly out of the window showing sunshine, but in a very short time Nigor's advertising broke into my thoughts again.

". . . and those areas, of course, are only for the Sighted. If an unSighted guest enters one of them, he or she is required to wear a white badge, just as the servants wear white uniforms. The badges have strict time limits on them, however, and even with the badges we recommend against the unSighted entering the areas. No matter how careful everyone tries to be, accidents do happen, and under no circumstances will the Realm allow itself to be held accountable."

"But you still haven't said what makes those areas so dangerous," Rik pointed out, and I turned to see him looking intently through a section of window toward the other side of the room. "If I decided I wanted to go in there to make the acquaintance of that beautiful redhead, say, why would I find myself being advised to forget it?"

"My dear sir, those are the areas the Sighted play their games of traps and conquest," Nigor protested, sounding as though he was being asked to tell someone how to breathe in and out. "Stepping into the wrong circle, speaking to the wrong person—just standing there rather than moving in the proper direction! Any of it might cause you embarrassment at the very least, serious harm at its worst. You really must be able to defend yourself; should you be unSighted, defense simply isn't possible."

"Defense is always possible, if you know what you're doing," Rik came back with a sound of amusement, then turned away from the window. "Now about this system of entries you use; what restrictions are there on where they can take you, and how do they operate?"

Nigor told him the entries could take him anywhere in that sector of the Realm, and to use one all he had to do was touch the jewel next to the destination on his transfer. By then the transfers were ready, and Rik took his strip of jeweled leather and tried to examine it. Needless to say there was nothing to *see*, and I noticed that Nigor didn't mention the other sectors that were available only through specially issued transfers. Special issues were expensive, and weren't paid for in coin any more than our stay there would be. You had to be Sighted to be able to pay, and apparently Nigor had come to the conclusion that Rik wasn't Sighted.

Nigor told us what residential area our suite was in, and then led the way through the entry. InThig, of course, didn't need a transfer any more than any other demon did, and came with us without the least amount of trouble. The hall leading to the suite was gorgeous, but once we stepped into the first of the rooms the hall was put in proper perspective. Palatial wasn't a bad word for our accommodations, but somehow that much opulence didn't feel right. When you're in the middle of rushing off to save someone in trouble, you really shouldn't be luxuriously comfortable.

"This, of course, is your reception salon, your dining hall is to the right, and the bedroom sets are off the hall to the left," Nigor said as he looked critically around. "The services available to you are listed in that slender volume sitting there on that marble table, and if you require something that isn't listed, simply ask for it. If you should need me, send for me at any hour."

He bowed to all of us—including InThig—then turned and left the suite. Even before he'd pulled the door closed behind him, Graythor was in one of the deep velvet chairs, Rik had walked over to pick up the book on what the Realm had to offer, and InThig was off investigating what might be found in the rooms we hadn't yet seen. Even though we'd had something of a long day, I didn't feel like sitting down and relaxing, but the idea of going looking for my bedroom was one I was seriously toying with.

"After we have our meal, I'm going to turn in," Graythor said, using his left hand to twist a menu out of the air beside his chair. "Their food is worth taking time over, but even if this were a resort I enjoyed, I doubt if I would indulge. I'm too impatient to be where we're going, and as close as we are I need sleep to help me deal with the delay. Why don't you get menus for you and Rik, Laciel."

"I don't really want a menu," I said, knowing the—dissatisfaction? indecision?—I felt could be heard in my voice. "Just order anything for me, Uncle Graythor, it won't matter what it is. When we finish I'll probably do what you intend doing."

"And a menu won't do *me* much good either," Rik said, looking up from what he was reading. "Since you know this place and I don't, why don't you order for all of us. As long as there's meat of some sort, I'll be perfectly happy. I'll need a good, solid meal to keep me going while I look over as much of the resort as I can."

He smiled at Graythor and went back to reading about available services, but Graythor didn't return the smile. The wizard looked surprised and the least bit disapproving, but then his expression cleared. He took a moment to run his finger over certain items on the menu he held, twisted the menu back to the nothingness it had come from, then got out of his chair.

"Since our meal will be waiting, we can go into the dining hall now," he said, obviously for Rik's benefit, then added, "And if you intend having Laciel show you the resort, I'll have to give you a proper wardrobe. As you move from area to area you'll need appropriate clothing, but the spell is a simple one. All the Sighted here use it, and I know Laciel is familiar with it."

"I appreciate that, Graythor, and I gratefully accept the offer," Rik said with another smile, moving toward the dining hall with the man he spoke to. "As far as Laciel goes, though, I won't be bothering her. She said she wanted to go to bed, so there's no sense in ignoring that and trying to impose. I'll start looking around on my own, but I'm sure it won't be long before I find someone willing to guide me."

He chuckled then and strode ahead to open the doors to the dining hall, and Graythor's stricken silence was so thick even InThig, who had returned from exploring, was sharing it. Wizard and demon exchanged glances behind Rik's back, but they firmly kept themselves from looking in my direction. Why they didn't want to look at me I wasn't quite sure, but I suppose it was a good thing they didn't. From the way Rik had spoken I knew the guide he'd find would be female, and my reaction to that had been very—strange.

Which, if you thought about it, didn't make much sense. As I trailed along into the dining hall after unexplainably having stopped short, I told myself silently but fiercely that I was being a mindless fool. I had tried very hard to get Rik to lose interest in me, and now that he had I should be happy. I *was* happy, *very* happy, and the fact that Rik intended finding a woman companion was nothing to be bothered about. He was a vital, attractive man, and it was only natural for him to . . .

I noticed then that I was not only still holding my transfer but was also pulling on it, so I tucked it into my belt to get rid of it. It was strange how fully grown adults had to play with things like children when those things were in their hands, and I really didn't understand it. Possibly it was something I ought to look into once I began studying what Morgiana and Uncle Graythor wanted me to study. . . .

"Now, that's what I call a well set out meal," Rik enthused, just about rubbing his hands as he circled the large dining table to take the single chair on that side. "I intend eating as much of it as I can, but not so much that I'll have trouble moving afterward. There are too many things to see and do around here, and I mean to get to most of them. Will they have trouble finding me with that gate alert if I don't happen to be in an open, public place?"

He looked at Graythor with the innocent curiosity of his question, apparently not noticing the way Graythor grappled with an inner struggle as he took his own seat at the table. I took the last chair to Graythor's right, and InThig settled to the marble floor to my right wearing an expression that was closer to a growl than a grin.

"No, no, they won't have trouble reaching you with the alert no matter where you are," Graythor answered at last, pointing to the large soup tureen rather than looking at the man he spoke to. I had the oddest feeling the wizard would have been happier if he'd lied rather than told the truth, but couldn't understand why that was. As I pointed to the cheese salad and one of the bottles of wine, it came to me that there seemed to be quite a lot of things lately that I didn't understand. I thought about all those things while I watched my salad plate and wine cup being filled, then conceded the fact that I didn't care about not understanding. Understanding things was usually important to me, but right then I simply didn't care.

Conversation faltered after that, but Rik was too busy being delighted with the dinner service to notice. Once he discovered he only had to point at something for it to appear in front of him in the proper plate or cup, he began playing with the arrangement. Those who are unSighted tend to enjoy the novelty of pretend power the serving spell gives them and I'd seen the reaction before, but that time I must have been too tired or impatient to see anything humorous in his behavior. Even the fact that the plates were gleaming silver moonbeams and the cups were jewel-encrusted golden mist didn't impress me, and the crackling red flames that made up what was usually silverware or flatware was just short of boring. It was nothing but silly children's games, and with something important to do ahead of me, I was in no mood for games.

As out of sorts as I felt, I shouldn't have had much of an appetite, but I was really hungry in spite of everything. The food was as outstandingly good as ever, and very briefly I once again wished I could get access to some of their recipes.

The first time I'd tasted their food, I'd tried to See exactly what was in the various dishes so that I could reproduce them at a later time. After all, just tasting something great doesn't tell you what's causing the greatness; you have to know exactly, or trying to reproduce it is a waste of time.

Morgiana had laughed when the first dish I tried Seeing had splashed up and almost covered me, letting me know the direct way that the resort's recipes were guarded. In a place that catered to the Sighted I should have expected something like that, but at the time of my first visit I'd been so young . . .

As opposed to the woman of advanced years I was right then. I leaned back in my very comfortable chair with a sigh, looking down at the light pink wine that was left in my cup. The meal was just about over;

when it was, Rik would go out to see what the resort had to offer in the way of entertainment. I knew he'd have no trouble finding exactly what he was looking for, and I couldn't decide whether I wished he would hurry up and get on with it, or whether I wanted the meal to drag on and on instead. Wanting it to drag on wasn't being very fair to *him,* but a very small part of me didn't seem interested in being fair.

"That just might be the best meal I've ever eaten," Rik said suddenly, breaking the long silence he apparently hadn't noticed. "I can't remember ever feeling this kind of satisfaction when I wasn't in my linkshape, and believe me, that's saying something."

"It's to be expected that the senses of your linkshape are a good deal sharper than those of your human shape," Graythor commented, and I glanced up to see that he, too, was leaning back in his chair with a glass of wine. "I wonder if that also applies to the area of sensitivity in emotional feelings as opposed to physical ones."

"No, emotional sensitivity is greater in human form," Rik answered, the words distracted, and then he made a sound of resignation. "And I think it's time to admit I can't simply leave this table and go out looking for fun. Now now."

"Oh?" Graythor said, suddenly sounding a good deal happier. "Emotional sensitivity has made you change your mind?"

"Hardly," Rik laughed, and I heard him pushing his chair a short way away from the table. "Involuntary overeating has made me change my mind. It looks like I'm going to have to order up a couple of bath girls, and give them the chance to help me work off the ton of food I just swallowed. After that, I should be able to get on with it."

"By the EverNameless!" Graythor snapped, sitting forward in his chair while InThig raised its head with a very cold look in its eyes. I had glanced at the two of them before finishing off my wine, but once those things were done I couldn't think of what to do next.

"What's wrong?" Rik asked Graythor, sounding seriously concerned. "The lists said bath girls are included as part of the services of a suite like this one. If that's not so and we'll be charged extra, then I'll certainly do without them."

"The matter of extra charges doesn't enter into it," Graythor said, his voice as cold as InThig's stare as he kept his eyes on the other man. "Sensitivity is the issue here, a sensitivity I hadn't thought you were lacking so completely. How can you keep speaking like that in front of Laciel?"

"You think I'm being ungentlemanly?" Rik asked, now sounding surprised, and then he laughed. "But that's ridiculous, Graythor. Laciel isn't an innocent little girl, she's a quest companion and entitled to be treated like one. She doesn't mind if I say I'm going to order up bath girls or go out looking for friendly guidance, do you, Laciel?"

I know I wasn't expecting him to speak directly to me; the fact was proven by the length of time it took me to understand that he had. When I finally looked up to see him smiling at me and waiting patiently for my answer, I almost didn't know what to say. My mind scrabbled around very briefly, and then came up with the only words it could.

"No, of course I don't mind," I got out, loud enough for the absolute silence they slipped into, more than a little whispery under any other circumstances. What it cost me to say those words I won't mention, but once again Rik wasn't noticing anything but his own reactions.

"See there, I knew she wouldn't mind," he said with a beaming smile to Graythor, totally vindicated, totally happy. "I wonder if they'd find it possible to send two redheads for bath girls. I've always been partial to redheads, and . . ."

By that time my wine glass was returned to the table, my chair was pushed back, and I was on my feet and heading out of the room. No, I didn't have the right to tell Rik what he could and couldn't do, but that didn't mean I had to sit there and listen to every one of his eager plans. Somehow I hadn't thought he would behave like that, as though he were delighted to be unattached and free to do as he pleased, but obviously I'd been wrong. When we'd first started that journey, I'd been glad Rik was with us, but right then I wished he had gone back to his home world instead. If he had, I would have been left with *something* pleasant to remember. . . .

I thought I heard someone call out my name as I swung the dining hall door closed behind me, but I hadn't been paying attention so I wasn't sure. All I knew was that I no longer wanted to go to my bedroom, no longer thought that I'd be able to sleep. I needed some place where no one would bother me, so without the least hesitation I left the suite and headed for that place.

CHAPTER 7

The transfer in my belt took me through the entry in the suite sector to the entry hall we'd been in earlier, and a few steps around the circle of entries put me nearer the one that was mostly restricted to those who were Sighted. The area the entry led to was dangerous for those who couldn't handle magic, but it was also the perfect place for a Sighted to lose himself. Or herself. With all the power they played with, with all the strength so much in evidence, one Sighted among so many others would not be easily found. I knew Graythor could do it if he really made the effort, but there was no need for him to waste the strength. It wasn't an emergency, after all, only a case of emotional oversensitivity.

I sighed as I looked at the ghostly outline of the entry I stood in front of, then reached out with my right hand and gestured it fully into line. There was no guard needed to keep the unSighted from going through it, for the simple reason that no unSighted could bring it into the necessary alignment for use. The entry was self-guarding, and would return to its former out-of-line condition as soon as I moved through it. Which summation woke me up to the fact that I was just standing there staring at it.

I sighed again without the exasperation I would have preferred, then stepped through the entry. Being annoyed was so much better than being depressed, but my store of annoyance seemed to have run dry. I wondered briefly why depression never did that, then shrugged the question into dismissal. I didn't particularly care about getting silliness answered, and since I'd passed through the entry I had to decide where to go from there.

And I did have a definite choice. The sector I'd emerged into was mostly out of doors, but not the sort of out-of-doors to be found in other sectors. With everyone there being Sighted there was no need to settle on one overall theme, so it hadn't been done. Bright sunshine played over fifty feet worth of grass to my left, while just beyond it another fifty feet was being rained on. To my right there were two or three dark areas bathed in bright star- and moonlight, and just beyond that snow was falling.

Directly ahead of my feet was a stone path, and white-clad servants were using it to move from one specialized area to another. The servants carried their own transfer slips, I knew, to be used as focal points for the delivery of whatever the Sighted in the sector might happen to want. Without foci the delivery would have been erratic at best, and in most cases wouldn't have made it at all. With all that power being used so casually, the atmosphere was almost pure static.

I could feel my automatic warding thicken as I moved away from the entry to the right, using the stone that circled around to find another path that would go deeper into the sector. There were a lot of people sitting and walking around in the sunshine and the rain and the darkness and the snow, and I had no interest in joining them. They were laughing, and playing, and having a really good time, which was, after all, what they were there for. It wasn't the reason I was there, though, so there was no reason to commit intrusion.

I had to walk almost halfway around the wide stone circle before I found a path that showed nebulous gray toward the end of it. The gray meant no one was using that particular area, and so it had no weather or worldslant dominating it the way the other areas had. I used the path to head for it, glad there were fewer servants in that general area, then realized why it was emptier. The areas to either side of the stone path were unusual or bizarre worlds recreated in narrow circumstance, where unSighted servants would have trouble surviving. Those who were having fun living underwater, or in the middle of sunlike flames—or in hovering, breathing blackness—had to pay for the privilege by providing their own service.

When I reached the end of the path and the gray area, I discovered that the path didn't really end. It continued on to separate gray to either side of it for as far as I could see, and would probably keep continuing on as long as there was someone who wanted his or her own area. All I needed was one area, though, so I ignored the rest and stepped off the path to the right into the nearest formless gray. Speaking a very short spell got me the comfortable chair and small table with a glass of wine that I wanted, and that was *all* I wanted. I walked over to the chair and sat, picked up my glass of wine, then leaned back in the peace and quiet of the swirling gray.

"Why did he have to do that?" something in my mind was finally able to ask, the thought filled full of disappointment and hurt. "Why did he have to act so—unfeeling and uncaring? Is that what he's really like, once all the pretense and glamour are stripped away? If it isn't, it's just too bad; that's all you'll be remembering of him from now on."

Which was horribly and completely true. My hand closed more tightly around the cup of wine, but there was no denying it. The memories I'd had of Rik fighting to protect me, trying so hard to get me to laugh—holding me in his arms and making love to me—all of it was gone behind his casual dismissals, his unfeeling observations, his uncaring questions. I'd become totally unimportant to him—and I didn't think I could bear ever seeing him again.

"Which you might not have to," that inner voice said, combining with the formless, swirling gray. "InThig and Graythor were right there with you, so if you tell them you'd rather leave Rik at the resort while the rest of you continue on, you won't have to explain why. And Rik certainly won't mind, now will he?"

No, Rik would definitely not mind. I had to take a sip of wine to ease the dryness in my throat, but that didn't change anything. Rik would have a great time at the resort while the rest of us went after Morgiana, and on the way back InThig could—

"Excuse me, but I couldn't help noticing how wrong this all is," an unfamiliar voice came suddenly, causing me to look up. The man standing there was very big and very blond, with light green eyes and a strongly handsome face. He wore a high-collared, short-jacketed formal suit of wine red over a pure white shirt full of ruffles, and his black boots were so highly polished no speck of dust or dirt would have dared land on them. I'd heard what he'd said but didn't understand a word of it, something he picked up immediately from my expression.

"This is all wrong because gray is too lifeless a setting for a woman like you," he explained with a smile, gesturing at what I sat in the middle of. "I'm sure you left it like this only because you couldn't be bothered, but for me the effort demands to be made."

He spoke his spell, then, gathering and using power with an easy confidence in his deep voice, and I didn't have to look around to know what he'd created. He'd turned the grayness into scintillating jewels that almost lived, deep-pelted furs that lay at my feet in all the shades of splendor, wide strips of breath-soft fabric weaving in and out and around it all in the most breathtaking of colors. My chair had been turned to gold and the table to silver, and a second golden chair had appeared beside mine.

"Now that's more like it," the stranger said, moving

forward to seat himself in the chair he'd created, at the same time gesturing a cup of wine into being. "Isn't this a much better setting for getting acquainted in? I'm Jaral of Phidor, and I curse the fates for not having brought us together before this."

"I'd say our being together is more your doing than the actions of any fates," I came back, resenting the way he'd intruded on my brooding. "And I'd also say no one ever bothered teaching you any manners. Before you barge in on someone's privacy, it's considered common courtesy to first ask if that someone wants your company. Since the answer in this case is no, you've wasted your time *and* your spell. Goodbye, Jaral of Phidor."

"You expect me to leave so that this time the tears can actually roll down your cheeks?" he asked very quietly, his green gaze serious. "You weren't far from it a moment ago, and I don't care how much prettier some people consider a woman's eyes when there are tears in them. I prefer seeing laughter, but I don't believe you can manage that. Would it help if I volunteered my services? As a sorcerer, I'm rated rather high."

The gentle offer should have exploded me out of the chair in insult, but I discovered I was much too miserable to bristle up the way I usually did. If it had been possible for someone else to help me, I would have taken that help, but some things have to be stood up to alone.

"Even a wizard would be out of his depth in the mix-up I'm in right now," I answered, working to produce something of a return smile. "I appreciate the offer, but there's nothing you can do. And I'm Laciel."

"Are you sure, Laciel?" Jaral asked, leaning forward just a little in his chair. "Some of the Sighted in this crowd play too rough for beginners to handle, not giving a damn how much damage they do. I've been trying to temper that when I can, because I care about those who are just starting out."

Caring and doing damage. I lost whatever amount of smile I'd been able to manage when those two phrases reached me together, and I realized they were rarely together unless someone was talking about them.

When you care, you try to prevent damage, but doing damage goes unnoticed when caring falls by the wayside. It wasn't right, it simply wasn't right—but that hadn't stopped it from happening.

"Jaral, what's taking you so long?" a throaty but petulant female voice came then, making us both look up. The girl who entered my newly redecorated area was fairly tall with a rather beautiful face, but she would have been more beautiful still without the pout she was working very hard on. Her short red hair was arranged around her face for the cute look, her blue eyes were almond shaped, her figure was spectacular in the low-cut, tight-fitting gown she wore, and she was really very annoyed.

"You told us you would be right back, and here you are settling in for the season," she accused my visitor, making sure he knew just how much she disliked the idea. "It's never any fun in the group unless you're there, so you have to come back right this minute."

"Ranni, you're being very rude," Jaral told the girl, a touch of sternness and disapproval in his voice. "This is Laciel, and she's our brand new neighbor and all alone. She and I have just started getting acquainted, so rushing away now isn't something I intend doing."

"Oh, Jaral, you always have *someone* you want to 'get acquainted' with," the girl Ranni answered in exasperation, one shapely hand resting on a well-turned hip. "If you absolutely must bring another little flower into the group, drag her over and have done with it. Although why you want *her* as one of your adoring crowd is beyond me. She isn't even up to dressing properly."

"Ranni, that's enough!" Jaral snapped while I straightened where I sat, my original faint dislike of the girl beginning to slide downhill. "No one starts out at wizard level, we all have to work up to it. If I recall correctly, you weren't up to much yourself when we first met."

"But that was when we first met," the girl answered with a purr, her eyes now resting lazily on me. "Would you like me to guess how much of this area *you* spelled, and how much Jaral did, little flower? I'm just about up to sorceress level now, and I've learned to recognize Jaral's work. Wasn't he sweet to help you out with something you're too low class to do?"

"I thought it was very sweet of him," I said calmly while Jaral leaned forward in his chair with a low growl. "If he makes a habit of helping those who are low class, you must have had more help from him than anyone."

"How dare you!" the girl gasped with great originality, straightening in insult as Jaral leaned back again with a laugh. "Are you stupid enough to think *he* can protect you if I decide to issue a challenge? The rules around here won't allow stand-ins or champions, so you'd have to face me yourself. I'd better hear an apology real fast, or you'll find out exactly what that means."

"Now, Ranni, you know I don't allow any challenges among my people," Jaral said very comfortably, smiling at the girl after sipping his wine. "If you want to continue on as one of us—and I'm sure you do—it's time you excused yourself and went back to our area."

"Maybe I'm not as interested in continuing on as one of you as you think, Jaral," the girl said, her pale face flushing faintly, her voice a little too high but still fairly steady. "You hardly look at me any more, and I'm tired of being pushed aside all the time by the new ones. If you want me staying with you, you'll prove it by getting up and going back with me *now*, otherwise you can stay here and watch a challenge being answered."

"Are you giving *me* ultimatums?" Jaral asked in frowning disbelief, looking up at the girl Ranni in a way I hadn't expected. Ranni wasn't pouting like a child any longer, and the man she spoke to wasn't happy about it. Right about then was when I woke up to what was really going on, actually hearing and understanding the various things Jaral had said to me.

He—and Ranni—thought I was new to my abilities as a Sighted, too new to be much good with what little strength I'd developed. From what the girl had said,

Jaral liked his women on the weakly-talented side, and once they began to gain in strength his interest shifted to the next—"little flower." So much for the caring I'd thought he was capable of, so much for there even being such a thing.

". . . said it wouldn't be all that long before I was just as good as you are," Ranni was informing Jaral stiffly as I put my wine cup on the table and stood. "He also said I would end up being better than you, because I wasn't afraid to let my abilities take me as far as possible. Back then I couldn't believe you were afraid of anything, but now I can see he was right. You surround yourself with a group of people who aren't anywhere near as strong as you, and that way you can tell yourself you don't *have* to try growing any more. You're as good as you'll ever be, Jaral, but some day I'll be worlds better than that."

"But some day is so far off, love," Jaral said with his own brand of purr, flipping his wine cup into nothingness as he got to his feet. "Right now you're *not* worlds better than me, you're not even close to being as good. Shall we take a moment to remember that excellent advice you gave Laciel about challenges?"

"Leave the girl alone, Jaral," I said as Ranni went pale and silent with the knowledge that the man she'd been ready to fight for intended having a lot of fun hurting her. "She did you a favor by telling you the truth. I don't believe in letting people get hurt for telling the truth, so back off. If you try jumping on someone you know is weaker while I'm around, the half-baked rules of this place won't do *anything* to save your skin."

"I don't need any lightweights trying to protect me, so back off yourself!" Ranni snapped, the heat again in her cheeks as her hands curled to fists at her sides. She thought she was being defended by someone weaker yet less afraid, and the humiliation was too much for her. She was really upset right then, but not nearly as bothered as Jaral.

"So now *you* think you can talk to me any way you please?" he demanded, his fury breaking into Ranni's protests and trampling them unnoticed. "I've heard it said that the arrogance of beginners should be put down hard for the beginners' sake, and I think I'm ready to agree with the point. Do you involve yourself in Hellfire combat at Conclave, Laciel? Possibly you don't because you're not yet strong enough, but that's something you should have thought of before you mouthed off to me. Now you get to learn the lesson the . . ."

Talk about anger and interruption. The three of us were so deep in our disagreement we hadn't noticed the arrival of newcomers, but when Jaral was interrupted in the middle of his tirade we couldn't help but notice. A resort attendant had been used as a guide, and suddenly shouldering past Jaral was a white-badged, unexpected—and unwelcome—complication.

"Laciel, I want you to come back to the suite with me," Rik said, his bronze eyes sober and concerned as he looked down at me. "If I'd known you would run out like that I would have— Well, I wouldn't have carried it quite so far. I have something to tell you, and I want to tell it to you now."

"I think you've told me more than enough for one day," I muttered, turning away from him to my right. "You and I are the best of buddies, and that's the way we both want it. In case you hadn't noticed there's a redhead behind you, and I'm sure if you ask her nicely, she'll be glad to show you the resort. As for me, I'm being paged elsewhere."

I tried to step around Rik to get out of the area, but Jaral and his chair and his outrage were in the way. If anything the blond sorcerer was even angrier than he had been, and he wasn't about to let me get away.

"Why am I not surprised you're here with an un-Sighted?" he sneered, obviously having seen Rik's badge and feeling raw over not being able to challenge him. "Lack of ability in one area often means the same lack in others, and I'd say it's clear you haven't even been able to satisfy someone with no talent at all. Poor little thing, no wonder you paled when I mentioned Hellfire combat. Isn't it a shame you won't be getting away with it that easily. We're still going to . . ."

"Laciel, this nonsense isn't important, but what I have to say to you is," Rik interrupted Jaral again, his hand coming to my arm to keep me from moving away. "It won't take long to straighten everything out, and then if you want to come back here, I won't stop you."

"He won't stop you!" Jaral crowed, but his delight was very much on the fey side due to the fury consuming him. "He, an unSighted, can actually stop you from doing as you please, and because of that is stupid enough to treat the truly Sighted with the same lack of concern. You're not going anywhere until we've settled our differences to *my* satisfaction, and if your— pet cripple interrupts me again, I'll have the skin off him in bloody, shrieking strips!"

Jaral was just about foaming at the mouth by then, and Rik finally noticed that something was going on. My—former quest companion turned to look at the furious blond sorcerer and began in a very soft voice, "What did you call me?" but I'd had enough of all of them.

"Point one you'd better listen to and understand," I announced to Jaral in a very loud voice, overriding everyone including the extremely nervous resort attendant. "You can't take his skin off in strips or even in curliques, because he's warded by a wizard who's stronger than the two of us put together. Point two covers *why* he's warded so thoroughly, and the answer is, to protect him from me. Point three says he needs protecting from me because I'm *not* a beginner, and point four gets around to mentioning that you're trying to challenge an Adept—namely me—to Hellfire combat. Even if you're also considered an Adept at Hellfire combat, I strongly urge you to find a different way of trying to soothe your injured pride. The way you've got now won't do the job."

"You expect me to believe all that?" Jaral asked with a nervous laugh, his rage and confidence suddenly a good deal lessened. "If you were all that good you'd be known around here, and I've never seen you before. Claiming to be an Adept is easy, but none of the Adepts *I* know turn down a challenge when it's offered. Anyone who really was an Adept wouldn't be using words to keep from joining me in a combat cylinder."

"They would if they'd had an experience like the one *I* had," I countered, annoyed to see his overconfidence almost back to the level it had been. "Hellfire combat at Conclave *seems* like a great big brave accomplishment, but there are wizards at Conclave who control the Hellfire after the combat and keep it from really hurting anyone. I had a—problem with someone who wanted to keep me from doing something very important, and like a fool I faced him in a cylinder. He knew the basics but wasn't Adept, and there weren't any wizards around to turn the confrontation into a game. When he lost, the—Hellfire—ate him—and I'll—never forget that—as long as I live."

Talking about the time made me feel almost as sick as when it had first happened, but happily the effort wasn't wasted. Jaral *knew* I wasn't simply making excuses, not after he looked into my eyes, and the realization shook him.

"But that doesn't explain why I haven't seen you before," he blustered, holding up this other point in an effort to forget the first. "There isn't a powerful Sighted on any civilized world who doesn't come here on a regular basis, for the food if nothing else. If you haven't been coming here, it's because you're a beginner who's only now starting to travel alone."

"Or I could have been too busy for the last couple of years to have the time for vacationing," I counterpointed before he pumped himself up too far. "I started coming here with the wizard who trained me when I was very young, and even back then I was advised against getting involved with the people who hang out in this area. I was told it was like the old saying goes: those who can, do; those who can't, pretend. If you people had any real talent, you'd be out using it instead of sitting around here pretending to be special."

It came to Jaral then that I was too calmly confident, too passing critical to be doing anything but telling the truth. His face took on that drawn look that contact with reality so often brings, but Ranni didn't react in the same way.

"You know, the idea of being out and doing sounds better than I thought it would," she mused, seeing nothing of the way Jaral crumbled a little on the inside at her words. "I thought the worlds had nothing to offer no matter how good I got, but that isn't true, is it? There are lots of opportunities out there—for anyone who has the good sense to go looking for them."

Her eyes were on me at that point, but not to see if I agreed or would offer her encouragement. She already knew she was on the right track, and when you *know* something like that you don't need anyone else confirming it. Her smile was bright and easy, and then suddenly it was being aimed at Rik as the girl herself stepped over to stand in front of him.

"Something tells me you have a weakness for redheads, you good-looking hunk of man," she purred, putting her palms flat to his leather shirt as she looked up into his eyes. "Since I'll be leaving this place soon, why don't we have a good-bye celebration to mark the accomplishment? Just you and me in suitable privacy; the resort can cater the occasion, but we'll provide our own entertainment."

For the briefest moment I didn't understand what Ranni was doing, but when I saw the vexation flash in Rik's eyes just before he began trying a graceful refusal, I suddenly understood. Ranni was thanking me for the help and support I'd given her by distracting the man she'd seen I wanted to get away from, and I really appreciated the effort. She'd told me she was returning a favor when she'd talked about Rik liking redheads; the only way she could have known that was from what *I'd* said, and I wasn't about to waste the opportunity.

Jaral, happily, had turned away to gloom over inner thoughts, so my path to escape was free and clear. Without making a fuss or being obvious I walked back toward the stone path lying beside my former area, and even the resort attendant waiting there didn't notice me. He was busy watching the time and fidgeting over how involved the unSighted he was responsible for was becoming in a place they had to leave soon, and didn't see me turning up the path to the right. What I wanted was complete privacy deeper in the gray of nothingness, and that's what I was going to have.

I expected to have all the time I needed to find exactly what I wanted, but for some reason it didn't work out like that. Rather than letting himself finally be distracted by Ranni—as I'd been sure he would—Rik was suddenly following almost directly behind me. The sound of his boots on the stone was as determined as the way he called my name, but the only determination I was interested in was my own. I didn't want to see or talk to him ever again, and if I had to go out of my way to accomplish that, I would. I had never learned to be very good at running—standing and fighting was more my style—but what I really lacked was practice. That struck me as a great time to practice, so I took off as fast as I could, heading even farther back into shapeless, formless gray—trying desperately to leave uncaring hurt behind.

I was so busy going flat out at top speed, it took a short while to realize I hadn't left much of anything behind. The pounding of boots was still unbearably close behind me, and he was calling my name again. But it wasn't *my* name, of course, only a use-name, so I was able to ignore it while trying to run even faster. The swirling gray to either side of the stone path made me feel as though I wasn't going anywhere, as though I ran and ran in one place and didn't move an inch. But I had to keep going, had to keep trying, or all the uncaring pain behind would catch up and touch me again. After a while even the strongest will break from that sort of touch, and at that point I was willing to admit—to myself—that I was far from the strongest.

And then a hand brushed my arm, a hand with fingers that were trying to close around my arm and pull me to a stop. Fear exploded inside me at the thought of being caught, as bad as anything I'd experienced as a child on the streets of Geddenburg, and that fear helped me find a little more speed. My lungs screamed pain and my chest heaved with the need for air, but I took that extra speed and used it. I still believed I could get away, needed the escape as badly as I ever had as a child, but I'd never before run from someone like Rik. He had his own reasons for chasing me, reasons I wanted to know nothing about, reasons he'd decided I would know *all* about.

If he'd been in his link-shape he would have caught me in three bounds, and even in human form he should have had me in next to no time. When he tried to reach me and couldn't, when I still kept ahead of him despite everything he could do, he must have decided to end the race in the only way he could.

One minute I was running with everything I had, and the next there were two arms being thrown around me and taking me down to the ground with the body belonging to the arms. I cried out and tried to struggle, but hitting the ground—even with Rik hitting first and cushioning me—was too much of a jolt. I was down and stopped, caught and netted, but I still struggled against the pain ahead even as I throbbed with the pain of the fall.

And that was when it happened. We'd started out rolling into soft gray, supposedly the gray of unformed possibilities, but that had been a disguise. As soon as we were on the ground a silent flash of lightning came, and rolling gray became unyielding black. The path was gone, the empty areas were gone, all of it—gone from sight and detection. I heard Rik curse in a low, confused voice, just as though cursing would do some good.

But, of course, it wouldn't. We'd been caught in a trap, and there would be only one way of getting out again.

CHAPTER 8

"First things first," I heard Rik mutter from where he sat near me in the blackness, a voice without any hint of a body. "Laciel, you seem to be breathing more easily now, so I want you to answer me. Are you all right?"

"No," I told him shortly, speaking the complete truth in more ways than one. I hurt from the fall I'd taken, hated the idea of his still being close enough to talk to me, was having trouble catching my breath as quickly as I should have—and was caught tight in a trap. I was furious at how stupid I felt over that last point—and wasn't doing too well with the rest of them, either.

"What exactly does that 'no' cover?" Rik asked, well-controlled worry in his voice that I guess I was supposed to believe. "You don't sound like you're at death's door, but I've learned that you rarely do, even when you *are* in a bad way. Were you hurt in the fall?"

Instead of answering him, I got to my feet, put my arms out in front of me, then walked forward slowly to find the dimensions of that trap. I knew better than to try to use magic there, even to kindle a light. Traps like that were made to hold their victims inside no matter how much strength those victims could bring to bear, and there was only one way of doing it. I couldn't See anything of the fabric of what held us, and that meant it was made out of absolute and utter nothingness. Nothingness has an affinity for magic, and if I tried even a small spell, our prison would draw out every bit of strength I had.

"Is that heavy silence supposed to mean you *weren't* hurt in the fall?" Rik asked, a shadow of annoyance creeping over the sound of controlled worry. "Or does it simply mean I'm not asking the right questions? If I do manage to come up with the right questions, will I earn another one-word answer?"

I let his talk drift past me as I reached one wall of the prison, then turned left along it to find a corner. When you build with nothingness, you find it solid enough to the touch, but touching it is just about all you can do once you *have* built with it.

"Why don't you call up one of those little suns you're so fond of?" Rik suggested after another silence-filled gap, the deep breath he'd taken apparently enough to banish the annoyance. "I'll feel better if I can see for myself that you're all right, and then you won't have to bother with any words at all."

The wall I'd found was about twelve paces in length, and when I reached the right-hand end of it, I sat down in its corner. Twelve by twelve that trap would be, a nice, neat square to keep us where they wanted us until they were ready for the rest of it. How long it would take before they were ready depended on a number of things, none of which I had the least control over. All I could do was sit in the midst of that nothingness and wait—while trying my damnedest to pretend I was alone.

"All right, so light is another thing we'll be doing without," Rik said with a sigh after a time that was becoming usual. "Maybe it's for the best, since there's now no reason to put off telling you what I have to. And every reason to get to it as fast as possible. Laciel—all that talk about us being nothing but former quest companions, and the women I showed such interest in—it was all done deliberately in an effort to get your attention."

Well, it had certainly gotten my attention. I leaned my head back against the corner of nothingness, vaguely curious about what Graythor had threatened Rik with to get him to come up with a story like that. That Graythor had sent him after me had been clear from the beginning, but for what purpose I couldn't quite figure out.

"You're still not saying anything, and I'm not used to that," Rik pursued, some of the calm in his voice having faded. "I also didn't expect you to take my act the way you did, and I suppose that's the reason it ended up being pushed to such extremes. When I began looking at other women in such an obvious way, you were supposed to get insulted and start an argument with me. When you seemed to be ignoring me instead, I began pressing harder, until finally I tried the bathing-girls idea. When I asked if you minded, you were supposed to get furious with me, tell me how little you thought of me, call me all kinds of names. You weren't supposed to—agree that you didn't mind and—sit there as if you really didn't and—then get up to go to your bedroom."

His voice hadn't really grown ragged, only the least bit uneven, and for some reason he wasn't sending me anything of the way he felt. If I believed what he was saying I might have gotten upset, but I wasn't *about* to be fool enough to believe him.

"Laciel, what I was trying to do was make you understand how *I* felt when you did all those things to push me away from you," he said, and now there was something in his voice I couldn't quite identify. "I wanted so badly for something real and deep to grow between us, but you were so desperate to have me gone off somewhere safe that you almost lost your life trying to make it happen. I thought that if you cared so much for me I had to care at least as much and agree to leave, but women must be stronger than men. I discovered rather quickly that I didn't *want* to keep to the agreement, that the last thing I'd be able to do when Morgiana was free was simply turn and walk away. I don't want other women, and I don't want to be safe; what I want is you."

Closing your eyes in absolute darkness is a wasted gesture, but sometimes gestures like that are necessary. I could still remember how I'd felt when I was very small, afraid to close my eyes in the dark for fear of the monsters that might come at me unseen. I hadn't known then there were worse things than monsters that could come at you, but like many monsters of the imagination, some of the worse things often disappeared if you refused to think about them.

"I still don't hear anything from you," Rik said. "If you expect me to believe you really don't care anything about me, you can forget it. If you didn't care, you wouldn't have left the suite; you'd have gone to bed the way you said you were going to. InThig had to point that out to me, but once it was said, I knew it was true. I also know I wasn't wasting my time completely with that plan I came up with. You didn't like the idea of me going after other girls, now did you? Graythor said you were good at not showing how you really feel, but he's known you long enough to see things that I couldn't. He said I'd hurt you, and once I believed him I laughed out loud in delight. People who don't care don't *get* hurt."

"And people who do care don't try to hurt on purpose," I said suddenly, the words spilling out of me by themselves. "When I did what I did to try—chasing you away, as you put it, my very first consideration was to neutralize any interest you might feel so there wouldn't *be* any pain. What you did was take the interest you already knew was there and twist it hard for a reaction, a reaction, by your own words, you were delighted to find. Well, since that first reaction pleased you so much, here's another one for you: once we're out of this trap, I never want to see or speak to you again for as long as I live."

"Why, because this time *you* were the one being hurt?" he demanded, the words accompanied by the sound of his shifting in place. "All that consideration you used to ruin my interest in you was supposed to be a kindness? When all it showed was that the woman I loved considered me a useless incompetent? If that's your idea of doing things the painless way, I'd hate to see you getting deliberately nasty. What you need most is to learn how to see things from other people's viewpoints, not just your own!"

"Well, since I *don't* know how to do that, I guess you're in luck," I returned, noticing that I was now glaring in his direction even though I couldn't see him. "Being rid of someone that inconsiderate can't be anything but a blessing, now can it?"

"Damn right," he said with heat, sounding just the way I felt, and then we were plunged into a silence that had two participants instead of just one. For my part I was furious that he would dare try making what had happened *my* fault, especially after admitting that he'd done it deliberately. You can't trust people who act like that, and there was no doubt in my mind that I was truly well rid of him.

After that pleasant little exchange I was just about ready to try breaking out of that trap no matter what the potential danger, but I was saved the trouble. The ghostly outline of an entry appeared, and I may not have noticed it when it was hidden in rolling gray, but there was no way of missing it against the nothingness. I quickly got to my feet and strode to it, and once I had stepped through became aware that my fellow prisoner was right behind me. That, however, was totally unimportant; what did matter was arranged in seats all around the area the entry let out on.

A stir of satisfied laughter went through the people who sat in the seats, their numbers showing that one reason for the delay in letting us out had been to give them all time to get there. There was red sand under my booted feet and a pale yellow sun high in the blue-green sky above, and the glare of light after the absolute darkness wasn't as bad as it might have been. Those people obviously weren't interested in blinding their victims, but the gesture wasn't one of kindness. They had other things in mind, things they would find a good deal more entertaining.

"Well, not only a clever pair, but also rather interesting," a woman's voice came suddenly, just as though she stood right next to us. "Neither one of them wasted their strength against the nothingness, so now they can spend it for *our* benefit. I find that very thoughtful, especially on the part of the man."

While the crowd laughed in appreciation of the woman's supposed wit, I looked around and managed to spot her. She sat to the right of where we stood, her section of the oval seating arrangement draped with bright and expensive cloth and decorated with gems and precious metal. My first reaction was to think how barbaric that looked, and then I understood that that was how it was supposed to look. We were being given a hint of what was ahead, but not a hint that was meant to be encouraging.

"What is it you people want?" I said to the woman who sat at least a hundred yards away, making no effort to keep the impatience out of my voice. Under normal circumstances she never would have heard me at that distance, but I was sure her spell would take care of the problem. When she and the others laughed again, I saw I was right.

"Why, dear girl, we want you and your friend to amuse us," she answered, the words, once again, sounding absolutely clear. "It's the price you must pay for trespassing on our territory."

"These areas aren't yours," I retorted at once, disliking the lazy sneer I could hear but not see on the woman. "They belong to the resort, and since they're not part of the private residential sections, as a guest I have as much right here as you do. Unmask the exit entry. I have better things to do with my time than stand around exchanging clever dialogue with you."

"Then you should have been doing them instead of barging in on us," the woman returned with a purr, still very relaxed and comfortable in her section of seats. "And as far as these areas not being ours goes, you seem to miss the point. If they were under the jurisdiction of the resort people, they would be here looking after things—and you. Take a good look around, and tell me if you see any resort personnel."

She gave me a moment or two to do the looking she'd suggested, and didn't seem upset when I didn't bother. I knew the situation, and she knew I did; her suggestion had been aimed at rubbing it in.

"What a shame, it seems we're all out of resort personnel today," she said after the pause, and her people chuckled their appreciation of the comment.

"I'm afraid you two will have to make do with us, but don't be disappointed. We fully expect to be entertained, so you won't have to work *too* hard—except possibly you, handsome man. Have you developed anything I would find—impressive?"

"He isn't Sighted," I told the woman quickly before Rik, who stood to my right, could ask what she meant. I had a fairly good idea what she meant, and hadn't realized Sighted men might actually do things like that.

"Oh, what a pity," the woman in the decorated seating said, and I could almost see her disappointed pout. "So many of the best ones turn out to be ordinary, and ordinary is such a bore. Except, of course, for those who don't know any better. I've half a mind to let you try one of my favorites, dear girl. After that, you'd never settle for the ordinary again."

"Half a mind is a good description for you," Rik said suddenly, an insulting drawl in his voice. "And if being ordinary means getting away with not having to tickle your vanity, I'll bet more than half of those men around you wish they were ordinary, too."

With a choked growl of furious rage the woman in the stands sat stiffly rigid, and then her right hand came up. Her spell was more spat out than spoken, but once I heard it I knew she was in for even more disappointment. Her strength was adequate for just about anything she cared to use it on, but neither it nor her unimaginative wording would find a way through the warding Graythor had given Rik. The man beside me had nothing to fear from the woman he'd insulted, but I still didn't understand why he'd done it. He might have been absolutely impossible, but I'd never before heard him be deliberately rude to someone.

The purple tongues of flame that appeared around Rik tried to engulf him, but all they could do was rage against his warding while he stood unconcernedly with his arms folded across his chest. The woman was so angry it actually took her a few minutes to realize she wasn't burning him alive, and then she turned her fury on me.

"Banish that warding this instant!" she screeched, so close to being out of control that the people around her made no effort to mix in or try calming her down. "Do you hear me, you little bitch? Banish that warding!"

"I didn't cover him with it, so I can't banish it," I answered, ignoring what she'd called me. "Have you lost it so far you can't tell wizard's work when you come up against it?"

She jerked her head back toward Rik, and I could imagine how her eyes narrowed as she really looked at the way her flames were behaving. The less power in the warding the closer the flames would be to the intended victim, and her flames weren't close at all. As a matter of fact they were closer to *me*, but it wasn't anything to be worried about.

"So I can't reach him that way," she growled, again using her right hand but this time to banish the flames. "That only means he can't be reached by magic, not that he can't be reached. I think I'm going to enjoy this more than I expected to, much more. It's too bad, dear girl, but you should have been more careful of the company you kept."

I could see her leaning back in her seat again, but when her right hand went up for the third time I couldn't hear anything of the spell she was speaking. That was a very bad sign, and the conclusion must have shown in my expression.

"What's the matter?" Rik asked, looking at me with his own version of narrowed eyes. "You don't think we'll have trouble with anything *she* can throw at us, do you?"

"*We* are going to have nothing *but* trouble," I answered without really looking at him, trying to figure out something clever before the sky fell on us. "If I had to guess I'd say she was summoning something, and if she isn't letting me hear the spell she's also warding whatever she's summoning. When we finally get to see what it is, just remember how much fun you had insulting her. It may make your final moments more pleasurable."

"If she's warding whatever-it-is, then you can't use magic against it any more than she can use magic against me," Rik summarized brilliantly, now frowning full out. "You can't stop her from doing that?"

"Sure I can stop her," I said, still looking around. "But only in the same way I stopped some of those creatures during the quest. Is that the way you want me to do it?"

"No," he answered immediately, unhappy with the necessity for the decision, but not unsure. "During the quest we had no choice, but this isn't the same. She may be no more than a brainless female playing queen of the heap, but that doesn't mean she deserves to die in the way those creatures did. Or at all, for that matter. No, I'll take care of whatever she throws at us, and you come up with something else to break us free."

"Is that your final word on the matter, O Fearless Leader?" I drawled, finally turning to look at him. He started in surprise at the name I called him, for an instant thinking I was joking with him the way I had during the quest, but I didn't like him well enough to joke with him and I certainly wasn't taking his orders. Whatever I did or didn't do would be *my* decision, and once I could see he understood that thoroughly, I turned my back on him again.

Which gave me an excellent view of the three awful beasts that now stood on the red sand, just below the section of oval seating on that side. They were yellow with brown spots that looked more like dirt than natural markings, and that's very possibly what they were. Slime smeared the fur of the beasts, mixing easily with the drool coming down from the things' fangs. Their claws were crusted with garbage and dirt and old blood, and their slitted green eyes were filled with delight over the tender morsels they were looking at. Each of them was big, almost as big as the white beast that had attacked us during the quest, and the only thing holding them back was the laughter of the woman in the decorated seat.

"What's the matter, dear girl, don't you like charzins?"

she asked, her voice back to being close. "I must admit I usually can't abide their stink, but this time I don't think I'll mind it. How much can the two of you take, I wonder, before you'll beg me to banish them? Well, we *will* find out, now won't we? Shall we begin?"

A flick of her finger loosed the charzins from where they'd been held, and they immediately began advancing toward us. Since they weren't too bright, I guessed they'd been leaning on the woman's invisible fence or wall, hoping it would let them free to play with their future meal. They were the sort of beasts who enjoyed the playing part even more than the eating part, which was why the woman had summoned them. She could watch them chewing off bits and pieces of us almost as long as she liked, and could still be fairly certain that we would be alive at the end of it.

"Charzins," Rik said with disgust in his voice, clearly familiar with the things. "But if you stop to think about it, what would be more fitting from someone like her? Stink and all, of course." He didn't quite glance at the woman as he said that, so he didn't see her stiffen again in fury. Instead he continued, "I'll be busy for the next few minutes, but don't forget what I said. Find a different way."

He didn't make the effort to look at *me*, either, which means he missed a second interesting reaction. Instead of looking at anyone at all, he was starting to move toward the advancing charzins, and as he went his form began to blur. Rik was shifting into link-shape, changing to the great bronze beast that was his other self, and the transformation was something the people in the stands hadn't been expecting. Mutters of shocked surprise ran through the audience, a gasp coming clearly enough that it had to be the woman in the decorated seat who produced it. We were supposed to be helpless victims, but Rik was already beginning to bend *that* theory.

And that made it my turn to go next, assuming I could clamp down on my anger long enough to do what was necessary. As I watched the great bronze link-beast moving with sure confidence toward one of

the three confused charzins, I was trying to remember
the last time I was so tempted to leave the protection
of someone out of my spell. After a moment I realized
the last time was during the quest, and the someone
was the same someone I was glaring at right then, so I
reluctantly let it go. Getting even would have to wait
for a more convenient time, when I could give it all of
my attention.

And wanted to give it that kind of attention. Right
then there was someone else I preferred paying attention to, someone who considered herself very clever. I
wondered how many of the Sighted she had caused to
be mutilated, and simply thinking about it made me
furious. It wasn't possible to permanently mutilate
someone with a strong enough talent, but that applied
only to the physical side of it. Mentally, the scarring
remained even when the body was blemish-free, and
that didn't even cover the topics of on-the-spot hyste-
ria and those who *weren't* strong enough to restore
themselves. The woman obviously never stopped to
think about others, but I intended changing that.

Everyone seemed to be watching closely when Rik,
in his link-form, suddenly attacked one of the charzins.
Since most life-forms tended to avoid them, even the
charzins were surprised, but the surprise didn't last
long. The one under attack fought and the other two
circled looking for an opening, and even the woman
who had started it all didn't notice the first of my
spells. She had cut off our close-up communication
link when it suited her, and right then the same thing
suited me.

As soon as I couldn't be overheard any longer, I
began speaking the second, more complicated spell. I
was taking a nasty chance with part of it, but I was
working on the theory that if things were going to
blow up under me, I'd prefer having them do that as
soon as possible instead of after a long time of being
safe. The entire concept of being safe was a rather
touchy subject with me right then, but I didn't have
the time to mull it over.

The heat of that small sun overhead seemed to be

increasing, but none of those in the stands appeared to be bothered by it. I wiped away the sweat on my forehead with the back of my hand as I watched Rik swing around fast from the charzin he was engaged with, to swipe hard at the one that was trying to flank him. The first charzin tried taking advantage of his momentary distraction by immediately moving in, but that turned out to be a bad idea. The fangs and claws of the bronze link-beast were there to stop the attack, and the charzin backed off with a half-snarl of pain and frustration.

Since the third charzin was working its way in closer, we had obviously reached a good point to stop that nonsense. I used a gesture to reconnect the voice link I had disconnected earlier, then raised both arms and spoke the single word I'd keyed my second spell to. Lightning flashed and thunder boomed, and when the sound effects were over the charzins were gone through the black holes that had opened under their feet, and the spectator stands were sectioned off in a very special way. Heavy black lines that weren't really lines surrounded those who had expected to be entertained, and after shouts and cries of fear and shock they all sat very, very still.

"What's the matter, folks, aren't you having fun with the spell I just devised?" I asked, knowing none of them would have trouble hearing me. Any Sighted who has had the least amount of training knows better than to believe a complex spell can be accomplished by the use of a single word, but the superstitions of the unSighted affect everyone to a certain extent. They'd heard a word they didn't understand and then my spell had come into being, and most of them *knew*, deep inside, that that was an accomplishment far beyond their own ability.

"What have you done?" the woman in the decorated seat tried to demand, despite the shrill unevenness of her voice. "What in the name of the Diamond Worlds have you done?"

She was no longer relaxed in her seat, most particularly because her seat couldn't be relaxed in. It tilted forward toward the wide black gap I'd positioned at her feet, and it took a bit of effort on her part to keep from sliding off the seat and into the blackness.

"I've dissolved certain key sections of the world-stuff around us, laying bare the basic fabric of the universe," I answered, making it sound as difficult as folding a piece of paper. "Those are fracture lines you see all around you, ready to snap off clean at the proper time. Theory says the bunch of you will be swept away along with the rest of this section of world-stuff, but no one has made any guesses about where you'll be swept away *to*. Maybe you'll be protected by your warding."

"No!" the woman screamed, but she was almost drowned out by the horrified reactions of her friends and followers. We all knew that warding could do only so much, and for the most part only against magic. Personal defenses were called warding, but they were really spells of protection. During the quest I'd learned how to deal with those who were warded, and right then I was putting that learning to use.

"But—but you couldn't have done something like that!" the woman babbled, so frightened she wouldn't have noticed even if she'd soiled herself. "What you're talking about— It's impossible! No one knows the shape and texture of world-stuff, so no one can work with it! You're just trying to frighten us!"

"If you believe that, why don't you call my bluff?" I asked very mildly, refraining from pointing out that if I was just trying to frighten them, I was doing a smash-up job. "I've discovered I enjoy showing off now and then, so why don't you challenge me to take out only *one* section of the stands? I'll even let you say which one."

Hysterical screams and protests sounded as I began to raise my arms again, showing most of them didn't think I *was* bluffing. I turned my face toward the woman I spoke with, the woman I still hadn't seen clearly enough to recognize, giving the impression I was waiting for her to choose, and the people around her went wilder still. Taking out one section could conceivably take out the rest as well, and none of them were prepared to risk that.

"No, don't, don't!" the woman begged in a shriek, needing no one's help to recognize the wisest response to make. "Please don't do any more of that—please, don't! We'll give you anything you want—anything!—if only you'll return things to the way they were!"

"You mean to having the charzins getting ready to play with my companion and me?" I asked, seeing in a glance that said companion had returned to human form and was standing quietly only a few steps away, an equally quiet smile on his face. With the beasts gone, Rik was free to enjoy the show, which was exactly what he was doing.

"No, no, of course not," the woman immediately denied, visibly dividing her attention between the gap at her feet and me. "An entry out of this area is right there on the sand, and you two will certainly be free to use it. With our apologies for having interrupted those—better things you had to do."

"Studying," I told her with a satisfied smile, one that should have increased her trembling. "These days I'm getting back into studying, even though it wasn't originally my idea. Once I qualified as a sorceress I thought I'd be through with studying for half of forever, but after only a couple of years I'm right back to it again."

"But—there isn't that much *to* study at your level," the woman objected, the frown in her voice showing she was close to being distracted by the confusion she felt. "It takes years and years to reach wizard strength, and then the only thing left to study is—"

I could feel her eyes on me when her words ended abruptly, and in the absolute hush all around there must have been a large number of faces paling. I smiled again, having the distinct feeling the woman could see me a lot more clearly than I was seeing her, and the way she froze seemed to prove the contention.

"UnSeen magic," she whispered, her lips barely moving, her eyes locked to me. "You're studying un-Seen magic. If you weren't, you never could have done this— But you're too young to be doing that, too young to be a wizard—"

"That's what I said, but apparently it isn't true," I told her with a shrug. "I've been informed I'm not far from wizard strength right now, and I'm not the only one who doesn't look it. As far as studying unSeen magic goes—I certainly am. They say I have a talent for it."

There were a lot of open mouths and staring eyes, but absolute stillness continued to reign until I asked to have the location of that entry pointed out to me again. Dozens of fingers indicated a place in the middle of the red sand, and as soon as I was close enough the transfer slip tucked into my belt began blinking. I touched the jewel for the residential area that was mine, gestured Rik through the entry first, then snapped my fingers before stepping through myself. The snap was my prearranged signal for everything to return to normal, which it did, and the first sight to greet me on the other side of the entry was Rik's grin.

"Laciel, that was beautiful," he applauded, letting out the laughter he had previously been holding in. "You scared the hell out of them, especially when you started them on the subject of unSeen magic. And telling them you weren't the only one who looked too young to be involved with that. It'll be years before they have the nerve to start up with anyone else—if they ever can again. They'll never know if they're netting a helpless victim—or a predator who ignores nets. If I had to bet on it, I'd say you cured them for good."

He was so pleased with the way things had turned out, that he didn't seem to notice I was doing nothing more than heading toward our suite. I walked right in, ignored Graythor and InThig where they sat looking as though they were waiting for something, and went directly to the bar. Pointing at a decanter of wine got me a cup filled, which I took to a chair and then immediately began to drink.

"Well, Rik, apparently you managed to find her," Graythor said, his voice on the strange side, a tension of sorts seemingly gone out of him. "The resort attendant you left with came back in a terrible flurry, babbling something about the two of you having been caught in a trap and the resort not being responsible. InThig and I decided to give you a short while to get yourselves out of the trap, and go after you to help only if you weren't back in a reasonable amount of time. Truth to tell, that reasonable amount of time was nearly gone."

"Come on, Graythor, you and InThig should know you don't have to worry about Laciel and me," Rik answered with a laugh, clearly enjoying himself. "I handled the physical part and she handled the magical, and it's highly unlikely that trap will ever be used again."

"It certainly wouldn't be if *I* had been there," InThig said in a growl, its claws flexing into the carpeting it lay on. "What sort of trap was it?"

Rik described what we had gone through, including what was said, not really noticing how closely Graythor was paying attention. I noticed it, but I was too busy swallowing wine to do anything beyond that.

"You really should have seen them," Rik finished up with a chuckle, stretching out on the couch he'd appropriated. "If they'd gone any pastier they would have looked like ghosts, and all because of a well-staged trick."

"You knew it was a trick?" Graythor asked in a strictly controlled voice, his gaze unmoving from Rik. "If it was that obvious, why didn't your captors know?"

"Probably because they weren't on the quest with us," Rik answered comfortably, tucking his hands behind his head. "You remember, InThig, when you and Laciel scared the hell out of those soldiers keeping us from the gate we needed to use. It was almost the exact same attitude, but this time she did it to a bunch of Sighted."

"Rik," InThig began, those blazing red eyes looking elsewhere than at the man, but he was off the hook for the comment he was having trouble coming up with when Graythor interrupted.

"Rik, I think you'd better understand she couldn't have been bluffing," the wizard said, and his dark, furious eyes slid to me. "Those black gaps you mentioned were looked at by those with the Sight, and *that* was what made them so frightened. She actually did what she said she'd done, and it was a miracle nothing went horribly wrong."

"But—but it was all so theatrical!" Rik protested, sitting up on the couch with nothing left of his amusement. "It was so terribly dangerous, so awful a threat, I knew it couldn't possibly be true. Are you sure it was?"

"Even if I had no other way, I would know from the way she's trembling," Graythor answered, flicking two fingers in my direction. "She may be irresponsible enough to do something like that, but she's not too ignorant to suspect you and she would probably have been swept away with all the others if anything had gone wrong. We haven't any idea what the fabric of the universe closes us off from, but if her toying with the world-stuff had ruptured it, you might have been in a position to find out. For a very, *very* brief period of time."

"I used anchors," I muttered, pointing at the bottle of wine to refill my cup. "Since I wasn't sure what would happen, my spell included anchors for him and me. But right there at the end, I discovered the anchors hadn't hooked in properly—"

Which had scared me at least as badly as I'd scared our erstwhile captors. I quickly swallowed down more of the wine, trying to get myself to stop shaking, trying to stop picturing what could have happened if any other part of my spell had failed. . . .

"Laciel, you and I are overdue for a long, serious talk," Graythor said in the hardest voice I'd ever heard him use, those eyes burning me with black fire. "It isn't as if you didn't know what harm it was possible to cause, and not only to those in your immediate vicinity. If those fracture lines had ruptured, everyone in this resort could conceivably have been swept entirely out of this universe, and probably out of their lives! What could possibly have given you the idea you had the right to put others in such jeopardy? How could you . . ."

"Please, Uncle Graythor, save the lecture for another time," I interrupted, holding one hand up. "I did something very stupid, and nobody has to spell it out for me. What I need right now is . . ."

"What you need right now is something a little more memorable than a lecture," Rik interrupted in turn, his tone now a growl as those bronze eyes flared at me. "I told you I didn't want those people hurt, especially not after I provoked that woman's reaction, and this was the better way you were supposed to find? The only reason people are irresponsible is because they've never been taught better, so it's more than time you had a few lessons. You and I are going . . ."

"Nowhere," I finished quickly, continuing the circle he'd forced his way into. "The concept of 'you and I' no longer exists, something we both agreed to, so stop acting as if we hadn't. And stop talking to me. You have nothing to say that I want to hear."

"Now what's wrong?" Graythor asked in exasperation, but at least he was asking only Rik. "When you found her, you were supposed to explain to her about what you'd been doing. Were you trapped before you had the chance?"

"Yes, but then I did have the time, so I did it," Rik answered, annoyed enough to glance away from me. "After that, I found the argument I'd been looking for, but we were interrupted before it could be ended properly. Listen, Laciel, you can't use what was said in that argument as ammunition against me. We were both too angry for it to really mean anything, so . . ."

"No," I pronounced before he could suggest whatever it was he had in mind. "You were the one who wanted an argument, and you can't claim you didn't get one. You got yours, and now I get to have what *I* want: no more talk."

"Laciel, it would be foolish to be unreasonable about this," InThig put in while I stood. "Rik was forced by your actions to behave the way he did, which means the situation could well be interpreted as being entirely your fault. Putting the blame on others when it's rightfully yours is not a character flaw you *used* to suffer from."

I looked at the demon after he'd made his very pointed point, and those blazing red eyes made no effort to avoid mine. InThig was in the mood to indulge in self-righteous accusation, so all I did was nod.

"You're absolutely right, InThig, the whole thing's my fault," I agreed. "I'm the one who gave my word about something and then broke it, and I'm the one who played hurtful games in an attempt to justify my broken word. It was all me, and there's only one way to treat someone so dishonorable: with high-minded disdain and dismissal in everything, except when working together is necessary. I'll understand when you ignore me completely until it's time to go through the gate."

InThig's tail swished in annoyance as I began to walk past the demon, but there was nothing it could say on its original tack. My intention was to take my glass of wine to my bedroom where I could relax in peace and quiet for a while, but some people prefer war and discord and enter into that state as often as possible.

"There's another way to treat people who break their word and play—'hurtful'—games," Rik said, stepping directly into my path. "You try to understand how desperate they must be to do such things, and when you find even a small amount of that understanding you make the effort to forgive them. Forgiving people isn't easy, I know, but sometimes they're such fools there isn't anything you can do *but* forgive them."

"Forgive people who hurt you?" I echoed, looking up at him in confusion—and with the dizziness caused by drinking so much wine so fast. "But when you forgive them, you're saying they had the right to hurt you, that it didn't matter if they hurt you because you're the type to forget about being hurt. When you forgive someone, you're leaving yourself open to be hurt again, because you've said it's okay to do that to you. They can do anything they like—pretend they love you and then abandon you—"

His expression made me realize I was saying too much, that I was letting too much of how I felt be seen. The wine had caused me to do that, but it didn't keep me from seeing the pity and guilt Rik was experiencing. I hated when people pitied me, but sometimes there's a benefit in having them react that way. When I walked around Rik to find a bedroom to use, he made no further effort to stop me.

CHAPTER 9

I didn't know how long I'd been asleep, but I couldn't shake the feeling it was "morning." The Realm of Dreams *had* no established morning, not unless you were in an area decorated with that sort of thing, but my mind had no interest in being corrected. It was too busy agreeing with my body that it was time to get something to eat, so I shrugged and gave in to the two of them.

Since I hadn't bathed the "night" before, I took care of that chore before dressing in my freshened clothes and leaving the bedroom. InThig padded out behind me, as silent as it had been since I'd opened my eyes, a mood that sometimes took the demon. This time its silence also seemed to be filled with thought, but I made no effort to ask any questions. If it was ignoring me the way I'd suggested, I intended enjoying the situation for as long as it lasted.

The dining hall was pleasantly empty when I entered it, so I twisted a menu out of the air, chose what I wanted to eat, then went to the table to sit down with the food. At least that was one thing about the Realm of Dreams: the food never failed to live up to your expectations. I was enjoying myself thoroughly when a number of other dishes appeared on the table, and then Graythor was there and sitting down.

"There's no doubt I was in need of the sleep I had, but I find it impossible not to consider it a complete waste of time," he grumbled, pointing first to something in a pitcher. "The gate should begin cycling down soon, I'm told, but they still refuse to commit to a definition of 'soon.' "

"Within the next century or so, I'm beginning to believe," I said in my own grumble, glad to see I wasn't the only one feeling like that. "But just in case it happens sooner, we ought to be ready to jump. Did you intend paying the bill yourself, or do you want me to do it?"

"I've already taken care of the matter," he answered, glaring at the food he pointed to. "They had some childish idea of a special play area they wanted spelled into being, but whoever built that spell was a blithering idiot. He or she and they couldn't understand why the area kept collapsing when someone of sufficient strength spoke the spell, and I very nearly had to explain it to them in words of one syllable. Once I corrected the spell and spoke it, they had their play area; this time it won't collapse. If I should ever be foolish enough to come this way again, I've been assured I'll be most welcome."

"Aren't they generous," I said, pointing at the pot to refill my cup of coffee. "You give them another whole area to collect gold or spells from, and they tell you you'll be welcome if you come back. Maybe no one corrected the spell before this because no one could handle generosity of that magnitude."

"The spell was too subtly wrong for that to be the case," he answered with a small headshake. "It was simply inferior workmanship from someone who should have been able to do better, considering the level of ability required to develop the spell to begin with. Lack of proper inSight was what it was, that and an inability—or absence of desire—to see a pattern as a whole. And, of course, a shortage of imagination."

"That's what we could use a better supply of right now," I muttered, sitting back with my coffee. "More imagination, or at least enough to get things moving for us." I let my mind spread for a minute, trying to think of something we could do, and then it came to me. "Hey, I know!" I enthused, leaning forward again. "InThig can get through that gate without waiting for it to cycle down all the way. Why don't we see if we can come up with a spell that will let us do it the way InThig does?"

If Graythor hadn't immediately choked on what he was drinking, he undoubtedly would have gotten to comment first. Since he did choke, though, InThig won the race by default.

"Laciel, what in the worlds have they put into your food?" the demon demanded, apparently having gone straight up into the air in shock. "Whatever it is, the substance must be highly illegal due to the way it warps judgment and destroys common sense! Have you any idea of what you just suggested?"

"What I suggested was a possible way for us to get on with Morgiana's rescue," I replied, not caring much for the demon's tone as well as its words. "What's the matter, InThig? Afraid of having someone steal your thunder?"

"Young woman, what InThig is afraid of is that you've lost your mind!" Graythor finally managed in a strangled roar, his linen napkin squeezed into one fist, his entire being projecting outrage. "Haven't you ever been taught what it can mean to attempt a duplication of sophisticated nonhuman abilities? Most especially demon abilities? Their life base begins at an entirely different point from ours, and in order to duplicate an essential part of it, you would need to alter your own base! Do you know what happens when someone tries to alter his life base?"

"No, Uncle Graythor, what?" I asked with very innocent and completely phony rapt attention, leaning one elbow on the table and my chin on the resulting fist. Graythor began purpling, everything he wanted to say at once keeping him from saying anything at all, fully aware of the fact that I knew exactly what he meant. It was one of the first things you were taught when you began developing magical strength, but the second thing you learned was that it was all no more than theory.

"You seem to believe no one has ever made a true attempt to disprove the theory, Laciel," InThig observed, somehow just about reading my mind. "In point of fact more than one attempt has been made, but each of them were such disasters most humans find it easier to avoid talking and thinking about them. I've had the details from some of the demons involved, and I rather agree with the human point of view."

"But what if those who tried the experiments were sloppy or unimaginative?" I countered, then looked back at Graythor. "You said yourself that someone with a particular level of strength and skill isn't expected to be sloppy, but I'll bet it happens more often than with just that play area incident. If you and I did it, it would be done right, Uncle Graythor, and you can't deny that. Let's just . . ."

"No!" the small, bent man shouted, fury still coloring his face. "You haven't even yet begun your studies, but you've already reached the point of believing you know everything there is to know. Some of the spells used in the attempts were written down—along with descriptions of the stomach-turning results obtained —and you will kindly read *those* before you again inform me how easily you and I will accomplish something. Until then the subject is closed, and I had best not hear another word about it."

"Uncle Graythor, that's unfair," I began to protest, actually feeling the heat of his anger radiating at me in waves. For some reason he was so furious, he was losing a small amount of control over the spread of his personal defenses. I intended demanding to know why he refused to discuss the matter even in general, but an unwelcome interruption came instead.

"What's all the shouting about?" Rik asked, coming up to the table to take the seat to my left. "Are we under attack already?"

"We certainly are, and the attack is from within," Graythor huffed, but at least that blazing edge of heat retreated. "Laciel had another brilliant idea, but at least this one is potentially devastating only to those who are foolish enough to indulge with her. But there won't be any devastation of any sort, will there, young lady?"

"Why are you afraid to even discuss it?" I demanded, totally out of patience with his stubbornness. "Simple talk doesn't hurt anything, and it seems to me . . ."

"No!" he shouted again, this time hitting the table with his hand. "Simple talk *never* hurts anyone, unless one of those indulging in the discussion is the sort who considers talk a prelude to acting. This time you will *not* act, no matter the stubbornness you attempt to bring to bear."

His left hand came up as he mouthed words I couldn't quite hear, but although I felt the stirring of power, I had no idea how it had been applied. He'd spoken a spell of some sort, but I couldn't imagine what its purpose was.

"You'll find out what that does if you attempt to try the spell on your own," he said with a great deal of satisfaction, apparently reading my mind the way InThig had. "All fractious children need stern and proper curbing."

"But adults have to learn how to curb themselves," Rik observed, paying more attention to choosing food for his plate than to looking at anybody. "If you have an adult who hasn't learned the trick yet, that's the lesson you start with. Don't you think so, Laciel?"

"If you don't experiment, how are you supposed to learn?" I demanded of Graythor, ignoring Rik entirely. "There's only so much studying and theorizing can give you; after that you *have* to experiment, that or give up working in the field."

"If the studying and theorizing aren't thoroughly gone into, experimenting becomes an act of attempted suicide," Graythor pronounced, staring directly at me with no amusement whatsoever. "Do you by any chance recall what happens to those who attempt complex spells before they have a thorough knowledge of the language of spells? Luck may keep them safe during their first half-dozen or so attempts, but after that, disaster lies all about them, waiting for their very next incautious step. Which comes rather quickly, due to the overconfidence they've become infected with because of the luck—which they've interpreted as supreme ability. Success can sometimes be the most devastating of results you can hope to attain, child, and I refuse to allow it to destroy you. And I also refuse to allow an exhibition of extremely poor manners. Answer the question that was put to you, and be polite about it."

"You want an answer, Uncle Graythor?" I said, suddenly so furious I could have spit. "I'll be glad to give you an answer. Yes, I certainly do recall what happens to those who try things they're not yet ready to do. Was that polite enough for you?"

"I think you know that wasn't the question I was referring to," he responded, still looking at me with that very direct gaze. "You're angry because you feel you were embarrassed unnecessarily by the way I spoke to you, and yet you consider ignoring a member of this group to be fully acceptable. If your sort of rudeness is proper, you must consider mine the same."

"But I haven't been rude to a member of this group," I countered, leaning back just a little to match his stare. "I may have been arguing with you, but that wasn't meant as rudeness. If that's the way you took it, you have my most sincere apologies. And, as far as I know, I haven't been rude to InThig. InThig, have I been rude to you?"

"Laciel, neither Graythor nor I consider that amusing," InThig returned, a clear growl in its voice. "Rik is just as much a member of this group as any of the rest of us, and if we can forgive the way you nearly ruptured the fabric of space all around us, you can find it within you to forgive the mistake *he* made. Which was, you must admit, of slightly less consequence than your own."

"What I'll admit is that what *I* did was *almost* a mistake," I snapped, turning my head to the right to glare at the demon. " 'Almost' doesn't count nearly as much as 'accomplished,' so you mustn't give me anything like that amount of credit. It simply isn't fair."

"No, no, let's take a minute to admit the lady's right," Rik said just as Graythor and InThig both tried to answer me, surprising his two supporters. "What she did may have been irresponsible and poorly considered, but it still worked out without hurting anyone. My efforts *did* manage to hurt someone, and I've been thinking about what she said on the subject of forgiveness. Telling someone you forgive them *is* like telling them it was perfectly all right that they hurt you, so I'm no longer asking her to do that."

"You're giving up?" InThig demanded, now sounding as annoyed with Rik as it had with me. "Don't you humans find it unbelievably dizzying to constantly change your mind like that?"

"I didn't say I was changing my mind or giving up on anything," Rik replied, his tone so mild that InThig blinked. "All I said was that I wasn't going to ask her to forgive me. What I intend doing instead is acting as if none of it ever happened, including my agreement to walk away from her. Laciel, I intend making you my wife, so I think we'd better get started with finding ways to get along. Predominantly peaceful marriages are the happiest ones, so why don't we start with carrying on normal conversations instead of the jumping-down-each-other's-throats the way we've *been* doing?"

Seeing a wizard and a demon with their mouths hanging open isn't an everyday occurrence, but I was too annoyed to give the picture the appreciation it deserved. Apparently Graythor and InThig didn't know Rik as well as I did, so what he'd said had surprised them. At one point I might have been just as surprised, but quests apparently prepare you for life in more ways than one.

"I think you'll both agree we have an important choice to make here," I said to my two true companions, speaking quickly to take advantage of their shock.

"Since he obviously needs the sort of help we haven't the time to give him, we can either leave him here, or find a Sighted willing to take him back to his world. We won't find it possible to rescue Morgiana if we try dragging around a crazy man with us, so which way are we going to do it?"

"And that's another thing," Rik put in with continuing mildness while Graythor and InThig just stared at first me and then him. "If you keep on calling me all kinds of names, getting along in a friendly way may become something of a problem. And I'm sure you didn't realize it, but conversation between you and me means us talking to each other, not me talking to you and you talking to them. Turn this way and look at me, and tell me you understand."

"You see?" I said to Graythor and InThig, silently thanking Rik for his help. "He's getting worse by the minute, and simply letting it go on would be cruel and inconsiderate. The only thing we can do now is . . ."

"I said, turn this way and look at me, and tell me you understand what I said to you," Rik repeated, and then his hand was on my face, turning it toward him. "I should never have let things go on like this for so long, but I don't know nearly enough about you. That's the first thing we'll change between us, and after that all the rest."

"Rik, this may not be the proper time to insist on things with her," Graythor said, his voice showing how disturbed he was over the way I struggled to free myself from Rik's basically gentle but stubbornly unyielding grip. "You must remember that she isn't used to being treated like that, and . . ."

"No, she isn't used to being treated the way I intend treating her," Rik broke in, his voice no longer mild, his bronze eyes unmoving from my face. "She's used to having people betray and hurt her, use her and fear her. They've taught her not to love anyone because those you love will always turn around and walk away, and I nearly added to that. I was such a damned fool I tried to make her jealous with the thought of me being with other women, but since she wasn't expecting me to behave any other way it wasn't jealousy she felt. Now I have to change all that, make her know she's the only one I'll ever want, and then make her believe it."

"Don't waste your time," I said, finally able to pull my face away from his hand, and then I looked back at Graythor. "I'm for having someone take him back to his own world, to save us the annoyance of running into him again when we return this way with Morgiana. If you and InThig don't have a better idea, we can see about getting it done right now."

"Laciel, you keep missing the point," Rik said, his voice returned to mildness as he elbowed his way into the conversation again. "I can't do any of the things I intend doing with you if I'm not right there with you, so I'd appreciate it if you'd stop making plans to get rid of me. I'm not going anywhere you don't go, and as part of that from now on you'll be going where you should have been right from the start. When the need for sleeping accommodations comes up we won't need as many as we did, because you'll be sharing mine."

"The hell I will!" I snarled, finally too far into outrage to ignore him any longer. "How dare you say something like that, as if I were a—a—"

"A grown woman?" he asked, the expression on his face very helpful and friendly. "Since you and I will be getting married as soon as this rescue mission is accomplished, there's no reason we shouldn't share a bed. You're entitled to have a little pleasure in your life, and the rest of us could use having you in a *good* mood for a change."

Sputtering incoherently at someone doesn't do anything but make them work harder to cover the grin they're trying to hide, so I went back to ignoring Rik in favor of working on Graythor. The dark, sallow-skinned wizard was rubbing his lips with one finger while InThig, with a typical demon-type sense of humor, chuckled deeply, but all I got to say was, "Uncle Graythor!" His dark eyes were immediately on me as he put his hand down and shook his head, then straightened in his chair.

"No, Laciel, complaining to me will do you no good," he said, all traces of his former disturbance gone. "Rik is absolutely right in believing you're not *able* to accept him, which leaves him no alternative than to make the decision *for* you. Your pairing off with him needs time to see if it will work, and you do deserve a bit of pleasure in your life while that time passes by. Our group will remain having the same number of members it had to begin with, and the only changes made will be the ones suggested by Rik."

"So you're on his side," I said, taking a moment to glance at InThig. "Both of you are on his side, and to hell with what *I* want. Well, you may see it that way, but I flatly refuse to. Since we're obviously into bald statements, it's time I made one of my own. You have the choice of seeing me as part of the group or having him, but you can't have us both. Make your decision now, and make it fast. Which one of us goes?"

"Laciel, there's really no need to be that unbending," InThig began while Graythor frowned and opened his mouth, but I'd had more than enough of words.

"I didn't ask for a discussion, I asked for a decision," I said, ending InThig's attempt to smooth things over and cutting off Graythor's comment before it began. "Don't worry about hurting my feelings. At this point I couldn't care less one way or the other. If you want me to be the one to go, just say so."

"I'd say they aren't the ones who most want to see you gone," Rik commented, taking up the slack the other two didn't seem prepared to tackle. "As a trained military observer, I've spotted someone much more eager than them to see you ride off alone."

"What are you talking about?" I demanded, even more annoyed with him for interrupting what should have ended all that nonsense. "There's no one else involved in this—unless you're talking about yourself."

"Hardly me," he said with a snort, and then that bright, eager smile was back. "The person I'm talking about has tried two or three times to get you out of this group, and didn't miss by much any of the times. Now it looks like she's finally succeeded."

"She?" Graythor echoed, stealing what would have been *my* question, but someone else got the point immediately.

"Of course," InThig said, a sleek satisfaction coating the words. "The one who has been trying so hard is Laciel herself. That was quite a clever observation, Rik."

"That's the most ridiculous accusation I've heard in a long time," I blustered as Graythor joined InThig in staring at me, for some unknown reason feeling very uncomfortable. "I haven't been trying to get myself out of this group, it was just the way things almost worked out. It wasn't anything *I* started, unless you believe I should have asked someone's permission before feeling insulted."

"You know, that's one of the things I've been having trouble understanding," Rik drawled, leaning back in his chair as he took over direction of the conversation. "You claimed you started out angry with all of us, got angrier still because we didn't notice you weren't talking to us, and then couldn't help blowing up because we didn't believe you were as good as new. That was when you picked up and walked away from us, heading off for the house of a friend."

"So?" I said, the only thing I could think of *to* say. Graythor was paying *very* close attention to Rik, but his stare was still completely mine.

"So, if you were as strong and recovered as all that and could prove it, why weren't you sticking around to demand a proper place in the group?" Rik obliged, the question tossed out with devastating mildness. "Why did you start to walk away instead, telling us you were going to stay with a friend until we got back? You couldn't have helped Morgiana from your friend's house, and isn't that what you most want to do? Help Morgiana? How could you have helped her by keeping your recovered strength away from—"

His over-detailed explanation cut off when Graythor struck the table with both palms and stood with a growl, and that was the point I simply closed my eyes and slumped back in the chair. I'd talked a very powerful wizard into feeling guilty about insulting me, and now that wizard had just found out he'd been fooled. No one enjoys feeling like a fool, but wizards tend to enjoy it less than most; I didn't know what he would do to me for it, but I did know I had absolutely no desire to see it coming.

"So that's what's been behind all of this nonsense and noise!" Graythor shouted, absolutely livid and probably not even noticing the way I flinched. "That obsession of yours to go after Morgiana and rescue her by yourself! I should have known better than to believe you were giving up on the idea, simply because I grew angry with you! Everything still has to be your way, as though you were still a child on the streets of Geddenburg, and not getting your way could well mean your defeat and death! This time, young woman, you've gone entirely too far, and I'm going to—"

"Attention, please, attention please," a bodiless voice broke in suddenly, saving me from having to hear about the way I was going to be killed. "The gate your party has been inquiring about has just begun cycling down. If it's still your intention to use that gate, we suggest you start making your way to the departure point. Your mounts, of course, will be there and waiting."

"Thank you, we'll be right along," Graythor said, paused very briefly, then added, "At least, most of us will be. Do you have an unformed area I might use as a detention cell of sorts, for someone who is long overdue for punishing? The cell will be self-sustaining until I return, and . . ."

"Uncle Graythor, no!" I shrieked, my eyes flying open in shock. "You can't leave me behind like that, you just can't! Morgiana needs me, and I *have* to be there!"

"Morgiana needs *us*," he corrected in a voice like grinding stone, his eyes burning with black fire. "That's a truth you seem incapable of understanding, and I won't see our efforts ruined because of it. If you were to go strutting around on your own and got caught, we'd not only have two to rescue instead of one, not only have Morgiana's strength to struggle with but yours as well, we'd also have them warned and alert against anything we tried to do. Have you at any time taken *that* into consideration?"

I sat forward in my chair where my first reaction to his threat had taken me, silent against the points he'd made but not conceding all of them. With as little as we knew, there was nothing to say they could convert me the way they'd done with Morgiana, and even before that there was no guarantee I would get . . .

"Do you remember the blind world, Laciel?" Rik put in at just the wrong time, the mildness of his tone having sharpened a bit. "We found ourselves in the middle of a very regimented society, where even making the right move didn't guarantee our safety. In places like that, you don't *have* to do anything wrong to trip, and from what InThig has said the world we're going to is very much the same. Would you really prefer being all alone in a place like that?"

I turned my head to look at him then, seeing in his eyes how pleased he was to have been able to remind me how I'd gotten myself taken without actually coming out and saying it and thereby breaking his promise. If Graythor found out now what I'd done on the blind world I'd be left behind for sure, but for some reason the thought of that wasn't bothering me as much as the other thing Rik had said. Do you really want to be all alone in a place like that, he'd asked, almost as though he knew how I'd felt in that cell they'd locked me up in, all alone . . . with no one on my side . . .

"It's no use," Graythor said, anger and impatience still dominating him. "It's always been nearly impossible to reason with her, and although I understand why, I choose not to accept it this time. We'll leave her here in a cell of nothingness . . ."

"No!" I said at once, snapping my head around to look at him. "I won't let myself be locked away while the rest of you go off. Morgiana needs me, and if I have to fight I'll—do it."

"So you'll fight," he said, the small, calm smile he

wore emphasizing the blazing black of his eyes even more. "With the expectation of winning?"

He knew damned well how I'd do against him, and in the mood he was in he was making no effort to soften the look that would have sent unSighted by the dozen running and screaming in terror. Graythor was one of the most powerful wizards ever, and he was still absolutely furious with me.

"I—don't mean I'll fight *you*," I stumbled, tangentially aware of how sorry he would be for hurting me—after it was already done. "I think I have a way of breaking out of a nothingness cell, and if you put me in one I'll have no choice but to try."

"Breaking out of a nothingness cell is impossible," he stated, apparently unaware of the frown he had suddenly developed. "Since we all know that, your statement is nothing but a bluff. You leave me no choice but to . . ."

"I'm not bluffing," I interrupted hurriedly, knowing how big a chance I was taking. "I didn't say I *knew* I could break out, I said I had a theory. If you force me to it, I'll test the theory."

"Excuse me, Graythor, but I believe we would do well asking what her theory is," InThig put in, sounding vaguely worried. "If she hasn't already jumped forward eagerly to test that theory—"

"It must be more dangerous than any of us can imagine, yes," Graythor agreed sourly, immediately understanding what InThig hadn't said in so many words. "Very well, young woman. Say it now, but make it *brief*."

"I don't know if I *can* be brief," I began, but seeing Graythor's eyes made me hurry on. "It's—just a thought I had when those idiot Sighteds trapped Rik and me. In order to make a nothingness cell you have to bend the nothingness, which means at least one side of the cell is drawn away out of full contact with all the nothingness in the universe. That side would be the cell's weak spot, so that's the side I would attack. It would absorb and draw out any magical strength exerted against it, but if the reservoir for the strength was being refilled as fast as it was being emptied, wouldn't something eventually have to give?"

I asked my question and intended doing nothing more after that beyond waiting, but I got a reaction almost before the words were entirely out. Graythor paled in a way I'd seldom seen him do before, and then his eyes were closed as though he were in pain.

"Those—openings—you developed to restore yourself faster," he said in a gravelly whisper, his voice trembling faintly. "Drawing in unlimited power and feeding it into absolute nothingness—the meeting of all and nothing—the concept causes my very soul to quaver— And you would dare consider *trying* something like that?"

His eyes were open again so quickly and looking at me so sternly I couldn't help swallowing hard, but that wasn't the time to lose the tiny amount of ground I'd gained.

"Only if I was forced to," I reminded him, working very hard to sound responsible but desperate. "If I'm not there, Morgiana won't be rescued, so I have to be there no matter what. If you consider me too big a risk to be around, you three can be the ones to stay here."

"You, young lady, are clearly a risk to be near no matter *what* the circumstances," Graythor rasped, those eyes refusing to let up. "At this moment, for instance, my sense of personal honor is gravely at risk. Many long years ago I swore an oath never to lose my temper so far that I would do something I would afterward regret. Possibly the oath could be gotten around by anticipating nothing in the way of post-punishment regrets— "

He seemed to be seriously considering the idea for a moment or two, and I didn't dare try reminding him how close we normally were. It was always possible we weren't quite as close as I'd thought, and that was hardly the best time for him to find it out. All I could do was wait for him to make up his mind, which didn't take very long at all.

"All right, we haven't really the time for this," he said, his mind fully made up. "Laciel, I will have your word right now that you won't try separating yourself from us again, or I'll leave you in a nothingness cell no matter what the possible consequences. The choice is yours, and you will make it quickly."

"But what if it becomes necessary to Morgiana's safety for me to—" I began, but the way he started drawing himself up again ended *that* in a hurry. "Okay, okay, you have my word. I won't try separating myself from you three again."

"You had better not have any hidden arguments qualifying the word you just gave," he warned, still not at all happy with me. "We continue to have the matter of your behavior until now to settle up on, and to add to it would be the height of foolishness on your part. Take my word on that."

"May I suggest that we now make haste to the departure area?" InThig said as it stood, a smooth calming hidden in its voice. "That gate can hardly be counted on to cycle down in the usual manner."

The best reply to that suggestion was for all of us to begin leaving the table, with Rik hurrying to finish up the last of the food on his plate. After getting me in it neck-deep with Graythor, the bronze-eyed man had done little beyond sitting back and watching my life be put on the line. He must have really been enjoying himself, but one day he would pay that enjoyment back—with interest.

CHAPTER 10

The same two entries that got us to the suite brought us back to the departure area, and although our horses were saddled and ready to go, the gate was not. It was definitely cycling down toward opening, but hadn't yet reached the point of doing so. Rik asked a hovering gate attendant for coffee, and once he had it he carried it over to Graythor, who stood just a couple of steps to my right.

"I'm curious about something you said during the—warmish—discussion just past," he put to the wizard after offering coffee to the rest of us and being refused. "You said Laciel was almost impossible to reason with, and that you knew why. I've noticed the same thing about her myself, but haven't yet come across a real reason for it. Would you care to share yours?"

"Awareness of the reason comes from having known her so long and well," Graythor grudged, giving me a glance that said he'd be a lot happier in the future if he could forget all about me. "The key to interpreting her actions lies in remembering that half her life—the formative half—was spent as a gutter rat and a leader of gutter rats. A mature leader, secure in his or her position, can afford to take advice on a regular basis from others; a frightened child, constantly in danger of losing her position if that fright—or indecision—is detected by others, is quite unable to do the same. Anyone attempting to reason with her during an emotionally trying time—"

"Is simply trying to undermine her position," Rik finished when Graythor just shrugged, those bronze eyes now resting on me. "A lot of her behavior seems to stem from that same set of rules, especially when something upsets her. I appreciate your confirming my own general guess, Graythor. Now I know what to do about her."

"If it involves the use of heavy weapons, I'd really rather not be told," Graythor said sourly, his stare downright baleful. "It would disturb my sense of the proper if I discovered myself debating the point of whether or not to protect her."

Rik choked on his coffee at that and InThig chuckled deeply, but I didn't find anything amusing in the comment. Whatever I did seemed to bother *somebody*, and I was beginning to believe I would also find Morgiana sharing the attitude. Before that whole mess started, I'd made a decision about going off on my own, and right then the decision looked like the best one I'd made in a long time. Once Morgiana was safe, I would tell her it was time I left, and then I would go. I owed her at least that much, and with it the determination not to let myself be talked out of it. She would probably try, but only because that was the kind of person she was.

Our wait descended into a silent one after that, and the turn of my thoughts shaded it most definitely into the realm of the unpleasant. My imagination was in the midst of picturing Morgiana happily sending me on my way rather than trying to talk me into staying, which made the sudden opening of the gate more welcome than the end of a normal wait. All of us but Rik and the attendant knew at once that the time had come, but our sudden flurry of movement told those others all about it.

We wasted not an instant moving our horses through the gate, and once we were on the other side we paused to look around—out of necessity rather than out of desire. The world we stood on was dead, but that single word does nothing to really describe the feel of the place. No trees, or grass, or shrubs, or animals, or birds, or insects, or anything a normal, live world would be expected to have. It was empty, totally and completely barren, and the fact that it still had air we could breathe managed to make it chillingly worse.

"Magic," Graythor said as he seemed to sniff the air, reaching out and yet almost subdued. "Magic holds and refreshes this air, but magic is also what killed their world. It took the strength of many more than just one to do all this, but why and how aren't the most pressing questions. What I would enjoy knowing is who or what could be maintaining the residual spells."

I couldn't help looking around quickly at that, trying to See if anyone or anything was trying to sneak up on us, but both the Sight and the too-glaring bluish sun above us showed the same nothing we'd been shown all along. We stood on a flattened mud ball of a world, we and our horses the sole representatives of life.

"It might be best if we simply continued on to the next gate," InThig said from where it sat, the only one of us not trying to look in five directions at once. "The desolation of this world is enough to reach through even to me, and we do have something of a distance to cover. Passing through it was considerably easier when I traveled the way I do when alone."

"No!" Graythor and Rik said together at once, but they weren't talking to InThig. I closed my mouth again without voicing the suggestion I'd been about to make, seriously considering being good and insulted. They couldn't have known for certain what I'd been about to say, and it would have served them right if I'd been going to suggest something really practical and usable. And what was so unacceptable about trying to do it InThig's way anyway? What was the use in being Sighted if you were too afraid to try something new?

I was just about up to muttering to myself as we mounted and started off, and not only because of the way InThig was chuckling again. As far as that rescue team went, I was at the very bottom of the ladder, and that wasn't a position I was used to or enjoyed. If I'd known they were going to treat me like the family idiot I never would have made that promise to stay with them, even if it meant having to try out my theory on a nothingness cell. Except that I couldn't quite forget Graythor's reaction to the theory. I stirred uncomfortably in my saddle, searching around for something practical to think about or do, but nothing came. It was possible my practical side had abandoned me for a while, but it would come back, it would come back.

When nothing in the landscape around you changes, you begin to believe you aren't going anywhere, no matter how long your horse keeps moving. That bluish sun in the sky moved, changing the angle of the shadows we cast, but that was it until we saw something a couple of miles ahead of us. Rik was the first one to notice it; when he pointed it out to Graythor, we all turned to look at InThig.

"Ruins of some sort," the demon supplied, sitting down and wrapping its tail around its feet. "Half walls of stone and brick, occasional petrified timbers, blasted and glazed earth—nothing that contains or maintains life. It's the first of a small number of ruins between here and the gate we're riding toward."

"Then that's where we'll stop for a meal," Graythor decided, giving up on trying to peer ahead. "I'd like to take a look at those ruins, to see if there's anything to be learned from them. The other dead worlds in this sector offer not the slightest clue, and certainly not the presence of breathable air."

"A clue to tell or show what?" Rik asked as we began moving again. "And how many dead worlds like this *are* there?"

"Exactly how many?" Graythor countered with a shrug. "No one knows for certain. Thirteen are easily reached and identified in this sector, but those are the ones linked together in some way. You might almost say they're variations of the same world, but no one knows how similar or different they were. There are also a number of dead worlds beyond the ones we can easily reach, but no one has bothered to follow the trail to its end. With the number of gates each world has, and the number of worlds reachable through each of those gates—"

"It would take a demon to investigate thoroughly and properly," InThig contributed. "We, however, find the dead worlds extremely distasteful, so we've by and large avoided them. If one of us should become curious about them, the information you desire would then become available, but . . ."

"But first some demon would have to see how basically amusing all those worlds were," I finished up for InThig, at the same time giving it a very sweet smile. "Demons have very—special—senses of humor, and they can often find something to laugh at in situations where poor normal humans would just stand and shake their heads."

"Oh, good, Laciel, you're attacking me again," InThig came back immediately, those frightful fangs bared in a grin. "You've been so polite to me lately, I was certain you weren't feeling well."

That time it was Rik and Graythor's turn to chuckle, and we were already moving on again before I could think of anything to say in return. At first I was annoyed that it had taken me so long, and then I realized I didn't actually care. InThig wasn't the one I really wanted to fight with, but *who* my target of choice was, was something I couldn't pinpoint. With those all around me and those ahead yet to be met—largesse, if there ever was any.

It didn't take long for us to reach the ruins, and InThig's uninspired description had been completely accurate. The site could have once held anything from a small village to a section of a large city, but by the time we looked at it even the color had gone out of what remained. Gray and brown stone, gray and brown bricks, gray and brown formerly blackened wood, gray and brown ground. The area was actually no colder than the rest of the world seemed to be—which was basically uncold rather than warm—but an out-of-place chill breeze hovered just at the edge of imagination.

"And now we can all be comfortable during our meal break," Graythor said after speaking a spell, his gaze moving around to be sure everything had come out the way he'd wanted it. "The pink tent is for you, Laciel, the blue for the rest of us, and the grass-filled corral for the horses. We can have our meal at the table set up in front of the tents, and then see to any private requirements. We won't stay for more than a short while, of course, but I see no need for roughing it."

He began dismounting then, seeing nothing of the way I sighed and shook my head before doing the same. A pink tent for the girl in the group, and a blue tent for the boys. I wanted desperately to say something about his forgetting a clear tent for InThig, or mentioning that I liked blue better than pink and so wanted to swap, but I really didn't dare. He was so eager to investigate the ruins he seemed to have forgotten his previous mad at me, and the last thing I wanted was to bring it all back to him. He'd remember eventually, most likely when I did the next thing he didn't like, but the longer I could put it off, the better it would be.

The three of us put our horses in the relatively small corral that was carpeted with lush green grass and mounds of oats, but although we took their bridles off we didn't unsaddle them. Unsaddling didn't pay for the short amount of time we'd be there, and we still had ourselves to look after. Graythor led the way to the fancy table he'd loaded with all sorts of food, but rather than sitting down he turned to me and Rik instead.

"Now that I think about it, I find I'm not quite as hungry as I'd thought," he told us casually with all the cunning of a baby mouse. "If you two don't mind, I'm going to take a look through the ruins before I eat, but don't let that stop you from indulging yourselves. I'll certainly be back before you know it."

"As a matter of fact, I'm not very hungry myself," I said, looking to my right where a large body did *not* block the view. "Maybe a stroll filled with thinking time will produce an appetite to match your future one."

"I can't say I'd mind sitting down right now, but if you two aren't going to be eating until later, then I'll wait," Rik put in to make it unanimous. "Ruins have always interested me, so I think I'll go with you, Graythor."

I'm almost ashamed to admit it, but I really thought that was going to be the end of it. I was no more than half a breath away from walking off in the direction I faced when a big arm swept me around, and then I was very close to Rik and looking up at him.

"A certain girl would interest me more than the ruins, but the girl in question says she wants to think while she walks," he told me in a rather soft voice. "Only because of that am I going to be looking at ruins rather than her, but at the same time I've decided to give her something else to think about."

With that he leaned his head down and kissed me,

and I was so surprised I forgot all about struggling. I mean, it isn't every day a man does something like that to you, and my reaction—or lack of one—had absolutely nothing to do with how well Rik kisses. Or how long it had been since the last time he'd done it. After the surprise passed I did begin to struggle, though, which eventually made him end the kiss.

"Most of that was as nice as I remembered it to be," he said as he looked down at me, and then he grinned. "But I think you're out of practice. We'll have to go over it again later, just to make sure you don't embarrass yourself."

He let go of me then and began to walk away, heading left toward that part of the ruins where Graythor waited with a very amused look on his face. I didn't have to be facing InThig to know it was just as amused, and it's possible that grating chuckle was what really woke me up. I suddenly realized that that beast Rik had taken advantage of me, and all *I'd* done was stand there and let it happen!

Well, better late than never has never been one of my favorite sayings, but there are certain times it really fits. Rik was warded by Graythor against my magic, but there was no reason to let *that* stop me. With thoughts of cats and skinning bouncing around in my head beside the furious anger, I raised my right hand and quickly spoke my spell. It was on the simple side as spells went, but that was no reason for it not to work.

Rik, however, *was* a reason. No sooner had I spoken the first syllable of the very short spell than the miserable beast was moving faster than I would have believed he could, throwing himself forward to hit the ground and roll and then go back up to one knee. The pit that had opened in the ground under where his feet should have been was thereby avoided entirely, and so was the heavy length of wood that was meant to drop on his head. It dropped harmlessly into the pit instead, and then Graythor gestured and the pit and wood were gone.

"Nice try," Rik called as he got to his feet, his grin

keeping Graythor's annoyance wordless. "I wasn't expecting you to use this particular way to keep me
limber for tonight, but you ought to know it isn't
necessary. Or maybe it's been so long that you just
forgot. If you like, we can use that pretty pink tent
right now to—"

His words broke off as I turned and stalked away,
so furious I could have chewed holes through that
pretty pink tent, metal braces and all. Graythor had
been standing there next to him, ready to counter
anything else I tried, and that simply wasn't *fair!* How
was I supposed to beat him over the head when he had
a bodyguard like that?

I had already gone a brisk distance through the
so-called ruins before I realized I had company, and
that company, was having no trouble keeping up. Those
who are into uselessly wasting their time can try to
outrun a demon, but since I had other things that were
more important to waste my time on, I didn't bother.
As I slowed my pace and sank into the subject I had
originally intended thinking about, InThig disappeared
from my awareness.

But not for very long. No more than a few minutes
could have passed before I blinked back to the realization that InThig had stopped directly in my path, and
if I kept going I would walk over the demon. I didn't
know what it was up to, but I decided to spend a
moment or so trying to find out.

"I know, you're curious about how it would feel to
be a carpet," I guessed, folding my arms as I looked
down at it. "Well, what are you waiting for? Go ahead
and stretch out on the ground, and I'll help you find
out."

"If you need to use me as a carpet before telling me
what's bothering you, by all means do so," it answered, those blazing red eyes looking at me soberly.
"It distresses me to see you like this, Laciel, and I
insist on helping—even if that help consists of nothing
more than listening."

"You've already helped, InThig," I said with a smile,
moving forward to put a hand on the demon's soft,

smooth neck. "You're the one who found Morgiana, after all, and got back to tell us about it. In a little while it will be our turn, and I only hope we're up to it."

"You're worrying about freeing Morgiana?" it asked, sounding and looking a lot more surprised than I'd been expecting. "Why, Laciel, I anticipate no real problems of any sort. What with you and me and Graythor and Rik, those people will spend years trying to understand what happened. They couldn't possibly come up with nastiness our group can't cope with."

"You're forgetting about something, InThig," I came back with a sigh, sitting down on the gray and brown dirt next to the demon. "Morgiana isn't an inexperienced child, and she isn't a beginner in magic use. She must have been guarding herself a dozen different ways, not to mention being fully alert, but they still managed to take her. And if the use of magic is as rare as you say, how did they do that? How did they overcome her strength and experience? If we don't find that out, we're walking in as blindly as she did."

"I may be mistaken, but I suddenly have the oddest thought," InThig said slowly, staring at me with those burning eyes as it stretched out long on the ground. "All that twisting and turning you did, trying to separate yourself from the rest of us— Your idea was to go in first and alone, as a decoy, to find out what we others would need to know in order to prevail. You intended sacrificing yourself for *our* benefit."

"For Morgiana's benefit," I muttered, looking away from that accusing stare. "If not for her, I'd still be the nothing I was when she found me—doing nothing, being nothing, good for nothing. I owe her, InThig, more than I can ever repay, and making sure you three have the information you need to rescue her is nothing more than a drop of water in that proverbial well. I'd give my life for her if I had to, and I'd even stand up to Uncle Graythor—which I may still have to do. If it comes down to needing a decoy, promise or no promise, I'm the one who'll be doing it."

"Graythor won't be pleased to hear you say that,"

the demon observed—as though I needed the observation. "He's as determined to see you kept safe as he is to free Morgiana, and you've no idea how close he is to punishing you for the way you've been acting. And we'd do well not to forget about Rik in all this. If Rik learned you meant to put yourself in jeopardy, his punishment would come first, I think."

"Don't waste any time worrying about Rik," I said with a wave of my hand, looking back at the demon. "He's too busy trying to jolly me into bed to get involved in other things, most especially serious things. Tell me: just what did Graythor threaten him with, that he's been trying so hard to show an interest in me?"

"Laciel, you don't believe that?" InThig demanded, even more surprised than it had been a moment earlier. "To begin with, Graythor would never do such a thing, and in the second place—how determined does Rik have to be before you'll believe he intends acting as he says?"

"It isn't possible to get that determined," I answered with a snort. "I'd forgotten for a while that I couldn't believe anything he said, but I won't forget again. I don't like being taken for an idiot, and I'm not blind or deaf. Graythor is the one who wants Rik to be interested in me, he's made *that* plain enough ever since they turned up at Morgiana's house, and now Rik has no choice but to go along with him. But he can't be blamed too much for *that* part of it. Graythor is someone no one in their right mind wants mad at them."

"I'm beginning to believe this penchant for making oneself dizzy you humans indulge in is definitely contagious," InThig stated, its agitation showing in the way its claws flexed in and out of the dirt. "It so happens I was there when Rik nearly broke down over what he thought was the failure of his plan, and despite the utter conviction you project when you speak of what *you* believe to be the truth, I refuse to forget the evidence of my own senses. The man cares for you exactly as he says he does."

"If you and Graythor believe that, I can see why you were on his side," I said, lifting a fistful of dirt and pebbles that I could let stream out of my hand. "I'm sure you saw *something* during that well-advertised time of Rik's near-breakdown, but I'm willing to bet it was a reaction to Graythor's anger more than anything else. Rik claims his interest in all those other women was playacting rather than real; did *you* take it for playacting?"

"Not at first, no," InThig grudged, glittering fangs showing briefly in reaction to the memory. "Since you seemed to be taking it all so well—in fact, not even noticing—I kept silent for your sake. When he went so far as to ask you if you minded—had he and I been alone, as soon as that door closed behind you, he would have been far too busy to even consider women."

"But you two weren't alone," I said with a nod, now looking directly at the demon. "Graythor was there, and once I left he may have stopped being so roundabout in his expressions of outrage."

"May have!" InThig exclaimed with its own sound of ridicule. "There was nothing of may-have about it. He began telling Rik exactly what he thought of him, in phrases I refuse to repeat in front of a lady, and I felt certain he was no more than heartbeats from speaking a spell which would have—made Rik rather unhappy. I've become willing to concede the fact that there are times when all-out attack is merely the second-best option."

"And then, just in the nick of time, you and Graythor noticed how—upset and contrite Rik was," I hazarded as a wild guess. "He calmed you both down with his story of a plan, and then he went looking for me to try it again. If there's one thing Rik isn't, it's stupid, and I'm sure he saw rather quickly how much trouble he was in. That's why it suddenly turned out that he'd been trying a plan, and why he was so upset over its not working out. Now that he has no choice but to be absolutely determined to win me, he's decided to enjoy himself while he tries."

"Which you have no intention of allowing him to

do, I'm pleased to see," InThig said with a growl, red eyes bright with a muted blaze. "I'll need to speak with Graythor, and then the three of us can decide how best to solve the problem."

"If you can get Graythor to stop protecting him, we can put our heads together over more important things," I said with a gesture of dismissal for Rik. "We still don't know what we'll be facing on the other side of that gate, and using a decoy may turn out to be the only way we'll find out. If the need arises, I don't want to waste time fighting opposition from my own people."

"Very well, I'll join you in trying to convince Graythor," InThig allowed with a sigh, finally seeing things in the right perspective. "I'm sure he'll see reason, once he understands the necessity. We'll have to—"

InThig's words broke off abruptly as those big, black cat ears swiveled, and then the demon was up on its feet, body tense, nostrils flaring, red eyes searching in a careful arc. I quickly did my own looking around, but there was nothing there even to See.

"InThig, what's wrong?" I asked, very aware of the fact that the demon still hadn't relaxed. "Not only is there nothing out there, there can't possibly *be* anything."

"But there is," InThig contradicted with a low, chill-making growl, its eyes continuing to sweep the area. "I'd nearly convinced myself I was imagining things, but now I'm certain I wasn't. Something *is* out there, but what and where, I can't quite—"

Its voice broke off again and then it was racing toward one section of the ruins, a black streak of coldly calm destruction. By then I was up on my feet, and even though I still couldn't see anything, I pitied whatever InThig was after. It wasn't possible to outrun or outfight a demon, and even magic couldn't be used to stop one once it launched itself in attack. I watched carefully to see what would happen next, but when it came, I didn't understand it.

InThig attacked, and *nothing* happened.

I shook my head and blinked my eyes, but that didn't change anything. InThig bit and clawed, then whirled around to do it again, but nothing was happening. The demon itself knew that, and I had rarely seen it so deeply in the grip of frustration. It stopped still for a moment, looked around before trying one last slashing strike, then backed up before moving toward me again.

"Laciel, I can't *reach* it," InThig called, and I couldn't decide if its voice was more angry or plaintive. "I'm positive it's there, but I can't affect it in any way."

"Maybe it's one of those ghosts we've heard about," I suggested, still peering hard. "I'm not getting anything at all, but you're much too practical to be imagining it. But why let it bother you? Just because it's there doesn't mean we have to—"

"Look out!" InThig shouted, its head only just turned toward me, but the warning came too late. There was sudden agony in my left shoulder and arm, the pain so great it almost kept me from throwing myself out of the way. I still couldn't detect what I was throwing myself out of the way *from*, but it proved to be the right move. The agony receded quite a lot, as though teeth had been withdrawn from my flesh, and I backed up along the ground toward InThig with a lot less grace than Rik had shown a little while earlier.

"Are you all right?" InThig demanded, agitation making its voice shake in time to its swishing tail. "If only I were able to *reach* them! How badly did that one hurt you?"

"Bad enough," I answered as I rubbed gently at my arm, glad I'd been able to keep from screaming at the first bite. InThig was almost crazy over not being able to protect me; if it thought I was really hurt, I didn't even want to try imagining what would happen. "So now 'it' has become 'them.' What I'd like to know is why my automatic defenses didn't work. Whatever-it-is shouldn't have been able to reach me, but you can take my word for the fact that it did. And why the hell can't I detect them unless they *are* reaching me?"

"A better question would be on the subject of how *we* are to reach *them*," InThig growled, looking around carefully. "My attack on one had no effect whatsoever, and I can think of nothing else to do. With the possible exception of an orderly withdrawal."

"Run away?" I asked with a snort as I began getting to my feet again. "Without even *trying* to fight? InThig, you may not be able to reach them, but they're not reaching you either. Since they *are* reaching *me*, I should be able to return the favor. If I could only tell where the hell they are."

"That's not difficult," InThig answered, its fur bristling as it took a half step forward. "Right now there's one coming directly at you from *that* direction, and I think it's going to—"

InThig's guess was lost as I raised my right hand and sent blazing blue fire toward the place the demon was looking, then played the fire across in a straight line. I felt faintly ridiculous defending myself from thin and harmless air—until one piece of that air began flaring and crackling with furious blue sparks.

"You hit it!" InThig crowed, not far from jumping up and down with glee. "And not only hit it, but hurt it! It's running away as fast as it can move."

"How about the others?" I asked, wishing I was able to see more than a small corner of my great victory. "Are they doing their own running?"

"No," InThig said, but now the growl in its voice was pure pleasure. "There's another one over there, by that jagged stone wall, and it's definitely moving in this direction."

By using InThig to spot for me, I was able to reach the second thing and three more. The last almost got to me before InThig detected it, and although that seemed to clear the area my demon companion wasn't pleased.

"Now that we've shown how capable and fearless you are, we'll go back to the others and leave this place," InThig announced in its favorite no-arguments tone, its attention still on our surroundings. "Graythor and Rik should be told about this at once, and— By the EverNameless, Laciel! What if they were attacked, too?"

My only answer to that was breaking into a dead

run, desperate to get back and find out if it was true. I didn't waste any breath cursing at myself for not thinking of the point before InThig brought it up, but that doesn't mean the cursing was left undone. I might have been busy trying to keep my own neck safe, but that was no excuse for forgetting about other necks—

InThig kept itself down to my best speed, and I knew there was no use in my telling it to go on ahead without me. If InThig wasn't there to spot the things, I'd be as helpless as Graythor and—and anyone else, so InThig wasn't about to leave me. All I could do was run not nearly as fast as I wanted to, kicking up a cloud of gray and brown dust under my feet, trying to gasp in air rather than the dead remnant of a dead world. If we were too late, I would— I didn't know what I would do, and I couldn't bear to think about it.

Racing around one partial wall that stood considerably taller than the rest almost caused more harm than the whatever-they-were had accomplished. With what seemed like no warning we were faced with two bodies pelting along at what must have been Graythor's top speed. If they'd been going any faster, we would have crashed right into them. As it was, we were just able to avoid a collision, and then we were all busy talking at once. The babble went on a lot longer than was amusing, and then Graythor held up a hand.

"I think we would be best off taking turns at this," he panted, but not so badly out of breath as someone else his age would certainly be. "I take it, Laciel, that you and InThig discovered the same thing Rik and I did—that this world still contains life of some sort, life which you and I are unable to detect."

"We certainly did," I answered with a nod, using my right hand to brush sweat-soaked hair out of my eyes. "What I—and I'm sure InThig—would like to know is how *you* two found out about it."

"I'm sure you would say I found out the hard way," Graythor answered with a grimace, flexing his right hand. "Rik kept saying there was something around us, but since I saw and Saw nothing I paid little or no attention. It took my touching one of them before I believed, and then I needed Rik to tell me where the rest of them were. I take it you and InThig handled the matter in the same way."

"Most likely the only way," InThig said, and then its blazing red eyes shifted to Rik. "I really must commend you on the sensitivity your link-shape shares with your human shape. If not for that, Graythor would have been taken entirely unawares."

"A sensitivity I was hoping wasn't limited to me and those like me," Rik answered, his eyes elsewhere than on InThig. "I was sure those things couldn't hurt a demon, but after seeing the way Graythor reacted to touching one, I was suddenly worried about what they would do to a tender young sorceress."

"Most of the doing was the other way about," InThig said with gloating smugness, sitting down so its tail could wrap around its feet. "I wasn't able to touch them any more than they were able to touch me, but after Laciel had a run-in with one she more than showed herself able to do all the touching necessary. I doubt if any of hers will bother us again."

"I doubt if *any* of those chased off will bother us," Graythor said, "but just the same we'll be leaving as soon as we get the horses. InThig—do you recall if you sensed those life-forms before we reached these ruins?"

"In point of fact, I do recall," InThig answered, its fangs showing in a grin. "There was no sign of them at all before we reached this place. Do you consider that significant?"

"I consider it significant that Rik confirms your observation," Graythor answered, still rubbing his hand. "Your two opinions together should mean we'd be safe stopping somewhere other than in the ruins, but very frankly I'd rather not take the chance. That none of us was seriously hurt is a gift we'd be fools to throw away, so we'll eat in our saddles and rest once we've passed through the gate. Does anyone object to that?"

Rik and InThig saw his pain and so said nothing, but I didn't need an awareness of anyone else's pain. My arm still hurt more than I was trying to notice, and

I had no interest at all in playing big and brave with
another batch of those whatever-they-were. Since no
one felt a burning need to stay on in that place, we
didn't dawdle, but it still took a while for us to get
going. Graythor let Rik order him to see to the food
while he saw to the wizard's horse, and InThig kept
Graythor company while I saw to my own horse. If
my mount had had to be saddled, I would have had a
problem, but I was able to manage the bridle with no
more than some teeth-gritting. My arm seemed to be
working better the more I used it, which was another
reason not to mention the matter to anyone.

Once we were mounted we circled around the ruins,
then rode straight until we had the next one in sight.
When we got close enough it was circling time again,
and by then we were trying to figure out why the
horses hadn't been bothered. The only guess that wasn't
immediately laughed off by someone centered around
the "scent" of magic. Those things that were magical
in nature rather than capable of magic—like InThig,
Rik and the corral the horses had been in—were of no
interest to the life-forms. Only sources that were capable of the manipulation of power—like Graythor and
me—could draw them, but for what purpose we didn't
know. To be frank, Graythor and I didn't *want* to
know, so the others left it at that.

It was late afternoon on that dead world when we
reached the gate we wanted, and we drew rein and
dismounted about a hundred feet away. Being that
close meant none of us *wanted* to stop, but we intended being extremely clever in our sneaking-in
method. Our disguises would all be in place *before* we
went through the gate, and that way none of the
natives would see us changing and thereby grow suspicious. It was all Graythor's idea, and one of the things
he was completely determined about.

"There's no need for looking so sour, Laciel,"
Graythor remarked as he moved a few paces away
from the horses, getting ready to speak his spell. "If
you feel that helping me take the wagon through the

gate will be too much for you, I'm certain I can manage it alone."

"That has nothing to do with it and you know it, Uncle Graythor," I said, wondering why I was wasting my breath repeating myself. "I don't see the need for a wagon in the first place, not when my horse is going to be one of the two pulling it. Without the wagon, I can continue to ride him, which also means I won't have to pose as a peasant woman, which in turn will . . ."

"Let you continue bedeviling me," Graythor finished before I could, his crooked half-smile showing annoyance soothed by satisfaction. "That, however, I will not allow, so you'd best resign yourself to the role which is yours. You'll ride beside me on the wagon where I can keep an eye on you, and only Rik will have a horse under saddle."

"But I won't be wearing my sword," Rik put in, trying to sound like a martyr and not quite making it. "The less we look like a rescuing and avenging force, the more rescuing and avenging we'll get to do. And even InThig is sacrificing something for the cause."

"I'm only sacrificing a semblance of something," InThig replied, its voice to the left of neutral. The demon hadn't been able to speak privately to Graythor yet, and it was feeling the nip of frustration.

"Semblance or not, the size you usually adopt is part of your natural comfort," Graythor said, almost sounding as though he were lecturing. "Compressing yourself down to the proportions of an ordinary house cat is more of a change than the one Laciel will be suffering through. If luck rides with us, we won't any of us need to suffer long, an end I'm sure we all mean to strive for. Isn't that true, Laciel?"

"You're really enjoying yourself, aren't you, Uncle Graythor," I said, suddenly understanding a point I'd missed before. "How long has it been since the last time you were able to throw your weight around like this, without having six other wizards filing formal protests?"

"Too long," he answered with an honest-to-Pete grin, and then his arms were up as he spoke his spell with a precision few others could match. It didn't take more than a moment, but once he was through, the changes were more than a single moment could be used to classify.

To begin with, he and I and the horses no longer looked like our usual selves. He was still small, but he looked more like a spry seventy with white hair, a bit of extra weight in face and body, and no sense of power at all. He wore loose brown pants and a faded brown and yellow tunic, very old brown boots, and a thin leather tie belt of brown. Although I couldn't see it, I knew that although my face was its usual oval, my hair was darker blonde, my eyes blue, and my comfortable traveling clothes were gone. Instead I wore a dark green skirt of shoe-top length, a white, long-sleeved tunic-blouse tied with a white cloth belt, and worn brown sandals. The horses all looked brown, overworked and old, and if they could have seen themselves they wouldn't have been any happier than I was.

"Is that wagon all right, InThig?" Graythor asked, tugging at the bottom of his tunic. "If it isn't close enough, just tell me and I'll change it."

"It seems to be perfect, Graythor," InThig said as it studied the thing, moving around to look at the back. "All of wood and rounded on top, with steps hanging down from the back. Yes, that's what most of the peasants used, and that dark red is also just right. A few of the wagons had other colors as trim, but I suspect there might be a class difference or some such involved in that. We'll be best off with a plain wagon, I think."

"Unless we discover we need the trim to get closer to the palace," Rik said, stepping forward in a two-shades-of-blue version of Graythor's clothes. His black boots were scuffed and dirty, but his leather tie-belt looked slightly less aged—and his eyes were no longer bronze. He now had merry dark brown eyes, the only disguising he needed beyond the clothes.

"If we find we need the trim, it won't take more than a blink to add it," Graythor said, then turned his head to me. "I've considered your suggestion, Laciel, and although I dislike the idea I find it impossible to deny the good sense in it. I've already seen to the matter for myself, so if you'll do the same we can be on our way."

"What suggestion was that?" Rik asked, and his new brown eyes narrowed a little. "Not that I don't think Laciel can make useful suggestions, it's just that I prefer hearing them before they're put into practice."

"Her suggestion was in reference to our personal defenses," Graythor said hastily, managing to keep me from demanding what business it was of Rik's. "As she pointed out, automatic defenses go off automatically, sometimes when we don't want them to. We've also discovered there are times they don't go off when they should, like with those undetectable life-forms in the ruins. All in all, we'll be better off without them, and then the choice of when to use defensive force will be entirely ours."

Rik didn't seem to like my suggestion, but since Graythor had already done his part and I spoke my own quelling spell without waiting for anyone's permission, there wasn't much he could do. Graythor kept the scene from growing awkward by asking Rik to help him with hitching up the horses, and once that was done InThig was asked to go through the gate to make sure no one was watching on the other side. By changing to vapor, InThig was able to sneak through and do its peeking around, and was quickly back with a report of all clear.

By then we were all ready to go, so Graythor started off leading the horses through. I was up on the back steps of the wagon, dividing my strength between helping Graythor shift the horses and wagon through the gate, and helping InThig, who came last, to get Rik and *his* horse through. It wasn't as hard as the first time I'd stood anchored in a gate to let four people and six horses make it through, but it wasn't as easy as just us and the horses would have been. Many people consider wood as once-living and therefore easier to handle than something like stone or steel, but you can bet those people never tried shifting a wagon through a gate.

As soon as we were all on the other side, InThig began compressing even as it got into the wagon, Graythor and I climbed onto it, Rik mounted up, and then we took off through the pleasant little woods the gate stood in. Hanging around the gate could have given us away, so we put the second part of our plan into effect and began putting distance between us and our true origins. It happened to be late afternoon on that world, too, so we had the time to cover a number of miles before we would have to stop.

We hadn't yet run out of woods, when we discovered we were almost out of light. Rik sniffed the air and said there was water not too far away, so that became our choice of campsite. Graythor let Rik point out the exact spot, tied the reins off on the wagon brake once we were completely stopped, then climbed down before stretching and looking around.

"I must say this is a much prettier world than the one before it," a tired-looking wizard said with a muffled yawn once he had finished stretching. "As soon as our meal is down, I, for one, am going straight to bed."

"That sounds like a decision we'll all be wise to indulge in," Rik said in a very sober way as he led his horse over, and then he momentarily dropped the nonsense. "Damn it, Laciel, hold still until I can help you. If you were trying to break your neck, you'll be happy to know you're only about one quick fall away from it."

I was too busy trying to untangle myself from the wagon to answer him, with that stupid skirt I had on refusing to let go. It had somehow grabbed a part of the wagon as I was trying to climb down, and getting it to unhook while keeping my balance wasn't working out well. I was just about ready to pull on it hard enough to tear the material, but that became unnecessary. A thick arm around my waist lifted me higher, a big hand slid the skirt loose, and then I was down on

the ground with a broad body blocking my path away
from the wagon.

"You also haven't listened to me about the conversation I said I wanted from you," his quiet voice
informed me, most of the amusement apparently gone.
"I let it go today because Graythor asked me to, but
tomorrow and the days after aren't covered in the
agreement. Starting tomorrow we talk to one another
like real live adult human beings, or you can expect
more trouble than you ever counted on. I'm not joking, Laciel, and I'm not bluffing, so don't make the
mistake of thinking I am."

I folded my arms and stared at the chest in front of
me to show just how impressed I was with his threat,
and even in the dimness he had no trouble understanding my meaning. His hands came to my arms
with a growl, but before he could put his displeasure
into words Graythor interrupted again.

"Laciel, I wonder if you would be kind enough to
come here and help me," he said, and for some reason
he sounded even more tired than he had. "You and
Rik can finish your discussion later, once everything is
seen to."

His wonderful Rik took his hands back and stepped
out of my way, and I walked over to Graythor without
rubbing my left arm the way I would have enjoyed
doing. The miserable beast had hurt me, but that
wasn't anything new.

"Laciel, I can See there's no one around watching
us, so I want you to create a campfire," Graythor said,
then pointed to a spot about ten feet away from the
wagon. "Over there, if you will, and large enough to
last us the night. If bringing the wagon through the
gate hasn't tired you too far."

"I'm not too tired for anything," I answered, privately including mayhem on the list. "One campfire,
coming right up."

I pointed to the spot and spoke my spell, narrowing
my eyes against the expected brightness, but I needn't
have bothered. Not a single spark appeared where it
should have, and suddenly the silly little chore had all

of my attention. I reworded my spell and spoke it again, this time demanding fire with my fist closed tight, but I was still wasting both time and breath. Looking around hard showed the Sight was still with me, but my spells were getting no response.

"That's what I was afraid of," Graythor said with a sigh, lowering himself to the ground to sit slumped over. "I was hoping I'd merely exhausted myself with overdoing, but good luck hasn't seen fit to make that so. We still have the Sight, Laciel girl, but you and I are no longer magic users."

CHAPTER 11

The fire that crackled about ten feet from the wagon wasn't as large as the one I'd tried making, and certainly wouldn't be lasting through the night. We hadn't been able to find enough wood for that, but it would still have to do. Rik had made the fire, and had also cooked us a meal over it from the provisions of food Graythor had put in the wagon as props. Props. Right then it didn't matter if natives of that world were watching us or not; we'd be doing nothing that gave us away.

"Well, at least we now know how Morgiana's strength was overcome," InThig said from its place beside my right knee, a miniature, toylike InThig. "It's ridiculous on the face of it and should be completely impossible, but there it is."

"In all my years, I've never heard of a situation like this one," Graythor grumbled, putting aside his empty bowl. Despite the heavy dark he seemed stronger than he had, as though the meal he'd eaten had returned something he'd lost. "Our previous spells are being maintained and we still have the Sight, but new spells fall as if on deaf ears. The strength is there, but something prevents us from using it."

"Which makes us one hell of an effective rescue team," I said in my own grumble, ignoring the bowl of food I'd been given. It sat on the ground beside my left knee, and I hadn't even looked into it. "We now have the choice of going on and doing what we can, or turning back to try figuring out the trick while we camp on the dead world. At least we know our magic *works* on the dead world."

"You think the failure of our spells is a trick of some sort?" Graythor asked, his frown full of creases in the firelight. "What leads you to believe that?"

"Well, we know *some* people can make spells work," I pointed out, wondering just how obvious that fact was. "If *they* can, and Morgiana's being held because *she* can, there has to be a way for us to do the same."

"We don't know all there is to know about Morgiana, Laciel," InThig corrected, the blaze in its now small red eyes muted. "We know the High King has her in his palace and is using her for *some* purpose, but not necessarily because she's able to use magic."

"If not that, then why her?" I asked bluntly, controlling myself hard at the thought of anyone using Morgiana for anything. "Morgiana may be one of the best people ever born, but she uses her own face and body. The best that can be said for her is that she's pretty, and kings usually have their choice among the beautiful. The reason she's being held *has* to relate to her magical strength, but being certain of that only generates another question—how did anyone find out about her magical strength to begin with?"

"The answer to that is obvious," Graythor said, leaning down on one elbow. "Either she discovered the—trick—we haven't as yet seen for ourselves, or something occurred which we can know nothing about."

"She can't have discovered the trick," I countered at once, beginning to feel very short-tempered with all that obviousness. "If she had, they wouldn't have been able to touch her. I refuse to believe that someone from a world like this, where using magic is so difficult most of the Sighted never manage it, can possibly have developed enough strength to overcome a wizard. That's not just beyond reason, it's stupid."

"But it still may be the truth," Rik put in from his own spot at the fire, his body stretched at ease along the ground. "Just because you don't like a theory doesn't mean it's false, and we can't afford to rule out anything at this point. Until we know for sure, everything gets tagged with a 'maybe.' "

"You know, she could have been caught in the simplest way of all," I said to Graythor, the notion suddenly popping up in my mind. "It isn't likely that she went straight to the palace and stuck her tongue out at the King, so there had to be something that brought her to his attention. I think she had some kind of trouble, and her automatic defenses were set off. The incident was enough for word to spread, and that's how the King heard about it."

"That could very well be it," Graythor said slowly as he considered my idea, his head nodding in distraction. "Yes, considering the circumstances, there's an excellent chance of it. It had occurred to me that she might have gone to the King to ask his help when she discovered her spells no longer worked, but that theory is shaky at best. Even assuming she could have gotten an audience with him, which isn't particularly likely, I doubt very much whether she would have done something like that without being too well aware of the risks. Her likeliest course of action would have been to return to the gate, which she would have had no trouble Seeing."

"Unless the King happened to be handy enough for her to have no trouble talking to him," Rik said, apparently enjoying himself throwing in his uninformed point of view. "If he seemed sympathetic and possibly even asked for her help with a problem of his own, she could have gone with him of her own free will. After that the two of them could have lost to his problem, or he could have turned out to be lying to her."

"And since we can See that gate as well as she could have, we still have my original question to answer," I said to Graythor, needing to know where he stood on the matter. "Do you want to go back and try to figure out what the trick is, or do you want to stay here and tour the countryside? Either choice could give us the answer, so which one appeals to you most?"

"I—dislike feeling this helpless," the small man answered, his voice held carefully steady as he sat straight again. "My first urge would be to return to the dead world, where it would be possible to think in comfort, but, Laciel . . ."

"And I think my best bet would be to stay here," I said with a lot of approval, trying to show him he was doing the right thing. "With the two of us working at it from different directions the problem should be solved in half the time, and the one who gets it first goes after the other to share the method. By then I'll also know something about this place, so we won't have to waste time looking around. We'll go to the palace together, zap that King of theirs, then lead Morgiana home in our own private triumphal procession."

"Now that you mention it, the idea of separating does seem to make sense," Graythor agreed in a musing way, none of the determined refusal I'd been half expecting showing anywhere. "If the two of us attack the problem from opposite sides . . ."

"Absolutely not," Rik said suddenly from where he lay, his pose still relaxed even though his tone had hardened. "This group doesn't split up under any circumstances, and especially not in a way that leaves Laciel here on her own. Or even with InThig, which is most likely the way she was about to arrange it. I'm surprised at you, Graythor. I thought you knew better than to let her talk you into something like that."

Graythor abruptly looked very confused, but that wasn't the emotion *I* was feeling. Every time I turned around I tripped over an unwanted millstone, and I was getting more than tired of it.

"Why the hell don't you learn to mind your own business?" I demanded of Rik, giving him some of that conversation he'd been so eager for. "This is between Graythor and me, and even beyond that you have no right to a say in what I do. I've been a big girl for quite a while now, and I get to go where I please and do what I like. Since that state of affairs obviously bothers you, look somewhere else. Like around the area of the gate, for instance, until one of us comes for you."

"But I *am* minding my own business," he returned at once, giving me no chance to go back to working on Graythor. "What size girl you are has nothing to do with the things you can do, or if you look at it another way, it has everything to do with it. From what InThig has said about this world, it's obviously more primitive than the one you come from. Remembering what almost happened to you before we stepped through even the first gate, would you like to guess how things will go for you now that you can't use magic any longer? They'll probably be as delighted that you're a big girl as I am."

"I see you've finally listed yourself with the group of people you fit with best," I countered, knowing it was my imagination that the fire seemed to make his eyes glow. "I won't have to worry about the warm reception I might get from the natives of this world if I stay away from towns and cities, and anything else I can handle. Or if I can't handle it, InThig can."

"Certainly InThig can," he agreed with a brisk nod. "And leaving a string of shredded bodies behind you won't attract any attention at all. And InThig can hunt for you, because you sure as hell can't hunt for yourself, or even find water. The only thing InThig can't do is mix with town and city natives to ask questions, the answers to which are probably the only things that will let one of us figure out the answer to the magic puzzle. If the answer was out here in the woods, we'd probably have it by now."

"You always sound so sure of yourself, when you really haven't the faintest idea of what you're talking about," I said with a growl, hating the way he did that. "You announce your opinions, and everyone's supposed to take them for facts. Well, I haven't any interest in your opinions, and I *don't* have to take them. I've had enough to be very bored, so go play leader somewhere else."

"But I can't play leader somewhere else," he protested, his tone more amused than plaintive. "I've given my word to play leader here, and I really hate going back on my word. All teams and groups need a leader, so I've agreed to be the leader for this one. That's what makes your proposed arrangements very much my business."

"Don't waste my time with lies," I told him with a snort, determined to put an end to being treated like an idiot. "With two magic users in the group, who's going to make *you* leader?"

"One of the magic users," another voice put in, a voice that had gained in strength and determination. "Magic or no magic, in a place like this Rik has the expertise we need. I asked him to be leader of our group, and he accepted."

"Then he can be leader of *your* group," I said with all the disgust I felt, giving Graythor my own baleful look. "*My* group wouldn't have him on a bet, not even if it meant crawling all the way to the palace on hands and knees. You can keep each other company on the dead world. At first light we'll separate, and . . ."

"Laciel, you gave your word not to try separating from us again," Graythor reminded me, that dark look pushing its way through his disguise. "Your word used to be rather important to you; are you serving me notice that that's changed?"

"Not at all," I said with a headshake, then stretched a little in preparation for getting up. "I promised not to *try*, which isn't the same as actually doing it. And as for whether or not I'd break my word for Morgiana's sake—you'd better believe I would. Any sense of honor I have is due entirely to her; throwing it away for her benefit is no trouble at all. As I started to say a moment ago, I have a lot to do tomorrow and you have the dead world to get back to, so . . ."

"Young woman, you're trying my patience!" Graythor snapped, and I could see he'd straightened where he sat. "You've done nothing but make trouble since this journey first began, and I've had more than enough of it. I am *not* going back to the dead world, and *you* are not going off on your own. We're all staying together, and Rik will do the job of leading."

"I'm sorry I've upset you, Uncle Graythor, but I'm afraid you're going to have to live with that upset until we're back where you can use magic," I said, having the excuse of getting to my feet to let me look away from him. "I *am* going off on my own, because that's the only way we'll find out what we need to know to free Morgiana. And I'd rather be attacked by every man on this world, than be within a hundred miles of that wonderful leader you've chosen. As I said, let him lead *you*."

I began to move away from the fire, intending to get a blanket out of the wagon, but a hand closed around my right arm, holding me where I was.

"Why do you sound as if you really hate me?" Rik asked, the bewildered hurt in his voice a joke in itself. "It can't be the arguing we've been doing, we always argue. I wanted to get it stopped so we'd have a chance to— Laciel, tell me what's wrong."

"Possibly she dislikes associating with people who lie to those around them," InThig answered for me, rising slowly to be a darker shadow among the shadows cast by the fire. "People who lie in such a way do so for their own sake rather than the sake of others, for their own protection and pleasure. Take your hand off her arm."

"No, I won't take my hand off her arm," Rik said with a headshake, now sounding confused. "InThig, what's wrong with you? Who have I lied to?"

"Have you forgotten already?" the demon asked with a sound of scorn, those blazing red eyes showing limitless strength despite the tiny size of the body containing them. "You lied to Graythor and me about what you were really doing in the Realm of Dreams, and since you were given no choice, you then tried lying to Laciel. Unfortunately for you, she saw through your storytelling, and now we *all* see you for what you are. I've kept silent until now, but if you don't let her go . . ."

"InThig, wait just a moment," Graythor said, by that time standing with the rest of us. "I would appreciate your telling *me* when Rik lied to us, for I must confess I have no clear memory of the time. As a favor to an old friend."

"I had difficulty of my own at first when I tried to remember," InThig assured Graythor without losing any of the—readiness—it was projecting. "After Laciel left the dining hall that time, you were about to remonstrate rather severely with him for hurting Laciel in the way he had. Don't you recall what he did to stop you?"

"Yes, as a matter of fact I do recall," Graythor answered, speaking slowly and clearly. "I told Rik he was about to feel the same pain he'd given Laciel, and he laughed bitterly and told me to go ahead and do anything I liked. He'd gambled and lost, and felt he'd probably had no chance to win to begin with. He also said he didn't believe he'd hurt her, but I could still do anything I cared to. Isn't that the way *you* remember it?"

"Well—of course it is, but—he had to be lying to us," InThig said with uncertainty, now shifting in place. "He feared the power you could bring to bear against him, and so fabricated a story about having been trying a plan. He had no need for a plan, Graythor, for he had no real interest in her to begin with. His interest was instigated by *you,* and once you became angry he had no choice but to continue going along with it."

"I see," Graythor said as he rubbed his eyes, the two words accompanied by Rik's sigh. "InThig, listen again to what you just said, and then tell me if those are your words and beliefs, or Laciel's. You and I were there together at the time, and we saw and heard the very same thing. You believed Rik then, though not for the same reason I did, but now you've changed your mind. Do I need to ask *who* changed your mind?"

"Laciel merely pointed out the truth to me," InThig protested, but it no longer sounded as convinced as it had been. "Perhaps I did believe Rik then, I'm beginning to remember now, but—why did I change my mind so radically? And what was your reason for believing him if it wasn't the same as my own?"

"My reason was the Sign of Truth," Graythor said, his sigh a full match to the one Rik had sounded. "I was careful to shield the gesture from both of you, but I was determined to know the full truth for Laciel's sake. I had no intentions of encouraging and supporting a man who wasn't absolutely and completely dedicated to winning her. As for the way your mind was changed so . . ."

"That can't possibly be true," I said to Graythor, beginning to feel dizzy over the way that conversation was going. "You couldn't have used the Sign of Truth on him, or you would have found out he was lying. You're the one who wanted him to be interested, and so he was. He knew what you would do to him if he wasn't, and he was afraid."

"Laciel, child, Rik isn't afraid of magic," Graythor said very gently, all signs of impatience gone. "He has a healthy respect for it the way *anyone* with sense would, but he isn't afraid of it or those who wield it. Surely you remember how he behaved with the female Sighted who had trapped the two of you? One of the things you yourself have taught him is that being warded is no guarantee of safety, and yet he still defied her. He's a fighter and a man of pride, and would rather be killed or badly hurt sooner than allow himself to be pushed into something he considers dishonorable. If pretending to love a woman when you really don't isn't dishonorable, I'd like to know what is."

"But none of that makes any sense," I said as I stared at nothing, distantly wondering why I sounded so plaintive. "All he wants is a female, any female, and since you've been pushing him at me he's decided he might as well take me. Morgiana tried that once with a young sorcerer, and didn't stop pushing him at me until she caught him—involving himself—with every witch and sorceress in a six-world radius . . ."

"Oh, my very dear," Graythor said, sounding horribly upset. "Between my interfering efforts and Rik's playacting, no wonder you thought you were in the same situation again. You really aren't, you know, and I'm sure that will be proved to you in a very short while."

"And probably would already *be* proved if you weren't so stubborn," Rik added, sounding more than just a little angry. "I admit a good part of this mess is my fault for letting you get away with being stubborn, but that doesn't make you an innocent victim of circumstance. You could have stopped what was going on at any time by trying to find out the truth, but since you were already convinced you knew the truth, you didn't bother. It looks like one of the first things I'm going to have to teach you is not to assume you know it all."

I finally turned my head to look up at him, but I didn't see anything in the firelight to ease that dizziness sitting right on top of me. I still couldn't quite bring myself to believe his intentions really were what he said they were, and even beyond that had a different problem entirely. If he *was* telling the truth as Graythor maintained, and the Sign of Truth was just about infallible, I wasn't sure I wanted him doing that. All I could remember was how hard it was to discourage him. . . .

"All of which brings us back to the last of my questions," InThig said, still sounding out of sorts. "I strongly believed Rik was telling the truth at the time of the occurrence, but my mind was changed for me because of no more than a simple conversation. I'm able to say that now after thinking about it, but an explanation is entirely beyond me. I've never before been so effortlessly swayed."

"No more have I," Graythor said, the response both filled with annoyance and faint embarrassment. "When I was finally able to consider the matter a few moments ago, I realized that, despite knowing better, I've believed an inordinate amount of what Laciel has lately told me. Asking myself why I've been doing such a foolish thing was fruitless—until I looked at Rik and remembered the odd thing that happened when Laciel was felled by that poison. Rik's talent of Persuasion was then able to reach through to her, and afterward he assured me the link between them remained strong and sure. Although he hasn't yet been able to affect *her* the way he does others . . ."

"*She's* been using *his* talent to affect *us!*" InThig said in pure outrage while I looked back and forth in confusion. "Filtered through her, a magic user, it touches those Rik *can't* touch. Graythor, that's not only intolerable, it's positively obscene! Magic users and beings *of* magic aren't supposed to be touchable like that; the practice goes against nature itself! I now no longer need to ask why this has happened, but I *must* know what can be done about it!"

"Calm yourself, InThig," Graythor said with a chuckle, stepping closer to clap Rik on the shoulder. "When our leader firmly disagreed with what Laciel was forcing me to believe, I suddenly no longer believed it. The talent is, after all, his, and full control of it apparently remains with him. You and I must simply make certain not to speak to Laciel alone until a permanent solution is found to the problem."

"But that's absolutely absurd," I protested as I watched the fur of a cat-sized InThig finally relax from standing straight out. "Not only wouldn't I ever do such a thing as use Persuasion on the unsuspecting, I agree with InThig that it isn't possible to do it to *you* two. It sounds like a good explanation, Graythor, but it isn't good enough as a reason for InThig not being able to be alone with me. If you need a reason for believing me beyond the fact that there's really no reason not to, you'll just have to look for another one."

"Possibly you're right," Graythor conceded in a distracted way, InThig just short of nodding in agreement. "Since there *is* no rational reason not to believe you, the proper explanation must lie elsewhere."

"Like hell it does," Rik said with a short laugh, and suddenly Graythor and InThig were looking confused again. "I was wondering myself about how accurate your guess was, but now I can see you were as right as you usually are. She isn't doing it consciously, but Laciel *is* drawing on my talent when she talks to you like that. Laciel, girl, if you stop trying to convince them you're right, you'll find you're not projecting the Persuasion the way you've *been* doing. And no issuing orders under any circumstances. I don't want to have to spend my time constantly pulling them out of it."

"This is ridiculous," I stated, looking from a pained Graythor to a blinking InThig and back to a very amused Rik. "You're all making this up, probably to get me to go along with whatever you say instead of pointing it out when you're wrong. Well, I'm sorry to disappoint you, teammates, but it isn't going to work. If there are orders to be issued I'll be issuing them, and furthermore . . ."

"No, no furthermores," Rik said, and suddenly he stepped forward to sweep me off the ground into his arms. "You're not boss around here, I am, and we won't be having the same fight for leadership we had during the quest. I'm the one who gives the orders and you're the one who takes them, without fuss, without argument, and without pointing out how wrong I am."

"And if I refuse to agree to that?" I demanded as strongly as I could, trying not to notice how struggling against being held by him wasn't doing me any good at all. "What if I tell you what to do with your orders, and then go ahead and act as I please? There's nothing you can do to stop me, and you know it."

"Oh, I don't know," he mused, dividing his attention between me and where he was carrying me. "I've learned lots of things to do in the face of mutiny, and I know those things work because I've tried most of them. You'd be surprised how often you get challenged when you're brought in cold to lead a bunch of experienced fighters. There's always at least one in the bunch who's determined to prove he's better than you are, and you have to know how to quiet him down without losing him for your force."

"And you do it with Persuasion," I said, caught up enough to show my distaste at that idea, but then I realized where he was carrying me. "And put me down! When I'm ready to get into the wagon, I'll manage it on my own."

"You'll go when you're told to go," he answered very affably, sounding as if he was just disagreeing on a color choice or something. "Once we get you used to taking orders as well as giving them, discussing something reasonably with you won't be an impossibility any longer. And no, I didn't use Persuasion on most of the men who challenged me. Here, this is where we'll be sleeping."

Just after entering the wagon he turned slightly to his left, and put me down on a built-in bunk bed with a lantern on the wall, a bed that would become wider than normal. Graythor had made the wagon bigger on the inside for our comfort, but hadn't wanted to make the fact too obvious. Part of his spell had specified that when one of us got onto the bed and drew closed the blanket-curtain that hung on a stretch of rope along the right side of the bed, the area would widen out to give more sleeping room. Four sleeping areas had been created to match the arrangement native wagons had, but only three of ours widened. The fourth was there for any unexpected events or guests, ones we didn't care to share our origins with.

But interior decoration wasn't what concerned me just then. I'd been told, calm as you please, that I'd be sharing my bed with a man, something I'd been able to ignore the last time I heard it. Right then, ignoring the arrangement wasn't quite as easy; after putting me down Rik had opened his leather belt-tie and was pulling his tunic off over his head. Once off, the tunic was tossed toward the foot of the bed, and my captor sat down to work off his boots.

"But I don't want to share a bed with you," I said, fighting to keep my voice from trembling. "You can't force me to share it with you."

"Of course I can," he answered, setting his boots to one side before swinging his legs up onto the bed. "If I keep on letting you go your own private way, you'll never get used to the idea of being my wife. Now, take that blouse off and let me see how bad your arm is."

"How did you know—?" I began to demand, but the look in those brown-rather-than-bronze eyes cut me short.

"So it *is* true," he said, the words and his expression mostly on the grim side. "At first I was convinced I was imagining things, specifically because InThig was acting unconcerned. I was expecting the demon to know whether or not you'd been hurt, just the way I knew Graythor had been hurt. When InThig wasn't worried in the least, I thought it was because there was nothing to worry about, but then I took you by the arms— Your face didn't show anything but your eyes did, and afterward I saw you rubbing gently at your left arm. Do you think a man never looks at the woman he intends making his wife?"

"Stop saying that," I told him with all the annoyance I was feeling toward myself. He'd tricked me with the oldest routine in the worlds, pretending he knew something when he was only guessing. "You can't make me your wife as long as I refuse to allow it, and I do refuse. Talk yourself blue in the face if you like, but talk won't change a damned thing. I've made up my mind, and have no intentions of unmaking it."

"And I've made up *my* mind," he said, reaching over to grab the edge of the blanket curtain and pull it completely closed. "You're going to be my wife, and I won't let anything stand in the way of that. Now, do you take that blouse off on your own, or do I have to help you?"

He turned back to look at me with that, and I barely noticed the way the bed under us spread and softened with better quality covers and pillows. Rik sat barefooted and bare-chested, his shoulders looking twice as wide as mine, his arms thick with the muscle even Kadrim hadn't been sure he could match. I'd tried my own hand at fighting with Rik once, and I still felt appalled at how much stronger he was. I knew I really had no chance against him, but I couldn't simply give in without a murmur.

"If you think I'm going to strip naked just because you tell me to, you haven't got the brains of a flea," I said as firmly as I could, making sure I didn't swallow hard enough for him to notice. "If you don't get out of this bed, then I'm going, and if you try to stop me, I'll . . ."

"If being undressed bothers you that much, you can turn your back," he interrupted, ignoring everything else I'd said. "I remember now how modest you are and I'm not trying to humiliate you, but I *am* going to see what was done to your arm. Graythor got only a glancing touch, but I have the feeling you were given more than that."

I didn't want to do it his way, I really didn't, but there was just the chance he would look at my arm and then leave me alone. There wasn't much hope things would actually go like that, but I didn't want anyone trying to claim I was totally unreasonable. Giving them the chance to claim that had already caused enough trouble, specifically by giving Rik a reason to insist on having his own way. He wasn't going to get his way because I wasn't unreasonable, and there was no more to be said on the subject.

With a good deal of reluctance, then, I turned my back on him and began working at getting my tunic off. The long green skirt made shifting around on the bed awkward as well as difficult, and I decided to talk to Graythor the very next day about finding something else for me to wear. He'd put all sorts of supplies and things into the wagon against need, and when it came to more flexible clothing I certainly had the need. Once I pulled my head free of the tunic, I also carefully withdrew my left arm, then held the bunched cloth up in front of me and shifted my arm back a little.

"For your information I'm not modest," I said while I stared at the wagon side in front of me, feeling cool air on my back and arm. "I just don't happen to enjoy parading around naked for the benefit of those who find fun staring. Just because you like showing off doesn't mean everyone does."

"Being without clothes isn't automatically showing off," he said distractedly, his fingers touching my arm very gently. "And someone without clothes isn't necessarily inferior to those who have them. Everything depends on context and intent— Damn it, girl, why didn't you mention this to someone?"

Without a sleeve covering it, I could see how black and blue my arm was, and glancing at it brought back a brief memory of unseen teeth biting down hard. The thought made me shiver a little on the inside, but only because I hadn't been able to see the attackers myself.

"I've been hurt worse than that without finding it necessary to go crying to someone," I answered, making sure the bunched tunic stayed where I wanted it. "There's nothing you can do about bruises but wait for them to heal, so I don't know why you're bothering me about this. And if your curiosity is all nicely satisfied now, you can just—"

My words broke off as his left arm circled me, and then I was down flat on the bed with him leaning over me.

"I'm bothering you about it because I care about you," he said very slowly and mildly, a patient teacher repeating the lesson for a thickheaded student. "What you can do about bruises is be careful of them, and make sure the person who has them isn't touched any way but gently. When you don't let people know about the pain you feel, you deny them the chance to share that pain and thereby show you how much they love you."

"Rik, don't—!" I began as his head lowered to me, but my left arm just didn't have the strength to keep him away. His lips found mine and touched them briefly, softly, with all the gentleness there ever was, and then his kiss was as full and direct as I remembered it. I was overwhelmed by that kiss, as badly as I'd been on the blind world, and when it was finally over my eyes didn't want to open.

"Mornings tend to come early on most worlds, so we'd better get some sleep," I heard after a minute, a big hand stroking my hair as an accompaniment. "If you'll get out of the rest of your clothes, we can get under the covers."

"And then you'll kiss me again," I said, hating myself for loving the way the words sounded. "And after the kiss you'll show me what I can look forward to as your wife."

"No, as a matter of fact I *won't* be kissing you again," he answered, and this time what I heard forced my eyes to open narrowly. He was still looking down at me, and when he saw my expression he grinned. "Stop trying to carve holes in me with that stare," he ordered with a laugh. "I didn't say I don't want to kiss you again, only that I won't. Kissing you tends to lead to other things, and other things will have to wait until that arm gets better. Since I expect to have to fight for what I want, you have to be in good enough shape to put up that fight."

"You're not funny," I told him bluntly, still holding the tunic to me as I squirmed around trying to sit up. "If you expect me to believe you forced me in here with the intention of doing absolutely nothing—! Come to think of it, anyone who did that would have to be crazy, so I guess I believe it after all. Get out of my way. I'm finding some place else to spend the night."

"You're spending the night right here, and so am I," he countered, moving himself back to block my way out of there, the grin still on his face. "A man doesn't always make love to his wife, but that doesn't mean he has no interest in sleeping next to her. And if I can stand it, so can you."

That wasn't anything like what I wanted to hear, but when I tried to put the tunic back on, he pulled it away from me and threw it after his own. I was furious enough then to try fighting him, but it did exactly as much good as I'd thought it would. I lost my skirt, underskirt and sandals, and not once did he come close to hurting my arm. Not having full use of the arm was frustrating enough to cause me to try a spell, but that did as much good as fighting had. I was finally forced to scramble under the covers, and the miserable beast chuckled as he blew out the lantern, got out of his trousers, then joined me under the covers. I thought he might change his mind at that point, but all he did was turn to his right and move around a little to get comfortable—what's usually called settling down for sleep.

As I lay there on my back, I tried very hard to maintain my anger, but I could feel the warmth of his body even though we weren't touching. Memories of my childhood floated up, of the closeness of my pack and the way we would usually sleep huddled together. It had been so long since the last time I'd experienced that sense of closeness I'd thought it was gone for good, but it looked like there were sources of it I hadn't known about. And Graythor had made sure he wasn't lying, that he had been telling the truth about how he felt.

As if that made any real difference. I'd only been kidding myself when I'd insisted that Rik let me out of the bed, that I didn't want to have anything to do with him. I wanted everything to do with him, wanted to feel his hands touching me and his body pressed hard against mine. I wanted the joy he was able to give so easily, the pleasure of him in all things—everything I had no right to want. He was risking his life by associating with me, and I simply couldn't allow that. I turned to the right myself and put a hand to his back, but rather than being burned by the touch my hand was only warmed.

"It won't work, you know," I said very softly, loving the feel of the hard-muscled back under my fingers and palm. "Nothing has changed from the beginning of all this, so nothing can ever come of it."

"But something *has* changed," he disagreed immediately, turning to face me and draw me close. "When this first started, I wasn't sure how you felt about me, so I hesitated and tiptoed up to the door instead of striding right in. Now that I know you feel the same way I do, I'll be knocking that door right off its hinges. Have you ever faced attack military style? Most people find it hard to stand up to."

"And most magic users don't even bother paying

attention," I countered, rubbing my cheek against the hair on his chest. "You seem to have trouble remembering what I am—and what I'm able to do. You can't overwhelm me with superior force no matter how hard you try, so an orderly withdrawal is the only option left open to you. That's part of military tactics, I'm told."

"Retreat without even trying to fight?" he asked with a snort of amusement, his hands holding me tightly to him. "A good military commander won't consider that unless there's absolutely no chance of winning, which doesn't happen to be the case here. I might have some trouble launching my attacks against a magic user, but all I see facing me is a soft, cuddly girl. You see something more?"

"Just because I can't make my spells work doesn't mean I'm not a magic user," I informed him with faint annoyance, trying to understand why he was being so stubborn. "Before this is over my spells *will* be working, no matter what I have to do to make it happen. After that, your campaign will be over, and if you keep hoping really hard, the disappointment won't be easy for you to take."

"But as of right now you *can't* make your spells work, so my campaign is only beginning," he answered with a soft chuckle, putting his lips to my hair. "I have nothing more than a cuddly girl to face and work on, so that's what I'm going to do. Disappointment can be worried about when it happens."

"Rik, you're not going to try taking advantage of me while I can't do magic, are you?" I asked, the silly idea having just occurred to me. "I mean, you *do* understand I won't be like this forever, so it would be really stupid to act as if I will? Rik? Tell me you understand that. Rik?"

I tried to get him to answer me, but despite the fact that he held firm to his decision not to kiss me again, there wasn't another word out of him that night.

"You look like the frog who couldn't decide which way to jump," Graythor commented the next morning, once we were on our way. "If you keep it up much longer, you'll turn into a statue the way he did. If you have a problem, you could try telling me about it."

"I have more than one problem, and I'm not *allowed* to talk to you," I grumbled, watching the forest we rode through. "But that's undoubtedly for the best, because I don't *want* to talk to you."

"You're not angry with me for siding with Rik earlier?" he asked, the innocence so thick in his voice that it would have stopped the wagon if someone spread the stuff on the ground. "Laciel, child, there was nothing else I *could* do. How would it look if I failed to support the man I, myself, chose as our leader?"

"I told you before—since you chose him, he can be *your* leader," I answered with all the surliness I was feeling. "I already have a leader, and she isn't too fond of yours. Just wait until I figure out how to make my spells work again. My very first project is going to be how to get through warding, that or growing twice my normal size. I'll teach him how stupid it is to take advantage of someone who's only temporarily helpless."

"You would prefer it if he took advantage of someone who was permanently helpless?" the second very innocent question came, showing how much Graythor was enjoying himself. "I hadn't expected you to support a point of view like that, and I must say I'm rather disappointed . . ."

"Oh, shut up!" I snapped, in no mood to be the cause of *anyone's* amusement. "If he can take advantage of the helpless, then so can I, which should suit you just fine, considering how much you like it when it happens to *me*. All you men are alike, and I hate the bunch of you."

"What you seem to hate most is being told you can't do something," Graythor said in a musing tone, ignoring my outburst as he guided the horses to the right of a big tree. "Rik answered no to everything you tried insisting on this morning, and he was perfectly right in doing so. It was also well within his province to assign you chores, and if you attempt disobeying him as you said you would, you're destined to grow even more unhappy. Didn't you sleep well last night, that you're so out of sorts today?"

It so happened I hadn't slept well the night before, and that was part of the reason for my rotten mood. I felt as though I'd had bad dreams all night, and the worst part was that Rik had been there when the screams or the sobbing had brought me awake. I was used to InThig being there, a reassuring presence of support that never intruded; Rik had tried to hold me and comfort me, and I hadn't been able to stand it. He'd also tried questioning me when daylight came, and hadn't been pleased when I'd simply turned and walked away from him. That was probably one of the reasons he'd been so hard-nosed with my perfectly reasonable requests, and a reason I wasn't about to accept.

"How soon do you think InThig will get back?" I asked, wishing the demon had already returned. That world was making me feel downright strange, and the sooner we got on with what we were there for, the happier I would be.

"InThig will be back when it's gotten the information we need," Graythor answered, sounding unbearably patient. "We can't very well ride into the nearest village or town without having a place we're supposed to have come from, or having a reason for having left. We also have to have something we do, and a reason for knowing almost nothing about this area. InThig will move as quickly as only a demon can, but it does have to stay out of sight. Do you have something you'd like to discuss with InThig?"

"No," I answered shortly, dropping that line of conversation as well. What I wanted to do was test Graythor's theory about my tapping into Rik's talent, and see if I could talk InThig into going along with my original plan. If the demon watched while they did to me what had been done to Morgiana, it could then go back and tell Graythor exactly what he needed to know. I had awakened with the conviction that simply searching for the key would never find it for us, which meant something more had to be done.

With the morning mist burning off, the day began to grow warmer even though it was still cool under the trees where we rode. I shifted on the wagon seat beside Graythor, unhappy and uncomfortable, beginning to hate the skirts I still wore. When I'd tried to tell the wizard I wanted something else as clothing, Rik had interrupted and flatly stated that I would stay with the skirts. It was what the women on that world wore, so it was what I would wear. That was when Graythor had chimed in and said I couldn't even have one of the two clean outfits stored for me in the wagon. The day before I'd hardly worn the one I had on, so I could wear it for the rest of *that* day, and then wash it in whatever body of water we camped near that night.

Wash it! No automatic refreshing spell had been put on our clothing, not when we expected to move around among people who might notice something like that, so the clothing had to be washed. And then Rik had announced that one of my jobs would be doing the washing for everyone, as well as cooking our meals and cleaning up afterward. He would hunt for our food, Graythor would drive the wagon, the two of them would take care of the horses, and everything else would be mine to see to. When I told him what he could do with all those jobs, Graythor cleared his throat and turned hastily away, but Rik was more annoyed than embarrassed. He was just beginning to go through some sort of vague threat when I walked away from him, and that had been it for the moment.

"Laciel, when we stop for lunch I expect to see you eating something," Graythor said suddenly, drawing me out of introspection. "You failed to eat last night and again this morning, and it isn't possible to be rational and reasonable when your insides clang emptily."

"I wasn't hungry last night or this morning," I said, still not really looking at him. "And if His Majesty expects me to do the cooking at lunchtime, don't look forward to an appetite of your own. In case you've forgotten, I was never taught to cook."

"Why, so you weren't," Graythor answered, and I could hear his frown. "There was no opportunity before Morgiana found you, and afterward there was no need. Under normal circumstances you might never notice the lack, but lack it remains, most especially here. Well, there's obviously nothing to do but remedy the situation. When we stop for lunch, I'll begin teaching you."

"You?" I asked in amazement, finally turning to look at him. "You know how to cook, Uncle Graythor? I never would have believed it."

"Why not?" he countered with a small smile, his glance at me filled with amusement. "We all start out young and full of fire, eager to learn nothing but magic and more magic, but after enough decades have passed, you discover that magic isn't all there is to life. Ordinary people do ordinary things without once speaking a spell, and most of them enjoy life quite a lot. If you were to look around, I doubt if you would find a single wizard who didn't have a hobby, usually one that was completely unrelated to magic."

"I can't imagine *wanting* to do without magic," I said, shifting on the wagon seat as I thought about it. "Magic makes everything so much easier, giving you all the time you need to work on things that are more important than ordinary day-to-day living. If I had to live in a world like this for the rest of my life, I'd either go crazy or die of boredom."

"As pretty as you are, you'd hardly be bored," he responded with a chuckle, using the reins to guide the horses around another tree. "And it would do you good to learn what satisfaction it's possible to experience when you accomplish something with your hands and mind, rather than with your talent. Some of us have hobbies that rely on magic, like Morgiana's traveling, but it's the traveling itself that interests her, the seeing new places and meeting new people. Aggan, our current house-and-spell sitter, writes music as his hobby, and he's really quite good."

"And your hobby is cooking," I said, remembering all those years I'd had nothing *but* hands and mind to accomplish things with. Very little had gotten accomplished beyond barely staying alive, and the amount of satisfaction I'd gotten could be used to fill the dot of a very small letter i.

"Which hobby *I'm* rather good at," he said, actually sounding proud. "Rik's cooking isn't bad, but it's very plain and wholly uninspired, the sort of effort you use to keep yourself alive while other things absorb your attention. Once you learn what I have to teach, he should be rather pleased."

"I have a better idea," I said, going back to looking at the woods all around us. "Since you two are so interested in cooking, you can teach *him*. I'll be spending my time on inconsequential things, like trying to make my spells work, but don't worry about interrupting me if something really exciting happens. I'm waiting breathlessly for the first time he manages to create a soufflé that doesn't fall."

"You're determined to fight him every step of the way, then," Graythor said with a sigh, and I could feel his eyes resting on me for longer than a glance. "I think you know as well as I do that we won't be likely to find the answer to the puzzle until we have a good deal more information, but you're going to use research as an excuse to challenge Rik's authority. I'd thought by the end of the quest you'd accepted him as leader."

"Ordinary people don't become leaders over magic users," I stated in a very flat way, making the effort to leave no doubt about the way I felt. "He may have been the leader to the others, but not to me."

Graythor said nothing more to that, which was hardly a surprise. If he couldn't threaten me with his greater strength, which he couldn't, there wasn't anything much he *could* say. If he hadn't been silly enough to appoint Rik leader of our group, there wouldn't have *been* a problem, but he had so there was. I *had* to refuse Rik's authority, just the way I'd always done with anyone who wasn't a wizard, so whatever happened would be all Graythor's fault. Besides, didn't he know that if you started taking someone's orders in one area, before you knew it you were taking orders in everything? With some things it didn't matter, but with others, like getting married . . .

I spent part of the rest of that morning brooding, then shifted over to the less satisfying but more productive area of experimentation. It had occurred to me that the people of that world might be prohibited from using the language of spells, which meant they had to make do with ordinary, everyday language. That sort of requirement would limit the amount of detail you could put in a spell and still take less than a day to speak it, but it would make doing magic possible. As a possibility it was at least possible, and the only way to find out for sure was to try it.

I looked at the hem of my skirt, Saw down to the base fabric of it, then began to describe it in moderate detail. It was really tedious doing it like that and it took quite a few minutes. Graythor knew immediately what I was doing, of course, but watched and listened without comment. When I finally decided I had a good enough grip on the cloth for anything simple, I raised my right hand and said, "Skirt hem, rise one inch!"

"Possibly the material is deaf," Graythor suggested, but his sigh told me he wasn't any more amused with my failure than I was. The stupid hem hadn't even twitched, which killed that idea as a possibility.

"How about rhyming?" I said as I slumped back on the wagon seat. "I think I heard somewhere once that rhyming works in some places."

"I know the world-dimension you refer to," Graythor answered, and if I didn't know him better I would have sworn he shivered. "We've erected warning walls around every gate to it we could find, to be sure no Sighted accidently blunders in without knowing. The power there is wild, which means there's no need to gather it, only to wield it. Any Sighted can exert the strength of a wizard if his or her rhyme is properly worded, but most don't know how to handle that much power. The disasters that occur are almost con-

stant and nearly beyond belief, and the more one tries
to fix things, the worse they get. If this world should
be like that one, our only option will be to leave at
once and then return with an unSighted army to rescue Morgiana."

I didn't like the sound of that, but we did have to
know. I said, "Skirt hem even, skirt hem fair, ride the
power an inch in the air."

"Thank the EverNameless," Graythor said with another sigh when the skirt didn't budge, and then he
glanced at me with a smile. "I'm pleased to see, though,
that precision is more important to you than meter.
Someone without your training might well have simply
ordered the skirt hem to rise, specifying nothing in the
way of distance. As one of your teachers, it gratifies
me that you twice recognized the need."

"If you're not going to use the language of spells to
establish control over something, you have to do it
somehow," I answered, finding myself as pleased as
ever when Graythor complimented me. "Besides, I
didn't want to take any chances since we're no longer
alone."

I nodded my head in the direction Rik was appearing from, slightly ahead of us and to the left. Our
mighty leader had gone hunting, and as he rode up to
the wagon he was able to announce success.

"Wild birds," he said with a grin, holding his tro-
phies high. "We'll probably camp out tonight even if
InThig gets back, and there's no need to use our
supplies unnecessarily. Graythor, there's a nice little
pool about a mile ahead of you, and that's where I
want you to stop for lunch. I'm going on to see how
much forest we have left before we reach that town
InThig said was there, and I'll meet you back at the
pool."

Graythor nodded pleasantly to acknowledge receipt
of his instructions, and once he did, Rik took the birds
he'd tied together and tossed them onto the wagon
between the wizard and me.

"Laciel, cleaning those birds is part of your job," he
said, his smile just as pleasant as Graythor's had been.

"When there isn't a feather left on any of them, bring them to me and I'll tell you what to do next. Do you understand?"

"Oh, absolutely," I assured him, making no effort to return his smile or say anything else. He stared at me briefly as his horse paced the wagon, an expression of indecision on his face, and then he decided not to press the issue. He raised a hand to Graythor and me as he touched heels to his mount, and not long after that he was gone into the woods again.

"Have you been wise enough to change your mind?" Graythor asked once Rik was no longer in sight, the words coming out puzzled. "I'll admit I hadn't hoped to see something like that, but the sight would nevertheless be welcome."

"I'm really glad not to be dashing your hopes, Uncle Graythor," I answered, moving my feet away from the feathered, unmoving bodies that lay in the wagon boot between us. "I told Rik I understood what he was saying, which was, after all, the only question he asked. If he and you assumed something else from that answer, it's certainly not *my* fault."

"Of course not, of course not," Graythor agreed with yet another sigh, shaking his head in a distracted way. "None of this is anyone's fault, really, but circumstances rarely end up with the consequences of blame. Our current situation being what it is, you would do well to consider that, child."

I wasn't quite sure what it was I was supposed to consider, but I also wasn't about to ask for details. We lapsed back into silence for the rest of our ride, and when we reached the pool Rik had spoken about, Graythor pulled the horses to a halt.

"I'll water our faithful beasts of burden," he said, tying off the reins before beginning to climb down from the wagon. "After that I'll put together a light meal for us, and I expect you to eat every bite of your portion. And if I were you, I would start plucking those birds. If Rik returns to find them untouched, I very much doubt if you'll remain the same."

"I'd like to *see* him try to touch me," I muttered,

giving most of my attention to getting me and my skirt down to the ground without a major mishap. "If he ever does, he'll need his sword to defend himself, and that no matter *how* strong he is. If he ever makes the mistake of getting me really mad, he'll find out I don't need magic to settle his hash good."

"Which would leave just InThig and me to go after Morgiana," Graythor said, and I heard him unhooking a bucket from the other side of the wagon. "With that pleasant thought in mind, perhaps it would be best to let nature take its course after all."

He reappeared to look at me briefly over the horses, then took his dry attempt at humor off toward the pool. Since I didn't find the situation quite as amusing, I took the opposite direction, needing a little exercise to get the kinks out of my body. Riding on a wagon seat may be better than walking, but that's the only thing it's better than.

It wasn't far from local noon on that world, but for the most part that fact was hidden by the trees all around. Occasional clearings let you check the sky, and there was one not too distant from where we'd stopped. I walked over to it and stood in the sunshine for a moment or two, needing the warmth even though it wasn't cold, and then I began moving around it in an aimless sort of way. Without magic I wasn't enjoying being out in the woods, not after having grown up in a city. I knew how to survive amid cobblestoned streets and soulless, padlocked buildings, but the knack didn't carry over well into tall trees and bushes and uneven ground grass.

"And it's also boring," I said out loud, feeling sullen enough to give my opinion to anyone who cared to listen. "The buildings of a city are all different, but when you've seen one tree you've seen them all. Green and brown and boring."

I scowled around at the objects of my displeasure, but none of them seemed to care that I wasn't oohing and aahing in admiration. Spoiled, that's what they were, so used to people raving over how wonderful unspoiled nature was that they probably didn't even hear it when someone tried telling them the truth. Unspoiled nature was a pain and a bore, and so were those who managed to live in it with next to no effort. How in the name of the Silver Sphere did you catch birds without leaving a mark on them—?

"He probably ordered them to death," I muttered, stopping where I was to examine my hands. "Or caught them walking instead of flying, and took advantage of them. I wonder if any of *them* had trouble deciding whether or not they wanted to be taken advantage of?"

I thought about that for a minute with my hand to my throat, but it was fairly obvious birds would be much too smart to find themselves with a problem like that. Only half-witted humans would jump happily into waist-deep mud, then wonder why they were having trouble getting somewhere. The full truth was they didn't *want* to get somewhere, which was why they'd jumped into the mud in the first place.

"And how the hell am I supposed to win, when half of me is fighting on *his* side?" I demanded of the golden sunshine, which ignored me exactly the way the trees had. "It's *wrong* to want things to work out the way he insists they will, but that isn't stopping part of me from wanting it. Letting him involve himself with me is like urging him to jump off the top of a cliff, but part of me refuses to see that. It's trying to help him make it happen, and all the rest of me can do is cause as much trouble as it's possible to think of. Maybe he'll get sick and tired of the way I'm acting, and simply lose interest."

My middle churned with the thought of that possibility, an indication of how much my traitorous part didn't want it to happen, but the rest of me stood firm. I wasn't about to let Rik get hurt, and that was bound to happen if he stayed anywhere near me. That he was willing to take the chance didn't matter; an adult was irresponsible if she let a child play too near the fire, and where black magic was concerned Rik was even less than a child.

With my resolve bolstered a little, I decided I might

as well get back to the wagon, and turned to cross the clearing again. I was even beginning to think about taking a bath in that pool, but looking up made me forget all about being clean. It occurred to me fleetingly that I might have been hasty in insulting the trees and the rest of nature out loud, but if that was what my mistake had been, it was far too late to take it back.

Just entering the clearing from the other side was a huge, golden-brown bear, and then it rose to its hind legs with a hungry-sounding snarl and came right for me.

CHAPTER 12

Without stopping to think about it, I snapped out a freezing spell, but the bear ignored the word and gesture alike and simply kept coming. Fear wasn't anything like a stranger to me, but what I felt right then was close to the worst it had ever been. I backed away through the clearing, trying to decide if I should look for a sturdy branch to defend myself with or simply turn and run, but the speed the bear was moving at didn't give me much deciding time. Because of that, my best bet seemed to be to *start* running, and if I happened on a proper branch I could always stop and try fighting. Liking the sound of that, I turned fast to run—and almost immediately tripped on the hem of my skirts and went down.

Hitting the ground hard jarred me enough that I couldn't quite curse those skirts, and then I was too busy trying to scramble back to my feet to have the time. A large block of ice lay around my heart and chipped into the rest of me, caused primarily by how close the bear was, but I'd learned a lot of years earlier that you couldn't let the fear freeze you. If you did, you were done for, and it didn't much matter if it was a bear behind you or a city guardsman. You had to run, and keep running, and try, and keep trying—

I screamed as one set of bear claws hooked into my skirts, the snarl accompanying the swipe almost one of triumph. My scream was one of frustration, an attempt to deny that I'd been caught, but it wasn't working. The claws stayed hooked in, refusing to let me go, soon to be joined by another set sinking into my flesh, and then—

And then there was a deeper, more chill-making snarl, a sound of outraged challenge that came just before the thud of heavy bodies. It took an instant to realize that I was no longer caught, that the bear had been pushed away and into a serious fight. I swallowed hard as I fought to control the way my body was trembling, and once I had a small bit of success, I forced myself to sit up and turn around. I needed to know if it was Rik who had saved me or InThig, but once I was able to see the growling, snarling fight I felt almost as confused as relieved.

The bear was fighting hard for its life, but not against a great bronze link-beast or a dead-black demon. Its opponent seemed to be a huge brown dog, a giant slavering monster with dripping claws and fangs and madly-glaring yellow eyes, and the dog looked to be winning. Even as I watched, it sank its fangs into the bear's throat, and with a single jerk of its head tore out fur, flesh, throat and all. The bear tried to scream as its final act in this life, but the try came too late. With blood spurting and body convulsing, it crashed to the ground, and the huge dog stood over it with paws leaning on the beast's chest, watching to be sure it really was dead.

Or that, at least, was the way it looked to me. As I ran a still-shaking hand through my hair, I realized most animals didn't do that sort of thing, a detached and intelligent sort of watching. I'd been wondering if I would be the next object of attack after the bear, but suddenly I didn't think I would be. The huge dog was enough to scare the hell out of anyone who saw it, but

I had the definite feeling its horrific appearance was no threat to me. I toyed with the idea of slipping away into the forest while the thing was still occupied, then chose a riskier course of action.

"Thanks for saving my life," I called, forcing my voice to sound as normal as possible. "Are *you* all right? Was the bear able to hurt you?"

Those glaring yellow eyes snapped over to me with the first of my words, giving me the distinct impression that I might have made a terrible mistake. It was hard believing there was intelligence behind that stare when it was being sent in my direction, but if it turned out my first impressions were wrong, it was already too late to change tactics. All I could think of was the way InThig looked at things and people—including me—and remember at the same time how gentle InThig basically was. The huge dog stared at me for what seemed like an hour, and then it stepped down from the chest of the bear.

"No, this puny beast had no power to harm me," it told me then, walking a few steps toward me before stopping. Its voice was snarly and growly, but the words still came through clearly. "Why are you asking me how I am and thanking me instead of running? Don't you see what I am? Do you want to be killed?"

"If I was going to be killed, I think it would have happened already," I said to the dog, right then knowing it was true. "You sound more bitter than bloodthirsty, which leads me to wonder why you saved me in the first place. If you didn't expect thanks and concern for what you did, why did you do it?"

"I've always been a fool, and probably always will be," the dog answered, sitting down where it was to continue staring balefully. "When I see someone who needs help, I can't keep from giving it, even if I know that that someone will run screaming as soon as they're free to do it. After all, who *wouldn't* run screaming from a hellhound? I ran away to the forests to get away from all that, but my fate continues to haunt me. What are you doing out here all alone, with no one to protect you?"

"Usually I can protect myself, and I'm not all alone," I said, feeling how ridiculous it was to get yelled at by something called a hellhound. "I'm traveling with two other people, but I wanted to be by myself for a while. If that bear had had the least sense of decency, it would have attacked someone who *wanted* the company."

"You nearly lose your life and you joke about it," the hellhound said, paying no attention to the blood smeared on its muzzle and paws and body. "I've seen men do that but never women, and I can't say I like it. You should be taught not to wander away from where you belong, and that might keep you alive. No guarantees, of course, not these days, but it might."

"I belong wherever I say I belong," I returned with a growl of my own, getting to my feet and beginning to brush at those stupid, now-torn skirts. "If you think saving my life gives you the right to tell me how to live, you have a big surprise coming. Maybe hellhounds get away with that sort of thing where *you* come from, but that's not the way it works around *me*. Thanks again for saving my life, and good-bye."

I began marching across the clearing with the intention of going back to the wagon, but the hellhound was up on his feet in a flash and a second later was blocking my path. I thought of the dog as "he" without the smallest sense of doubt, and the narrow-eyed way he looked up at me only confirmed the opinion.

"You've never before seen a hellhound," he stated, sounding utterly convinced and very curious. "Not only aren't you afraid of me, you also act nothing like the proper woman your clothes proclaim you to be. Who are you, and where do you come from?"

"I would say that was my business," I countered, putting my fists on my hips as I returned his stare. "Are you going to get out of my way, or do I have to walk around you?"

"If I were still a man, the answer to that would be neither," he said with a sharp-fanged grin, those yellow eyes looking me up and down. "Unfortunately, you now appeal only to my memories, which is a great shame. If I took you as my woman, you would undoubtedly live longer. Try to make at least a token effort to stay alive since I, for one, would have missed not knowing you."

He moved off to my right with that, letting me continue out of the clearing with no further trouble. I could feel his stare for quite a few minutes, but I was much too busy thinking about what he'd said to bother about a stare. If he was still a *man?* What was that supposed to mean, and how did it figure into what we were there to do?

I got back to the wagon to find Graythor happily engaged in putting a meal together, but he did a double take when he looked at me. I'd done the best I could in brushing away the dirt and grass and leaves that had gotten on my tunic and skirts, but I still looked less than neat and tidy. Not having the use of magic was beginning to be a real pain, and I suppose it was too much to expect Graythor to pass on commenting about my lacks.

"Laciel, where have you been and what have you been doing?" he demanded, putting a bowl down to stare at me. "I really don't think you should be wandering far from this wagon. When I called you, I got no answer, and now that you've come back, just look at you. What happened?"

"These skirts happened," I said with a near growl, seeing no reason not to take advantage of a true situation. "I tripped and fell and almost killed myself, and all because you and Rik have to play stubborn. Are you waiting for the sight of blood before you'll change your mind, or do you intend settling for a couple of broken bones?"

"I understand there's a trick to lifting the skirts out of your way before starting to walk," Graythor answered, shifting his attention back to the meal that seemed nearly done. "If you made some effort to practice the knack instead of simply striding off in all directions, you'd be a good deal less likely to fall down—not to mention looking more ladylike. Or do you expect appearing more gently feminine is likely to kill you?"

"Sometimes you can't tell *what* will turn out to be fatal," I countered, folding my arms as I continued to stare at him. "You're not going to try to find anything else for me to wear?"

"Talk to Rik," the most powerful wizard of our time said with a helpless little shrug. "He's in charge of this group, and I can't countermand his decisions. It's rather silly to appoint a leader if you're simply going to ignore what he says."

"But everyone else is fair game for being ignored," I said with a nod, coldly furious. "Okay, if that's the way you want to play it, it's fine with me. It won't be the first time I've been ignored, and once you have the experience you discover certain advantages."

"What advantages?" he asked with a frown, but I was already turning away from him and heading toward the pool. The first and most obvious advantage was that anyone who ignored you could be ignored in turn, but that wasn't what I really wanted to do to Graythor. The temptation to try using Persuasion on him was one step short of overpowering, but that I refused to do. If you can't win your fights fairly, you don't deserve to win them at all, and using Persuasion wasn't fighting fair. Even if I wasn't completely convinced it would work in the first place.

When I reached the pool, I looked at the water, then sat down beside it to do some thinking. I would have preferred bathing in it to sitting near it, but Graythor hadn't even offered a fresh set of the clothes I hated. Bathing doesn't do much if you can't put on clean clothes afterward, and I was wasting enough time on that world without deliberately adding to it. When InThig got back that might change, but first the demon had to get back.

And now that I had time to think about it, where did that hellhound fit in? From the way he talked he wasn't one of a kind, but chances were he didn't fit in well with the others. He had run away from being feared and shunned, and that told me more than he probably knew. If someone is around who spends most of his time saving people, after a while people stop being afraid of what he looks like and start paying more attention to what he does. Once it's firmly established that he's a friend, he could have five heads with bad breath on top of it, and most people won't care.

But if he happens to be one of a group who, in general, hurt rather than help, his own occasional good deeds get buried under the mountain of their bad ones. He's hated and feared because of what *they* do, and probably isn't very popular with his equals, either. When people work for a fearsome reputation, they don't like having one of their own ruin their efforts. The hellhound who saved me had run away from attackers and victims alike, and he'd started out life as a man.

As a man. I shifted uncomfortably where I sat, reaching out a hand to trail fingers in the nearby water, then brought the water back to cool my face. It wasn't especially hard to turn ordinary people into something else, but most magic users had more of an ethical sense than to indulge in the nonsense. It wasn't pleasant to be turned into something you didn't especially care to be, and unless the spell was watched on a more or less constant basis, the victim tended to revert to normal after a time. Living things strive for a proper balance, and what they started out life as being was always the most proper.

But my hellhound acquaintance remained a hellhound despite not enjoying the state, and he wasn't the only one being kept like that. The others were feared and hated with reason, and times weren't what they once had been. There was no guarantee about staying alive, not "these days," and that made me worry even more about what Morgiana had gotten herself into. If it turned out she was responsible for any of that, I didn't want to see her face when she found out about it.

I was still sitting next to the pool when Rik walked over to me, but I didn't bother looking up. He'd gotten back not long after I'd walked away from Graythor, but hadn't come over until he and the wizard had finished their conversation. I hadn't been able to hear what was being said, and wasn't sure I wanted to know. The only thing I *did* want to know was when InThig would be getting back.

"Laciel, Graythor told me you took a walk," Rik said, and I could feel him looking down at me. "I thought you knew better than to wander around all alone, but since you don't, let me make it as clear as possible. These woods aren't safe for someone who can't defend herself, so there won't be any more walks. There's an unfamiliar scent I keep picking up, and I don't want you running into whatever's making that scent unless I'm there to protect you."

"What if I don't want your protection?" I asked, the words nothing more than conversational, my eyes still on the cool green water of the pond. "What if I prefer protecting myself, and don't happen to be interested in substitute protectors? It would save you some trouble, after all, and you'd be free to spend all your time protecting Graythor."

"From time to time, *everyone* needs someone else's protection," he answered, sounding as horribly patient as Graythor had. "During most of the quest the rest of us needed *your* protection, but that didn't mean we were any the less for it. We ran into things we weren't equipped to handle, so you did the handling for us. Right now, you're not equipped to handle these woods, so it's my turn to do the handling. Once you figure out this puzzle world, the job will be yours again."

"You didn't answer my question," I pointed out, still not looking at him. "I didn't say anything about whether or not I need your protection—which I don't—I asked what would happen if I didn't want it. You're more than ready to give it, I can see, but I'm telling you to keep it. Now that you know my preferences in the matter, what do you do about it?"

"You're asking if I would nod with a pleasant smile before going about my business elsewhere?" he said, and then he was suddenly crouching beside me, his hand on my face forcing me to look up at him. "The answer to that is no, I would not simply accept your preferences in the matter, giving you the chance to run around all over this world on your own. Doing something like that could get you killed, and for some silly, unexplainable reason I don't think I'd enjoy seeing you killed."

"So we go with *your* likes and dislikes, and to hell with mine?" I demanded, pulling my face away from his hand but still glowering at him. "That really shows how wonderful a leader you'd make, thinking about no one but yourself. A proper leader considers the feelings of those she leads, otherwise she's more dictator than leader. Just like someone else I could name."

"Are you trying to start a fight?" he demanded, his eyes blazing, and then his expression changed. "Of course you're trying to start a fight; why else would you be saying such idiotic things? Okay, the question now is *why* you're trying to start a fight. Are you expecting it to distract me from everything you've done and haven't done today?"

"Don't you get tired of thinking about no one but yourself?" I asked, letting disgust show in my voice. "You're the only one capable of saying anything intelligent, the only one capable of doing any real protecting, and also so terribly special you have to be distracted. Has it ever occurred to you that not everyone thinks about you first? That some of us have less egotistical things and people to take our attention? You . . ."

"Egotistical?" he repeated in a strangled roar. "You have the nerve to call *me* egotistical? If you're not in charge of the entire universe, you expect it to break down and never start up again. And you're totally incapable of following other people's orders, mostly because you've never grown up. In your mind you're still that wild little pack leader you were in Geddenburg, and if someone dares to suggest something to you, you immediately decide they're trying to take away your pack. Well, I think it's time someone *did* take away your pack, and then you might be free to forget about running everything—and might also be free of those nightmares."

"The only way to take away my pack is to hurt me

so badly I stop coming back to the ground line," I told him very softly, giving him a half smile I hoped would make him even angrier. "If you want to challenge a pack leader you make a line in the dirt, then you step up to it with your stick in your hand. When the pack leader answers your challenge by meeting you at the line, the two of you go at it until one of the two is knocked down. When that happens the one still standing goes back to the line to wait, and the one who was knocked down has to get up and also go back. The fight is over when one or the other can't make it back to the line, usually because they can't even crawl any longer. When did you intend drawing your line?"

His jaw tightened as he stared at me, but he didn't come back with an immediate answer. He seemed to think he could solve every problem I ever had by showing how well he understood me, but *his* biggest problem was that he didn't understand me nearly as well as he thought. I watched the expression in his eyes shift around as he tried to decide whether or not to continue with his supposed challenge, and then all of that was gone and he stiffened as his head came up.

"That strange scent I noticed earlier, the one I told you about," he said in a very low voice, his lips barely moving. "I'm picking it up again, but this time it's close enough to be right on top of us. You get ready to get back to Graythor and the wagon as soon as I give you the word, and I'll . . ."

"And you'll probably start something neither of us will enjoy," a growly, snarly voice interrupted, clearly coming from the bushes only a few feet away from where I sat. "It will certainly do us all a lot more good if we try introducing ourselves first."

"Since the suggestion is yours, why don't you start us off?" Rik said at once, straightening as I twisted around, and then stepping directly in my way. "And since it isn't very interesting talking to a bunch of bushes, you might also come out where I can see you."

"Nothing simpler," the growly voice answered, and then the hellhound padded out into the open from the

side of the bushes before sitting down beside them. He
made no effort to move any closer to Rik or me, but
those sharp-pointed fangs seemed to be spread wide in
amusement. By then I was up on my own feet and
standing next to Rik rather than being blocked by
him, but I still couldn't see anything particularly funny.

"All right, now I can see you," Rik said to the
hellhound in a very neutral way, at the same time
having the nerve to push me back behind him again.
"Since you went that far, I'll introduce myself as Rikkan
Addis and ask who we're welcoming into our camp."

"My names are Fillik Kop Togor, and I'm very
pleased to meet you, Addis," the hellhound said, fangy
grin widening, only glancing at Graythor as the wizard
hurried over. "The female is out from behind you
again, Addis, which isn't very surprising considering
the sort she is. What are *her* names?"

"None of your business!" I snapped, trying to decide whose attitude annoyed me more, his or Rik's.
"If I want to be introduced to you, I'm perfectly
capable of saying so. What do you want around here?"

"Laciel!" Graythor said in a very severe way, Rik's
glance agreeing completely. "If you don't know how I
feel about rudeness by now, you're completely beyond
hope. Fillik Kop Togor is our guest, and if you can't
be polite to a guest, you can be sent to the wagon
instead. One more word out of the way, and that's
where you *will* be sent. Now then, what can we do for
you, my friend? May we offer refreshment?"

"I've already had my refreshment, thank you," the
hellhound returned with a chuckle while I threw my
hands up and turned away. "A bear I happened to
have a disagreement with, one that lacked the least
sense of decency. What you can do for me is tell me
where you all come from, and how long you expect it
to take you to defeat the High King."

CHAPTER 13

The hellhound's questions settled a silence onto Rik and Graythor, but it wasn't anything that took *me* by surprise. I'd tried to warn my intrepid companions by being deliberately rude to our visitor, but they'd been blind to the warning and had only seen the rudeness. I turned back and folded my arms, waiting to see how two paragons of good manners avoided answering questions we hadn't yet worked out answers *for*. Telling someone to mind their own business was *my* way, but since they didn't like my way, I was dying to see what *they* would come up with.

A couple of long moments went by while Rik looked at Graythor and Graythor looked at Rik, and then our esteemed leader cleared his throat.

"What do you mean, where do we come from and when will we defeat the High King?" Rik asked, trying to sound honestly puzzled and innocently confused. "We may not come from this immediate area, but we certainly have no intentions of doing anything to the High King. What made you think we did?"

"The very fact that you don't come from this immediate area," the hellhound answered, stretching out along the ground without rising from his seated position. "Those who *do* come from this area, those who dress the way you're dressed, and use wagons like the one over there, would never have welcomed me into their camp. You can't have it both ways, my friends. Either you're complete strangers and shouldn't look the way you do, or you belong here and shouldn't be talking to me the way you're doing. How will you have it?"

Rik and Graythor exchanged looks again, but it was fairly obvious we were caught in the sort of predica-

ment I'd been expecting. Without enough information
to build a good story, all you can do is refuse to
answer; if you do it in just the right way, your ques-
tioners will pick up the sense of an official secret, one
they'd be much better off not knowing. The technique
of a dodge like that was apparently beyond Rik and
Graythor both, but they were the ones who had taken
over running "our" effort. I'd been threatened with
being sent to my room, and the prospect of a punishment like that made me quake in my sandals.

"And what other names come before the name Laciel,
Laciel?" the hellhound asked, possibly in an effort to
give his new friends time to consider what they would
say. "From the size of your self-esteem, you should
have earned five at the very least. Do you have other
names, Laciel—or just the one?"

"Where I come from, the single name has a very
special significance," I answered with as mysterious a
smile as I could manage, one that was also half smirk.
"The same could even be said for here—under equally
special circumstances. Didn't your superiors ever tell
you about that?"

The hellhound lost his amusement at that, heavy
brown hackles actually starting to rise, and then some
prior line of reasoning intervened.

"No, I don't believe you're some sort of King's
agents, out looking for whatever you can find," he
said, a ghost of his grin returning. "The King doesn't
need agents like that, not any more, and even if he did
he would hardly choose ones like you three. Your tall
friend over there has senses almost as keen as mine,
the small man has more presence than all the nobles of
the court put together, and you—you have the arrogance of the King himself, and that in spite of your
being a most obvious candidate for the Chosen-Blessing.
I suspect I know how well you'd like the Blessing, but
you still can't be bothered with keeping modestly silent. If you *are* deliberately looking to end your life,
you might have the good manners to mention that to
those around you."

"But despite the inconsistencies, you're still sure

your conclusions are the right ones," I said, not having followed parts of his reasoning but still able to cast doubt on them, especially with more of a smile. "It's fascinating to speak to people who are absolutely certain—no matter what."

That time the hellhound's hackles did rise, and his yellow eyes glared more balefully as his head went back. The less you argue with someone the more they begin to doubt themselves, and my smile of confidence was really bothering our guest. His claws ripped through the grass as he began to sit up again, and it was at that point Rik interrupted.

"Don't let her upset you, friend Fillik," he said, taking a step forward with one hand raised in a calming gesture. "We *don't* work for the High King, you have my word on that. Laciel has a habit of starting any number of fights she can't finish, but we don't want one with you. Can you tell us why you came here and introduced yourself?"

"Obviously, it was my intention to join forces with you against the High King," the hellhound growled, clearly forcing himself to stay seated. "The only way I'll ever become a man again is if the High King is defeated, but none of our own people have a chance against him. When I heard the things you people were talking about—nothing that would be familiar to anyone I know—you have no idea how long I've waited— Can't either of you make her behave the way a woman should?"

His final question was so close to being plaintive that Rik had to rub at his face with one hand, and Graythor almost squeaked with the effort of keeping his expression serene. Our guest had obviously forgotten that he was the one who had started the conversation with *me,* not the other way around. He seemed to be used to women who let themselves be walked on, which meant he was in for something of a rough time if he did join forces with us.

"Our Laciel has always been on the undisciplined side," Graythor finally answered, managing to keep from laughing in the hellhound's face. "Her talents are

certain to come in handy during our efforts here, but
we just as certainly don't want to draw unwelcome
attention to ourselves. Can you tell us how she *should*
be behaving?"

"Why, with proper modesty and reasonably silent
obedience, of course," our guest answered, still glaring in my direction. "Women are there for the pleasure of men, and there's little pleasure in unrestrained
female foolishness. No woman has ever earned more
than a single name, and there's a very good reason for
that."

"Of course there is," I said with a very nasty grin.
"You men are too afraid of the competition, so you
play whatever game it is only among yourselves. You
don't want to have to make up a bunch of excuses as
to why you lost to a mere woman, which would happen to at least some of you, so . . ."

"Laciel, leave him alone!" Rik ordered, the words
sharp in reaction to the hellhound's immediate bristling insult. "We aren't here to tell these people how
to live, only to make sure they get to do it their own
way instead of somebody else's. And if you intend
going into a town or city with us, you'd better listen
good and hard about the way you're supposed to be
acting. If you don't act that way, you don't go. Why
don't you join us at our fire, friend Fillik? That way
we can all get comfortable while we find out how we
can help each other."

The hellhound glared at me one final time before
joining Rik and Graythor in heading for our fire, and I
was left to bring up the rear. Rik was worrying about
my not fitting in in whatever city or town we went to,
but he needn't have bothered. As soon as InThig got
back, I intended solving the problem for him.

Our guest settled down between the two male members of our party, but politely refused the bread stew
Graythor had made. Both offer and refusal were pure
form, something to be gotten out of the way as fast as
possible so that more important matters could then be
paid proper attention.

"This earning of names you mentioned," Rik began, pouring himself a mug of coffee. "Where we come from, only titles are earned, not the names themselves. Can you tell me how it works?"

"Titles come here with certain positions, so they aren't in the least important," the hellhound answered, settling himself more comfortably on the grass. "Names are what count, how many you get and when you get them, and some men start collecting even before they're considered men. If a boy kills a wild animal, for instance, or manages to complete a hard, intricate job, he's given the name of someone who performed a similar feat in the past. These names are ages old, and it's a very great honor to bear one."

"If you have to do one of these marvels in order to get the name, how did these ancient heroes get *their* names?" I asked, choosing my own piece of ground by the fire. "I mean, if everyone *always* started out nameless, then it stands to reason . . ."

"Once a man becomes a man, he tests with the other young men of his age in their village or town," the hellhound went on in a louder voice, riding right over the question I'd been trying to ask. "What he's testing for is his first adult name, and how well he does in the testing determines what name he's given. Many people think a man should be allowed to cooperate with his twin during the testing, and then the two of them could earn the same name. The laws don't allow that, however, so everyone has to compete separately."

"Are there that many multiple births that the question would come up?" Graythor asked, his brows high. "Where we come from, multiple births are the exception rather than the rule."

"It's pretty much the same here, so I don't understand your question," our guest said with a frown that could be heard. "'You don't often hear of tris or quads or pents being born, it's usually just your ordinary twins, but I suppose that's why the laws *don't* get changed. If a man is allowed to cooperate with his twin, what's to say he can't cooperate with two or three twins if he has them? It's the first time you really act alone, completely without your twin, and afterward it's never the way it once was. That's the point—and the reason—most twins go their own way."

Graythor nodded as though some confusion had been clarified for him, but probably only to avoid long explanations. If everyone of that world-dimension was part of a set of twins, they'd have trouble with the idea of single births. For all we knew there could be laws or moralistic stands against such a thing, maybe even infanticide on the occasions it happened. Graythor was certainly wise to avoid so potentially touchy a subject, but it was something we should know about and I had no good reputation to ruin.

"What about those who *have* no twin to separate from?" I asked, wondering if I would be ignored again. "Aren't there any people around whose twin died in childhood—or was never born?"

"I can understand why you would be interested in that sort," the hellhound came back, yellow eyes resting on me again. "Virtually every Chosen female is half-born, and if anyone bothered with their male counterparts they would probably find the same thing. There are never that many of them—even though for some reason most men consider half-borns very attractive—but the High King's been rounding them up to give them his Blessing. Once they're Chosen, no one ever sees them again, but there are rumors about what's done with them after the third or fourth time they've experienced the Blessing. The rumors are enough to turn even my stomach, but maybe you'd care to let me know if they're true once it becomes *your* turn."

"Why do you think Laciel would be a—Chosen?" Rik asked, the question deliberately calm and easy despite the hellhound's grin. "You don't know anything about her beyond the fact that you and she don't get along, but you sound very certain. Since she isn't one of your people, how can she be anything in your society at all?"

"I heard you talking to her about her nightmares," the hellhound responded, still grinning faintly at me.

"I happen to know that that's how the Chosen are found out, the ones who are silly enough to show their faces in towns and cities. They start having nightmares because of the High King's spell, and once it gets bad enough someone always hears them and turns them in. But just the females. Male half-born never have the nightmares."

"For the simple reason that the High King has no interest in giving *them* his Blessing," Graythor said, and I thought I detected an undercurrent of anger in his voice. "Tell me, my friend—how many people know the High King himself is half-born?"

"Almost no one," the hellhound said, turning his head to look at Graythor with heavy surprise. "It isn't something most people would have the nerve to say about him, but it's true. How did *you* find out?"

"It was only a logical deduction from what you've told us," Graythor admitted, leaning slightly forward. "And your own source of information? Are you absolutely certain it's true?"

"I heard the High King talking once, when I was one of those guarding the palace," came the answer, along with an uncharacteristic sigh. "I was still a man then, and had just about decided that the life of a guardsman didn't suit me as well as it did the others. And I couldn't make myself really believe the High King had the right to do anything he cared to just because he was High King.

"It got so bad I even would have tried saving *that* female from him, but I waited too long to hand in my resignation. My section of the force was marched out of the city and into a temporary camp, and when we woke up the following day, we were as you see me now. We were told we'd been honored by the High King, and if we served him loyally and well we would be returned to the forms of men. If we didn't, we would stay hellhounds, and we didn't need to have it pointed out that there were no females of our kind. . . ."

"Which meant there was no running away and settling down elsewhere in your new form," Rik summed up, compassion clear in the words. "Either you stayed and did as you were told, or you faced an empty, lonely, painful life. Nice guy, this High King of yours, but I'd like to go back to the question of nightmares. We're not *in* a town or a city, so how can Laciel's nightmares have anything to do with the High King's spell?"

"I believe I can answer that," Graythor said when the hellhound all but shrugged. "Our friend here was attempting to get some of his own back by suggesting Laciel was half-born, I think, and merely used the nightmare incident to support his contention. You weren't suggesting it seriously, were you?"

"Not really," the hellhound admitted, his wide grin back. "I wanted to shake her up a little, but obviously she doesn't know enough about it to be properly frightened. Any woman from around here would be terrified by the suggestion, and would undoubtedly do anything she could to prove it wrong. That one just sits there staring at me with those big blue eyes, daring me to say anything at all, she couldn't care less. It makes a man *want* to shake her up a little."

"Oh, I don't know," I drawled, my return stare a little less intense than his yellow one. "I would have been much happier if you hadn't said what you did, because I got the same thing from Graythor's guess that he did, even if he did get it first. It looks like you were right after all, and for this area I *am* half-born. Isn't that so, Uncle Graythor?"

"I was hoping you'd missed that," Graythor answered with a sigh while Rik's head came up and the hellhound lost his grin. "The half-born of this world are for the most part untrained, which means their range is significantly less than yours. They would need to be *in* the town or city, while you—"

"Can feel it all the way out here," I finished when he simply shrugged. "I think we may be close to the answer to one of our questions, but I have another that's even more important." I moved my eyes back to the hellhound and said, "What did that slimy King of yours do to the small woman he probably picked up as a Chosen, the one who's currently living in his palace? Tell me if he hurt her."

"So that's who you are," our guest said quietly, all of the amusement gone from his attitude. "The friends of hers we were told would be coming, the ones every guardsman and hellhound in the kingdom is looking for. The ones who will steal away our chance to take over the rest of the world, to rule it as its masters, which we all know is our true destiny."

Those glaring yellow eyes had gone unfocused by then, and if he had started foaming I wouldn't have been in the least surprised. Rik and Graythor edged back as a deep growl began in the hellhound's throat, and it was clear the beast's body was demanding that he jump to his feet and start destroying everything in reach. His muscles spasmed as those fanged jaws opened and closed, but instead of jumping up he began rolling on the ground, fighting himself rather than someone or something else. The growling and snarling brought a chill to the warm forest afternoon, silencing the birdsong and small-animal noises for some distance around. The fight wasn't a short one, not nearly as short as the one he'd had with the bear, but slowly, slowly, he forced himself back under control. When he finally rolled to his feet and shook himself, Rik, at least, relaxed from the ready-stance he'd taken at the start of the incident.

"I hope you'll excuse that, but the High King's spells aren't easy to fight against," our guest said as he sat again, looking and sounding very tired. "It takes a lot to keep from giving in to them, but I've had more of mindless destruction than any man should be able to stomach. They didn't think I'd be able to desert my assigned prowl area either, but I managed that as well. I think you now know what sort of reception you'll get if anyone finds out who you are and why you're here."

"Talk about convincing propaganda," Rik said with a frown, slowly settling down in his original place. "Those ideas *have* to be backed by magic, which means I don't understand how you can fight it. With most spells, fighting isn't possible."

"I suspect that the High King hasn't established as total a control over Morgiana as he believes," Graythor said, still standing in the place he'd retreated to. "She must somehow be affecting the spells he formulates, making it possible to break out of them with enough determination. How that would be done I haven't any idea, but it seems the most likely explanation. Without something of the sort, resisting the spells should be virtually impossible."

"And that brings us back to my original question," I said, filing away Graythor's guess for later consideration. "If that pig is so hard on Chosen that even the idea terrifies women, what sort of thing has he been doing to Morgiana?"

"You know, I think I'm beginning to feel sorry for the High King," the hellhound commented, a faint gleam starting to fill those eyes again. "I don't know what it is about you, but you give the impression there won't be anything he can do to stop you taking vengeance on him for whatever he's done to that woman. There isn't all that much, though, not with her. She lives almost as well as he does, and he's the only one who's allowed to visit her in her apartments. No one knows why he's so careful of her, and there are those who would *like* to know, but aside from telling everyone she's necessary for the conquests we'll be making, he says nothing."

"I'd say his comment about her being necessary should be more than enough," I told him, only partially relieved to learn that Morgiana wasn't being tortured or some such. "If he could make those conquests without her, he would have done it already, so she isn't just necessary; she's downright vital. Why would that be so difficult for anyone to see?"

"Girl, you're missing the point," the hellhound objected, on the way back to grinning. "His saying she's necessary is a *joke*, we all know that. Since she's only a woman, she can't be anything like necessary, not to mention vital. And he hasn't started the conquests yet because he hasn't been High King that long. He only took the throne at the beginning of last winter, after the old High King died of the deep cough, may the Ancestors have taken him safely into Their arms. The old High King was fairly powerful and well-liked, but our new lord—he seems to have ten times the strength."

"And a tenth of the popularity, I'll wager," Graythor muttered, his brow wrinkled in thought. "Laciel, stop grinding your teeth. You should know by now what these people think of women, and their attitude may well be the only thing keeping Morgiana safe. Our friend Fillik has just said the High King has enemies, and I doubt they'd hesitate over striking at her to reach him. Even if it would do them no more than partial good."

"You're really amazingly sharp," the hellhound said to Graythor, his grin now for my companion. "Yes, the High King has acquired an unbelievably large number of enemies for the short time he's been on the throne, and no, they can't hope to replace him with one of their own. The High King *must* be a member of the royal family, otherwise the power isn't there for him. The laws permit challenges for the throne before any coronations are enacted, and the last challenges ended the way it's said they always do. No other man was able to call up the power, so Triam was crowned without opposition. But there's one point I think you and friend Addis are missing."

"What point is that?" Graythor asked, exchanging a surprised glance with Rik. The hellhound hadn't included me in on those who were missing things, but he might have been trying to ignore me.

"My conversation name is Togor," he replied, looking back and forth between the two he addressed. "You've both been calling me Fillik, which is my advanced award name and never used by anyone but myself. My first award name, Kop, is used with my trial and conversation name if someone has to call or mention me, and if I find it necessary to answer or introduce myself, I use all three names. They say Kop Togor, I answer Fillik Kop Togor, and friends simply say Togor."

"Does that mean I get to call you, 'Hey, you'?" I

asked while the others made noises of enlightenment.
"If strangers call you Kop Togor, friends call you
Togor, and no one but you calls you Fillik Kop Togor,
that doesn't leave me much of a choice."

"Why, not at all," the hellhound Togor came back,
and the gleam in his eyes had grown really bright.
"There's a very definite name for lovely little darlings
like you to call me. You call me 'sir.' "

I started to suggest something else entirely to call
him, but Rik and Graythor managed to drown me out
while they also kept me from surging to my feet. It's
hard enough to accomplish successful surging in skirts,
but when two men have their hands on you, the act
becomes impossible. During it all, that miserable hellhound just sat there chuckling, his tail going back and
forth in time with his amusement, enjoying the thought
of me trying to reach him. What I really wanted to
reach him with was one of my nastier spells, but I was
mad enough to be willing to settle for my hands.

"I'm glad to see your arm is better," Rik grunted
from my left, having gotten an elbow in the middle to
prove it before both of his arms wrapped around me.
"If you'll calm down enough to think, you'll realize
you're not likely to do him any harm even if you do
reach him. And if you don't stop trying to commit
bloody murder on *me*, I'm going to be doing some
harm of my own. If you can't take it, you shouldn't
have started up with him."

"What I can't take is stupidity in the amounts *he*
keeps showing," I snarled, glaring at the idiot hellhound. "He thinks he's so good, but he isn't even
bright enough to understand what Graythor told him.
And he has the nerve to claim it's the thing he's most
interested in."

"That's another sign that the High King's spell is
reaching her," Togor the magnificent said calmly, my
sneer in his direction doing no more than adding to his
amusement. "Nightmares at night and flights of temper during the day, both starting off relatively mild but
getting worse and worse the longer the Chosen tries to
resist going to the palace. It's hard to hide both reac-

tions and gets harder the longer it goes on, but I don't remember hearing that the spell makes them imagine things. I wasn't told anything, lovely little darling, so there's no need for me to make any claim at all."

"But you *were* told something," I pounced at once, ignoring Graythor's look of puzzlement and the rest of what the hellhound had said, at the same time shaking off Rik's loosened grip. "Graythor told you how to stop being a hellhound, and it's so obvious even a lovely little darling is able to see it. What a shame you're just too stupid to see it for yourself."

"This is a flight of temper with a vengeance," Graythor said with a scowl while our guest stiffened where he sat, all amusement gone again. "I've never seen her this tauntingly vicious, not in all the years I've known her. Rik, we'll have to see if there's anything we can do about it, but first I think Togor needs his question answered."

"Then let him answer it himself!" I snapped, furious that Graythor intended interfering. There wasn't anything wrong with me, not anything at all—or at least nothing that wouldn't be cured by seeing that hellhound laid out in neat little strips.

"Have you been watching her to be sure she's taking proper meals?" the hellhound asked suddenly, still very much on the sober side. "Once they start falling under the influence of the spell, one of the first things they do is stop eating. That takes away their strength to resist the rest of it, and then they don't *have* to be turned in by others—they turn themselves in. I keep forgetting you're strangers and don't know about these things, but every time she opens her mouth she reminds me. Even I can tell she's getting worse."

"By the EverNameless!" Graythor exclaimed over my attempt to demand just who was getting worse. "It slipped my mind completely! She hasn't eaten anything since before we arrived here, but I thought it was no more than moodiness. Laciel, do you remember we talked about that? Laciel, do you remember?"

"Of course I remember," I answered with all the vast annoyance I was feeling, especially over the way his hand gripped my arm. "You were bothering me again, just the way you usually do. And in case you didn't know it, you're hurting my arm."

"I'm trying to get your attention," he came back without apology. "Stop glaring at Togor and listen to what I'm saying. It's more than time you ate something, so I'm going to get a bowl of bread stew for you and you're going to finish it. Do you understand me?"

"Why would I eat if I'm not hungry?" I demanded, finally willing to turn my head to look at him. "Do *you* eat when you're not hungry? Does Rik? Does anyone with any intelligence? Of course they don't, so why should I?"

"Because if you don't eat it yourself, I'll feed it to you," Rik said from my left, strangely sounding half patient and half annoyed. "I'm tired of getting an argument out of you over every little thing that comes by. You have to eat whether you're hungry or not, and if you don't do it yourself, I'll do it for you. Does that answer your question?"

"You've decided to fight with me?" I asked at once, feeling both better and worse. Part of me wanted a fight with him, to show him what I could do, but another part stupidly wanted nothing to do with hurting him. "I'll try not to hurt you much," I said to quiet that stupid second part of me, "and it ought to be a lot of fun."

"Aha, now I know what her problem is," that idiot hellhound announced while Rik's face went through a series of the strangest expressions I'd ever seen. "She's *afraid* to eat that bread stew, that's what she is. *Anyone* can fight or argue, but it takes real courage to do something more. Can't you two see she'll never be talked into agreeing with you while she's still that afraid? She's only a female, after all . . ."

"Who's afraid?" I roared, trying to rise up onto my knees to reach across the fire toward that idiot. "You'll never see the day you can do something that I can't! There's nothing I'm afraid of, nothing in this whole entire universe! And I can tell you exactly what *you* are! You're a . . ."

"I'm someone who's saying you're afraid to eat that stew," he interrupted flatly, those yellow eyes picking up a glint from the fire even in daylight. "I don't have to worry about you proving me wrong by doing it, because you'll never do it. You're a small, helpless female, and you simply don't have the courage."

I was so mad I wanted to go after him with nothing but teeth and nails, but then there was a bowl of that stew there in front of me, with somebody urging me in whispers to show the fool how wrong he was. It was a really marvelous idea, so good that I grabbed the bowl and began stabbing at it with the wooden spoon, then started stuffing my face. I wasn't hungry at all, in fact I felt overfull, but I'd show that stupid hellhound just who was afraid of what.

It was the strangest thing, but the more I ate the bread stew the hungrier I became. I also suddenly noticed how good it was, and all the time I was eating there was a soft voice in my ear, urging me to fight for control, telling me not to let the spell get the better of me. For a while my mind seemed to be floating as I ate, but then things settled down to the sort of clarity I was used to, without the clouds of unreasoning irritation and rage. There was a spell that had been affecting me, and the arguments I'd gotten into with the hellhound Togor had shoved me right over the edge and fully under its influence.

". . . so you must fight hard to free yourself, Laciel, something you ought to be able to do," Graythor's voice whispered in my ear, just the way it had been doing all along. "The spell is formulated for use against the untrained, and designed by a Sighted who is only partially trained himself. Your strength is far greater than his, so you should be able to shake it off."

"I think I have, Uncle Graythor," I said with a sigh, looking down at the empty bowl in my hands. "I don't understand why I needed food to help me concentrate, but apparently it did the trick. Not to mention the fact that you did a wonderful job. Thank you, it was really delicious."

"I doubt if I've ever been happier to receive a

compliment," he answered with a wide smile, taking
the bowl from me and putting it aside. "You must
remember that you'll lose the urge to eat again, but
you mustn't let that stop you. One *does* concentrate
when one is eating, and obviously the concentration is
enough to distract from the spell. We need you free
and rational if we're to get where we must on this
world."

"Where did Rik and Togor go?" I asked, looking
around to see that we were alone at the fire. "I think I
owe Rik an apology, and as for Togor—I don't believe
he pulled me out of it after what I said to him. And
before I could tell him what he needed to know. You
or Rik should have hit me over the head with something."

"Believe me, the temptation was there," Graythor
said with a chuckle, then put a gentle hand on my
arm. "It was difficult for all of us, but most difficult
for you, I think. But you needn't worry about Togor's
not having been told what he should know. He understood the idea almost as quickly as I did once you
pointed it out, and right now is most likely off trying
to make it work."

"By fighting the spell," I said with a nod, reaching
for the cup of coffee I'd just noticed near my right
knee. "If he can fight the compulsion he's been put
under, he might also be able to best the original spell.
Did Rik go along to try to help?"

"Rik apparently felt the need for a walk in the
forest," Graythor answered, just short of a shrug. "He
left his horse, I know, so he's most likely looking for
exercise. I seriously doubt that we need to worry about
his safety."

Remembering the expressions that had crossed Rik's
face when I'd challenged him to a fight, it wasn't his
safety that I was worrying about. He'd looked very
annoyed, totally out of patience, almost downright
disgusted—in other words, just about sick and tired.
Of me. That was what I'd wanted him to be, of course,
but success was making me feel just as sick as I'd
known it would. I was also tired, to complete the
match, but it wasn't yet time to rest.

"We've learned quite a lot from our new friend, and you and I need to discuss it," Graythor said, pulling me out of unpleasantly deep thoughts to see he'd poured a cup of coffee of his own. "We now know most of the people of this world are born as twins, but not the Sighted. They're what these people call half-born, and the High King is one of them."

"All half-born may not be Sighted, but no Sighted is anything but half-born," I said, sipping my not-terribly-warm coffee. "At least, that's the impression I get. And female half-born, those who are Sighted, are called Chosen and summoned to the palace with a general-broadcast spell. After that they're never seen again, which leads me to wonder if the royal family isn't trying to cut down on the competition."

"Probably so, but that's surely not the whole of it," Graythor said, his eyes on his own coffee. "They also need ones like themselves to keep their family from losing the talent, possibly even more than they need to keep female Sighted from ordinary male Sighted. You must remember that the royal family have learned how to use their talent, whereas the ordinary Sighted have not."

"And they couldn't have learned purely by accident," I said, willing to bet on the point. "Some time in the past someone Sighted came through a gate, wondered why no one was using their talent, worked out the puzzle, then took over and settled down here. If we knew how their society was arranged before that happened, we could probably figure out the puzzle ourselves, but that's a lost cause. These people have even stopped asking themselves the obvious questions, so it must have happened a really long time ago."

"You're assuming that from the names matter," he said with a vague nod. "They earn their names by what they do, but the names must have come before the deeds at *some* time. And the fact that they compete for their adult names individually seems to be to allow those without twins a chance to do the same as those who are part of a pair, such as male half-born. But from Togor's attitude, I would say male half-born are no longer *allowed* to compete, not as thoroughly as they're looked down on. I still don't see, though, why you assume the rest."

"It's only a guess, but it *feels* so right," I said, trying to put the certainty into words. "For instance, if the natives of this world found the answer by accident and all by themselves, why hasn't more than one tiny group done it? Accidents like that tend to repeat themselves, especially with a working example in front of your face. If they had to be shown, there's a reason for no one else having joined the game, and I also think I know how they kept it a secret so long. Only one person in the royal family knows at a given time, with nothing more than the absolute basics written down for emergencies. Each King is supposed to train his successor when he gets tired of kinging, but somewhere near the beginning the thing broke down. A King was killed unexpectedly by accident, and his successor was left with nothing but the basics and no one to train him."

"Confound it, Laciel, you can't possibly know that," Graythor objected, really put out. "You're jumping from one guess to the next, with nothing concrete to base them on. Wild speculation won't get us our answers, and . . ."

"But don't you see I'm doing more than guessing?" I interrupted, gesturing with my cup and almost spilling the coffee. "How far have these people gotten with developing their strength? Judging from their spells, the answer is not very far, which doesn't make sense from the length of time they've had. They should at least have the learning of whoever taught them to begin with—unless that learning was lost early on. They had to start from the only thing they had, the bare basics, and only one person each generation or so has worked to advance their knowledge. At that rate they *couldn't* have gotten very far."

His face had clouded up to start arguing facts with me, but he didn't have any. It came to me that I might be jumping around a little too fast for someone who was used to the slow and methodical way of doing things, so I backtracked and tried to put things in order.

"Okay, okay, let's take this one point at a time," I conceded. "Can you counter the argument that some-one had to show these people what to do, otherwise more than the royal family would be exercising their talent?"

"That's not necessarily true, but I can't think of a proper argument to set against it," he grudged, not happy but trying to be reasonable. "When I think of something, I'll bring it up, but for the sake of discussion I'll temporarily grant the point."

"Good," I said with a smile. "Someone came through a gate, figured out how to make magic work, casually mentioned it to whoever happened to be standing nearby, then left this world again."

"Very well, if one is to assume a visitor from else-where, one must also assume he stayed," Graythor grumbled, trying not to laugh at the picture I'd drawn. "Even had he done as you suggested, the Sighted he told would have been able to do little or nothing with the knowledge. Merely being Sighted isn't enough."

"Using magic takes practice and knowledge, right," I agreed. "So our visitor stayed and set himself up as King, and made sure no one else found out his secret. How do you keep people from finding out your secret, Uncle Graythor?"

"The only way is to not tell anyone, Laciel child," he answered in a very slick tone of voice, showing he'd decided not to be baited any longer. "You pre-pare a sight-and-sound sealed room against the time you'll *want* to share the secret, but until then you keep everything to yourself. And chances are excellent that the one who was killed unexpectedly was this visitor himself."

"Your reasoning, sir?" I demanded with mock fero-ciousness, loving, as always, to work with someone as wonderfully quick as Graythor.

"It's quite simple, child," he replied in a very superior, very educated way. "If he had continued to live, those around him would have known certain things were possible even if they didn't know how to accomplish them. Longer lifetimes, for instance, and spells to ward off sickness and cure wounds. The 'old' High King died of a disease, and no one considered it strange or bemoaned his untimely loss. I heard that in what Togor said just as you did, but it meant less to me than it obviously did to you."

"Which gives me the blue ribbon for finding things to back up my wild assumptions, but still leaves us short," I said, resisting the urge to slump where I sat. "We probably now know how things got this way, and have also convinced ourselves we'll never find the magic answer by accident. What we still don't have is a way to find it on purpose."

"And the one person who has the answer will never tell anyone but his heir," Graythor gloomed in agreement. "What we do have on our side is a knowledge of magic greater than anyone on this world, and likely even greater than the one who originally came here. If he found the answer, surely we can do the same."

"If we could just get the least little hint," I fretted, beginning to be annoyed. "What about this twins business? If everything normally comes in sets of two, maybe you need two people working at once. Don't forget what Togor said about the new King being 'ten times as strong' as the old King. That has to mean he's using Morgiana's strength, and teaming up may be the way he does it."

"That's an excellent idea, Laciel, excellent," Graythor enthused, putting his cup aside in his excitement. "And if we presuppose the presence of an outsider, we can also assume that the language of spells is being used. Let's try it now."

"Something simple, like lifting your cup," I suggested, catching his eagerness to a small extent. The idea still felt the least bit off, but exactly how I didn't know. "We can use the standard learning exercise, since we both know that precisely."

"But not too precisely," he said with a small laugh, meaning, of course, that the spell wasn't as involved as it could be. The more you learned, the more you Saw;

the more you Saw, the more you described; the more you described, the better control and greater strength you were able to bring to bear. Practice spells were very simple, since they were designed to be used by those just beginning to learn. Graythor and I could speak one of them together without worrying if one or the other of us would put in more. We looked at each other, took individual deep breaths, then spoke the short, simple spell.

And afterward watched the cup continue to sit there.

"So it's back to square one," I said for both of us, not as disappointed as Graythor probably was. "I have the feeling we're close, but close in which direction? I'd hate to find out we had all the necessary information, but just weren't seeing it."

"Better than not having it and ready to see all," Graythor grunted as he stood, looking tired and depressed. "If we do have the key, we'll soon find the lock to match it to. Would you like another cup of coffee?"

"No, I think I'd prefer a bath," I said, moving the skirts out of my way before getting to my feet. "That pool is cold, which means it's being fed and refreshed by an underground spring or something, so I shouldn't be ruining our water source. And I'll even walk around to the far side, just to show my heart's in the right place."

"I consider it more important for our surroundings that your body be in the right place," he came back, glancing at me before turning toward the wagon. "I'll draw what water we'll need before you bathe, and that way walking to the far side of the pool will be unnecessary. You'll bathe as close to our camp as possible and won't be overlong in doing it. The fact that we have no soap should speed your efforts to a great extent."

"No soap!" I echoed in a yelp. "Uncle Graythor, how could you forget the soap?"

"If I'd tried putting everything conceivable into my spell, I'd still be beyond the gate speaking it," he returned, not in the least bothered. "Be grateful I included a small amount of bar silver and gold, which should allow us to buy what we need in that town just ahead. If InThig hasn't returned by the morning, we'll rely on Togor's guidance in the ways of the natives. I have the very strong feeling we need to experience these people in proper numbers before the answer we seek will have any chance of coming to us."

He took the two water barrel buckets and went toward the pool, leaving me with something to think about. Graythor was getting feelings about that world just as I was, but they weren't the same feelings. Did that mean both of us were right, neither of us, or maybe just one of us? If only one of us, then which one? If we were both wrong, what did we have left? And if we were both right, then—I had no idea what it meant. That place was making me dizzy in more ways than one.

I went into the wagon to rummage around, but there were no drying cloths to match no soap. A few of the compartments underneath and above the bed areas refused to open for me, and that was annoying; Uncle Graythor had things he didn't want little Laciel getting into, which probably included a supply of the kind of clothes I'd tried demanding. I felt a very strong urge to break into those closed compartments, but I couldn't find anything to do the breaking with and I really did want that bath. Muttering nasty things under my breath I appropriated an extra blanket, then carried it out of the wagon and to the pool.

Graythor was busy pouring water into our water barrel when I came out, so I didn't disturb him. Instead I walked in among the bushes and trees around the pool, then moved left away from the part of it that was easily accessible from the camp. I didn't know why he was suddenly so worried about my safety, but between him and Rik—and even Togor—I was beginning to feel claustrophobic. I knew the forest could be dangerous—that bear had made the point perfectly clear—but I had no interest in bathing in the middle of our camp.

I stopped at a point where the bushes came right up to the edge of the pool, put the blanket down, then began getting out of my clothes. It felt like it had been months since the last time I'd bathed, and even though I knew it hadn't been, I couldn't wait to get into the water. While I'd been growing up, swimming had been a warm-weather luxury, and it had taken me quite a while in Morgiana's house to learn that bathing was even better than swimming—and not only allowed but expected. I could still remember how Morgiana had laughed when Yallah had complained to her about my taking four baths in one day. . . .

I put a bare foot into the water to reestablish the temperature I needed to expect, then sat at the edge of the pool before sliding in. The water was colder than I normally liked and the air wasn't quite as warm as it had been when I'd had all those clothes on, but there was nothing I could do to change any of it. Even if I spoke a spell, it wouldn't work, and the frustration of that was really beginning to get to me. I wanted to beat at everyone and everything around me, force them to do as I demanded—

I used a shallow dive to take all of me underwater, and when I reached the surface again I was mostly back in control. That broadcast spell was tearing my temper into shreds and tatters, and even I was willing to admit my temper couldn't afford it. There must have been a reason for doing that to female Sighteds, but for the life of me I couldn't figure out what. What possible benefit could there be in having one of us lose her temper, even in the matter of identification? There were so many other emotions that could be used for purposes of self-betrayal, so why anger?

All those questions were doing nothing more than adding to my frustration, so I forced myself to forget about them and concentrate on swimming. The pool was deep and wide enough for enjoyment, and despite the coldness of the water I was determined to have that fun. I used both hands to wipe the water clear of my face, then began swimming across the pool to the far side. The water was a fresh dark green, shaded by the trees all around and therefore kept from being crystal—

The big body rose up in front of me so suddenly that

I nearly cried out, and my first thought was that I was being attacked again by one of those stupid forest dwellers. I hit at whatever-it-was and tried to swim away, but two wide arms had wrapped around me and my efforts at self-defense were being laughed at in a low, deep voice. My second idea was that it was Rik who was playing mindless games, but by then I was able to see water-darkened blond hair and was able to tell something else as well. It answered a few questions, first among them who this intruder was.

"So you managed to overcome the hellhound spell," I told the man who was Togor, ignoring his laughter. "Now if you can just do something about that other spell, you should be completely back to normal."

"I've only overcome the hellhound spell temporarily," he answered, tossing his head to get water and wet hair out of his eyes. "If I don't exert every ounce of will I have, I'll be right back under it, but this is better than nothing and I wanted you to be the first to know. But what's this about another spell?"

"That should be obvious," I said, very aware of the fact that his arms were still around me. "There must be another spell that's wiped out even the memory of good manners in you, or you would have let your news wait until I'd finished my bath. Now, if you don't mind, I'd like you to go away until I am finished."

"Oh, but I do mind," he said with a grin, his broad, rugged face very close to mine. "I felt the draw of you even when I was a hellhound, and now that I'm a man again—however temporarily—I'm not about to let an opportunity like this be wasted. My hellhound body would hardly be able to appreciate it the way this one can."

"I'm here to take a bath, not give you opportunities," I snapped, feeling my cheeks redden even as I pushed at him. "It's too bad you don't come from where I do. You would have learned a long time ago not to try taking advantage of a woman even if you *are* Sighted."

"By the long-fingered hands of my First Ancestor!" he said, mostly surprised but partly annoyed. "You have the nerve to call me a half-born even after what I told you about my family? Haven't you any idea what an insult most men consider that?''

"Now that makes sense," I said, seeing the point at once. "Female Sighteds are culled from the general population, and male Sighteds are made to feel like less than men. If they don't take pride in being what they are, they're bound to make less trouble for the royal family. But that doesn't really apply to you. You know you're Sighted, and it doesn't make you feel inferior."

"Woman, you can't possibly justify that with anything but guesswork," he accused, and now the annoyance was growing. "If I were half-born the way you claim, there would be no way for you to know it, and even beyond that, no way for you to know my feelings in the matter. You're striking out in all directions in the hope of reaching vitals, but all you've struck is empty air."

"I think you know better than that," I said with some of the satisfaction I felt over having been partially released, continuing to tread water. "I couldn't tell when you were a hellhound, but now I can feel the presence of your talent. It explains why you've been successful in fighting those spells, even to the not-quite-full extent that you have. We tend to know each other, we who are Sighted, and the more strength we have, the harder it is for one of our own to hide from us. You knew this could happen, but you came here anyway."

"Is that why you believe I'm not ashamed of being what you accuse me of?" he asked, and his very light eyes looked directly at me. "Isn't it possible I knew nothing of what you claim I knew, and am no more than a victim of your overactive imagination?"

"You're more interested in making *me* the victim," I said with a snort, pushing my wet hair back with one hand. "You probably decided you could distract me if I did notice, and if the distraction didn't work, you could then try calling on kinship. Only someone who *wasn't* ashamed would react the way you've been doing,

so don't expect any apologies from me over having
insulted you. And whatever it is you're after, you can
just forget about it. I don't make a very good victim."

"But I don't want to forget about what I'm after,"
he said with a sudden grin, those arms pulling me
close to him again. "You're an absolute handful and a
half, little darling, and you draw me like sweets draw a
child. You're bright and sassy and ready to give as
good as you get, and other women are pale shadows in
comparison. I want a taste of you, and I usually get
what I want."

"Not this time, you don't," I began in a snarl, but
one of his hands came to tangle in my hair, and then
he was kissing me as if I belonged to him. I fought to
get loose, struggled to break away, but his strength
was as impossible as Rik's and as hard to escape.
Water splashed gently all around and eventually lapped
up to our noses, and that was what finally made him
let me go.

"Yes, very definitely a tasty taste," he said with a
soft laugh, still holding my arms. "You'll probably try
attacking me when I talk your uncle into giving you to
me, but I'll consider it worth it. It's about time you
had a real man in your life, a man like yourself, not
one like that Rik who lets you walk all over him. I'll
teach you to love me, and then you'll know what being
happy really means."

What he'd said was so outrageously ridiculous, all I
could do was stare at him with my mouth open. Of all
the idiotic, overconfident, *mindless* people in uncounted
numbers of worlds, Fillik Kop Togor had to be close
to the top of the list. He wasn't even able to maintain
himself in his true body yet, but all his plans were set
and his mind made up. And most bizarre of all, it
looked like his intentions were *honorable!*

"You can't talk my uncle into giving me to you," I
said at last, using that as the first item of argument on
my list. "He doesn't have the right to give me away
without my agreement, and wouldn't even if he did
have the right. I'm the only one who gets to decide
when it's time for a man in my life, and when the time

comes I'll say so. As for my walking all over Rik, that's the most ridiculous thing I've ever heard. I . . ."

"The hell it's ridiculous," Togor interrupted, his grin completely unchanged. "I've heard how he talks to you, how he tries to reason you into doing as he says, and all you do in return is divert him into arguments he had no intention of getting involved in. He knows—or *should* know—it can mean your life if you do the wrong thing out here, but he still lets you get away with not listening to him. You'll never find *me* caring that little about you."

"Whether or not what I do risks my life isn't the point," I countered, ignoring how tired I was beginning to feel from treading water so long. "The point is that it's *my* life, and if I want to risk it—or even throw it away—you have no say in the matter. No one has the right to tell me how to live, and that goes for you and Rik and Graythor and every other being who ever lived. Just because Rik is learning that doesn't mean he's being walked over."

"He may be learning something, but not what *you* think he is," Togor countered my counter, the look in his light eyes now sharper. "You may believe that what you do with your life is no one's business but your own, but that only holds true for someone who lives entirely alone. When you live and associate with other people, what happens to you affects them as well. If you throw your life away for no reason you're not just hurting yourself, you're also causing *them* anguish. Only the most selfish of small children will cause pain to those who care about them without giving it a second thought, and small children need to be taught better. If the same was done to them, they'd resent it bitterly."

For some reason I couldn't think of an immediate answer to that, but it did give me the opportunity to notice that I'd had enough of swimming for one day. I pulled out of his loosened grip and headed back toward the bank where I'd left the blanket and my clothes, but apparently hellhounds weren't satisfied with having only a single last word.

"Of course, some small children let themselves get hurt in order to *punish* those who care about them," Togor said, needing only two long strokes to be swimming right beside me. "They haven't been allowed to get their own way, or they were punished for doing something foolish, so they hurt themselves to make those around them sorry. The only problem with that little ploy is that it can't be used too often. If it is, the people around the child get to the point of being too sick and tired to care *what* happens to her. Trying to show they care becomes a boring waste of time, and after that they simply stop trying."

I really didn't know what point he thought he was making, and I was too anxious to be out of the water to care. The air had gotten a lot cooler and the water temperature hadn't warmed much from the time I'd first gotten into it, and the thought of a nice warm blanket to wrap up in sounded really good.

"But sometimes there are those around who care more than a little about the child," Togor persisted, grabbing my arm as we reached the bank together. "They know the child is unhappy and want to help the child, but first they have to let the child know she really means something to them. Once they do that, they can help her with her unhappiness, but first they have to show her how much they care. The best first step in accomplishing that is to not let her hurt herself any longer."

"Let go of my arm," I said, holding to the bank with both hands and not looking at him. "I want to get out of the water, so let go of me."

"I felt you calling to me even when I wore the shape of a hellhound," Togor said softly, his fingers refusing to loosen. "I've never before felt this way with a woman, and I've never met one with your strength. The man Graythor knows you need a man to care for you and make you happy, so when he finds out the laws allow him to arrange that for you, I don't think he'll hesitate. The other, Rik—if he isn't already beyond caring, he's not far from reaching that point. In a very short while, you'll no longer have to be concerned with him. And now I agree with you—it *is* time to get out of this water. Ladies first."

As soon as his grip disappeared from my arm, I levered myself up onto the bank, needing to get it done before he decided to help me. Standing up, reaching for the blanket, and swirling it around me was accomplished in almost the same motion, and huddling into it felt almost as good as I'd thought it would. I ignored the splash of another body coming up out of the water, but when I heard a flurry of determined and vigorous shaking I thought I knew what had happened. I turned to find that I was right, and Togor stood there back in his hellhound form.

"I suppose it's for the best that I couldn't hold my true shape any longer," the hellhound said with a grin that showed lots of pointy fangs. "I don't have any clothes for that other body, and fighting you for possession of that blanket would be very undignified. Will you do me the honor of being my dinner partner tonight? If I can't find any clothes, I'll borrow a blanket of my own."

Rather than answer him, I picked up my dirty outfit and crumpled it all into the crook of one arm, then ran for the wagon.

CHAPTER 14

I lay unmoving on the bed for quite some time, the curtain-blanket pulled all the way closed, my body curled up in the blanket I'd used as a drying cloth. I hadn't wanted to think about what Togor had said, but the words kept coming back to me again and again, refusing to let me thrust them away. The bed was soft and comfortable and the area was dark with the curtain closed and the lamp unlit, but I hadn't fallen asleep the way I'd hoped I would. Even nightmares

would have been better than what I was then going
through, but I couldn't manage to make the trade.

Was I really so horribly self-centered that I gave
pain to the people around me without knowing it or
even caring? Is that what I'd really been doing with
my ideas of living my own life, simply hurting the
people who cared for me? Was I trying to hurt everyone else because I'd been hurt, trying to punish everyone for what my parents—whoever they were—had
done to me? Was it possible Yallah had been right in
trying to stop me, to get even for all the terrible things
I'd done?

I could feel a lock of still-damp hair under my right
cheek, but I couldn't gather the necessary determination to raise my head and brush it away. Of all the
things Togor had said, what had hit me hardest was
the part about Rik. I'd been trying so hard to destroy
his interest in me, but now that it looked like I'd been
completely successful I didn't know if I could stand it.
It wasn't right to want him near me, not when being
that close could cost him his life, but to never have his
arms around me again, to never have him kiss me the
way he did—

If it was right, why did it have to hurt so much?
Why didn't it feel good instead, the way things that
were right *should* feel? Why were the tears rolling
down my cheeks, a gesture of good-bye that I simply
couldn't bear?

All I had was question after question, a long procession without a following cavalcade of answers. The
only thing I knew was that I *was* being selfish about
Rik, begrudging the pain it cost me to keep him safe.
He'd be so much better off when he left me for good,
and Togor had said he wasn't far from doing exactly
that. When it did happen, I would be so happy for
him, so very, very happy—

But I couldn't make the silent tears stop.

I first realized that it had gotten dark when a knock
came on the wood beside my bed area, and Graythor's
voice told me our meal was ready. Eating was almost
the last thing I was interested in doing, but if I didn't

eat, that stupid spell would jump on me again, and I'd end up arguing and fighting with everyone in reach. Arguing was something else I didn't want to do any longer, and maybe not ever again. You hurt people when you argued with them, and I'd caused enough harm.

I found a clean outfit to put on, what looked like a dark blue skirt and beige tunic in the dimness of the wagon aisle, and then went out to join the others. There were two people sitting near the fire, and both of them rose to their feet just as I reached them.

"Laciel, child, look who's come back from exploring the woods," Graythor said, pointing to the other side of the fire. "Your cat, InThig, and after we'd decided he must be lost or eaten."

"She doesn't seem to care much for me," Togor said with a chuckle as I looked to see that a miniature InThig really was lying down on the far side of the fire, eyes mostly closed. "She won't come anywhere near me, but I suppose that's understandable. Once I'm permanently back to being a man, I can try making friends with her. Cats used to like me."

I wanted very much to be near InThig right then, but when I took a step with the intention of circling the fire, a hand closed on my arm to make the first step the last.

"Come and sit between Graythor and me, Laciel," Togor said, his tone gently urging. "We waited the meal for you, and it will be easier for all of us to serve ourselves if we're sitting near one another."

I hesitated very briefly, but the request was too reasonable to make a fuss over. Togor, I saw, had managed to borrow a tunic and trousers in different shades of brown, but apparently there were no extra pairs of boots. He stood barefoot without obvious discomfort, and it struck me that he might be the least bit larger than Rik. As I moved to the place between him and Graythor I looked around again, and the wizard caught the action.

"I saw Rik very briefly a few hours ago, but he must have gone back to the woods," Graythor said, he and

Togor waiting until I was sitting before taking their own places to either side of me. "I can't imagine what he's doing out there after dark, but I'm sure he's all right. When I caught that glimpse of him earlier, he seemed distracted."

"You look distracted yourself, little darling," Togor said, this time not sounding very pleased. "Your hair's a solid tangle, and it still feels damp. The weather isn't warm enough for you to be walking around with damp hair after dark. We don't want you getting sick."

His big hand had touched my hair, and I remembered then that I hadn't stopped to brush it. It didn't matter in the least, of course, not with Rik off being "distracted." He was undoubtedly trying to find a way of telling me I could forget about being his wife, which was the best thing that could happen. Not only didn't he need to be put in danger, he also had no need whatsoever for a female Sighted who walked all over him.

Graythor had prepared the birds Rik had caught earlier in the day, and along with a mixed vegetable dish the meal was very tasty. The only thing I found odd was the local version of table manners Togor guided us into, with me being the only one who was allowed to reach for things. Graythor and Togor had to wait until I got things like bowls and servings and slices of bread to them, but Togor was the one who poured the wine. Graythor wouldn't have provided anything but the finest vintage, but drinking it out of a clay cup took some of the pleasure out of it. I ate the delicious food I didn't want and drank the excellent wine that tasted flat, and paid only token attention to the occasional conversation going past me.

"Yes, there's no doubt about it," Togor said when his meal was swallowed, leaning back with his cup of wine. "There's no doubt you can pass as a master cook looking for hire at the palace, Graythor my friend. Once they get a taste of what you can do, you'll be lucky if they don't chain you in the kitchens."

"Is there really a danger of that?" Graythor asked, sounding worried. "I'm sure to need the freedom of the city and palace, and being confined would be more than awkward."

"No, there's no danger, I was only joking," Togor answered with a chuckle. "You have to remember that people want to be able to eat what a master cook produces, and if they get him annoyed or upset, they might not be able to. You can use slaves to serve your food, but not to cook it."

"And there should be no difficulty with my claiming to come from the village of Erbno?" Graythor pursued, still sounding bothered. "What if someone else from Erbno works at the palace, and tries to talk to me about the place?"

"Erbno is so close to the border into the next kingdom, most of the people there find the trip to Triam's city too long to be worth making," Togor reassured him. "If you do run into someone from there, you have two options on how to behave. Either you tell them you left the village at a very young age and therefore no longer remember it, or you look down your nose at them and don't speak to them at all. Master cooks are expected to act like the High King himself, so no one will get suspicious if you treat underlings like dirt."

"I think I'll do best keeping myself aloof from everyone," Graythor decided, his tone musing. "Making friends means sharing confidences at some point, and that would cause nothing but trouble. I'll certainly enjoy the cooking I'll be doing, but I won't enjoy having questions put to me that I can't answer. We'll only have a short while to look around in Avden tomorrow, and from that we'll have to draw a thorough understanding of how the natives of this world behave."

"Especially Laciel," Togor agreed, sounding fractionally more serious. "If she continues to be able to hold off the effects of the Chosen spell, she should be all right on that count, but she really must learn how women are expected to act. If she doesn't, she can't go with you when you apply at the palace, and I'm not sure she should in any case. They might find her a place as a maid just to please *you,* but they mostly employ slaves in the palace and there could be misunderstandings."

"Which would promptly turn into wars," Graythor said, the words faintly weary. "But if I don't take her to the palace with me, we won't be able to work on the problem together, and the suggestion also raises the question of where I *would* leave her. She certainly can't be left alone, not even with InThig. To keep her company, that is."

The hastily added words reminded me that InThig was being kept a secret from Togor, and even though I didn't know the reason for it, I considered it a good idea. All our plans and plots were suddenly coming from the hellhound, and if he turned out to be something other than what he claimed, we could find ourselves in need of a secret weapon. The food I'd stuffed down had begun making me feel a little better, but going from zero to one or two on a scale of a hundred doesn't mean much in the way of improvement.

"If you like, you can leave Laciel with me," Togor suggested casually, the words no more than warm and friendly. "I know a place in the city where we can stay, not too far from the palace, so you'd still be able to meet with her on a regular basis. You have my word that I'll take good care of her and keep her out of trouble, so . . ."

"No," I said before Graythor could accept that idea along with the rest, probably startling the two men. I kept my eyes on the fire the way I'd been doing all along, but I'd stopped listening and started participating. "If it isn't smart for me to go into the palace with Graythor, then I won't go, but I don't have to be 'left' with anyone, most especially if the anyone is you. We'll work out something else."

"There aren't too many other choices," Togor said, his voice still smooth and very, very reasonable. "Women in the city are either slave or free, and if they're free, they're always under a man's protection. Father, uncle, brother, husband—they have to have a man there and directing them, or questions are asked.

Since the wrong answers too often turn the free woman into a slave, it isn't smart taking unnecessary chances."

"We'll be taking enough of a chance simply going into the city," Graythor said, adding another voice of reason. "Since Togor is in this with us, it doesn't make sense not listening to his advice or taking advantage of his presence. We're here for an important purpose, Laciel, and if our personal preferences need to be temporarily sacrificed, we won't find it too high a price for eventual success."

"*Eventual* success," I echoed with a sigh, wishing there was another way out of that mess as I turned my head to look at Graythor. "He's already got you believing this is going to take more than a little time, but it *can't* take long or we've all had it. If the High King gets around to setting *Morgiana* on watch for us, the game is over then and there. Please tell him we're not interested in his offer, Uncle Graythor."

"I'm sorry, Togor, but I'm afraid I have to agree with Laciel," Graythor said, and he wasn't just throwing around words with no meaning. I'd pushed belief at him with every ounce of strength I had, and the Persuasion was *making* him go along with me. I'd also given him a good reason for agreeing, but that didn't mean I was pleased with what I'd done.

"Her point is a valid one, and we can't afford to ignore it," Graythor went on to a very surprised, currently-human hellhound. "You've told us there are guardsmen on the lookout for us, but guardsmen can be avoided or fooled. If the High King begins thinking of magic in terms of defense instead of simply for offense, he'll realize Morgiana can be used to detect us no matter where we are or what we look like. We *must* do what we came to do as quickly as possible, or chances are excellent that we won't be able to do it at all."

"And none of us can do anything until you two come up with the answer to your problem," Togor said with a sigh of resignation, those light eyes doing no more than glancing at me. "Very well, I can see where you can't afford to be separated right now, but the situation could change in some way. If it does and the girl's safety is at stake, I'd like to have your word that you'll give her to me."

"You have it," Graythor said, too fast for my shouted, "No!" to interfere. "Her safety is my primary concern, and you know that as well, Laciel. I've given my word now, so the matter is closed. Argument would be a waste of both your time and mine."

He raised his cup for a refill from the wine bottle, and Togor gave it to him after giving me a very pleased grin. The hellhound had caught me off-guard by pretending to be beaten, and now he thought he had what he wanted. He was looking at me as though I was already caught and caged, but he had a long way to go before that came anywhere close to happening.

The two men exchanged a few more words worth of conversation, but after that Graythor emptied his cup and put it aside, then rose to his feet.

"The thought of bed sounds good to me right now, so I'll bid you two a pleasant night," he said, all but stretching and yawning where he stood. "Togor, you're welcome to the fourth bed in the wagon if you decide to use it."

"I won't be able to hold this shape long enough to appreciate the comfort," the hellhound answered with a smile and a headshake. "Once I'm back in that other form I won't need to sleep either, so a bed would be a complete waste. What I'll do is watch Laciel take care of these dishes, and then find a place to stand guard while the rest of you sleep."

"Laciel doesn't need to take care of those dishes," Graythor said, and this time he did yawn. "By morning they'll be perfectly clean and ready to be used again. Magic is useful in many ways, Togor, not just for conquest."

He chuckled as he headed for the wagon, and I couldn't help wondering why he was leaving me alone with a man who was the next thing to a stranger. If that was Graythor's idea of being concerned about my safety, it was a good thing I could take care of myself.

"Well, I think it's also time for *me* to turn in," I

announced to no one in particular, then began moving my skirts out of the way. Togor had been sitting there just looking at me, and I could feel his stare even without turning my head to see it. I don't like being stared at, especially not by overgrown hellhounds, and most especially not when they aren't in hellhound form.

"Aren't you going to congratulate me?" the object of my thoughts asked, at the same time taking my left hand. "I've gotten your uncle to agree to giving you to me, so it's just a matter of time. And you were so sure it couldn't be done."

"Since I haven't been given to you *yet,* I'd say I was right," I answered, reluctant to look at him but not about to hesitate and let him know it. "You got an 'if' out of Graythor, not a 'yes,' and that makes all the difference. Not to mention the fact that you still haven't gotten a 'yes' out of me."

"Your 'yes' will come later, once you've been mine for a while," he said, the smile in his light eyes matching the one on his face. "You'll be a delight for me, lovely darling, and I'll be absolutely magnificent for you. You're a beautiful, desirable woman, and it's about time someone treated you like it."

"But what if I don't want you to be that someone?" I asked, finding it impossible to keep the question unspoken. "What if I want to look around for a while yet, or have already found someone I like better? What gives you the right to try forcing yourself on me?"

"I'm not trying to force myself on you," he answered with a laugh, briefly kissing the hand he held captive. "I've decided we'll make a wonderfully happy couple, and what I'm trying to do is get started with it. Don't you *want* to be happy?"

"Of course I want to be happy," I answered in exasperation. "Everybody wants to be happy, but that doesn't answer my . . ."

"Then if you want to be happy, why are you squirming around so hard trying to keep it from happening?" he pursued, the fire glinting in his very light eyes.

"The sooner you settle down and accept what I'm doing, the sooner I'll be able to make you happy. That's simple enough for anyone to understand, so I don't know why you're having trouble with it."

"I'm *not* having trouble," I fumed, hating the way he kept kissing my hand. "I just don't happen to think you're the man who *can* make me happy. And besides that . . ."

"How do you know?" he demanded in a mild but firmer way, his stare refusing to let me go. "How do you know I'm not the man who can make you happy? I say I am, and my opinion's at least as good as yours and most people would consider it better. How many men have you known really well? And I mean *really* well?"

"Why—that's none of your business," I faltered, feeling the heat move into my cheeks again. "It's also a question no man with the least amount of good manners would . . ."

"In other words, almost none," he said flatly, nodding his head in a knowing way. "I'd tell you how many women *I've* known really well, but I'm not trying to brag or discuss something that will embarrass you. All you need to know is that I never before decided I could make a woman happy, but with you I have. And I will. Struggle if it pleases you, but that won't change anything. As soon as you're mine, I'm going to make you happy. Now I think it's time for you to go to bed."

He got to his feet, then took both of my hands to pull me to mine, and I hadn't the slightest idea of what had hit me. I knew something had hit me and it must have been about the size of the wagon from the way it had left me stunned and dazed, but I couldn't remember seeing it go past. I was trying to decide if I actually felt as strange as the path my thoughts were following, but we reached the back of the wagon in just a few steps and Togor interrupted the rambling.

"If you dream of me, the nightmares won't be able to touch you," he said softly, putting his arms around me and drawing me close. "'And I want you to dream of me, and of the delight you're going to give me. Making you happy will be no effort at all."

He used the fingers of one hand to raise my face to him, and then he kissed me in the same way he had that afternoon. The kiss was gentle but very possessive, and I was too confused to try fighting him again. It was probably because of that that I noticed the—draw—I felt from his kiss, the need to return what I was getting, the desire for more. I finally found out what it meant to experience something that made your head swim; when he ended the kiss, I had to lean against him for a moment until it went away.

"And tomorrow I expect to see your hair neatly combed," he said when I was just about back to myself, his tone stern but his stroking hand gentle on the hair he discussed. "A woman as all-around marvelous as you has no business demeaning herself in any way at all, and especially not in a way so easily corrected. I don't want the world considering you as less for even a single moment. Is that clearly understood?"

All I could do at that point was nod, but it seemed to be enough. He patted my shoulder and then helped me up the steps, but by the time I turned for a last look at him, he was striding away toward the woods, already pulling off the tunic he wore. In another minute or two he would be back to having the body of a hellhound, and for some reason I didn't want to see that. I walked very slowly to my bunk bed, barely registering the fact that the lamp had been lit on the wall over it, and sank down to sit numbly with my head empty of thought.

In a year or a century or even a minute or two a flash of black went past my almost unseeing eyes, and then a chuckle sounded along with the plopping down of a small, furry body.

"My, my, what a charming flush I see on some young lady's cheeks," InThig said in a smooth purr. "She hasn't had much experience with being escorted home by a gentleman who needs no chaperoning, but apparently that lack is in the process of being corrected."

"What are you talking about?" I asked, fighting to

make sense out of words that nevertheless made me blush even harder. "InThig, I don't understand what happened."

"He took you in hand is what happened," the demon said in a very satisfied way, bringing a long tail around to its right to curl into a 6. "Graythor told me he thought you needed to get to know more men, and that this Togor would be really good for you. I was surprised when he out-argued you, but when he simply kissed you and then walked away, I was actually both shocked and delighted. True gentlemen are a vanishing breed, and I hadn't expected to come across one at the very end of the worlds of civilization."

"Is *that* why Graythor left us alone?" I asked, putting one hand to my head. "To give me the chance to get to know more men? But that doesn't make any sense. He wouldn't do that with Rik still around."

"Well—maybe he—thought Rik needed the competition," InThig groped, suddenly sounding a lot less pleased. "Yes, he thought he needed the competition, so— No, that doesn't work very well, does it? With Rik gone off into the woods somewhere, encouraging that Togor is tantamount to sneaking around behind Rik's back. Graythor is much too fair-minded to do something like that, so there must be another explanation."

"Which I might be able to come up with if my mind wasn't stopped dead," I muttered, then forced myself to look at the small, black cat-body. "InThig, talk to me and keep talking to me, make me listen to you no matter what you have to do. I've got to get rid of this mush in my head, and I've got to do it now."

InThig had no real idea about what was going on—as opposed to me, who saw everything with the clarity of rock—but it didn't try asking me all sorts of silly questions. Well, it *did* ask me all sorts of silly questions, but they were the kind that pulled me out of the fog rather than driving me deeper into it. I had to search my memory to answer the questions InThig asked, and after a frightening number of minutes I was able to tell I'd pulled out far enough to start thinking about more pressing subjects.

"Like what I was hit with," I said aloud, then turned to the glaring red eyes watching me so anxiously. "You do realize I was run over, don't you? Like the way a stampede runs over whatever happens to be in its way?"

"Laciel, if you don't want me to call Graythor, the least you can do is lie down for a while," InThig answered, obviously thinking I was still out of it. In a way the demon was absolutely right, but what it had wrong was the direction.

"InThig, he used something like Rik's Persuasion on me, and I'm willing to bet he used it first on Graythor," I said in explanation, one I hoped would calm my currently only friend. "I don't know if he can reach you as well as us, but frankly I'd rather not find out. You couldn't tell that's what he was doing to me? It didn't make you the least suspicious?"

"I—think I enjoyed his arguments too well to notice their lack of true convincing power," InThig admitted, blazing red eyes no longer looking directly at me. "He forced his own direction in the discussion while refusing to allow you yours, and the intentions he expressed were extremely attractive for me since they were being expressed to you. You *do* need a man who's determined to make you happy, you know, so—"

"So you decided this would be a lovely place for me to settle down," I finished when InThig didn't, almost too disgusted to stand it. "If all of you would just forget about my love life for five minutes and concentrate on the reason we're here, we could be out of here with Morgiana in no time flat."

"I would say that's exaggerating things a tad," InThig answered, but its sigh was a form of agreement. "What isn't exaggeration is our urgent need to know why Togor is doing what he is, why he's manipulating you and Graythor and possibly even our rescue attempt. Do you believe he's secretly working for the High King?"

"I don't know," I answered, closing the blanket

curtain and then taking the two quickly-appearing fluffy pillows to lean back against. "If he was he should have reported us already, and he does seem to have a legitimate problem. If he hates being a hellhound as much as he says, and something tells me he isn't lying, he *has* to be against the High King. If he was working for him instead, turning us in would earn him any reward he cared to name—like being permanently made a man again."

"But his being a King's agent does remain a possibility," InThig said with a distracted nod. "If he isn't, he's found another game to play, one which involves our plans and you in particular. Do you believe he's sincere in what he said to you?"

"I haven't any idea, but I sure as hell hope not," I said with the shudder I couldn't hold down, wrapping my arms around myself. "That kindly-but-firm way he has—with the sort of Persuasion he has backing it up, he walks all over me and I can't do a thing to stop him. I even get to the point of not wanting to stop him. If he ever did get me, I'd spend the rest of my life doing exactly as he said—and not even hating it."

"I think I've suddenly become incapable of understanding the language," InThig muttered, closing its eyes and giving a hard headshake. "I could have sworn you said you wouldn't hate it."

"Maybe I should have said he wouldn't let me hate it," I clarified, feeling the need to shudder again. "He'd make me enjoy the slavery he kept me in, but it would still be slavery. As long as it wasn't *my* decision that kept me with him, that's all it could ever be. The only real, true happiness involved would be his, and no one has the right to do that to someone else."

"He may not have the right, but he certainly seems to have the ability," InThig grumbled, shifting around to lie on its side. "How are we going to keep you and Graythor away from him, short of having me shred him into confetti? If it turns out he *isn't* working for the High King, he could be very valuable to us."

"Now that I know what he's doing, I'm hoping it won't work on me again," I said, pulling forward a bedraggled strand of my hair to fiddle with. "Graythor is another matter, and I don't think telling him what's being done will help. It didn't help keep him free of *my* influence, and that's a possible weapon I have to keep in mind. If Togor can work on me maybe I can do the same to him, using Rik's ability the way I did with you and Graythor. Truthfully, I was saving that as a last-ditch defense against the man, but I think I've gotten to the last ditch sooner than I expected to."

"But the question remains as to whether the ability will work against someone who also has the ability," InThig just had to point out, ruining my evening even more than had already been done. "You weren't able to affect Rik, you'll recall, but possibly that was only because you would have been using his own ability on him. Togor's ability and Rik's don't appear precisely the same, so it might work after all."

"Something better work, or I'm an absolute goner," I pronounced very firmly, then let myself get on to another point of fretting. "And speaking of Rik, where the hell is he? I don't believe he's simply out there wandering around enjoying the scenery, not at this time of night. He wouldn't have missed dinner and left us alone for so long—unless something happened to him."

"Laciel, in a manner of speaking something *did* happen to him," InThig admitted in a hesitant way, then quickly shook its head. "No, no, I don't mean he's been hurt, so please don't go jumping up and running out. Graythor told me Rik returned to camp right after you went for your bath, and he saw the man following you into the bushes when you circled the pool. It was the reason Graythor himself didn't follow after and insist you bathe nearer the camp."

"But—I didn't see any sign of him at all," I protested, beginning to feel confused again. "The only one I saw was Togor, and he made me feel terrible with what he said. He—also kissed me."

"And after that Rik went back into the forest without stopping to speak to anyone," InThig said with a sigh. "Graythor believes he saw and heard something that disturbed him quite badly, and won't return until the matter is resolved."

"I can't imagine what great decision he thinks he has to make," I said, the confusion giving way to upset—and maybe a trace of annoyance. "He should have realized by now that things just aren't going to work out between us, so the only rational move he can make is turning and walking away. But—do you mean to say he saw Togor forcing me to kiss him, and didn't do anything to stop it? He just stood there and watched, then went out for another walk?"

"Who's to say what he saw and didn't see?" InThig returned, definitely uncomfortable. "Possibly he thought you wanted to be kissed, and didn't feel it his place to intrude. By the EverNameless, my girl, how many times have you insisted to him that you're able to look after yourself? If he's finally made himself see it that way, how can you possibly have the nerve to complain?"

"I'm not complaining, and even if I were, that isn't what I'm complaining about," I told the demon's indignation. "What I mean is—damn it, I don't have any idea what I mean. I really do think I'm beginning to hate all men, and once we have Morgiana safe I'm going to become a hermit. Hermitess. Whatever the hell it's called. I may even decide to hate demons."

"Nonsense," InThig said with a chuckle, settling down again with its front paws tucked in. "No one can hate demons, we're much too lovable. Not to mention intelligent, capable, and all-around superior."

"You forgot modest," I pointed out, not for the first time, then sat up and threw the pillows back where they belonged. "And I think that's my cue for deciding it's time to get some sleep. Maybe parts of this mess will make sense in the morning."

"Things that make sense do so all the time," InThig was good enough to inform me, but at least most of the smugness was absent. "The trick is in being able to see that sense, which a good night's sleep might indeed accomplish for you. Sleep well in the knowledge that I'm here again, and nothing will pass me to harm you."

I smiled and hugged the demon gently, then got out of my clothes and under the covers, blew out the lamp, and finally lay down. Every part of life was endless rigamarole and boring effort when it wasn't possible to use magic, and as I got more comfortable under the covers I knew I'd never be able to do without it voluntarily. It would be like learning to see color, and then living in a black-and-white world, learning to hear music and singing and then living without sound. The loss could only be imagined in a vague sort of way if the ability was never experienced, but once it was . . .

And thinking about losses, magic was only one item on a list that was trying to grow longer. I'd almost lost my freedom that night, along with my memory of self and everything that went with it. What Togor had done to me was so frightening I shuddered again, and even worse was the thought of what would have happened if InThig hadn't been there. I didn't *want* to be taken over and made happy, that hellhound had no *right* to make me happy. . . .

I made a sound so rude that InThig stirred where it lay, but the action helped to bring things back in perspective. Togor wanted to give me *his* version of happiness, and the most frightening part about that was that everyone *did* want to be happy. If they couldn't be happy on their own terms, they eagerly settled for someone else's—just so long as they really were happy. I tended to be more stubborn than that, tended to want happiness on no one's terms but my own, but what was so wrong with that? If it made me happy to be miserable while I searched for happiness, who had the right to say I shouldn't?

I laughed softly at the nonsense while I stared into the dark, but then I stopped laughing. InThig had been so very impressed with how much of a gentleman Togor was, but I had the feeling I knew better. That kiss he'd given me—maybe I *didn't* have much experience with men, but that kiss had never been meant as anything but a physical wish good night. He'd gotten me to the point of not being able to refuse if he'd

invited himself in, and then he'd simply walked away—
but he hadn't walked, he'd hurried. That told me he
wasn't able to hold off changing back into a hellhound
any longer, not that he was being a well-mannered
gentleman. If he hadn't had the changing problem
crowding his mind—

He would have taken me to bed and made me be an
absolute delight for him. Even if the thought made me
furious, he would have made me an absolute delight.

And thinking about being furious . . . if Rik had seen
it, he would probably have stood there taking notes
and then would have gone back to the forest again.

I hated men, all of them, and once I was off that
world I would never let another of them near me
again. The promise helped me settle down a little, but
didn't help once I fell asleep. I dreamed about Togor
as he'd told me to, but knew for a fact that I would
have preferred the nightmares.

CHAPTER 15

The next day started out too early, and quickly went
downhill from there. After breakfast we packed up
and got moving again, and I rode inside the wagon on
my bed, pretending I wasn't feeling well. What I was
really feeling was furious; every time I thought about
it, the fury mounted higher and higher toward rage.
Togor had come in to join us for breakfast, and when
he'd taken my hand and kissed it, I hadn't been able
to keep from blushing. He'd grinned a very wide grin
at that, immediately realizing I'd dreamed about him
exactly as ordered, and that was when I'd announced
how sick I felt and stalked back into the wagon.
Graythor had brought me the breakfast I'd missed, his
face carefully neutral, and I'd almost choked stuffing it
down.

"And Rik still isn't back," InThig had pointed out, adding to the beauty of the new day. "I think you know I don't believe in being an alarmist, Laciel, and Rik is certainly capable of taking care of himself, but I can't see him abandoning us as he's apparently done. Something must be keeping him from returning, but I can't imagine what it could be."

"Well, he didn't take his horse, so it's possible he changed to his link-form to get around more easily in the forest," I said, sipping at what was left of my coffee. "If that's what he did, maybe someone caught him in a trap, skinned him, and is right now making a pretty bronze fur coat."

"Laciel!" InThig squawked, tail bottled and fur standing away from a very outraged feline body. "How can you say something like that and pretend it's funny? If Rik is hurt, it certainly isn't a joke, and to call your attitude irresponsible is to understate the entire . . ."

"InThig, will you please calm down?" I said in irritation, shaking my head at the demon. "If getting hysterical was likely to help, as well-prepared as I am I would already be doing it. Togor has me staked out as private property, Graythor is cooking for and serving me without a single complaint, Rik has come down with delicate male problems and has disappeared, and I—I'm trying to find the answer to a nasty little riddle that only one person has solved in who knows how many hundreds of years. At the same time I'm looking over my shoulder, afraid I'll see a marriage ceremony closing up fast. If it wasn't so godawful embarrassing, I'd tell you about the dream I had last night."

"Are you trying to say the situation is impossible?" InThig asked, down from the bottling stage but hardly its usual calm and coherent self. "I hadn't realized that part about Graythor, but now that you've mentioned it— What are we going to do? Leave through the gate, and come back only when we're better prepared?"

"Better prepared in what way?" I asked in turn, already having considered the point. "With an army around to protect us? How much good would they do against Morgiana's magic? With more prearranged spells? How far can we count on prearranged spells? With more magic users? What good would they be without the key for *using* magic? And how do you propose getting Graythor to turn meekly around and head back? Togor's got him even more fired up than he was to begin with, and if he lets Graythor go, he's got to do the same with me. Somehow I don't think that hellhound's about to let me go, but if you think I'm suffering from an inflated ego, please say so. I'd be deliriously happy to be wrong. And then there's Rik . . ."

"Yes," InThig agreed glumly, slumping rather than sitting down. "And then there's Rik. Wherever he is, he probably needs help. Even if we were able to talk Graythor into turning back, we'd be doing nothing less than deserting a comrade. And I would sincerely enjoy telling you that you were suffering from an inflated ego, but I watched Togor closely when you went out earlier. He does indeed want you rather badly, Laciel, and possibly for more purposes than the obvious one. That is, for other than the pleasure of your company . . ."

"I know what the obvious purpose is, InThig," I said, sounding wearier than I liked. "During the quest I may have had trouble believing men found me attractive, but the point was really hammered home during the time I spent with Su and Kadrim, taking over the Wolf tribe. After it was done and the dust had settled down, Kadrim had his hands full with the other tribal warriors who had stood with us against the Wolves. Most of them didn't understand who and what I was, but they still came to Kadrim with offers, wanting to buy me as a wife. If I'd wanted to, I could have tried each and every one of them in bed, and then told Kadrim which offer to accept. If I'd wanted to."

"But you didn't want to," InThig said quietly, and it felt as though the demon were speaking to me on a different, higher plane. "You had the opportunity and apparently the knowledge of what was involved, but you chose to pass on it. Do I need to ask why?"

"Certainly not," I said, then finished the rest of the

coffee in my cup. "I had this monstrous headache. So what are we going to do about our current headache?"

"A better question to ask would be: what *can* we do?" InThig countered, not pleased with my previous comment but knowing it was the wrong time to pursue the point. "We can't go back, we can't forge ahead—do we merely sit quietly while we're neutralized one by one?"

"We have to continue on at the same pace we're going, and under the same restrictions," I said, tapping my lips with one finger. "What we don't have to do is forget about planning, we only have to pretend we're forgetting about it. In a few hours we'll be at that town, and while Graythor and I are looking around at its people, you can be looking around for Rik. If he *is* in trouble, we'll have to get him out of it, preferably without letting Togor know we're doing it. And we've got to continue keeping *you* a secret, so you can go back for reinforcements if Graythor and I are taken. I'm going to tell you everything we've learned so far— all of which comes to two or three theories that are seventy-five percent guesswork—and then you can tell me what, if anything, you found of interest in your most recent travels."

So I told InThig the various ideas Graythor and I had had and what we'd tried, and in turn the demon told me about that kingdom. There were proportionately more guardsmen in the outlying districts and villages than closer to the King's city, and the people in those areas weren't buying the idea they were there because of the proposed wars of expansion. The guardsmen were giving the people there a hard time, forcing them to obey the laws in the same way town and city folk did, taking down men's names and registering them and their families, making them be specific about the work they did. If anyone refused to cooperate, they were given one warning; if they didn't heed the warning, the hellhounds took over.

"And that sort of example had no need to be set more than once for most," InThig said with distaste. "The hellhounds truly enjoy their work, and I was enormously tempted to tear a few of *them* apart, to see how well *they* liked it. Had it not been necessary that I remain unobserved, I would have done just that."

"This King Triam wants all of his people firmly under his thumb before he goes on to the next victims on his list," I observed, absently wishing there was more coffee. "He's obviously using terror tactics to beat the independents into line, to make sure that those who traditionally go their own way start going his way. Registering people, murdering those who won't cooperate, probably a lot of looting and rape into the bargain . . ."

"Looting, yes, to a small extent, but not rape," InThig corrected, a flick of its tail showing extreme unhappiness. "Anything of value that hasn't been officially granted to a man or family ends up in the ranking guardsman's possession, and loose coins of any sort disappear to the guardsmen themselves. Sometimes one man or another will be harassed by a small group of guardsmen, usually those called half-born, for instance, but women are never bothered. The guardsmen have female slaves for their—entertainment —and either ignore the local women or are simply courteous to them."

"I think that's stranger than almost anything else I've heard about this place," I stated, looking at InThig with a frown. "Are you sure about that? No incidents of *any* sort?"

"Are you complaining about the one decent aspect of this outrageous invasion of privacy?" InThig demanded, ready to fluff out again to twice its size. "I'm sure the King realizes there would be uprisings if his guardsmen went so far as to offer indignities to women, so . . ."

"Garbage," I stated again, knowing exactly what I was talking about. "If there's one thing guardsmen count on as a bonus to the pay they collect, it's taking 'liberties' with females who can't complain to the authorities up higher. They're miles and miles away from the King's city, InThig, and the only ones around to complain to are those who would condone whatever the guardsmen cared to do. If the men rose up, the forces would put them down again, and all the King would hear was that the people tried being uncooperative. If they're not attempting the women, the reason isn't decency, but I'll be damned if I know what it *is*."

InThig was highly skeptical and I really couldn't blame it, but I did know what I was talking about. Those guardsmen in Geddenburg were generally considered decent men, but most of them hadn't thought twice about helping themselves to females who weren't in a position to complain. The "decent" element of women were not only safe from them, they could count on protection, but those who were too low class to matter just didn't matter. Rural residents would be considered just as unimportant to occupying troops, so why . . .

"Have you considered that none of the women are attempted because none of them are considered individuals in their own right?" InThig offered, still looking faintly huffy. "Each female must have a man of some sort to stand her protection, else she's taken up by the law and dealt with rather harshly. Surely you can see where a situation like that . . ."

"Would be nothing more than legal blackmail, and therefore means only what chains would," I interrupted impatiently. "These men are working very hard to make sure women don't go their own way, but instead of locking them up in harems they lock them up with laws. I wonder what they're so afraid of?"

"Why do you insist on making assumptions based on no more than speculation?" InThig demanded, sounding very much like Graythor had. "You may not care for the circumstances under which women live in this kingdom, but that doesn't necessarily mean the men are afraid of something. It only means they prefer the arrangement to . . ."

"Wait a minute," I interrupted again, sending the demon another frown. "You said, 'in this kingdom.' Was that just an accidental choice of words, or are things done differently in other kingdoms? Have you looked around at some of the others as well as this one?"

"Just to be thorough, I did look at some of the others," it admitted, a definite shrug in its tone. "It so happens none of the other kingdoms do things in the same way they're done here, but that can't possibly be significant. Different places, different customs, you know."

"The only way for it not to be significant is for one or more of them to have the ability to do magic," I said, and if the words sounded like a challenge then that's what they were. "Do any of those other kingdoms have the secret, InThig? Do any of them have control of their talent?"

"No," the demon admitted, definitely with reluctance. "Not that that proves what you seem to think it does. The subservience of women in this kingdom offends you, so your mind is searching around for hidden meanings and dastardly plots. Has it never occurred to you that the women here may well *prefer* their treatment to what you consider freedom? Are you able to admit that they may well be happy and content?"

"'Of course I can admit that," I said with a beaming smile, leaning back just a little. "What thinking being *wouldn't* prefer being dependent on someone else's kindness to keep them from slavery? Not being thrown out into the street, not the possibility of starving, but inescapable slavery. All or nothing, take your choice of whose boots to lick. Is that the reasonable explanation *you're* looking at, InThig?"

Blazing red eyes stared back at me, but I didn't hear any words to go along with the stare. Different things are considered reasonable to different people, but if *no* one affected can consider a particular thing reasonable, you don't have a custom you have a puzzle.

"This fits in somehow with those laws Togor told Graythor and me about," I said, leaning forward again to rest my elbows on my knees. "I wish it meant that only women can do magic, but we've already tried that and it doesn't work. How about the half-born in those other kingdoms? Were you able to tell whether or not they're treated the way they are here?"

"The Sighted are well-integrated in other kingdoms, but mostly through the lower classes," InThig grudged, and I couldn't tell whether or not it was glad to switch to another topic. "Their being different is a virtual guarantee that they'd be looked down on in one manner or another, but their treatment is nowhere near as harsh as it is here."

"But only the men are treated harshly here," I pointed out, bothered by something but not knowing what. "Female Sighted are called Chosen, and forced to go to the palace for a Blessing. After that, according to Togor, they're never seen again. Where does *that* fit in, and does it fit in more than one place? And was that how the King got his hands on Morgiana?"

"That may very well be," InThig said, and then its head rose, as though something had occurred to it. "And, if male Sighteds are able to influence female as easily as Togor influenced you, that may account for Morgiana's behavior. The King interviews her as one of the Chosen, learns of her origins, then Persuades her to do as he says. After that—"

"Yes, after that," I agreed sourly, putting my head down and locking my hands in my hair. "After that he uses her strength for his magic, but how, damn it, how?"

Once again the only thing I got from InThig was silence, but that was also the sum total of my own contribution. I sat there wracking my brain for any sort of an idea, even one that was totally ridiculous, but nothing wanted to come. I tried for what seemed like forever, but all I got for my efforts was a headache.

When the wagon abruptly bumped to a halt, I was actually grateful for the reprieve. I stretched a little before getting to my feet, swearing to myself that I would never again joke about someone not being able to think. Serious thinking was damned hard work, but at least I'd satisfied myself on one point. Graythor and I had spoken our joint spell in the language of spells rather than in plain words, but I was convinced that didn't make any difference. The only way to get any real strength into a spell was to *use* the language of spells, and if Morgiana wasn't using it, the King's strength wouldn't be ten times more than his predecessor's. Besides, the language of spells *was* plain words, only adjusted and abbreviated.

"Laciel, it's going on toward noon," Graythor called from just outside the wagon. "If we're going to have the opportunity for a good look at the people of this town, we have to leave now. The walk isn't far, but the longer we delay the less time we'll have."

"Togor is with him," InThig said in a very soft voice from the place it still sat on my bed. "You go ahead, and I'll get busy with my own chore."

"Good luck to both of us," I said in a whisper, then headed for the steps out of the wagon. I was thinking hard about the possibility of finding the answer I was looking for among the people of the town, but only to keep from thinking about what InThig would be looking for. Rik couldn't possibly be seriously hurt, and I had to keep that firmly in mind.

"Are you feeling any better now, lovely darling?" Togor asked as soon as he saw me, his hands coming to my waist to lift me down before I could use the steps. "If you aren't, then Graythor can go alone, and I'll stay here to watch over you."

"I'm feeling fine now, thanks," I answered, pulling a little to get back from the hands that hadn't left my waist on their own. The hellhound was a man again, and I was willing to bet watching wasn't the only thing he wanted to do with me.

"Well, I'm delighted to hear that," Togor said with a grin, having let me go only because he didn't care to press the matter just then. "Since you *are* feeling better, I can plan on our taking a walk tonight, just the two of us and the moonlight. The moon will rise rather late, but you won't mind that, will you?"

"Of course she won't mind," Graythor said with a chuckle when I didn't answer, his hand coming to pat my shoulder. "She's basically a good girl, and she'll have had enough practice all day in doing as she's told. Come, Laciel, and let's get this over with. You walk to my left and immediately behind the line of my shoulders, and don't speak to anyone even if they speak to you first. I'll let you know if you're allowed to say something, and until then you're to keep quiet. Come along, come along. You can see Togor again when we return."

He bustled me away from the clearing where the wagon had been stopped, heading us for the road I couldn't see until we cleared most of the screening trees and bushes. The road ran left and right, but to the left was where the town lay. I could just see the way the road turned into the main street of the town, with dusty one-story buildings rising to either side of it. Deeper inside the town were probably larger and grander buildings, but no one wasted size and grandeur on outskirts.

"Uncle Graythor, there are people up ahead, but right now we're alone," I said in a low voice, following him the way I'd been told to. "I want you to make the effort to understand that Togor has been using Persuasion on you, but I don't want you losing your temper and making a scene. Do you understand what I'm saying?"

His cheerful, confident pace faltered very briefly, as though he'd just remembered something, but he didn't actually come to a stop. His head came up and his hands closed to fists, but he just kept walking the way he'd been doing.

"If you weren't here, child, my language would be of the sort I usually deplore," he muttered after a moment, the words hard and furious. "That man—the things he's made me say and do! If you hadn't used the Persuasion at your own command—!"

"You'd still be eagerly making dates for me," I finished when he didn't, keeping an eye on the people we were sharing the road with. "I know. What I don't know is what we can do about it. Now that you're aware of what's happening, is there any chance you can resist it?"

"Am I able to resist *you?*" he snapped, too angry to

be fussy over who he was snapping at. "You had a
short duel with him over dinner yesterday, I now
recall, and despite the fact that I'd had my orders from
him, you were able to momentarily sway me. My
knowing you were capable of doing it didn't stop it
from happening, so I feel confident in saying resistance is out as an idea. If only I could bring my
strength to bear—!"

"Well, you can't and neither can I, so that's another
thing we have to forget about for now," I whispered,
close enough to feel the blaze of frustration in him.
"Uncle Graythor—has Togor told you what he wants
with me?"

"If you don't know what he wants, you're still a
child rather than a woman," he growled, but then he
paused while visibly keeping himself from turning toward me. "Forgive me, Laciel, there was no call for
speaking to you like that. What I meant was . . ."

"I know what you meant, and I know what *he*
means," I interrupted, too aware of the shortening
distance between us and the nearest natives on the
road. "What I don't know is what *other* plans that
hellhound has. Did he give you any orders about the
magic question? Did he tell you to forget about trying
to find an answer?"

"On the contrary, he's most anxious that we find an
answer," Graythor came back, slowing his pace a very
little. "If I discover the key first, I'm to give it to him
without letting you know what it is. If you discover it
first, I'm to tell him at once. If neither of us discover it
by the time I'm ready to be settled into the palace as a
cook, I'm to officially give you to him. By that time,
he assured me, you would be properly trained and
obedient. Are you being properly trained, Laciel?"

"You should know, Uncle Graythor," I answered,
working hard to keep the growl out of my own voice.
"You were one of the ones who helped train me.
What do you think of Hellfire as a fitting present for a
hellhound?"

"That tells me exactly how angry you are, but you'd
best keep a good grip on your temper," he warned,

rubbing his face with one hand. "The Chosen spell will be stronger inside the town, and if you lose yourself to it the officials will step in. Our friend Togor cautioned me against staying too long, and to leave immediately if you feel your resistance weakening—and in that I must reluctantly agree. If you experience any difficulty put your hand to my shoulder, and I'll lead us out of there immediately."

"Lead us out of there," I repeated, almost distracted by the touching thought of how concerned the hellhound was over my well-being—but not quite. "Uncle Graythor—if you wanted to teach someone a quick spell, how would you do it? Wouldn't you—lead—them through it?"

"By the EverNameless," he breathed, and this time he did stop short. "Men in this kingdom always lead the women— Laciel, repeat after me: t'lan sh!"

"T'lan sh," I repeated, automatically including the left-hand gesture just as he had, but no comfortable pavilion with hot meal inside appeared in our path. All we got was the same nothing we'd been getting, and that time the disappointment was almost too much.

"I think I'm beginning to understand why some people go berserk and start destroying everything and everyone in reach," I said in a very low voice, extremely aware of Graythor's silence. "I would have bet everything I own—and would have lost it all. This is like the worst of all possible bad dreams, and I hadn't realized how fitting it is. The Realm of Dreams, a dead world that isn't really dead, and here, the Realm of Bad Dreams. Isn't it the worst possible foolishness not to admit it when you're beaten?"

"We're not beaten yet," he answered in an overly even voice, his eyes still on the road in front of us. "We know there's an answer, so we just keep looking. At this point finding the answer is the only hope we have, and not just for Morgiana's sake. Laciel, order me not to tell Togor the answer if—when—we do find it. I nearly went running back to him a moment ago."

I made the effort to put as much belief and strength into the order as possible, then followed along behind

when he continued on toward the town. What I really
wanted to do was lie down with my eyes closed and
curl up into a ball, which just might make that world
go away. I needed it to go away very badly, but the
Realm of Bad Dreams just kept refusing to cooperate.

Graythor and I had stopped on the road right where
it left the woods, and once we started walking again
we reached heavier traffic in only a few minutes. Most
of the people leaving the town took a road that curved
away to our right, but two riders went past in a moderate cloud of dust that accompanied them toward the
woods road. More people seemed to be leaving than
arriving, and considering the time of day that was
surprising. People who travel usually start out early in
order to make the daylight last long enough for them
to get where they're going, but possibly those people
weren't going too far.

We trudged on up the road and into the town with
other new arrivals, and it wasn't very surprising to
learn that the town was little more than an overgrown
village. Dusty wooden buildings gave way to painted
wooden buildings, but the only real activity in that
town was in the teeming market square that was its
center. It looked like every soul in a ten mile radius or
more had come to town that day, and Togor had been
right in his warning to Graythor. The Chosen spell *was*
pushing at me a lot more insistently, but as long as I
knew what it was, I could hold off the urge to start an
argument with everyone I passed.

We joined the flow of foot traffic into the market,
then spent a lot of time moving from one stall to the
next, looking at what was being offered. Leather goods,
metal goods, tools, cloth, food in every stage from
seed to ripened melon, calf to roasted side of beef, egg
to sauteed chicken parts, fruit to sweetened drink, and
mash to ale. It was almost dizzying to see how many
different things were being offered, and the movements of the people were almost as hard to follow.

Most seemed to be there to make specific purchases,
and after a while I had to grudgingly admit InThig
might have had something of a point when it had tried

to say their attitudes weren't all bad. Many of the women did follow along behind the men they were with, but that arrangement seemed mostly for older men and younger women. If the two were closer in age the woman most often held the arm of the man, or his arm circled her shoulders in a protective sort of way. If a couple like that entered a narrow aisle between stalls the man invariably stood aside to let the woman go first, and if a single package was being carried, he did the carrying. Every woman in sight was in the same sort of long skirts I was wearing, but I couldn't very well condemn the entire setup for that.

Sight of the first guardsman we passed made me hold my breath, but I soon got used to seeing the tall figures in boiled leather and helmets, wearing swords that looked very businesslike. The guardsmen were also businesslike, and they stood their posts alertly without bothering the people who were there to buy. They seemed to be paying more attention to the women in the crowds than to the men, but with the Chosen spell going full blast that was completely understandable.

After what seemed a very long while, Graythor bought the two of us lunch and soft drinks. When we finished eating, he made a number of purchases at various foodstuffs stalls, and then we headed out of town again. Our lunch break had had what might be called entertainment—a thief had been chased and caught by two of the guardsmen almost right in front of us—and we'd been able to watch as the thief was dragged off to be locked up. I'd had fleeting thoughts about *us* getting locked up when Graythor had paid for our meal with one of his small silver bars, but no one batted an eye. He was given coins in change by the food stall man, and had paid for his other purchases with the coins.

"That must be their lockup," Graythor said to me as we passed a cross street to the left after leaving the market area. "Those two guardsmen were the ones who arrested that thief."

I looked at the men without saying anything, but could see that Graythor was right. Those *were* the

same two guardsmen, and the building they were coming out of looked taller and blockier than the ones
around it. I had the urge to use the Sight on their
lockup to See what, if anything, was inside, but didn't
follow through any more than I had when I'd felt that
urge earlier in the market. Just because their Chosen
spell was weak enough for me to resist it, that didn't
mean there weren't any Sighted-traps which could give
me trouble. If I was pretending to be unSighted—
pretending!—then I'd damned well better *be* unSighted.

We followed the street out of town until it became a
road, then followed the road toward the woods where
we'd left the wagon. We weren't the only ones leaving
the town when we did, but the others turned off onto
the curving road, leaving us to continue on alone. We
walked along in silence for a few moments, letting the
distance between us and the others widen, and then
Graythor sighed.

"I have no idea how you saw it, but for me that visit
was no more than a waste of time," he said, shifting
his package from one arm to the other. "There was
nothing that gave me even the least hint of an idea for
an answer, and I hadn't realized how much I was
hoping we would find something. We're running out
of time even faster than *you* suggested, and it's occurred to me that we might be wise to retreat through
the gate to regather ourselves."

"We can't do that," I said, feeling all the gritty dirt
that had gotten into my sandals and hating the sensa-
tion. "I know you've probably been ordered to overlook it, but Rik is missing. We can't go back and leave
him in the middle of whatever he's in the middle of."

"By the EverNameless, that wretched native!"
Graythor exclaimed bitterly, telling me my guess had
been right. "Of course we can't leave Rik, even if it's
highly unlikely that he's in trouble. We have to know
for certain, not gloat over guesswork the way Togor
did. I remember now that he thinks Rik is afraid of
him, and has given up all claim to you and left, to
keep from having to fight him. Togor may seem rather

well-mannered and cultured, but he's really quite uncivilized."

"So I noticed," I commented, at least relieved to hear that Togor hadn't arranged something to lure Rik away. "And that reminds me. Under no circumstances are you to tell that hellhound what InThig really is. Right now InThig's our secret weapon—unless you've already said something?"

"No, no, happily the subject never came up," Graythor answered with a certain amount of satisfaction. "If it comes up in the future, I should be able to continue saying it's no more than your pet. What are we to do about Rik?"

"InThig left to look for him when we left for town," I said. "The best thing you can do is pretend you've forgotten all about Rik just the way you're supposed to, and I'll let you know what InThig finds out when Togor isn't around. Which, I fervently wish, could be from now on into forever."

"But you and I both know it won't be, don't we, child?" he asked very gently, turning to put a strong hand on my arm. "Do you fear him? If you do, then I'll distract him while you take Rik's horse and run for the gate. InThig will certainly find it possible to help once I've been brushed aside, and between the two of us you may very well make it through to the dead world. At the very least, you'd then be able to restore your automatic defenses, and once you did you could return. You know well enough that Rik would want you to."

"Which means I can't possibly break precedent and do it," I pointed out, smiling to ease the worry I could see in his eyes. "Since I haven't listened to Rik yet, now would be a terrible time to start. Don't worry, Uncle Graythor, I'm not afraid of the hellhound, or at least not in the way you think. I seriously doubt that he'll hurt me if he manages to back me into a corner, even if my intentions aren't the same toward him. What I *am* afraid of is that he'll make me feel like a fool, the way he did the other night. His Persuasion had me as solidly as it had you, and if InThig hadn't been there, I doubt if I could have broken out."

"I do believe I'd rather have the embarrassment of being taken over as mine alone," he said, shaking his head with faint disgust. "We'll certainly keep InThig as a secret weapon, but please don't hesitate to use that weapon if the need should arise. I would rather enter the city without Togor's assistance and guidance, than have you suffer through an unbearable time."

"Uncle Graythor, that's one of the biggest problems in this mess," I said, trying to break it to him gently. "If Togor gets me, it *won't* be unbearable, and probably won't even be uninteresting. He intends making me *happy*, but I'll be damned if I'll let him. And not necessarily figuratively."

"I don't think I'm up to translating that right now," he said, looking as though he'd enjoy closing his eyes. "Females have always been something of a mystery to me, and I'm much too old to change that opinion. Just remember that I'm with you whichever way you decide to go. And if you stop to think about it, only Togor believes we can't do without him in the city."

Which was an interesting point to think about. I tossed it around while we finished walking back to the wagon, then forgot about it in favor of looking around. Our unfavorite hellhound was nowhere to be seen, but he'd left us a present that was at the very least noteworthy. Half of a deer lay in front of the wagon, and Graythor actually made pleased sounds when he saw it. I wondered if he'd missed the fact that the other half of the deer was eaten rather than simply cut away, then I decided I'd be best off not asking. I hadn't given the wizard any orders concerning cooking, and if he picked up on that after we were out of that mess, I'd be much better off if I'd avoided the subject completely.

I left Graythor to appreciate his present, and went into the wagon to see if InThig was there. My empty bed said the demon hadn't gotten back yet, but just as I was trying to decide between staying in the wagon and going back out, the air not far from me began to darken. I watched as InThig formed in smoke before drifting over to my bed to coalesce into a cat, but I wasn't given the chance to speak first.

"Laciel, you'd better sit down and get a good grip on that hasty temper of yours," I was told with a long tail swishing back and forth in time to the words. "This is a situation where plans must be made, without anyone running off and taking hasty action. We must be calm and cool, in no way . . ."

"InThig, if you say hasty again I'll hit you with something," I growled, feeling that horrible clutch of panic on my insides. "What happened to Rik? Is he hurt? How badly is he hurt? How long will it take for me to reach him? Tell me, damn it, tell me!"

"Laciel, I'm *trying* to tell you," the miserable demon lied, since it was doing no such thing. "As far as I could tell Rik isn't hurt at all, but he's certainly not in the best of positions. Brace yourself, my girl, and remember what I said about staying calm. Rik—has been captured by the natives."

CHAPTER 16

"That lockup," I said, wanting to smash and break things. "If it was those town guardsmen who took him, Graythor and I must have walked right past him! We've got to get him out of there."

"In broad daylight?" the monster of a demon asked, staring at me with those blazing red eyes. "Using just your hands? We could, of course, use my teeth and claws, but we'll hardly be able to keep our presence quiet after that. Have you decided we should retreat after all?"

Retreat, the same word Graythor had used. I turned away from InThig and used one hand to brush back a strand of my hair, the hair I almost hadn't brushed just because Togor had told me I had to. It was irrational and unreasonable, but even if I *felt* beaten, I couldn't just pick up and run away. Other people can't claim they've beaten you unless you can't make it back to the line; if you *choose* not to go back, the only one who's beaten you is yourself.

"No, we're not going back, we're going ahead," I decided aloud, then turned again to look at InThig. "No matter what we have working against us, it can only get worse if we have to try it a second time. I just wish we could do it the way I originally intended, but I'm afraid that's out. Not only can't I walk away from Graythor while Togor still has power over him, something tells me this thing can't be beaten by one person alone. It has to be a team effort, like on the dead world, or it isn't going to work."

"What you originally intended was being a decoy," InThig said, down with tail wrapped around feet. "I'm extremely relieved you've given up on that, and I believe I understand why. If you put yourself in the clutches of the High King and he *does* have the Persuasion ability Togor shows, you'll quickly become converted the way Morgiana was. I'm sure you realize we can't have the two of you against us."

"Better me than her," I muttered, taking that strand of my hair to mess with while I tried straightening my thoughts. "I don't have anything like her strength, and if Uncle Graythor wasn't here to balance that off— InThig, there's one last thing you really have to know. If we get to the point of absolute bottom line and Graythor and I still don't have the answer, you'll have to try spying on that King Triam and Morgiana to see how they do it. I haven't any idea how you'll get past Morgiana's being on the alert for you, but you'll have to find a way and then bring the answer to someone who can help. If they come here already knowing the answer, they shouldn't have any trouble."

"And under the circumstances, you and Graythor will be where?" it asked, those eyes unmoving from my face. "Taken prisoner or dead, it seems, since you aren't suggesting I bring the answer to you. Do you really believe I'll allow anything like that to happen?"

"It could happen whether you expect to allow it or not," I pointed out, trying to be gentle. "If it does, don't waste time blaming yourself or looking for revenge. We still have to consider Morgiana, which is the reason we came here in the first place."

InThig certainly intended adding to what it had said, but it wasn't given the chance. Movement came at the back of the wagon, and then Togor stuck his head in.

"Ah, there you are, Laciel," the hellhound in man's form said. "Come outside, I want to talk to you."

A glance at InThig showed how annoyed the demon was, but it didn't say anything as I hesitated for a breath before going toward the outside. I didn't know what the hellhound wanted, but whatever it was I would be better off hearing about it away from a very unhappy demon. I stepped through the back of the wagon, then paused on the highest of the steps.

"What do you want?" I asked Togor, not terribly happy at being bothered. It might be true that we couldn't go after Rik until it was dark, but that didn't mean we couldn't start making plans.

"What I want is to talk to you," the hellhound repeated, his very light eyes looking up at me in the way they'd been doing lately. "You're back from town earlier than I'd expected you to be, so let's take an afternoon walk to practice for the one we'll be taking later under moonlight."

"I think I've done enough walking for one day," I said, needing to ask InThig how many doors that lockup had—if that's where Rik was being kept. If it wasn't, I needed details about where he *was* being held, and the sooner the better. You can't expect to accomplish a smooth and professional breakin without studying the place you're breaking into. "Why don't you check with me tomorrow," I added, "and see how I feel about it then."

"Tomorrow can take care of itself," he answered, quickly reaching up to me before I could turn away, putting an arm around my waist, and pulling me down to him. "I want a walk today, and you're coming with me. I can't very well talk to you if you aren't there."

"It's possible to arrange things so that my being there will be as useless as my not being there," I returned, angry enough to try making him let me go. "Just because you talk doesn't mean I have to listen."

"You may be harder to reach than most women, but you'll listen," he disagreed with a grin, totally confident, totally sure. "And you might as well stop struggling. Those skirts aren't letting you kick me very hard, so why waste the effort?"

With his right arm around my waist and his left hand holding my left wrist, I was "helped" into the woods away from the wagon. Graythor hadn't been far away, but he was obviously so wrapped up in working on the half deer that he hadn't noticed the exchange between Togor and me. That told me the hellhound had spoken to him before calling me, and his next words confirmed that.

"Graythor tells me you two thought you had the answer to the puzzle, but it turned out you were wrong," the hellhound commented, an interested party who was merely keeping up with the latest news. "He also said the visit to town wasn't any help, and he's feeling very dejected over the continual failure to find an answer. Did *you* get any bright ideas that you simply haven't told him about yet?"

"If I did and they work out, I guarantee you'll be the first to know," I growled, wishing I wasn't simply threatening. "Take your hands off me."

"No," he answered, still in an extremely good mood. "I enjoy having my hands on you, and if you'd let yourself relax, you would enjoy it, too. If you and your uncle don't find what you're looking for very soon, what will you do?"

"We'll sit down in the middle of a street somewhere and sulk," I said, using my free right hand to fend off a bush branch that wanted to get much too friendly. "Where are you taking me?"

"I'm taking you for a walk," he said, the answer all

but dismissive. "If you don't find the key you're looking for, will you try to leave this world?"

"Certainly not without first saying good-bye to all the dear friends we've made," I assured him, annoyed that his grip on my left wrist refused to loosen. "I want to go back to the wagon."

"No," he said again, beginning to sound less satisfied. "Your uncle tells me you'll probably be forced to leave, and if I like I can go with you. I've thought about that, and I've made up my mind. I don't want to go with you, and I don't want you going either. I may allow your uncle to go, but you'll be staying here with me."

"I don't want to stay here, with or without you," I said, starting to feel the first touches of ice on my insides. "You have no right telling me where to go and what to do, so don't waste your time trying. When it comes to living my life, I'm the one who makes the decisions."

"Nonsense," he contradicted with a small sound of annoyance. "Life makes our decisions for us, and we have no choice but to go along with them. If your friend's life hadn't led her to this world, your own life wouldn't have led you after her. And if your dissatisfaction with life hadn't taken you out walking alone, you and I would never have met. My own life brought me to the spot where I saved you from that bear, and from then on our lives were intertwined. Don't forget that if I hadn't saved you, your life would have ended there and then. Since it didn't, it now belongs to me."

"No," I stated clearly, borrowing the word from him to keep from being drawn into his contentions. Conceding one or two of his points was the way I'd lost myself to him the last time, and I had no intention of letting that happen again.

"Yes," he counterstated, convinced, positive, unbending. "I saved your life and now it belongs to me, but you don't have to be bothered by that. The bear would have hurt you, but I never will, not when we're going to be so happy together. The laws give me the right to claim you, your uncle has given his permission, and a bear sealed it up tight. Your life and mine will go forward together in happiness, and you'll be an absolute delight for me."

I tried to say no again, but suddenly my wrist was free and I was pulled around into his arms, his very light eyes looking down at me fiercely.

"Don't we have a *right* to be happy?" he demanded, almost accusing me of saying we didn't. "Hasn't there been enough in each of our lives that brought us pain and tears? There aren't any natural laws that say people have to be miserable, are there? Of course there aren't, so why can't we have *our* happiness? You know something? I can't think of a single reason."

His hand went to my hair and his lips lowered to mine, and even though I tried to push free I couldn't manage to do it. At first his kiss was something I wanted no part of, but then that—tingle and draw came through to me again, forcing me to accept it, making me want more. My head began to swim again, sooner than the last time, but the kiss refused to end. I was drowning and suddenly eager to drown, and the kiss just didn't end.

But eventually it did. I was no longer aware of the early afternoon all around us, or that we were in the middle of the woods. I knew only that I was being held in two strong arms I didn't want letting go, not when it meant I would also have to give up getting more of that tingling and drawing.

"You see?" Togor whispered, holding me close to his chest as he stroked my hair. "It isn't something to fight against and refuse, it's something to look forward to and joy in. I already feel that joy, and I very much want to share it with you. You believe that, don't you?"

I nodded my head, making no effort to speak words I knew I could never form. I did know he wanted to share the joy with me, but—

"Of course you believe it, because it's true," he murmured, this time bringing his lips to my hair. "I felt the pull of you the first time we met, lovely darling, and could hardly wait until you shared the feeling. You've known all along how badly I wanted you, isn't that true?"

I nodded again, this time with more certainty. Of course I'd known all along that he wanted me, but—

"Well, you could hardly have missed it," he said with a chuckle, the words and sound caressing me together. "Even in my other form I was all but drooling, quivering over the least touch of your hand. The first time I kissed you—it was extremely fortunate for the sake of my dignity that I had another form to shift into. Kiss me again."

I raised my face to him without hesitation, and his lips were as softly demanding as they'd been the other times. His desire was very strong, I could feel that as clearly as I could my own feelings, but—

"Do you know you're already a delight?" he asked, ending the second kiss much sooner than I wanted him to, strong approval in the eyes that looked down at me. "You're a delight and a marvel, and I very much want to feel your arms around me. You know how much I'll love that, don't you?"

I nodded for the third time, knowing the absolute truth of what he'd said. Being held was wonderful, marvelous, a tingling ecstasy almost as good as being kissed.

"Yes, of course you know, how could a delight like you fail to know?" he said in a murmur, his hands now holding my face, his kisses light and much too brief. "I'm sure you also know how much I want you to agree to sharing joy with me. If you do agree you must put your hand in mine, and let me lead you to our place of sharing. Show me you agree by giving me your hand, lovely darling."

He stepped back away from me and held his hand out, palm up, open and inviting. I stared at that hand for a moment, the thoughts in my head chasing one another around, and then I reached out and gave him my own hand. He smiled as he closed his fingers around mine, and then he was drawing me forward to a pretty little area that was mostly grass surrounded by lovely flowering bushes.

"I found this place especially for us, my darling," he said, lifting me in his arms before putting us both down onto the grass. "The High King may be the only one who can give a true Blessing, but I can and will give joy. You won't regret your decision, for that you have my word."

His arms were around me as we lay side by side in the bower, and once his next kiss began, I found it was mainly to precede the touch of his hands. He was gentle in all ways, keeping his earlier word to bring me no pain, and the joy he had was long in doing and longer in ending.

Togor took me back to the wagon, gave me a final kiss, then hurried away into the woods with his tunic already on the way to being pulled off. Graythor seemed to be as distracted as he'd been when we'd left, but as soon as the hellhound was out of sight he hurried over to me.

"Laciel, child, you have to pull out of it and listen to me carefully," he said, his hand hard on my arm. "Togor has been influencing you, but it's time to think clearly again. Did he hurt you? Did he make you tell him anything or promise things you really didn't care to?"

"I'm not under his influence, Uncle Graythor," I said with a sigh, not quite meeting the serious gaze searching my face. "He almost had me and I'm sure he thinks he did have me, but apparently my theory was right. Making up my mind not to let him take me over let me hold him off just enough to keep it from happening."

"Then why are you looking so distracted and—and—" He tried to find the right word, but since he wasn't feeling what I was he couldn't seem to do it. I was glad he wasn't feeling it; one of us was more than enough.

"I let Togor make love to me," I admitted in a whisper, getting it said before I found a dozen or so reasons not to mention it to anyone. "He thought he was Persuading me to do it, but it was entirely my own decision. There was a woman in the Realm of Dreams who assured me Sighted men were the best to be had. I know why she feels that way."

"You found him—superior, then?" Graythor asked, the question very gentle and entirely neutral. "He didn't harm you in any way, or cause you to regret your decision?"

"No, he didn't harm me," I said, looking down at my hands. "As for superior—no, not that either. There's a—draw—to be felt between those who are Sighted, and that's what that woman must find so impressive. For me, it was just—"

"Something that happened to be there?" Graythor suggested, almost as though he knew exactly what I was talking about. "You had a plan of some sort you were working on, a reason for what you did beyond simple impulse? Not that you need to account to me as though you were a child."

"No, I'm all grown up these days, aren't I, Uncle Graythor," I said with a smile that had no amusement in it, then straightened up a little. "Of course I was working on a plan. Now that Togor has what he wants, he won't be bothering me tonight when InThig and I want to be out freeing Rik. I'm assuming InThig spoke to you, so where is it? I'll need some details on the building where Rik is being held."

"InThig has gone off to gather more of those details you just mentioned," Graythor said, still rather reserved. "In its haste to tell us what had befallen Rik, it neglected to look at the building with an eye toward the needs of humans. Had you and I been demons as well, we would have had all the intelligence we needed."

"I think I would enjoy being a demon," I said, but the words used were much too indefinite. Right about then I would have given anything to be a demon, rather than a human. "Will you let me know as soon as InThig gets back? We have a lot of plans to make."

"Certainly," Graythor agreed with a small, warm smile. "And then we three can plan the rescue, for I'll be going with you and InThig."

"If you like," I said, then headed for the wagon. I wasn't convinced that Graythor ought to be going with us, but that was a point we could all discuss later. At the moment I had other things to think about, and I

wanted some privacy while I did it. I made it into the
wagon and over to my bed, and as I sat down, I was
glad the lamp on the wall wasn't lit.

"So much for the great experiment," I muttered,
lying down to curl up across the bed. I felt disappointed, and stupid, and very upset, not to mention
half ashamed and half resentful. It was all such a
muddle I couldn't figure out where to begin, and almost wished I didn't have to think about it at all. It
would have been nice to be able to forget about it, to
pretend it never happened, but since I wasn't the only
one involved, that simply wasn't possible.

Togor was one of the others involved, and the thought
of him was what made me most ashamed. Oh, I was
certain now that he had plans for me that had nothing
to do with "joy" and "happiness," but that didn't
change the fact that he sincerely wanted me as someone to share his life. He was an overbearing, manipu-
lative pain in the neck, but that didn't mean he wasn't
also sincere. He'd wanted to share something with me
he'd been convinced we'd both find wonderful, and I'd—

I'd agreed out of nothing but curiosity and an undefined urge to get even with someone else. And none of
it had worked out, not the least, smallest part.

"But now you can call yourself a woman of experience, can't you," I taunted myself in a low voice,
really needing to rub it in. "You let him make love to
you convinced it would be great because *he* was so
involved, but all it turned out to be was disappointing.
It wasn't awful, far from it, but when just one of the
two are sincerely involved . . ."

It became just a passing good time, nothing to remember and dream about, nothing to add that extra
tinge of rose to your outlook on life. It became wasted,
disappointing motion, and accomplished nothing more
than underlining the time it hadn't been like that at all.

"I hate him!" I whispered vehemently, wishing I
could bury my cheek in the blanket it lay against. It
was Rik I hated, Rik I wanted to bash into tiny pieces,
but I couldn't for the life of me understand why. I also
couldn't understand why I'd let Togor make love to

me to get even with Rik, when it was highly unlikely Rik would ever know about it. Or care even if he did find out. I'd chased Rik away, killing whatever interest he'd felt in me, and I'd done it on purpose. Why in all the worlds would I hate him, then, and want to blame him for everything that had happened? Why?

That final question hung in the air for the longest time, unanswered and likely to stay that way for the foreseeable future. I was so miserable I didn't know how I was standing it, but that wasn't really anything new. I knew what it was like to live with nothing but misery and hopelessness, to know that each new day would bring nothing but more of the same, but you had to keep going anyway. If you stopped it would all roll over you, and maybe that was the only real way of ending it.

"Laciel, are you asleep?" InThig's voice came suddenly, just as I felt small feet moving across the bed. "I'm back with the information we need, and we really should begin making plans."

"No, I'm not asleep," I said with a sigh, looking for the strength necessary to sit up. "And yes, by all means, let's make some plans. I'm the best there is when it comes to making plans."

CHAPTER 17

InThig tried to ask me what I was talking about, but I assured the demon it wasn't important and then led the way outside. Graythor was busy playing with the meal we'd be eating later, and the campfire was bright against the near fall of dark. Since we were where Togor could see and possibly overhear us, we had to be careful, but InThig kept its senses spread out and alert even while it was telling us what it had learned. That let us do what had to be done without the need for sneaking off somewhere, which would have made even the trees in that forest suspicious.

By the time our meal was ready and Togor showed up to help us eat it, we'd hammered out a plan of sorts. Rik *was* being held in the lockup Graythor and I had passed leaving town, and it wasn't going to be easy getting him out. I'd tried talking Graythor out of coming along, but the man I called uncle had refused to sit around waiting for InThig and me to get back. If something went wrong, he wanted to be right there and knowing about it, not sitting near the wagon *imagining* all sorts of catastrophes. InThig and I finally admitted that having him loose while the rest of us were captured would do no real good, so the point was taken as settled.

The first thing Togor did when he arrived was kiss me, which made me feel even worse than I had. I'd never heartlessly taken advantage of a hellhound before, and no matter how ridiculous that sounded it wasn't anything but the truth. That Realm of Bad Dreams was certainly living up to the name I'd given it, except on one very important point: none of that was a dream. I very much wished it could be, but I was no longer in a position where wishing could make it so.

Our meal of deer was delicious but very silent, with Togor sitting much too close to me and exuding an air of ownership that was almost thick enough to cut. If the food hadn't been really good, I never would have been able to eat any of it, and even so I was barely able to finish what I'd been given. Togor was very concerned about my not feeling well when he noticed it, and firmly ordered me to bed even before the meal was entirely over. Under other circumstances I would have ignored him, but I did need a good excuse for not spending any time in his company. I finished my wine and left the fire without speaking to anyone, and my "pet cat" followed me into the wagon.

It wasn't all that long before Graythor was able to join us, and we were relieved to see that Togor hadn't worked on him while he'd had him alone. According

to Graythor, the hellhound had been in too good a
mood of distraction to even pay much attention to
him, but that was something I didn't want to hear. I
changed subjects by asking for the clothes I'd need
that night, and Graythor went to get the tunic and
trousers and light boots he'd graciously granted me
temporary use of.

We waited until the time got closer to deep night,
had InThig check to make sure Togor was nowhere
around, then we snuck off into the woods. We used its
cover as long as we could, shifted to the road only
when we had to, then moved as fast as we were able to
go. The lack of a moon helped considerably, and once
we reached the town, I took the lead in front of
Graythor. Flitting through urban shadows without being
seen was something I'd learned to do rather successfully, and it was the sort of skill even the passage of
years doesn't erase.

I spent our shadow-glide through the town wondering if we should have worried more about what Togor
was doing, but once we reached a place directly across
the street from the lockup I had to let the question go.
The large, blocky building had two entrances, one in
front and one around the other side in back. Even
before InThig had told us about the extra guardsmen
in back, I'd known we had to go in the front. Only
honest people use a front entrance, and whoever was
inside would not be alert against the arrival of honest
citizens. Those in back would be alert against *anyone*
showing up, and that we couldn't afford.

"But, Laciel, there are torches on the front of that
building," Graythor protested in a whisper. "InThig
says there are no torches around back, so wouldn't we
be better off going in that way? What if someone sees
us?"

"There isn't anyone around *to* see us, but that isn't
our biggest concern," I whispered back, impatient to
be getting on with it but needing to reassure him first.
"If they've linked Rik with InThig's earlier visit, we'll
have to go back to the dead world whether we're seen
or not. If they haven't, simply getting out of this area

may take care of the problem. And the lack of torches
doesn't balance off the larger number of guardsmen
around back. Are you ready?"

"I suppose so," he answered with a sigh, bracing
himself against what was ahead. "I realize it was my
choice to come along and be a part of this, but my
active adventuring years are quite a distance behind
me. One must—take a deep breath and jump in without hesitation."

"Yes, Uncle Graythor, but don't forget InThig will
be right behind us," I said, patting him on the arm
while making sure my hair was tucked down into the
top of my tunic. The clothes I wore were a man's, and
I didn't want a glimpse of long hair to confuse the
impression. "If anything goes wrong, InThig will be
right there to help."

"The EverNameless be thanked for small favors,"
he muttered, but so low I probably wasn't supposed to
hear it. "Very well, let's get it over with."

I put my left arm around him before he could change
his mind and ask another question, and then the two
of us ran for the heavy wooden door that stood between two sputtering torches. I helped Graythor along
as though he wouldn't have been able to make it
without me, and we both were deliberately panting
heavily by the time we reached the door and burst
through it. We wanted it to seem that we'd run a long
way, and the dirt we'd smeared on our faces and in
our hair should have furthered that impression.

"Help us, please help us!" I said in a high, thin
voice as soon as we were through the door, ignoring
the way the three guardsmen inside were already reaching for their swords. "It's right behind us! Please don't
let it get us!"

"Calm down, boy," one of the guardsmen said as he
thrust his sword back in its scabbard, then he looked
at Graythor. "What's the problem here, old man?
You let that child have too much of whatever it is you
been swallowin'?"

"There's—there's something been following us, almost breathing down our necks," Graythor gasped

out, the words unsteady in a very realistic way. "Please—we know it wants to get us, but you mustn't let it!"

"A good fright's the least you can expect for bein' out so late, old man," the guardsman to the right said, looking and sounding annoyed. The three men had been seated behind a table in the mostly-bare stone room, and our sudden entrance had brought them all to their feet and reaching for their weapons. I had a feeling we were lucky none of them had spilled the cups standing in front of them, or they wouldn't have been even as polite as they were being.

"And if you don't want us askin' why you *are* out so late, you better get on home," the first guardsman added, his deep voice almost pure grumble. "You keep on runnin' around and botherin' folks like you're doin', you're gonna end up in a cell."

"But you have to believe us!" Graythor began in a desperate tone, possibly caused by seeing the three big men about to take their seats again. I really didn't know what he expected them to do other than what they *were* doing, but he must have forgotten that we weren't the ones who were supposed to convince them to come out from behind that table. When the blood-chilling snarl came from behind us out of the dark, Graythor actually jumped.

"What in the name of the First Ancestor was that?" the guardsman on the right demanded, his eyes on the open door rather than on the two harmless people who hurried forward toward the table. All three of them were standing straight again, and this time their swords were in their fists.

"We better find out what it was," the center guardsman decided, gesturing to his companions without taking his eyes off the doorway. "I'm goin' to take a look, and I want you two right behind me."

"Can't be one of them hellhounds, not after the King decided they was wasted here," the third guardsman said, moving out from behind the table the way he'd been told to. "Maybe we got us a rogue wolf or some such."

"If we can't see what it is from here, we get a couple of spears and a bow before we go out," the center guardsman decided, leading his small force forward. "Keep your eyes open now, just in case it attacks."

I admired the three as very brave men, but couldn't help shaking my head over the way they'd left two strangers behind their backs. As the three moved forward cautiously, I took a step away from Graythor, which let me reach the heavy sticks tucked into my tunic belt on the left. My supposedly helping along an old man had let me hide the presence of those weapons with his body, and it was almost time to use them. The three guardsmen hadn't stopped to put on their helmets, and for that I was very grateful. If they *had* put on their helmets, InThig would have had to kill them.

I handed Graythor his stick as we watched the guardsmen move slowly closer to the door, and then our signal to attack came. InThig made that snarling sound again, too low for it to carry far, but loud enough to take the full attention of the men in front of us. As they stared hard trying to see just what was making that noise, Graythor and I came up behind the rearmost two, and a double head blow later they were on their way to the floor. I jumped past my man while InThig thrashed around outside covering as much as it could of inside sounds, and then number three was out and on his way down. We could have had trouble with that third guard, but he'd been too well convinced his back was safe and that had done the job.

"Thank all the Powers there are," Graythor said in a low voice as InThig trotted inside fast to let me close the door. "If they had turned just before we reached them—"

"Then we would have claimed we wanted to help get the beast," I finished firmly, trying to calm a very nervous-sounding wizard. "If you're interested in drawing upsetting pictures, try imagining what would have happened if they'd managed to *see* InThig. It only increased the size of its voice, just in case someone did get a glimpse of it, so all that was out there was a cute little pussycat. How long do you think *that* sight would have held their attention?"

"I beg your pardon, Laciel, but I happen to make a very frightening and feral cute little pussycat," InThig said primly, obviously trying to help jolly Graythor out of the shakes. "If they'd seen me they most certainly would have fainted, saving you two the trouble of having to knock them out."

"Of course they would have, InThig," I agreed as though I really believed it, glancing toward the door behind the table that had to lead deeper into the building. "We only handled it this way to give Graythor and me something to do. As soon as we drag these three away from the door, you can lead us to the cell Rik is in."

"Why don't I do the dragging while you and InThig go after Rik?" Graythor said, still looking shaken but apparently determined to get it under control. "I gave myself a bit more than average physical strength when I suppressed my defenses, and once we reached this world I was pleased that I had. I can also be here on watch in case anyone comes in."

"That might be the best idea," I decided at once, itchy to get finished and get out of there. "I've never been comfortable in lockups, so the faster we're done the happier I'll be. Is it this way, InThig?"

"Yes," the demon answered, having no trouble keeping up with me as I strode toward the door the guardsmen had been guarding. "The keys are on a peg just to the left of this door on the inside, and there are two other prisoners in other cells. They won't have heard what went on in *this* room, but once we go through the door we should be as silent as possible."

I nodded as I reached the door, then put InThig's advice into practice by opening it quietly and slipping through. The demon padded soundlessly ahead of me, but waited until I had the door closed again and the ring of keys down off the wall before continuing on. We'd come through into an area of solid metal doors to either side of a fairly wide aisle, and there was only one torch near the door we'd come in by and one at the far end to light our way.

We had to go two-thirds of the way down the aisle to reach the right cell, and then I had to find the right key to open it. Choosing one metal key on a ring, sliding it into a lock, and then trying to turn it doesn't get done repeatedly but silently without a lot of effort, and by the time I found the proper key I was sweating. It was then necessary to pull the door open without waking up everyone in town, and that proved almost beyond me. InThig was into the cell as soon as I'd moved the door the least little bit, leading me to believe the demon had cheated in the matter of body solidity, and a moment later I was getting help opening the door—from the inside.

Rik needed more space to squeeze through than InThig had, but as soon as it was available he was out and ready to close the door again. He frowned and started to say something when he saw me, but when I put a quick finger to my lips he got the message and saved it. He turned instead and pushed the door the rest of the way closed, waited until I relocked it, then followed InThig and me back to the door we'd come in by.

Once the keys were back on their peg and I'd first peeked through the door, we were able to rejoin Graythor. He'd pulled all three of the guardsmen to the right of the front door, out of easy sight if anyone came in, and he waited until the cell block door was closed before coming toward us with a smile.

"I'm delighted to see our team completely back together again, but I'll be even more delighted to see it elsewhere than here," he said, making sure to keep his voice low. "Shall we save all greetings and questions until there's less of a chance of someone walking in and spoiling our reunion?"

"That's a very good idea, but I wish you'd had another, earlier good idea," Rik said, rubbing at his shoulder through his torn and dirty tunic. "I'm very glad that you came to rescue me, but you should have left Laciel at the wagon. This is no place for a woman."

"If you happen to get picked up again, I'll remember you said that," I put in very evenly in spite of the monstrous anger I suddenly felt, letting my hands go to fists at my sides. "As a matter of fact I intend remembering it from now on, to keep myself from ever again wasting time on something that obviously isn't worth the effort. InThig, will you please check to see if the street is clear? I'd like to get out of here right now."

"I'm not saying I'm not grateful you came, I'm just saying I wish you hadn't risked yourself," Rik told my back in that very familiar patient way when I followed InThig to the door. "There's no sense getting insulted over something that wasn't meant as an insult."

"It would be best, my friends, if we continued to be cautious," InThig said, pausing at the front door to look back at us. "By giving the guardsmen almost no time to pay attention to Graythor and Laciel and not speaking at all where the prisoners might hear us, we've given them a false impression of who's been here tonight. If we intend continuing on, we must keep it like that."

InThig's point was a very good one, so none of us said anything more while it checked the streets, then we followed silently when it returned to gesture us after it. I took us through the town shadows again despite Rik's effort to push himself forward first, then went up the road in my own way once the town was behind us. Neither Rik nor InThig was happy about *that*, but by then I simply didn't care.

I think getting back to the wagon without any trouble was something of a surprise for me. For some reason I keep expecting—*something*—to happen, and when it didn't the lack just added itself to everything else bothering me. The others were in a very good mood, so good they were just short of bubbling.

"Sit down, Rik, and start on this piece of venison I saved for you," Graythor directed as he began building up the fire. "I'll make a fresh pot of coffee and anything else you'd like, and then we can discuss whether or not to move on tonight."

"And I would enjoy knowing how and for what reason you were taken," InThig said, sitting down neatly not far from where Rik was already attacking the portion of deer Graythor had given him. "Did they have any idea you weren't alone, or that you were one of those they were supposed to be on the lookout for?"

"I think they know now that I'm not alone," Rik said as soon as he'd swallowed, forcing himself to interrupt his meal. "As for how I was taken, that was a combination of bad luck and stupidity. I made the mistake of not paying attention to where I was going, and ended up walking into a squad of those guardsmen who were out hunting for fresh meat. If I hadn't startled them, they probably wouldn't have bothered me, but I did and they didn't like it, so they began asking me all sorts of questions. When I refused to answer—Hellfire, I *couldn't* answer!—they knocked me around a little, then dragged me back to their lockup."

"And you, of course, couldn't afford to do anything to stop them," InThig said with a nod in its voice, just as though Rik had followed the only course possible. "If you had left their bodies behind in the forest, someone would certainly have gotten suspicious."

"And our breaking him out of jail won't look suspicious at all," I put in in a mutter, not really interested in joining the conversation. That entire rescue mission had turned into a farce, and we'd be lucky if we didn't end up needing rescuing ourselves.

"There's an excellent chance that what happened tonight won't be reported," Graythor said jovially to Rik, but I had the feeling his words were meant even more for me. "If those three men tell anyone what was done to them, they'll also have to admit they were made fools of by an old man and a child. Since they aren't likely to be too anxious to do that, and since the prisoner they'll find missing wasn't guilty of anything beyond refusing to answer their questions, they may very well decide to forget the matter entirely."

"And we can continue on as though nothing had happened," InThig agreed in a very satisfied way, joining the other two in ignoring the soft sound of ridicule I'd made. It was *possible* those three guardsmen would keep quiet, but there was no doubt they were brave men and they hadn't appeared to be fools. If they once stopped to ask themselves why an unimportant prisoner had been set free in such a strange way— and how anyone had known he was there to begin with—the next thing they'd do was report the entire incident. Better to look a little foolish, after all, than to be accused of treason for not obeying the King's orders.

"But something did happen, InThig," Rik countered, wiping the last of the deer meat on his hands off onto his filthy trousers. "As a matter of fact, more than one thing happened, and we're going to have to straighten it all out. Laciel, you and I are overdue for a long, private talk."

"Why don't you check with my appointment secretary when we get back?" I suggested, moving closer to the fire to see if I could tell how soon the coffee would be ready. "If she finds it possible to fit you in, we can have a nice chat then."

"Laciel, behave yourself," Graythor scolded, almost sounding like his old self. "Since we're all here together, the least we can do is be polite to one another. Insults and flippancies are entirely uncalled for."

"Why don't you tell that to *him*," I said, gesturing toward our mighty leader. "And while you're at it, you might try mentioning how smoothly his escape would have come off if this poor, helpless little female had been left home the way he thought I should have been. Go on, tell him."

"Rik, that *is* a point well worth mentioning," Graythor said after a slight hesitation, turning toward the man he spoke to as he fingered the stick tucked into his tunic belt. "I discovered that my expertise and enthusiasm in the matter fell a bit short of the level necessary for success, and if Laciel hadn't been there, you would likely still be in that cell. I'm forced to admit that she could have accomplished your escape alone, but I on my own most likely would have failed."

"Which is no excuse at all for having taken her," another voice chimed in, and we all turned to see Togor striding up to join us. "If that—friend of yours was careless enough to get himself taken, he had business to also get himself free or stay in the cell and rot. Risking Laciel in such an ill-thought-out venture was unforgivable, and I can see I was wrong to allow you to look after her. From now on, I'll look after her myself."

"The hell you will," I growled, paying no attention to the way Rik rose to his feet in reaction to Togor's anger. "I told you more than once you had no say over me, and I didn't do it just to hear myself talk. I'm not in the mood to be pushed right now, Togor, so do yourself a favor and save it for another time."

"I knew I'd have trouble with you if *he* came back," the hellhound said with a lot of annoyance, his fists on his hips as he glared at Rik. "When he lets you walk all over him, he makes you believe you can do it to all men, and I haven't had time enough to teach you permanently how wrong that is. Right now you're going to bed, and once I'm finished with these two, I'll be in to make sure that you did. In the morning you and I will have a long talk . . ."

"Don't you understand simple speech?" I demanded, so angry I took a step toward the hellhound. "I'm not a zero to be ordered around and sent to bed, and you'll never live to see the day that I am. Your talent doesn't have me under your control, and his patient lectures don't have me under *his* control. I'm sick to death of the two of you, and I'd be happiest if I never saw either of you ever again. If you still don't understand what I'm saying, let me spell it out for you: go away!"

"I don't think I'll ever get enough of the glow that flows out of you when you're angry," that idiot hellhound said with a grin, obviously ignoring everything I'd told him. "The only woman on this world who matches you in that is your friend, and Triam isn't about to let anyone else claim her. But if I had the choice, I'd still pick you, so there's no need for you to feel jealous. If you're not tired enough to go to bed yet, that's fine with me. Go in and change back to decent clothes, and we'll have our moonlight walk after all."

"Have you any idea how infuriating it is to be ignored?" I asked very softly, slowly walking forward to close the gap between us. "You enjoy my—*glow*—so that's the only thing that matters? You'll do what's best for me because *you* decided it's best? To hell with what I want, as long as you get yours? Then let's get this started right by *really* giving you yours."

With my last words I hauled off and kicked him, as hard as I'd ever kicked anybody and with the weight of the boots I wore behind it. He howled and grabbed for his shin, hopping around on one foot while clutching at the other leg, and once he'd rubbed at it for a minute or so he was able to look up and point a finger at me.

"Now that's done it," he growled, his very light eyes showing furious in the firelight. "I was too patient with you, and this is what I get for it. You've just earned yourself a good punishment, my girl, and trying to run won't help you. If I have to chase you, you'll regret it even more, so get yourself over here right now."

"If you didn't like the kick, consider how well you'll like it if I stop playing and get serious," I told him, sliding the heavy stick out of my belt. "Maybe you've been showing patience but I'm fresh out, and I'm tired of repeating myself. I'm not *your* girl or anybody's, and if you have to have a broken arm or cracked ribs before you'll believe that, I'm willing to oblige."

"Why don't we all try calming down?" Rik said suddenly as Togor's jaw tightened, moving quickly into the hellhound's path as he took a step toward me. "You know you don't want to hurt her, Togor, so why get into a fight where you might do it anyway? She has a nasty habit of not holding back when she swings a stick, and if she lands one, you'll be tempted to knock her silly head off."

"Who asked *you* to butt in?" I demanded of the

broad back between me and the hellhound, but my reaction was ignored in favor of a second and more forceful one.

"You'd dare to try telling *me* what to do?" Togor rumbled at Rik, the two of them almost eye to eye. "Just because you're afraid to teach the girl some respect for you, you expect me to be the same? Now that I've claimed her, I'll be the one to decide what's done with her, and it certainly won't be any of the spineless things *you've* tried. Now, step out of my way and watch how a *man* does it."

"If that includes hurting her, no one will be watching because it isn't going to happen," Rick came back, his voice as calm and even as it had been all along. "It doesn't take a man to hurt a girl, it takes a man not to—and your claim doesn't mean a thing. The girl isn't yours; if I have my way, she never will be."

"Ah, so you think *you're* man enough to claim her," Togor said in a sleek, insulting way, giving his opponent a faint but very pleased smile. "I was hoping it would come to this, I really was. Defeating you will be much better than having you walk away, both for my satisfaction and in having her forget you. And once you're bested, she *will* forget you."

"Now you two wait one damned minute," I began, just about ready to boil over, but no one heard me. With the last of his words Togor swung a big fist at Rik's face, and the other man staggered back a couple of steps from the strength of the blow. Before I knew what was happening, Graythor had his hands on my arms and was pulling me back out of the way, and I couldn't seem to break his grip.

"You're not going to be getting between them, so don't even consider trying," Graythor said in my ear while Rik returned the punch to the face Togor had given him, rocking the hellhound. "This has been building for some time in more ways than one, and I'm near to feeling sorry for friend Togor. He never should have stepped into the problem."

"Graythor, let go of me!" I hissed, silently cursing the extra strength he'd given himself. "If I do to them what we did to those guardsmen, they'll *both* leave me alone and we can have some peace and quiet around here. How are we supposed to find the answer we're looking for if we never get any uninterrupted thinking time?"

"Give it up, Laciel, because it isn't going to work," Graythor said while the two men fighting exchanged a few punches. Then Togor drove into Rik with all his body weight, knocking Rik down with himself on top. After that they rolled around punching each other, and it was all I could do to keep from flinching at the sound alone.

"You won't find it possible to influence me now, young lady," Graythor went on with annoyance growing heavier in his voice. "Rik must be blanket-broadcasting negation, and his efforts are protecting me from you as well as Togor. You're not going to interfere with that fight, you're going to stand here and watch it out to its end. After that you're going to face up to what's been going on, not turn your back and pretend it has nothing to do with you. It has everything to do with you, and I think you know it."

"That's ridiculous," I said with a snort, beginning to feel my anger switching to *him*. "You think it's *my* fault that those two idiots are fighting? Didn't you hear me say I wanted nothing to do with either of them? I wasn't joking, I meant every word. If you can stand there and say it's my fault, you're as bad as they are."

"Tangentially I'm exactly as bad as they are," he surprised me by agreeing, and this time his annoyance seemed self-directed. "Every time you smile and call me uncle, I begin to melt in nearly the same way they do. The only difference is I'm not in love with you, and they certainly are."

"Garbage," I said with another snort, then was yanked back again when the battle rolled closer to where we'd been standing. The two halfwits looked ready to keep the fight going all night—or until they'd beaten each other to pulp, whichever came first.

"They're not in love with me, they're in love with

their own ideas about what love should be," I said when the bodies rolled away again, this time heading toward the fire. "Rik is in love with the idea of saving me from myself, and Togor is in love with my 'glow.' If I could make a couple of mindless copies of myself they'd both be delighted, because neither one likes me with my opinions intact. But that's too bad about them, because that's exactly the way I intend staying."

"With opinions intact," Graythor echoed, and briefly I wished I could see his face. "I know that doesn't include the opinion that you started all this, which is only one of the things wrong with your opinions. You encouraged Togor, Laciel, first by giving him the impression that you had no real interest in Rik, and afterward by letting him believe he was influencing you. And the way you've been treating Rik—daring him not to lose his temper while you taunt him unmercifully. If a man can't cope with a sorceress without losing his temper, he has no business being near her. That's what you've been insisting in all but words, but when Rik *didn't* lose his temper you turned around and blamed him for *that*. Do you have any idea what you *do* want?"

"I told you, I want them both to leave me alone!" I said, even though I felt like screaming it out. "I'm tired of being ordered around and argued with, and I just want to be left alone!"

"That's not what your expression says when you look at Rik the times you think he can't see you," Graythor retorted, his voice hardening. "I've seen that look and so has he, which is the reason he refuses to give up. You love him as much as he loves you, but something is making you push him away, something beyond your supposed fear for his safety. You're trying to drive him away for another reason, and that reason was what made you encourage Togor. You were hoping the hellhound would be able to do it *for* you."

I stood there in the dark, watching the two men who were up fighting on their feet again, feeling the way Graythor's fingers bit into my arms nearly to the point of pain. He was wrong, of course, very wrong, but I suddenly didn't want to continue the argument.

"They're very well matched, Laciel, but I think Togor is learning that he won't be winning the way he's obviously used to doing," Graythor said, satisfaction in his voice as he watched Rik block one of Togor's punches, then connect with a blow of his own. Both of them had bloody faces and knuckles, and although it was nothing I hadn't seen all the time as a child, I wouldn't have stood there watching it if I wasn't being held.

"You had no doubt you could send Togor on his way when the time came, so you tried to use him to get Rik to give up in disgust," Graythor persisted, his tone terribly remorseless. "You might have succeeded if Rik had been around for more than the very beginning of it, and if Togor hadn't actually fallen in love with you. Now you have both of them to cope with, and you believe you can get away with saying this fight isn't your fault? I think not, young lady, I think not."

I still saw no reason to answer his nonsense, but then we both saw something that ended our conversation. Rik hit Togor in the middle, bending him over, then lifted a fast knee into the native's face which knocked him backward and away. It was Togor who began the sprawling roll to the ground, but suddenly there was the sound of ripping cloth and then a hellhound was there in place of the man. The beast used its fangs and claws to rid itself of the tatters of clothing, and then burning yellow eyes looked up at Rik.

"I hadn't meant to do this, but now that it's happened I'm glad," the growly, raspy voice said. "If I hadn't been about to lose I wouldn't have slipped from control, and I now *won't* lose. You must be the best opponent I've ever faced, so rest assured I'll make this as quick and painless as possible."

I stood frozen in place, refusing to believe Togor was about to *kill* Rik, confused that he'd politely apologized first. What difference does apologizing make if you intend *killing* someone? The hellhound began to move, slowly and with confidence, but then he paused

and those yellow eyes widened. Rik was in the process
of shifting to his link-shape, of course, something Togor
hadn't known he could do. Before the hellhound could
launch himself in attack against a human, the human was
no longer there; a great bronze beast stood in his place.

Graythor moved us both back a third time, right up
against the side of the wagon, as a matter of fact, but
our safety wasn't what I was worrying about. All I
could think of was Togor and that bear he'd saved me
from, the way he'd won against it so easily. I still held
that heavy stick in my hand and I struggled to break
Graythor's grip so I could try doing something, but the
wizard refused to let me go—and then it was too late.

Bronze link-beast and brown hellhound came together with a crash I could feel, the hellhound having
leaped, the link-beast having taken the attack. Out of
the corner of my eye I could see InThig sitting not far
away, tail wrapped around feet, red eyes watching the
fight with no more than easy interest. The demon
could have stopped that fight, it could have gotten
between them and forced them apart, but all it was
doing was sitting and watching. I wanted to scream at
it to stop just sitting there, but I didn't. I wanted to so
badly I was trembling, but I didn't.

Rik and Togor weren't just sitting there, and every
beast in the forest must have known it. They bit and
clawed at one another, growls and snarls loud and
horrible, each beast-shape trying to rip apart the other.
One minute they were up high, just about fighting on
two legs, and the next they were down and rolling,
locked together out of shared decision. They *wanted*
to fight, and that was why I hadn't said anything to
InThig. The demon could have stopped them this time,
but they would only have found another.

A clash like that wasn't made to go on long, and it
certainly didn't. They went at each other for only a
few minutes, and then it became increasingly clear
that the bronze link-beast was getting the better of the
hellhound. Snarls turned to howls as teeth sank into
the brown body again and again, and then the hellhound wasn't scrabbling around trying to get *to* the

link-beast but away from him. The look in the yellow eyes was shocked and appalled, and when Rik finally gave Togor the chance to break off, he took it with dizzying speed. The hellhound raced away into the woods limping only a little, and the bronze link-beast stood with legs spread wide and head held high, daring his former opponent to return.

"That should teach him," InThig said with a comfortable chuckle, raising one paw to clean its face. "Hellhounds are *created* magical creatures, not natural ones, and they haven't a chance against the real thing. Silly of him to have thought otherwise."

Graythor made a sound of pleased agreement and finally let my arms go, but all I could do was stand there for a minute trying to get my thoughts in order. I half-noticed that Rik was shifting back to human form, and realized that his tunic belt must be his silver belt in disguise. That silver belt held his clothes and things intertransition while he was in link-form, then returned them all when he shifted back.

"Okay, that takes care of the first fight," he announced with fists on hips once he was all the way back. "If you'll excuse us, Graythor and InThig, it's time for Laciel and me to get to the second. Now that I'm in the mood, it would be silly to put it off."

Graythor, over near the fire, gave Rik a sharp look before glancing at me, then he shrugged and gestured to InThig. The demon hesitated visibly, trying to make its mind up about something, but the hesitation didn't last long. Its movement seemed reluctant as it followed Graythor around to the back of the wagon and up the steps, but it still went.

"Finally," Rik muttered, annoyance strong in his voice. "I was beginning to think getting you alone would be impossible. Are you ready to talk to me about all the nonsense that's been going on?"

"I've already said everything I care to," I answered, then walked over to the fire to check the pot of coffee Graythor had set down on the ground. "If nobody wants to or is able to understand me, that's their problem rather than mine. I'm having a cup of coffee, and then I'm going to bed."

"So it *will* be a fight rather than talk," Rik said very flatly, and I glanced up to see the—hardened—way he looked at me. "I was right when I said you needed to be bested, and in his own way Togor was also right. You do need to learn how to treat people with respect, and now's the time for your first lesson. Here's the line you wanted to meet me at so badly, and I'm already at it."

He'd used his heel to scrape a line in the dirt while he was speaking, and once it was done he just stood behind it, waiting for me to respond. At another time he would have been bluffing, saying he was ready to fight when he really wasn't, but right then there was no bluff about it. His blood was still up from the fight he'd had with Togor, and that made him dead serious.

There were any number of things I could have said then, but rather than picking one or two I got a better grip on the stick I hadn't had a chance to put away, then went to meet him at the line. After being challenged, he had the right to demand that I face him, and I'd be the last to argue the point. The first time I'd challenged him I'd tried insisting that he have a stick of his own, but right then I didn't bother. I'd gotten to know him well enough to know he'd ignore me, so there was no sense in wasting the breath.

Stepping up to the line wasn't hard, not after all the times I'd done it, but I could feel Rik's eyes burning down at me as he waited for me to get it started. Technically speaking that wasn't proper, to have the challenger strike the first blow, but that was another point it didn't make sense for me to argue. He always gave his opponent first shot at him, I'd noticed, and I didn't expect he was about to change.

My grip on the heavy stick was as good as it was going to get, so I feinted at him with a jab, then tried bringing it across in a backswing. Tried, though, was as close as I got; his right arm came up to hit my arm rather than the stick, and then I was shoved back away from him. There was an instant of stumbling before I went down, and the ground was just as hard as I remembered it to be.

"Never attack from your unguarded side unless your opponent is too groggy to take advantage of the opening," Rik's voice came, as hard as the ground but considerably more even. "If you aren't ready and able to protect yourself, your attack gets blocked and you get hurt."

I sat up before getting to my feet, then went to stand at the line again. This time I tried a double feint before going for the strike, but it didn't make any appreciable difference. A hard-muscled arm was there to stop the strike, and the push of two broad palms against my shoulders sent me back down to the ground.

"Standing flatfooted is the best way of asking to get knocked over," that voice came again, just as even, just as hard. "The best stance is one foot behind the other, back foot angled out, weight distributed equally between the two. Think of your leading foot as the blocking side, and launch your attacks from behind the block. Once you're able to do that, you can learn how to attack from your blocking side."

This time I made it back to the line before the lecture was over, so as soon as the words stopped, I went at him again. Exactly what I did blurs into all the rest of the attacks, but since all the results were the same it really didn't matter. Every time I went down I got a lecture on what I was doing wrong, and after a while it made me mad.

The next time I attacked, I waited for what he called a block to go up, then I switched the stick around fast and rapped him hard across the knuckles. His breath hissed angrily as he snatched his hand back to shake it, and I felt a grim, low-grade sense of satisfaction. It was the first time I'd reached him, and all firsts are worthy of notice.

But it was also the last time, and a time he made sure I wouldn't forget. Instead of pushing me away, he was suddenly pulling me to him, and then he had bent me forward and was smacking my bottom hard. I struggled to at least free the stick I was still holding, but he hadn't forgotten about it. His left hand held it still while his right hand punished me for hitting him, and only once he was satisfied did I find myself back in the same place on the ground.

"And you can expect a lot more of that from now on," he growled, rubbing at the back of his hand while he glared down at me. "I'm through with quietly accepting anything you care to throw at me, and that includes your absolute refusal to take orders. You'll learn to listen to me at least as well as you did with that hellhound, or I'll know the reason why. You . . ."

He had to break it off then because I was back to the line and swinging with everything I had, and that time he had to work at it to keep me from connecting. But he did keep me from it and knocked me down again, and after that it all really did become a blur. I kept trying and he kept knocking me down, and after an endless, *endless* time I realized he was kneeling next to me with both of his hands on my shoulders.

"Stop fighting to get up again!" he ordered hoarsely, the expression on his face peculiar. "I thought you hit your head the last time you went down, but this time I'm sure of it. Are you trying to kill yourself?"

My head might have been hurting a little, but that wasn't the important part. What bothered me more was that I'd dropped the stick, and hadn't even been aware of it. I groped around with my right hand, trying to find it, but it seemed to have rolled out of reach.

"Laciel, the fight is over," Rik said, speaking the words slowly but forcefully. "I'm not going to let you go back to the line, so it's all over. Damn it, woman, stop trying to push my hands away and listen to me! If Togor had come back as many times as you did, he would have had me! If you want me to admit I can't take any more, then I'm admitting it."

I didn't know what he was talking about, I really didn't. Everything was a confusing swirl in my head, and I couldn't seem to follow what was going on.

"Why did you make me do this?" he asked, the words a husky whisper. "I love you so much, but you refuse to accept my love. You'd rather have pain from

me, and I don't understand why. You never expected
to best me, I'd bet everything I own on that, but you
still came to the line and kept on coming back. Why,
Laciel, tell me why?"

"I owed it to you," I said, looking away from the
pain in his eyes. "And I hate you. Let go of me."

It took him a minute to lift his hands from my
shoulders and another minute before I was able to roll
to sitting, but once I was on my feet it was a little
easier. I made it to the wagon and up the steps, climbed
onto my bed and drew the curtain, then let the flood of
tears come as hard as they wanted to. Nothing Rik had
done to me hurt as bad as what I felt on the inside, and
there were just no words to explain why that was.

It took a very long time before exhaustion brought
sleep instead of tears, and when I finally woke up it was
to find that we'd been captured by the King's guardsmen.

CHAPTER 18

"It's all my fault," Togor said again, his lowered voice
fighting with the rumble and jouncing of the wagon.
"If I hadn't been so distracted, I would have sensed
them moving in, but I didn't pay any attention at all."

"You weren't the only one," Rik said, his voice
almost pure growl. "If I'd paid less attention to you
and more to the woods . . ."

"None of us is without blame," Graythor interrupted, glumly trying to calm them down. "After last
night you two couldn't be expected to do anything *but*
watch each other warily, and that gave our enemy the
time to approach. Once they had their bows trained
on us, we had no choice but to surrender."

"And now we're on our way to Triam's city, but not in
the way we'd planned," Togor said, taking over Graythor's
glumness. "I'd still like to know how they found you."

"Most likely they had Morgiana's help," Graythor answered with a sigh. "You may remember Laciel mentioned the possibility, using it as an example of how little time we had. It distresses me to see how right she was."

"Speaking of Laciel, where is she?" Togor asked, his tone sharpening just a little. "I'm glad she wasn't there to see us back down from those bows, but shouldn't she be awake by now?"

"We had a late night, so if she's still sleeping let her sleep," Rik said, sounding more than a little weary himself. "When we were interrupted, you were about to tell me why you came back. Would you like to pick up now where you left off?"

"I came back because we were involved with more than fighting over a woman," Togor answered. "You beat me fairly—twice—and let me get away with my hide mostly intact, and that after I tried to backstab you. I wanted you to know I wouldn't have done that if not for this damned spell I was put under, and also wanted to say I was still with you if you'd have me."

"Well, I think it would be hard to argue the fact that you're definitely still with us," Rik said, and it was his turn to sigh. "Despite everything I wish you weren't, but we couldn't have been that lucky. All our luck disappeared as soon as we came through that gate."

"Togor, have you any idea what they mean to do with us?" Graythor asked, obviously trying not to sound worried. "Is there any chance we'll be brought in front of the High King and Morgiana? Close enough to speak to them, that is?"

"I seriously doubt it," Togor said, gloom covering every word. "If it was me alone, there would be no reason why not, but Triam will never chance it with you three. He may take a look at Laciel—in fact, he's almost certain to—but the rest of you?"

I could almost see his head shaking, an absolute denial of hope, but that wasn't the way Graythor took it.

"You mean he'll be bringing Laciel in front of them?" the wizard asked, delight beginning to grow. "But that's wonderful, my friend. All Laciel will need is a few words with Morgiana, and then . . ."

"No, Graythor, no, you're missing the point," Togor interrupted, and his voice suddenly grew softer. "When Triam sees Laciel, your other friend won't be any-where around, and Laciel will be—too occupied—to go looking for her. Triam will find Laciel just as at-tractive as I do—do you understand what I'm saying?"

Graythor's sudden silence probably indicated he un-derstood exactly what Togor was saying, just the way I did. The High King liked to give Sighted women his Blessing—from on top of them after he'd Persuaded them into accepting him.

"What will he do to her if she gives him trouble?" Rik asked, his voice now almost a monotone. "I don't mean just talking back—I mean if she actually tries to fight him."

"Women don't fight the King," Togor said with a little laugh of incredulity. "Not even men fight him, so that goes double for women. He'll have as close a hold on Laciel as I did, so it won't even matter that as soon as he was crowned he stopped the small amount of exercising he'd been forced to. He'll crook a finger and she'll run to him."

What sounded like a groan of pain came from what had to be Rik, since the words that closely followed the groan were Graythor's.

"Togor, my friend, we have deep trouble," he said, his tone hinting he wished he hadn't been beaten to the groan. "You said the King will hold Laciel as closely as you did— Didn't you hear her last night? She told you she *wasn't* being influenced by you, and she was telling the truth. She's learned how to resist whatever is involved in your talent, and she's certain to resist the King as well. And from Rik's reaction, I'd say we had another problem on top of that. Would you like to tell us about it, Rik?"

"What I'd like to do is wake up and find this was all a bad dream," Rik answered, a faint sound suggesting he'd run his hand through his hair. "Last night I thought I had all the answers, so when Laciel refused to talk to me as if I were a human being rather than an insect, I—decided to go for another victory. More than once she'd challenged me to meet her on a battle line, so I finally did."

"Damn it, you hurt her," Togor said furiously, and sounds came as though he were starting to get up. "That's why she isn't here with us now—you hurt her!"

"If he'd hurt her, we'd hardly be discussing the problem in the way we're doing," Graythor said soothingly, and the scraping sounds stopped abruptly. "Let's just listen to what Rik has to say, and if there's any accusing to be done we can take care of it when he's finished."

"By my First Ancestor, you have a grip like no old man *I've* ever seen," Togor muttered, and then he sighed. "All right, what you're saying makes sense, so I'll listen before I jump. What happened at this battle line you mentioned, Rik?"

"A little more than I expected," Rik answered, and now his voice was muffled as if his head was down. "She had that stick she was ready to use on you before our fight, Togor, but I've had enough training in unarmed combat to hold off three stick-wielding females her size. I was mad, and more than ready to push her around a little, and had convinced myself a few bruises would do her all the good in the worlds. She would learn she couldn't even match me, let alone best me, and then I would make her tell me what had really gone wrong between us."

Rik paused then, as if expecting a question or a comment, but nothing like that was offered. The silence was expectant rather than just for form, so he took a breath and then continued.

"The first thing *I* learned—and it took so long it proves what a damned fool I am—was that she already knew she couldn't best me. She even knew she couldn't match me, but when I told her I was accepting her challenge, she stepped up to the line without saying a word. Every time she came at me, I stopped her attack and pushed her down the way they'd do on a playground, intending to bruise nothing more than her arrogance. Over and over I kept doing it, waiting for the time she'd stop coming. And then it finally dawned on me that I wasn't working as hard to stay unbashed as I'd had to for a while, but she was still coming back every time. Once she even crawled a few steps before she was able to get back to her feet, and I thought she might have hit her head the last time she went down. I tried to stop it then, but she wasn't hearing me. She had made it back to the line, and what you do at the line is fight—"

"I suspect it was harder for you than it was for her," Graythor said then, smoothing over the unevenness that Rik's voice had fallen into. "Women seem to have this knack—they experience a hurt, and the men who care for them feel the pain."

"That's not a knack, it's a curse," Rik grumbled, but his voice was mostly back to normal. "Whatever it is, the next time she went down she did hit her head, and that made me realize I'd had enough. I went after her and held her down until she could understand what I was saying, and then I told her it was over. If I hadn't held her down, she would have gone back to that damned line again— Do you understand what I'm saying?"

"I'm afraid I do," Togor answered, and his tone was as bleak as the dead world. "If you'd fought her the way you fought me, you would have had to kill her to stop her. Why in the name of the First Ancestor is she like that? How do you people raise your girl children?"

"Laciel is somewhat different from your average girl child," Graythor said with another sigh. "Happily, most girls don't need to go through what she did. But now that you understand the situation more thoroughly, friend Togor, we need your opinion. How will she get on with the High King?"

"You mean if she lets him live?" Togor asked with a snort. "I didn't miss the part where Rik admitted keeping himself—unbashed—wasn't as easy as he'd expected it to be. I think I should have let her fight you first, Rik, and then I could have walked away winners. But with Triam— I don't even want to think about it."

"If he hurts her, I'll kill him," Rik said in a very—offhand way. "I don't know how, but somehow I'll get to him and I'll chop him into neat little chunks, and then I'll sit there and watch him die. Do you understand that, Togor? If he hurts her, he's dead."

"I believe you, Rik, and if it were up to me, you know nothing would be done to her," Togor said, the words coming tight and so fast they spilled over one another. "I would never hurt her, and I really want you to believe that."

"It's all right, Togor, I'm sure Rik believes you," Graythor said, and even *his* voice sounded strained. "Togor isn't the enemy, Rik, he's on our side, and we'll all do everything we can to keep Laciel safe. Are you all right now?"

"Only if this really is a nightmare," Rik answered, and his voice was muffled again. "By all the gods, I've never before wished so hard for a bad dream. What are we going to do?"

"In general, I don't think there's anything we *can* do," Togor said, sounding totally played out. "For ourselves we'll have to wait to see what happens, but for Laciel we'll have to talk to her as soon as she wakes up. If we're all very firm, we might be able to talk her into behaving herself with Triam."

The only answer he got to that was a chorus of short laughter from Rik and Graythor together, a reaction he wasn't terribly pleased with.

"Well, then, what do *you* two suggest?" he demanded. "In my world women do as they're told, and I have no experience at all with your obviously more advanced way of life. Since you're the experts, *you* come up with an idea."

"I'm certain Rik will think of something," Graythor said, back to being soothing. "He's the one most closely concerned with her, after all, so . . ."

"No, don't count on me for that," Rik interrupted quickly, and he, at least, hadn't been soothed. "If anyone does anything, it will have to be you, Graythor. I'm out of it."

"Much more likely, what you are is still upset,"

Graythor came back, working to sound forceful and assured. "What you went through with her last night would have shaken anyone, and you must give yourself time to get over it. The one thing to remember through it all is how she feels about you."

"Yes, that's exactly what I am remembering," Rik answered, the heavy tonelessness back. "I intended getting the truth out of her last night, and that's what I did. She hates me."

"That can't possibly be true!" Graythor protested, shocked. "In fact, I know it isn't true! She . . ."

"Graythor, she told me so herself," Rik interrupted again, and I heard the sound of rising. " 'I hate you,' she said, and she couldn't even stand to look at me when she said it. I'll still kill any man who hurts her, but beyond that I'm out of it."

The sound came of boots moving toward the front of the wagon, a short pause, and then the muffled flutter of a blanket-curtain being closed. All the rest was silence, which pointed up the following sigh.

"To fight so hard and win nothing but emptiness," Togor said, the words echoing with his sigh. "He's a man of honor, and I would have preferred winning in another way or not at all. A man should be able to keep what his prowess earns him."

"Togor, if I were you, I would hesitate before considering that I had won," Graythor said slowly and carefully. "I don't believe what Rik thinks Laciel told him, and from the way she behaved last night, she isn't considering you as a replacement for him even if a replacement were called for. She's more likely to attack you again."

"Nonsense, my friend, nonsense," Togor returned, a good measure of humor back in his voice. "The girl didn't attack me, she was just showing a bit of temper. And if she won't have Rik, who else do *you* think that leaves? I'd thought I'd lost her, but now she's mine even more thoroughly than she was."

"I think it's past time that Laciel was up and part of these discussions," Graythor said very firmly, accompanied by the sounds of rising. "She's at least as much involved in this as we are, and in certain instances even more so. We really do need whatever ideas she might have."

I heard a brief scraping, and then a gentle knock came at the side of my bed area.

"Laciel, child, it's time for you to wake up," Graythor called, the words gentle but inflexible. "Things have happened, and it's past time that you knew about them."

Rather than answer, I just sat there letting everything revolving in my head soak down deeper, but Graythor wasn't prepared to be patient.

"Laciel, you really must wake up," he began, and then his head peeked around the side of the blanket-curtain, a lamp held at the same height. "We have to—oh. You already are awake."

As soon as he'd moved the curtain, my bed had flickered back to being nothing more than a bunk bed, so when he moved the curtain all the way open, Togor saw nothing but that. I was sitting at the far side of the bed and leaning against the wall of the wagon, and the hellhound got quickly to his feet to grin at me.

"They say that every disaster has some shadow of benefit," Togor announced, letting his light eyes move over me. "If a man *has* to be captured by his enemies, it helps considerably if his lady is captured with him. Even if she does have a dirty face and is still wearing men's clothes."

"You climb onto this bed, and you'll find out the true meaning of the word disaster," I said as flatly as I could, stopping him just as he was about to do exactly that. "I'm not only not your lady, I'm seriously considering finding out how well you'll look covered in your own blood."

"Laciel, that's really no way for a young lady to talk," he scolded, but something must have told him I had the real answer to his burning desire for me. "You—look strangely different this morning, and you may be right about waiting until later before we exchange any personal greetings. Things have happened . . ."

"I heard," I said, leaning off the wooden wall at my

back. With the fluffy pillows gone, the position wasn't as comfortable as it had been, and I didn't need the distraction of pain.

"Laciel, child, you do seem strangely different," Graythor said, his eyes looking worried in the lamplight. "Just how much of our discussion did you hear?"

"All of it," I answered, making a face. "And since you'd probably like one of your most intense questions settled now, let me assure you that you don't have to worry about King Triam. If he tries to give me his Blessing, I'll settle his hash for him permanently."

"Now that's exactly the attitude we *don't* need," Togor exploded while Graythor closed his eyes and shook his head with a sigh. "Triam is a man and therefore stronger than you, so no matter how tough you think you are, you won't find it possible to best him. And what do you think would happen even if you did? What do you think you'd accomplish even if you killed him?"

"The least I'd accomplish would be to then have his successor to deal with," I answered, giving him something of a smile. "I might find getting along with the new King a little easier—since he would already know me. Or aren't you next in line for the succession after your brother, Togor?"

A small sound of startlement came from Graythor, Togor just stared at me—and Rik suddenly exploded from the bed he'd gotten into.

"What did you say?" he demanded, stomping over to stare at our newest companion. "He can't be the King's brother."

"But he is," I contradicted, watching the way Togor watched me. "I knew there was something—undefined—about him all along, but it took me until now to figure it out. He was supposed to have been a guardsman at the palace, but he knew too much about the wrong things. A guardsman would be expected to know certain things about his King, but he wouldn't know many personal things and he wouldn't speak of the King as if they were almost equals. How many times has he said 'Triam' instead of 'King Triam' or 'the High King'?"

"If that's your evidence, it's somewhat on the flimsy side," Togor said, returning my faint smile. "People call the King anything they like when he isn't there to hear them, and I'm no different from them."

"Aren't you?" I asked, folding my legs in front of me as I looked up at him. "Haven't we established beyond doubt that you're half-born? Considering the lousy way most people in this kingdom treat half-born males, how were you supposed to have gotten a position like palace guardsman? A job like that is hard to come by even for the best, and half-born males are being flattered when they're just considered inferior. No matter what story you told, they would have checked to be sure it was true, and then they would have found you out."

Annoyance flitted in and out of the eyes looking down at me, but he wasn't saying anything about flimsiness.

"So we have a half-born palace guardsman who couldn't possibly have gotten a job like that, and when a virtual stranger finds out his secret about being Sighted, he's no more than faintly amused," I went on. "He isn't frightened, or insulted, or particularly bothered that she found out. He doesn't *feel* inferior and obviously never did, and surprise, surprise. He also just happens to know that the King is half-born as well. That's the sort of unimportant gossip *every* mere guardsman would know. And if you consider . . ."

"All right, all right, there's no need to go on," Togor said, conceding defeat but only with his words. "I wasn't sure how sure *you* were, but now I know. So what happens next? Toss out the spy in your midst, hoping he'll break his neck when he hits the ground, and then forget about him? If that's what you intend, let's get it over with."

"Do you think you have a reason why we shouldn't?" Rik asked, studying the man who had turned away from me. "If you were really on our side, you would have told us the truth."

"Which would have accomplished what?" Togor demanded, turning his head toward Rik. "Either you would have thought I was lying, or you would have thought I was a spy for my brother. Either way you wouldn't have accepted me as one of you, and that was what I needed."

"Why?" Graythor asked, the word relatively gentle. "Why would you want to join us against your brother? Because he turned you into a hellhound?"

"That would be reason enough, but I also have others," Togor said, now looking at the wizard. "I was more than ready to support my brother as King just the way I supported our father, but Triam decided I couldn't be trusted to support him. I was friendly with too many of his court followers, distinguished myself to the point of earning a third name, had very dangerous ideas about honor and the way a King should behave. At that, I suppose I was lucky. Our two younger brothers disappeared months ago, and no one seems to know where."

"So you decided you could make use of our help in taking over your brother's throne," I said, bringing his attention back to me. "And to make it even sweeter, our group contained a female Sighted just like the one your brother had. If we could figure the riddle to doing magic on this world, you'd end up having it all."

"Using you was *not* the only interest I had in you," he stated, turning all the way back to lock eyes with me. "You're the most desirable woman I've ever met, and any man who didn't fall in love with you would be a fool. I may be a fool in other things, but not in that."

"No, in that you're simply a liar," I said, leaning my elbows on my thighs. "I'm such a sweet-tempered, delightfully obliging little darling that every man in the universe just can't wait to hear my silvery, tinkling laughter. You needed my strength and you liked the looks of my face and body, and those reasons overrode my lacks in the sweetness department. You also thought I was a match for Morgiana, but you would have been sadly disappointed. I won't have her strength for years and years, so your plans wouldn't have worked out anyway."

"You know, there's one thing you're right about,"

he answered, folding his arms as he looked down at me. "When it comes to sweetness, a wagonload of honey would have trouble balancing you out. You're the only woman I ever knew who tempted me to ignore my upbringing where females are concerned, and believe me, that's saying something. But it still isn't enough to make me not want you."

I made a very rude sound, but all that did was sharpen the annoyed look I was getting from him. He was lying in his teeth, and if he thought I didn't know it, he really was a fool.

"I think that's a side issue we can safely shelve for the moment," Graythor put in after clearing his throat. "What's more to the point is where Togor stands with us now, and how, if in any way, this revelation can help us. Togor—what can you tell us about how your brother handles magic?"

"Absolutely nothing," the hellhound answered, disgust heavy in his voice. "As our father's heir *he* got the preliminary training, and no one else is allowed to know anything about that. The secrecy is just as stiff as when magic is actually being performed, with special guarding spells to make sure of it. I doubt if there's anyone in this world who can tell you how he does it."

"I'll bet Morgiana could," I said. "If he's using her strength—and we know he is—for the best results she has to be as close as possible. If there was only some way of getting through to her."

"We're not likely to find one, so we may as well forget about it," Rik said, rubbing his face with one hand. "What we need more, I think, is some way of getting out of this trap. What are our chances likely to be if we try breaking out, Togor?"

"Our chances are probably nil no matter what we do, but personally I'd rather go down fighting out here than provide sport for my brother," Togor replied, meeting Rik's gaze. "There's a very large underground chamber beneath the palace, not far from the dungeons. In our father's time it was used as the execution ground for condemned criminals, the sort of criminals who had earned the worst and hardest kind of death. Triam changed that not long after he took the throne, and now the place is used to entertain him and his closest cronies. Their victims are usually from the lower classes, but in our case I'm certain he'd be willing to make an exception."

"No, Rik, that *isn't* the best idea," Graythor said at once, obviously seeing the sudden decision in Rik's eyes. "If we throw our lives away to escape a possibly worse death later, we also throw away any chance we might have of winning out instead of losing. Death is a very final happening, too final to rush into."

"But for some there could be worse ahead than the worst of deaths," Rik countered, his glance touching me so briefly I might have imagined it. "If that's the only future someone has to look forward to, the kindest thing you can do is help them to avoid it. Unless you think it would be better to wait until the last possible minute, and only then find out you waited too long."

"Don't let him upset you, Uncle Graythor," I said as quickly as *he* had spoken, bothered by the sudden look of extreme old age on the wizard's face. "I'm too mean to ever be offered a fate worse than death, and you of all people should know that. They save that sort of thing for the sweet young dears, who make it all worthwhile with their moist-eyed trembling. Honestly now, can you picture me moist-eyed and trembling?"

"More easily than you seem to think," Graythor answered, still looking drawn and old. "I know you considerably better than you believe I do, child, and I'd sooner see you dead than in the clutches of a man like this King Triam. Morgiana will have had little difficulty in withstanding his doings, but you would not endure it in any way the same. Have no fear, those who care for you will protect you from such a fate. But not now, not this soon."

He turned away then with the obvious intention of doing some thinking, and I caught a glimpse of Rik and Togor before they turned away as well. The looks on their faces were almost identical, and it was a good thing I didn't have to speak. After seeing the way they agreed completely with Graythor, I wouldn't have known what to say. For my own part, I didn't even want to think about it.

After a while Graythor came back to where I sat, and the two of us tried working on the magic puzzle. He started out by apologizing for the lack of anything for me to eat in the wagon, but I couldn't see that as our biggest problem. Far more important was the fact that we'd already tried our best ideas about magic, and I, at least, seemed to be fresh out.

"But we now have a confirmed addition to our information," Graythor pointed out from where he sat on the right side of my bed. Rik had gone back to the bed he'd popped out of so fast, and Togor, resting in hellhound form, lay on the floor near the front of the wagon. "You did hear our friend mention the preliminary training his brother had been given, didn't you? I'm certain that that training consisted of learning the language of spells."

"If it does happen to be the language of spells that they use," I said morosely, still in the mood to disagree. "What if it's a different language entirely, one we've never heard of?"

"Oh, come, Laciel, let's not be nonsensical about this," Graythor said with annoyance, shifting a little where he sat. "Aside from the language of spells, there *are* no other languages, which is certainly as it should be. How would people and beings converse if everyone spoke his, her, or its own language?"

"They wouldn't, which in any number of cases would turn out to be the best situation possible," I moped, chin resting in palm. "There's been a lot of conversation I could have done very well without."

"Another language would be entirely beyond the bounds of any sort of logic," Graythor said, grimly determined to settle the point before dismissing it. "Our assumed visitor who came through the gate would have had to bring that language with him, otherwise the tongue would be known to the people *here*. If it was known, it would have been experimented with, and our visitor would not have been the only one discovering the secret. And if it *was* here, why would our visitor bother learning it when everyone spoke *his* language? If he brought it with him, how could it possibly link to magic in *this* world? The language of spells does, but the language of spells *is* this language in a different arrangement, and this language applies everywhere."

"All right, all right, you've convinced me," I conceded, holding up one hand. "The training given Triam was in the language of spells, but I don't see how that helps us. We already knew it was either that or this language, and we've tried them both. Since neither of them work for us, we're right back where we started. And by the way, where's InThig?"

"Your pet is napping right now on *my* bed," Graythor said, giving me a look with Meaning. "He'll probably want to play later, so he's busy resting up. Now, about this training. It's occurred to me that possibly *simple* spells are the ones that don't work, and a magic user must be fairly deep into his talent before he can accomplish anything. It would explain why beginners have no chance of discovering the method on their own—they aren't using spells that are detailed enough."

"Now that's a possibility," I said as I straightened, already forgetting about what "playing" my "pet" InThig might be getting ready for. "Let's give it a try."

Graythor started with a medium-complex spell, I tried another in the same category, and then we did one together. After that we upped the ante a little bit each time, and by the time we were through we could have torn that entire world apart—if the spells had worked. Fortunately or unfortunately they didn't, but whatever produces frustration was going full blast.

Shortly after that the wagon stopped, we sat unmoving for a while, and then we were fed. I was able to get a glimpse out the back door before being warned away by a guardsman with a bow, and the sight wasn't in any way encouraging. There must have been more

than thirty guardsmen around, and that didn't include
the ones I could hear but couldn't see. It did include
the half-dozen hellhounds, though, lying on the ground
not far from the back of the wagon and simply watching it. There would be no catching *them* sleepy and
therefore less alert, which made for a problem even
aside from the bowmen. The King wanted us in his
city, and didn't seem terribly worried if we got there
whole or not.

Once our meal was over and we'd started moving
again, Graythor came back to his earlier place on my
bed. We'd all eaten alone, possibly using the privacy
to try telling ourselves we weren't really prisoners, but
for me it hadn't worked. I was beginning to feel again
as I had as a child, surrounded by people and forces
that were too big and strong for me to win against,
and I hated that feeling. I'd thought I'd never have to
feel it again, but that horrible world was bringing it all
back—with no handy gate that would let me escape it.

"Laciel, Togor tells me that at the rate we're moving, we'll be in the King's city tomorrow," Graythor
said, surprising me by not going immediately back to
our problem. "Have you thought about what will happen then?"

"I love the delicate way you discuss these things,
Uncle Graythor," I answered, forcing a faint smile for
him. "What has Togor said about the possibility that I
actually might be able to kill his brother?"

"He doesn't consider it a very likely possibility,"
Graythor admitted with a slight hesitation, making no
effort to return the smile. "And even if you should
manage it after all, the King's guardsmen would kill
you in turn before anyone would be able to interfere.
It seems we may have to use our secret weapon to
accomplish the King's ending—as an absolute last possible resort."

He was saying that for a reason, I saw, and I knew
without doubt that I'd hate the reason. When he saw I
was ready to hear it anyway, he rubbed at his face and
then plunged in.

"It has occurred to me that King Triam has had

ample time to establish a very close link with Morgiana," he said with a sigh. "Links like that are very sensitive, and it's almost certain that if Triam is killed—"

"Morgiana will go with him," I finished when he didn't, suddenly and horribly chilled. In my memory I could see that being we'd come across on the quest, the Singer who had held Su and Kadrim—and Rik— prisoner with her mind and will. If I'd killed her, they would have died as well, and the way I'd gotten around the problem couldn't be used in the present situation.

"Then Triam has to live," I said very simply, willing to accept no other possibility. "We'll have to find something else for our secret weapon to do."

"Our secret weapon is frantic," Graythor said, still staring at me with soft, dark eyes. "It refuses to allow you to come to harm, but it also cannot bring itself to harm Morgiana. It's currently tearing up one small corner of my bed with its claws, trying to resolve the dilemma."

"Tell it not to waste the time," I said, trying not to slump where I sat. "If that King decides he wants me, I'll find *some* way to handle it. And if I can't, then . . ."

"Whatever you do, don't say it won't kill you," Graythor told me angrily, his dark eyes no longer mild. "I'm aware that you consider yourself a woman of experience, Laciel, but your experience is hardly so vast that you would remain untouched by something like this. For some there *are* things worse than being killed, and as you mentioned I do know you rather well. It's come to me that Rik might possibly find some way to . . ."

"You're counting on Rik?" I interrupted with a snort. "Really, Uncle Graythor, I thought you knew better than to waste your time like that. Rik won't do a damned thing."

"Laciel, you can't possibly believe that," he returned with a laugh of incredulity. "Didn't Rik step in when he thought Togor was about to hurt you? Didn't he vow to kill the King if you were harmed? I know you couldn't see his face and eyes when he said that, and I'm rather glad you couldn't. Even I, who was in no danger at all, felt chilled. My dear child, he's very deeply in love with you."

"He's very deeply in love with the idea of keeping me from getting hurt," I countered, making no effort to bar the disgust from my voice. "That may seem terribly noble to *you*, but I know better than that. Getting hurt physically is nothing, nothing but a part of life, and you usually forget about it even before the bruises heal. If he really cared about me, he would have shown it in a different way, but he didn't. What he showed me instead was the truth, so from now on he can keep his vows to himself."

"And what truth was that?" Graythor asked, his voice gentle again, his head to one side. "I ask in order to be able to understand, child, not in an effort to pry. I've seen nothing that would substantiate your contention."

"But of course you saw it," I answered, wondering how a wizard of his ability could be so blind. "You were the one who saw it, and then told InThig about it. Didn't you say Rik was there when Togor came after me in the pool, while I was taking a bath? Didn't you tell InThig he must have seen everything that went on?"

"I believe I said it was *possible* he saw everything that went on," Graythor answered cautiously. "He was certainly there so he had the opportunity, but I still don't understand what that can have to do with . . ."

"Uncle Graythor, he saw Togor kissing me and it didn't bother him!" I spelled it out, as clearly as possible, in an effort to get that conversation over and done with. "If he really cared about me, it *would* have bothered him; he would have gotten jealous and tried to stop it! All he did, though, was turn around and walk away, pretending nothing had happened at all. Is that what someone does when they care for you?"

"I—hadn't thought to look at it in quite that way," Graythor admitted, finally having gotten the point. "Is that what Morgiana taught you, a way to judge the behavior of men who claim to be in love with you?"

"Don't be silly," I said with another snort. "Morgiana never mentioned the point, because she didn't have to. All the books I've ever read make that one point very clear, and even Dranna confirmed it during the quest. She said Zail and Kadrim would get jealous if I gave one or the other of them too much attention, and then the one *not* getting the attention would start a fight. She had more to do with men than I'll ever have, so you can't say she didn't know what she was talking about. And didn't Rik himself try to make *me* jealous? No, Rik has made it plain how little he cares about me, and that's why I hate him."

"I see," Graythor muttered, staring at me in a peculiar way. "You learned that outlook from books, Sofann Dra confirmed it, so it has to be true. I wonder if you've ever considered the possibility that there may be some people who don't look at it the same, who might consider making others jealous but who would rather think about the situation before rushing into anything themselves. If Rik were one of those, then . . ."

"Then he's too thickheaded to be let out alone, and I still want nothing to do with him," I finished firmly. "If everyone else in the worlds looks at it the right way, it shouldn't be beyond him to do the same. He probably *would* do the same if he really cared, but all *he* cares about is what *you* do—keeping me from getting hurt. Are *you* deeply in love with me?"

"No, child, I'm not in love with you," he conceded with another sigh. "I love you dearly, but I'm not *in* love with you. What I am the most is vastly confused, and if ever I wished Morgiana could be here— Well, idle thoughts, idle consequences. I think I shall take a short time to speak with our companions, to be sure they make no decisions to act foolishly, and then I'll return to continue *our* efforts."

He patted my foot, then got up to walk toward the front of the wagon, and in another moment I heard him talking softly with Togor. Instead of trying to make out the words, I lay down flat on my back, put my hands behind my head, and forced myself to think about magic. The only thing we hadn't tried seemed to be standing on our heads while speaking the spells, and I intended making that my first suggestion when

Graythor got back. If all we had left untried was pure silliness, then silliness had to be next on the list.

I drifted away into my own thoughts while I waited, and was only brought out of them once when I heard Rik shout, "What?" in a very outraged, disbelieving way. If Graythor was giving him reasons for not starting trouble with the guardsmen outside, he didn't sound as though he cared for the reasons. Well, that was too bad about him, just like a lot of other things. If he decided not to listen to Graythor, I wouldn't care in the least.

When Graythor finally got back, we discovered he might as well have stayed away a little longer. He closed his eyes and simply shook his head when I mentioned being upside down, and that was it as far as reaction to the idea went. It was also it as far as ideas of any sort went, and staring at each other while rubbing our heads did nothing to change that.

We stayed together until the wagon stopped again, waited for our meal, then ate it when it came. Graythor took his meal with Rik and Togor, muttering something about hoping they would make a remark to cause his mind to begin working again, but I was in no mood for human company. When InThig jumped up onto my bed and settled down wordlessly in the far corner, I didn't mind at all. Once I heard tiny claws ripping at the blanket there I was prepared to reconsider the decision, but it wasn't worth making a fuss about. InThig still hadn't resolved its problem, but there was nothing I could do to help.

After the meal I got up and walked back and forth between the back bunks for a while, but what I really needed in the way of exercise was a long walk outside. I'd spent most of the day being mostly motionless, and if the description sounds boring, it was only a shadow of the way I felt. I had just about decided to ask if I could take a walk before we slept, but then something happened to tell me not to waste the breath.

Despite its being dark outside, the wagon began moving again, and the guardsmen weren't simply looking for a better campsite. They didn't want a campsite at all, and we would be in the King's city a lot sooner than we'd expected.

CHAPTER 19

At one time or another all of us but Togor had gotten a little sleep during the night, but we were all wide awake when we reached the palace. The cobblestones let us know when we reached the city, and the crowd noises told us people were up and about. We weren't able to see any of it, not with the board they'd nailed over the back in the way, but we'd certainly been able to hear it. We had the feeling we'd reached the palace when the noises died away, and Togor confirmed our guess.

"Yes, this has to be it," he growled, his yellow hellhound eyes looking more unhappy than intimidating. "I'll wait until they start pulling off that board before I change back to man shape. There are people in the palace who were once friends of mine, and if we come across any of them, I want them to be able to recognize me. You never know who might be willing to lend a hand to a friend . . ."

He let the thought trail off and didn't pick it up again, especially since none of the rest of us agreed there was a chance of getting help. The King was able to do magic, and was the only one who could; even if one of Togor's friends *wanted* to help, what could any of them do that would make a difference? We'd be kidding ourselves if we thought it could happen, and it was much too late in the game to kid ourselves.

"If the King intends enjoying our demise, surely he'll want a personal hand in making it happen," Graythor said, rubbing his face as his eyes showed distraction. "What other way would he have to do that than through the use of magic? And if he uses his magic, we should be able to observe his method and copy it. Togor, Rik—do you think the two of you will

347

be able to protect Laciel and me from the physical
until one or the other of us is able to do that?"

"If we're all sent out at the same time and the
hellhound spell doesn't grow stronger and more com-
pelling," Togor said, "you can count on me to stand in
front of you as long as I continue standing. As for
Rik—do you really need to ask him?"

Graythor smiled and shook his head, which was
answer enough for Rik and Togor both. No one seemed
to be waiting for *my* answer to anything, and that was
just as well. Togor had said the Chosen spell was even
stronger in the city, and he hadn't been wrong; I could
feel my temper wanting to flare out at anyone near
enough, but I was still able to hold it down. I was just
hoping we would get to whatever was going to happen
in a reasonably short time; sleeping in the middle of
that spell was something I really didn't want to try.

The wagon slowed down to a pace that could only
be described as picking its way through, and after a
short time of that finally stopped altogether. We waited
for them to begin ripping the board off the back of the
wagon, but there seemed to be a delay of some sort
that no one bothered explaining to us. Togor waited a
few minutes, and when the wagon didn't start moving
again, he changed his mind about not changing his
body. He padded to the front of the wagon, shifted to
man form, then began getting into the replacement
clothes Graythor had given him the morning after the
fight.

Of course, I didn't get to see most of that with my
own eyes. Not that I would have stared at the hellhound once he had changed to a man, I do have better
manners than that. It was just that as Togor was
almost to the place where he had left the clothes, Rik
stepped in front of me and lounged there with folded
arms. I didn't know if he'd done that on purpose or
not, but I certainly wasn't going to ask. Despite the
really strange way Rik had been looking at me since
we'd all gathered together, I had nothing to say to the
man.

Whatever had delayed our release was finally resolved, and the board was pulled off the back of the wagon and thrown aside with a crash. A guardsman stuck his head in to tell us to come out one at a time and slowly, and when the head was quickly withdrawn Togor gave a humorless laugh.

"I think it's safe to say the fools are afraid of you," the ex-hellhound observed. "It's apparently not yet occurred to them that either you really are dangerous and their preparations are therefore useless, or you aren't dangerous at all and their overcaution is being wasted. In the long run I suppose it doesn't matter, but that sort of mindlessness is typical of Triam. Well, shall we go? Ladies first, of course."

"Let's save the gentlemanly gestures for another time, shall we?" Graythor disagreed as I was about to step forward. "I'll go first, then Laciel, then the two of you. And Laciel, of course, will carry her pet cat."

Togor shrugged, then gestured his agreement, never dreaming that Laciel was carrying her pet cat because that pet cat had insisted on it. InThig had also suggested the order of march, and Graythor had agreed immediately. Neither of them could tell me what good having InThig with me would do, but they refused to change their minds on the point.

Graythor moved warily as he climbed out of the wagon, and when I followed him I understood why. We were well inside the palace somewhere, but our guardsmen were behaving as though we were outdoors and would have someplace to run if we did get by them. The torchlight from the stone walls glinted off the steel heads of arrows aimed at us, and the hellhounds were spread out in a line that presumably cut us off from freedom. We were gestured around the wagon toward a wide corridor, and then we were directed up it.

As we walked along in single file, it became obvious what the delay in releasing us had been. The route we were sent by was just about littered with bowmen, and that remained unchanging even after we began going downward. The stairway was wide and straight and reasonably well kept, and every step of the way we were under one weapon or another. When that stairway ended, it was considerably cooler, not to mention darker, danker, and smellier. But the bowmen were still there, as well as guardsmen armed in other ways.

They marched us quite a distance from the stairs we'd come down, but finally we reached a section with cagelike cells lined up to the right, and four of the cage doors were open. Graythor walked down and entered the first cell, I was gestured into the second, Rik had the third, and Togor was awarded the fourth. With all of us inside the cell doors were closed and locked, and only then were most of the guardsmen allowed to relax. They were also gathered together and marched away, leaving only a handful to keep a distrusting eye on us.

"I love this decor," I said to no one in particular, walking over to put InThig down on the bare cot the cell contained. "Early bars over avant stone."

"They look like cages and that's what they are," Togor said from his end, easily seen through the side bars of my cell and Rik's. "I wonder how many of Triam's enemies saw this as the last comfort they were ever given?"

"Let's not be morbid," Graythor said firmly, staring at the bars that even covered the stone wall at the back of the cell. "We're still alive and we're still together, and those are two points in *our* favor. Hopefully there will be more of the same later."

He turned his head to look at each of us then, obviously trying to remind us about his final idea. If the High King made the mistake of using magic where Graythor and I could copy the technique, we were all home free. What he'd neglected to mention was how big an "if" that was; if the High King used magic we might conceivably win free, but if he didn't, we were positively done.

After that brief conversation we were all free to go about our own business, which for the most part consisted of giving the cell one extra glance and then either sitting on the cot or remaining standing. The wooden cot was all the cell contained, and its mattress of straw-filled cloth was beyond filthy and all the way down to nauseating. The stone floor was gritty with something that crackled under my boots, but even so it seemed cleaner than that cot. Not clean, just cleaner.

I decided to do my sitting down on the floor near the bars separating me from Graythor's cell, and a few moments later that position showed me what size the cells were. Rik stalked four and a half paces to the back of his cell, turned, then stalked four and a half paces to the front. Togor stalked the same amount from side to side, and I couldn't decide if watching them distracted from dullness or was making me dizzy. They seemed to think they were accomplishing something burning up energy like that, but I needed my energy for fighting off the Chosen spell.

No more than ten or fifteen minutes went by like that, and then I had a sudden visitor in my lap. InThig had been playing kitty-cat with great flair the whole time, keeping its eyes mostly closed so as not to give heart failure to our captors. It had purred and rubbed its head against me almost every time someone looked at it, but carrying it down into the bowels of the palace had almost flattened me. It didn't weigh what it normally did in big-cat form, but no real cat alive the size of InThig could have hefted as much as the demon did.

"Hey, take it easy," I muttered in a very low voice to a demon who was stomping all over my thighs. "If you keep that up, I'll have to crawl out to be executed. I've been wondering what I would have to do to put you on a diet."

"One doesn't diet away mass, Laciel, and I'm much too massive in this form to be a lightweight," InThig returned in a calm but very low lecturer's voice. "I apologize, of course, if I've caused you any discomfort, but I needed to tell you that I would be gone for a short while. I'm going to make another attempt to reach Morgiana."

"You think it will do some good?" I asked, pretending to stroke and caress my "pet." "If Triam has her sewn up tight, all she'll do is call the guard again."

"Perhaps so, but with our party captured there's no longer a need to stay away for fear of warning them of our presence," it answered, somehow managing to purr at the same time. "It's occurred to me that I was able to pull *you* out from under Togor's power by talking to you. It may not be the same with Morgiana, but the chance needs to be taken. I'll tell Graythor, and then I'll go."

"Good luck," was all I was able to think of saying, but I couldn't remember ever speaking two words I meant more. InThig rubbed against my hand one last time, then jumped down and walked easily between two bars into Graythor's cell. Being small had definite advantages at times, and it came to me again how nice it would be to be a demon.

The words exchanged between InThig and Graythor didn't reach me or our guards, and after quite a while with the guards unmoving from their places I decided InThig had gotten away clean. Despite the wall torches the whole area was dark and shadowy, and even a real cat shouldn't have had trouble disappearing. I shifted against the bars at my back, and tried to find something useful to occupy my mind.

Another chunk of unfilled time dragged by, enough of it to force Togor and then Rik down to sitting. It's a wonder that most prisoners don't die of boredom before their captors can put them to death, but maybe they do. Maybe the idea of executing prisoners is nothing but a hoax, developed to cover the fact that boredom was what really did them in. Captors do have to save face, I realized, and they would be terribly embarrassed if people found out their dungeons were so deadly dull. What would be more natural, then, than to spread the story—

"On your feet." The words took a minute to penetrate the silliness I'd been in the middle of; when I looked up, I saw that the guardsman was talking to *me*. He and two others had apparently just arrived, and they were standing in front of my cell.

"I said, on your feet," he repeated when I didn't

move, faint annoyance behind the words. "You can't have forgotten how to obey orders *this* soon."

"What will you do if I *don't* obey your orders?" I asked, still just looking up at him. "Drag me into a dungeon and lock me in a cell?"

"Seriously harming women may be forbidden, but punishing them isn't," the guardsman informed me, his helmeted head coming up a little. "If you don't get on your feet and come along, you'll find out what provisions for that my orders include. Which way will you have it?"

I looked at the big man and the two other big men behind him, then silently stood up. Arguing or fighting would have done no good at all, and I couldn't say I hadn't been expecting something like that.

"Where are you taking her?" Rik demanded from my left as one of the two guardsmen behind the spokesman came forward to unlock my cell. "Damn it, where are you taking her?"

Ignoring him and his question together, the guardsman who opened the cell reached in and pulled me out by one arm. He wasn't overly rough about it, but when the second guardsman came forward to take my other arm there was no doubt about how well held I was. The guardsman who had spoken, obviously an officer, led the way out of the area, and I was pulled along behind him. None of them paid the least attention to all the shouting Rik and Togor were doing, and once we turned a corner the noise was left pretty much behind.

The corridor I was hurried along was narrower than the one they'd used to bring us to the cells, and there were no bowmen anywhere. That told me they didn't consider me as dangerous as the men I'd been with, and I really wished I could take advantage of that. On a normal world I was even more dangerous than two out of the three, but on *that* world . . .

We didn't walk nearly as far as we had from the stairs, only about half the distance or less. The officer stopped in front of a heavy wooden door on the left, knocked twice, then motioned me inside when the door was opened. The two guardsmen holding my arms took care of getting me inside, and the man who opened the door for us studied me while the officer closed it again.

"Are you sure this is the right girl?" the stranger asked with a frown, his overfleshed face showing how unhappy he was with me. "She's filthy, and just look at the clothes she's wearing."

"She was the only female with them, my lord," the officer answered, standing at attention the way his men were doing. His face registered nothing in the way of ridicule for the ruffled and laced costume the newcomer was wearing, all in reds and pinks and ribboned in white. If I were male, I knew they'd have to knock me unconscious to get me into a rig like that, but the heavyish man didn't seem uncomfortable at all. I didn't much care for his attitude, though, so I decided to see what I could do about changing that.

"My clothes and I may be filthy, but that's considerably better than being ridiculous," I said, trying hard for a smirk while I looked him up and down. "Doesn't it bother you when people start laughing hysterically as soon as you walk in a room?"

"Insolence becomes ignorance when its source is the uninformed," the man returned with a haughty sniff, but his face did go a shade or so darker. "And I can see that your manners are well matched to your appearance and wardrobe. The High King is most unlikely to be pleased."

"Now I'm crushed," I answered, wishing I had a hand free to use for patting at a yawn. "Now I'll have to go back where I came from, to live out a life of unending disappointment. Do give him my regards anyway."

I tried turning away toward the door I'd come in by, but the two guardsmen holding my arms weren't having any. I hadn't been dismissed by the idiot in fool's clothing, so as far as they were concerned I wasn't going anywhere.

"You may give the High King your regards in person, girl," the man told me, a slight smirk of his own showing when it was clear I wouldn't be leaving the way I wanted to. "Should you please him despite your appearance, that won't be all you'll give him. I'm going to inform the High King of her presence, Captain, so keep a close watch on her."

"Yes, my lord," the officer answered, and then we all got to watch the fool disappear through a doorway in the wall opposite the one *we'd* used. The door was made of a much better quality wood and was even stained and carved, and undoubtedly led elsewhere than back to the dungeons.

Since there was obviously going to be something of a wait, I gave in and looked more closely at the room I stood in. It was a fairly large room, well lit by wall lamps, and the pretty blue and green silks covering the walls made one think the place was somewhere other than on a dungeon level. The carpeting under our feet was long and silky and white, and the furniture standing on it was darkwood and nicely carved. Two tables, a long, wide, padded lounge, three chairs, a sideboard holding pitchers and goblets—all the comforts of a home away from home. There was also a light perfume in the air, undoubtedly to cover any stray dungeon odors.

"How long is this likely to take?" I asked the officer, wondering if he and his men were as patiently uncaring as they seemed. "I have a few spells I wanted to work on, so—"

I broke off the nonsense when the officer paled and almost reached for his sword, and the two men holding me convulsively tightened their grips. Magic wasn't taken lightly at all by those people, and they must have been told I was involved with it in some way. After that all three of them stared directly at me, and conversation was definitely out.

The High King let me know how unimportant I was by the length of time he made me wait. I was shifting from one foot to the other when that fancy door opened again, and the three guardsmen went instantly to attention. I suppose I would have known King Triam anyway from the close resemblance between

him and Togor, but even if I hadn't, I would have
gotten the message from the way he carried himself.
He was alone when he came through the door and
closed it behind him, but he gave the impression of
leading a large, involved procession. He was light-
haired and light-eyed like Togor and just about as tall,
but he seemed a bit burlier than the man-form of the
hellhound. He wore a long-sleeved, light blue shirt of
very good material, wine-red trousers with knee-high,
dark red boots, and a wide belt all of silver. He
gestured once and the three guardsmen almost ran out
of the room, and then he smiled at me.

"Kitrum was wrong," he said in a voice that was
slightly deeper than Togor's, and possibly even a little
smoother. "It won't be necessary to have you cleaned
up before I can see how attractive you are. I see things
that Kitrum can't hope to."

"Before you sprain your arm patting yourself on the
back, you might remember there's a reason for that,"
I said, letting him know he wasn't impressing me.
"Assuming Kitrum was that overdressed fool who was
in this room earlier, he isn't Sighted while you are.
What's the matter, Triam, afraid that having other
Sighted males around will be too much in the way of
competition?"

"I'm the High King, sweet girl," he said with a
sudden grin I hadn't been expecting. "I'm not afraid
of the competition because no one can compete with
me. Do you know how marvelous a glow you have?
No wonder my brother couldn't keep away from you."

"Yes, Togor did mention something about my glow,"
I said, folding my arms as I stared at him. "As a
flattering come-on, it leaves quite a lot to be desired.
You'd better not have hurt Morgiana, or nothing in
this entire universe will save you."

"Ah, and how the glow brightens," he said in ap-
parent delight, in a way I could swear he was serious
about. "This gets better and better. Would you like a
glass of wine?"

"I'm fussy about the people I drink with," I answered, watching him walk the two steps to the side-

board. "With someone like you, I'd even pass up water in a desert."

"You don't seem terribly impressed with the fact that I'm a king," he said over his shoulder while filling two silver cups from a pitcher. "Are you so used to kings, then, that you feel free to insult them as much as you please?"

"Not long ago I was involved with two kings," I said, remembering the quest and deciding I might as well use whatever I had. "One of them was sweet, and wanted to marry me. The other was awful and wanted to own me. The second one died."

"But not by your hand, I'd wager," he said, turning with one of the cups to stare at me. "Despite your insults, you're not the sort of woman who could easily harm a man. You do much better giving him your love."

"You're an excellent judge of character," I said as I swallowed most of a laugh, remembering the delicious feel of a good, hard stick in my hand. "There are some men I can't harm easily at all, much as I'd like to. I guess I'm just too softhearted and meek."

"You think you're mocking me, but you really aren't, you know," he came back with a gentle smile after sipping at his wine. "Do you think I can't recognize a sweet, soft woman when I see one, a woman who's tired of running and fighting and hiding? Sneaking around is no life for a woman like you, not when you can have so much more. And you do want more, don't you?"

"That's a fairly safe question," I observed, keeping my voice even. "Even people who have everything usually want more."

"Why shouldn't they?" he countered, bravely defending the point. "There's nothing wrong with wanting more, even if you do seem to have everything. But no one can have everything, not even the mightiest of kings, and certainly not those who haven't even one really pretty dress to show themselves off in. You're a beautiful woman even as you are, Laciel, but don't you think you deserve at least one dress to make yourself even lovelier?"

"It's really strange having you mention that," I
mused, working to keep my face straight. "I remember Togor saying something about skirts . . ."

"My brother is a fool who couldn't give you even a
cheap skirt," he said, now sounding firmly superior
and faintly ridiculing. "I, on the other hand, can give
you the loveliest of dresses and gowns, all of which
will be worn for me alone. I can keep you safe and
comfortable, happy and secure, and all you need to do
in return is please me. That's not so much to give for
all you'll be getting, is it?"

"It does sound like a really great bargain," I wa-
vered, shaking my head just a little. "You'll give me
all of that, and all I have to do is please you. But what
if I can't please you?"

"Oh, lovely girl, there's no chance at all of that," he
said, his grin back and widened. "You'll address me as
High King and do as I tell you, and I won't be anything *but* pleased. Now come and stand closer in front
of me and take your glass of wine, and in a little while
we'll start you on your most important duty to me."

"That sounds wonderful," I said, smiling warmly at
him. "Except for one small thing . . ."

"And what would that be?" he asked with expan-
sive good humor, ready to grant me almost anything
my little heart desired.

"I've already told you I'm fussy about who I drink
with," I answered, letting the smile disappear. "It's
too bad about that very important duty, Triam, but
your talent for influencing isn't anywhere near as strong
as your brother's, and I had no trouble resisting *him*
either. Unless wasting time is a hobby of yours, you
might as well send me back to my cell."

"You really are remarkable," he said, the grin gone
but not quite as deeply into anger as I'd wanted him.
"Your friend Morgiana asked me not to involve myself with you, but her trouble is that she's jealous. She
doesn't want me to give you my Blessing, so she tried
making up frightening stories about you. She was right
about how remarkable you are, but as for dangerous—
you really must pardon my laugh. Now that you've

been separated from the others, there's nothing you can do, and even Morgiana admits you haven't her strength."

"Then why am I here?" I demanded, trying to hold down the fury I felt over the way he spoke about Morgiana. "If I'm so helpless and you know I can't match her, why are you bothering with me?"

"I was wondering if I would be able to resist your glow the way my brother obviously couldn't," he came back, his grin back as well. "I also couldn't imagine a glow more intense than Morgiana's, but now that you're in front of me I don't have to imagine it. Anger always increases a half-born female's glow, and by that glow a king can tell what potential she has. Morgiana has all but realized her potential, but you—you've barely begun to approach yours. You may not have her strength yet, but one day you'll have all of hers and more."

I stood there staring at him as my mind whirled, wondering if he could possibly be telling the truth. That part about anger answered the question I'd had concerning the Chosen spell, and it fit in another way, too. All strength seems to increase when someone gets angry; if you know how to control the anger, the same is true for your ability with magic. If that was the way the High Kings of that place chose which Sighted women would make the best partners . . .

"So I think that explains why we're both here," Triam said, taking a final sip of his wine before replacing the cup on the sideboard. "I'll need to work on you a good deal longer before I'll be willing to admit I can't bend you to my will, and while I'm trying there's no reason not to be enjoying myself at the same time. I *am* the High King, you know, and as one of the Chosen you're entitled to my Blessing."

"Even if I don't want it?" I said, not liking the way he began opening his shirt to take it off. "I thought women were treated better on this world."

"Surely you don't expect me to harm you?" he asked with an incredulous laugh, tossing his shirt aside. "The laws are excruciatingly clear on the point, and even the High King would feel the effect of the First

Spell if he tried breaking the laws. No, my lovely, I won't be harming you, all I'll be doing is giving you my Blessing. Every Chosen has assured me that it's more than worth having."

He began walking toward me then, and I had to admit there was no place to retreat to. Without his shirt I could see how easy living was already softening him, but he was enough bigger than me that that softening might not be of any help. It probably would have been a different story if I'd had a weapon of some sort, but all I had was myself alone.

"I don't care if your Blessing is worth having or not, I still don't want it," I said, finding it impossible not to back away from him. "If you try giving it to me anyway, you'll be forcing me, and that stays true no matter what you call it."

"But dear girl, that doesn't apply to *me*," he said with a laugh, shifting fast to my left to keep me from darting past him. "It's your duty as a Chosen to accept my Blessing, and as long as I don't cause you harm, it's my right to give that Blessing. Ah, now we'll have a small taste of you."

I gasped as his arms closed around me and tried to pull loose, but the table I'd backed into refused to give me the room I needed. I struggled to keep my face turned away from him, my heart beating so wildly I thought it would explode, but his hand came to tangle in my hair and hold my head still.

"I really don't understand why you're fighting me," he murmured, touching his lips to mine gently but hungrily. "I'm not going to hurt you, I'm just going to take some pleasure. If you behave yourself you'll have pleasure, too. If you don't, it will be more like a punishment. Wouldn't you rather be pleasured than punished?"

His demanding lips cut off any answer I might have made, and I was so sick with fear that I couldn't even feel the draw all male Sighteds have for female. He was going to force me—just the way I'd been forced all those years ago—and his strength refused to let me go—and if he did force me I would die—it wasn't the same as being willing—it wasn't—it wasn't—!

And that was when I learned what fear can do for you if you let it. It doesn't only weaken your knees and make you gasp for the air of life, it also lends you the strength of desperation and the frantic courage that comes from being cornered. Instead of uselessly pitting my muscles against his, I bit down hard on the lips that were trying to take what I didn't want to offer, making sure I didn't flinch back from giving pain while being held like that. In that sort of situation, giving halfhearted pain was worse than giving none at all; a half effort would bring no more than half freedom of movement, and the other half would be what you were trying to avoid.

Triam howled at the feel of my teeth and tried to simply pull my head away, but the urge to escape what I was doing to him also loosened his hold on me. After a quick moment I was able to pull free entirely, and that was when some of the lecturing Rik had done during our fight came in handy. Don't ever consider running away from a stronger opponent while he's still able to chase you, Rik had said, at the same time probably trying only to frighten me. Running is a good idea if you aren't going to be able to beat him, but first take the time to slow him down. Put everything you have into the effort, and *then* take off.

I didn't really have anywhere to take off *to,* but that could be worried about once I slowed Triam down. Using my desperate need to escape, I slapped the back of my hand down hard on his nose, and when he screamed and grabbed for the flaring agony, I slammed my knee directly into his groin. His eyes had been tearing too badly to see the kick coming, but when he felt it, he folded up and slid down to the carpeting, mewling and clutching himself.

Panic was still flickering through my body even then, so I just *had* to try running. I turned and made for the door I'd come in by, hoping desperately hard that the guardsmen were gone, but yanking open the door ended the hope. All three of them were still there, and when I tried running past, they just caught me and dragged me back.

"By the First Ancestor, what have you done to the King?" the officer demanded in shock when he glanced into the room, and then he was inside trying to help while his men forced me after him. I was still so wild I couldn't stop trembling, but it turned out I needn't have worried.

"She's—impossible!" Triam gasped out after a couple of minutes, glaring up at me through a film of pain. "She isn't a female, she's a demon. If she wants to die so badly with her friends, then let her! Get her out of my sight, get her out!"

His screaming orders and the officer's gesture were enough to have me dragged out of the room again, and then taken back the way I'd been brought. I was headed for that cell again, to wait to die with my friends, and the thought of that made me want to laugh and sing.

At least until I was thrown back *into* the cell, and the door was locked again behind me. It's fine to feel relieved when you're out of danger, but going from frying pan to fire isn't the kind of journey that's usually celebrated. I couldn't feel depressed, not when Graythor, Rik, and Togor were all demanding to know if I was all right, but sobered could not be ruled out quite as easily.

"Laciel, you must answer us immediately!" Graythor thundered, his entire expression one black cloud as he tightened his grip on the bars between us. "Where were you taken, and why were you brought back with such—such—"

"Unseemly haste?" I supplied, sitting down on the stone floor of my cell. I needed to sit down right about then, and the bare stone felt better than the white carpeting would have. "I was taken to see the High King, but he didn't think much of me. He told them to take me back to die with the rest of you."

"I can't understand Triam behaving like that," Togor said into the silence Graythor and Rik were suddenly producing. "His greatest weakness is a Chosen with a glow even slightly stronger than her sisters. He couldn't possibly have decided he didn't want you—unless there was more involved you just aren't mentioning."

"Well, there might be one or two points I've pretty much glossed over," I admitted, turning my head to look all the way through at him. "You were almost right about my not being able to do anything against him, but someone else was even more right. When you're not going to be able to beat somebody, slow them down before you try to run. The running part didn't work out very well, but the slowing down was able to turn the trick."

Out of the corner of my eye I caught Rik's frown, and then his expression cleared with pleased but grim satisfaction as he understood. What he'd told me had let me help myself, and he deserved to know that even if I *wasn't* talking to him. That, unfortunately, was it as far as pleasing revelations went, though, and all we had left was to settle down and wait for the end.

A lot of very slow time passed after my return, especially since we weren't given anything to eat or drink and none of us felt the urge to complain. After all, how do you complain to people who intend killing you that they aren't treating you properly while you wait? I sat on the stone floor in the middle of my cell with my eyes closed, but I wasn't sleeping or hiding or asking for help from the EverNameless as the ignorant usually did. No one with a mind failed to realize that the EverNameless had their own interests to look after; if you wanted help, you'd damned well do best looking in your own direction first.

And that was just the trouble. Ever since my visit with the King I'd felt I had the answer I needed right in my hand, but I couldn't close my fingers on it. The frustration grew so bad that I hit my forehead with the heels of my palms, but that still didn't jar loose what I needed. Men in that kingdom didn't *harm* women, even though they ruled them almost completely. The King was utterly in charge of the women around him, and as he did, so did the men of his kingdom. But they were forbidden to *harm* women, as if being held so close *wasn't* being harmed, but that wasn't the point. Kings usually did anything they pleased, but there had been something about a First Spell—?

"What in the name of sanity—?" Graythor blurted, and I opened my eyes to see what the sudden rumbling I heard meant. What it meant was that a stone wall was lowering down in front of all four of our cells, and the guardsmen who had been standing out there were already being marched away. It looked like everyone knew they wouldn't be needed again, not after whatever was about to happen.

"I can't believe Triam is actually going to put a woman to death along with the rest of us!" Togor just about blurted, obviously knowing what was happening. "It's monstrous, Rik, and if I could get my claws on him. . . !"

Rik nodded to show he understood, and I suppose Graythor and I did, too. Togor had relaxed back to his hellhound shape, but he had apparently kept his mind in a human mold.

"Togor, tell us what's happening," Graythor urged, his hands on the bars between us again. "Why have they dropped a wall over the doors to our cells? Do they mean to seal us in here until we die of thirst and hunger?"

"As bad as that sounds, what they have in mind instead will probably be worse," the hellhound answered with a shake of his oversized head. "In a very short while the wall on the other side of our cells will be raised, and then we'll be released to face whatever Triam's prepared for us. Whatever it is, you can count on its being slow and painful—not to mention horrifying. Laciel, you'll have to be very brave."

"She *is* brave," Rik said flatly, dismissing the point, and then his head came up. "Unless you're trying to say—we won't all be let out together. Do you mean we may have to face whatever-it-is one at a time?"

"That depends on how angry Triam is, and therefore how long he wants to drag it out," Togor answered as he sat, and then those yellow eyes were resting on me. "Would you like to make a guess about that, Laciel?"

"If I had to guess, I'd say we'll be going out one at a time," I confirmed his suspicions with a sigh. "When I last saw your brother, angry would be too mild a word of description."

"Well, that tears it," Rik said, turning around to stare at the wall that had been there when we'd arrived. "Now we have to figure out a way to stay together even before we decide on a battle plan. Maybe we'll have the time to—"

His words broke off at the sudden grinding sound, and he didn't bother starting them up again. Whatever he'd wanted the time for no longer mattered; the wall fronting our execution ground was being raised out of the way, and that meant we were all out of time.

CHAPTER 20

"Thick red fog," Graythor said once the wall was all the way up, describing what all of us were seeing. "And I believe there are gouts of flame appearing every now and then. Is the area as large as it seems, Togor?"

"Larger," the hellhound said morosely, and then his attention was taken by something. "But you should be able to see that for yourself in a little while. The fog is starting to thin."

"Is that significant in some way?" Rik asked, standing close to the bars as he stared out. "You make it sound unusual."

"It is," Togor confirmed, also looking out. "Triam likes to run his victims all around in that fog, getting them thoroughly lost while they spend their time fighting off *things* that attack them out of it. He and his cronies see everything clearly from where they sit, of course, and make wagers as to how long each victim will last. If the victim's mind is broken before his body, Triam automatically wins. It's a game he really enjoys."

"Game," Rik repeated with disgust, wrapping one hand around a bar. "But today he's playing at something else, because that fog is thinning so fast I can see it happening. Do you have any idea why he's doing it?"

"All I can do is guess," Togor said, back to sounding totally dejected. "It has to have something to do with Laciel, even though I don't know precisely what. It's possible even *his* friends would never stand for a woman being treated the way they would a man, so he's going to be easier on her."

"Eas*ier*," I muttered under my breath, still sitting in the same place on the floor, but now turned around to face the new outward. Rik and Graythor hadn't said anything to that bit of guesswork, but they were probably thinking the same thing I was. Easier didn't necessarily mean easy, only less difficult. And if I could just get my fingers around that damned answer—!

"You will now come out to meet your fate, girl," Triam's voice suddenly announced from thin air, and a door swung open in the cage side I faced. "You could have had the love of a King, but chose instead to spurn him. Come out and see what you'll have in his place, and know regret before you die."

"If you think I'll be regretting what I did to you, you're stupider than your friend Kitrum looks," I replied, getting to my feet in the slowest, most insulting way I could manage. "You've found you can't best me, so there's nothing left for you to do but kill me. If anyone tells you that makes you the winner, they're lying in their teeth."

"I'll be sure to remember that when you're gone," Triam's voice said with a chuckle. "I may even drink a toast to your memory. Come out of the cage and walk to a place where we can all see you."

Way over on the far side of the cavern a small group of people were becoming visible through the thinning fog, but they were so far away they were hardly more than an undefined cluster in their high-standing box seats. Graythor and Rik and Togor were all shouting, some of the words aimed at me, some at Triam, but making that kind of a fuss didn't pay. I'd only been fairly successful at living, but I'd decided a long time ago that I would sure as Hellfire die well.

Walking out of that cell wasn't very hard, and neither was moving closer to the distant seated figures. The wisps of red fog that were left still showed eruptions of occasional fire, but none of them came really close to me. The stone under my feet felt strangely hot, and I had the distinct impression it was usually hotter. I kept moving, hoping to get closer to those who sat and watched me, but suddenly there were six figures only twenty feet ahead which caused me to stop rather abruptly.

"What's the matter, girl, don't you like my hell-hounds?" Triam asked, his tone a perfect match to the way six pairs of yellow eyes stared at me and six fang-filled mouths grinned and slobbered. "I discovered that some men are beautifully well suited to being hellhounds, and these are six of my best. They love the taste of warm flesh and hot blood, but they've been ordered to take their time with you. After all, we wouldn't want it ending too soon for you, now would we?"

"Maybe these six will find it possible to remember that they were once men," I said, fighting not to let the ice inside me show in my voice. "Your brother was able to overcome your spell and throw it off, so there's no reason why these men can't."

"There's one reason, or possibly two," Triam answered, still chuckling and enjoying himself. "The first is that my brother has a talent these men don't, and the second is that that weakling fool always preferred having people like him. These six were never liked, but after what they did as hellhounds they were certainly feared. Later on, I may let them toy with my weakling brother, but for now he'll have to wait. As a gentleman and King, I could never let it be anything but ladies first. You six may now begin."

At least half of the hellhounds let out joyous howls at that as they all started slowly forward, but I was so stunned I just stood there staring at them with my mouth open. The answer! That *had* to be the answer, it all fit so perfectly! My best idea had been absolutely right, but I'd been looking at it backward! I had to get to Graythor and tell him—

But I couldn't, damn it, I couldn't! If I turned and ran, those hellhounds would have me an instant later, their speed letting them catch me with no trouble at all. I had to get back to Graythor, but I couldn't—and then I almost jumped out of my skin at the touch of something about mid-shin height. I looked down to see a small black shape finish its rub on my leg, and then walk slowly out to stand directly in front of me.

"InThig," I breathed, the relief making me almost light-headed. I'd forgotten all about the demon, but it had turned up just in time.

"Why, isn't that sweet," Triam's voice came again, sounding infinitely amused. "The girl's pet is going to protect her against my hellhounds. I wonder how many of them are going to be left after it's finished."

"None of them," InThig answered in a growl, undoubtedly shocking the great king down to his underwear, and then it was the hellhounds' turn to be shocked. Before their eyes the tiny cat shape grew and expanded to its usual giant cat shape, and then, with a sound of great satisfaction, the demon launched itself toward the six who had thought they'd have nothing but a helpless female to face.

Confidence is a good thing to have, but confidence combined with ignorance doesn't work out very well. The hellhounds, counting six of themselves and only one of InThig, decided to take out the demon before continuing on after me. I doubt if it took them very long to realize their mistake, but by then I was already backing away from the absolute destruction InThig was causing among them. Backing away, backing, and then turning to run—

"Okay, okay, you don't have to trample us," Rik said, keeping me from falling after I crashed into him. "We know we're late, but we came as soon as we could."

It took me an instant to realize that all three of them were there, but once I got a look at their cells, I didn't have to ask how they'd done it. Each cell had two bars pulled way out of line, leaving a gap between that none of them would have had trouble getting through. Graythor's extra physical strength—even more extra than he'd let on—

"Togor, can you show us the way out of here?" Graythor now demanded, part of his attention on the way InThig was dismembering hellhounds. "Once that's over, they'll remember about us, and we want to be gone before . . ."

"Uncle Graythor, I've got the answer," I said as fast as I could, then tried to calm the rush a little. "It was so obvious, we *did* have it all along, and it's a good thing because running won't do us any good."

"Laciel, child, calm yourself," he said, just as though I wasn't already doing that, walking nearer to where I still stood with Rik's arms around me. "How can you be sure this isn't just another false alarm? It might be best if we run first, then try your idea once we're out of this cavern. We can't afford . . ."

"Uncle Graythor, if you had just come through a gate and was trying to teach a Sighted here the language of spells, how would you do it?" I demanded, just about jumping up and down. "You'd speak the spell first, and then have the Sighted repeat it. And yes, I know we tried that and it didn't work. But ask yourself—what if that first visitor was *female*, and the Sighted she tried teaching was male? Ladies first, Uncle Graythor, ladies first!"

"By the EverNameless, I think that's it," he said, his eyes wide in shock, and then he pulled himself together. "Yes, all right, we do have to try it, but I almost wish this weren't the answer. When I repeat the spell I'll be drawing on *your* strength—but the King will be drawing on Morgiana's."

"Maybe it isn't only the female's strength that's being used," I suggested, but not very confidently. "Maybe she simply adds to the male's—"

He took my hand in his and squeezed it gently, but we both knew there was only one way of finding that out. It was stupid to think that male Sighteds could only use their own talents with the strength of a female Sighted, but unfortunately stupid doesn't necessarily mean impossible.

And it explained why women were held so horribly close in that kingdom. They were raised and trained to do nothing but obey orders, and that way female Sighteds were no danger to the King and his heirs. They would do exactly as they were told even if they *did* have to speak the spell first, and would never try to get stubborn or make an attempt to take control. Especially, make an attempt to get control. . . .

Graythor and I turned together to watch the end of InThig's fight, but there wasn't much to it. Those hellhounds had no more of a chance against a demon than their human victims had had against them, and bloody parts of bodies were scattered everywhere. The last hellhound was practically whole, but it certainly wasn't living any longer. InThig had its fangs buried in the thing's neck, and was shaking it like a leaf in a windstorm; after a couple of minutes of that it tossed the body aside to lie with the others, and two burning red eyes glared around.

"Is that all of them?" it asked in a ridiculing tone, finally turning its head to look at the distant King. "They were barely worth my time and trouble, but it *was* faintly amusing. What a pity they were your best. Now you have no one to send after them."

"What *are* you?" Triam's voice demanded, sounding more than simply shaken. "Magic doesn't affect you, and you—*tore* them *apart!*"

"Why, I'm nothing more than a pet protecting the girl I belong to," InThig answered very sweetly, sitting down to begin licking one paw. "Don't all girls have pets like me?"

"If they don't, they damned well should," I muttered, making Graythor chuckle, and then I raised my voice. "Now that you've met our secret weapon, Triam, possibly you'll be interested in another happy surprise. Look at what *we've* found."

I have to admit I had my fingers crossed tight when I spoke the spell, but as soon as Graythor repeated it and ended with the gesture, it all fell into place. To be perfectly accurate, it was the section of box seats containing Triam and a figure that just had to be Morgiana which fell into place, the place being down on the stone opposite where we stood. Since I hadn't wanted to hurt Morgiana, the fall wasn't *too* hard, but I'd made sure it would be enough to shake them up.

"How could you have possibly found out?" Triam raged, staggering to his feet after the seat section had landed. "*No* one has ever found out before, no one!"

"How many Sighted visitors have you had that your statistics are supposed to mean something?" I asked, long since out of patience with the fool. "Release Morgiana and let her come over here to us, and you may escape with your skin intact. Try anything cute, and you'll learn what magic is really all about."

I gave him the ultimatum with my fingers still crossed, hoping hard that he didn't know about the link he'd almost certainly established to Morgiana, but that time the balance swung the other way.

"Release her?" he repeated with a scornful laugh, glancing at the small, quiet figure at his side. "If I release her, I'll have nothing, and considerably less than nothing. Let's see how well you fight when I can do anything I please to you, but you don't dare do the same to me. Especially when I control the greater strength."

He turned to Morgiana then and began to speak rapid words to her we couldn't hear, so I hastily spoke a spell that would encircle us with an unSeen wall. As soon as Graythor heard me he repeated the spell, then looked at me with worried eyes.

"Laciel, he's absolutely right," the man in the wizard fretted, dark eyes also furious with helplessness. "He can and will do anything he likes to us, but we can't retaliate without harming Morgiana. It won't be long before one or the other of them finds a way to affect us, and then we're *all* done."

"But we're not done yet," I pointed out, then turned my head to look toward our opponents. Fiery red-orange lightning was raging against the unSeen wall I'd erected, and even as I watched, the lightning was joined by angry bright blue daggers. Triam was doing the directing, but it was *Morgiana's* strength handling it all . . .

"Uncle Graythor, I think I have a way for us to win, but it's a little on the risky side," I said. "Do you think you can repeat my spell *exactly*, like you did for the unSeen wall, even though you don't know it the way you know the wall spell? You won't be able to fix or adjust it the least little bit, or there's no telling what will happen. Can you do it?"

"You obviously intend using black magic," he said, and now the look in his eyes was one of more than worry. "It once occurred to me that those killer spells in Black grimoires, the ones that look as though they *should* work, even though they destroy every Sighted who speaks them— Possibly no more than a single sound is wrong, and that's the reason why they don't work. One single sound. Yes, Laciel, I do believe I will be *very* careful to repeat your spell exactly."

I wished right then I could have taken his hand, but we needed one hand each for the gestures in the spell, and couldn't afford to make those gestures awkward and therefore imprecise. If we didn't get it right, we could end up erasing ourselves, and that would mean the end of Morgiana and Togor—and Ric—as well. My second wish was that there could have been something else for us to try, but that one was even more impossible than the first.

There was no sense in wasting time Triam could use against us, so I visualized the spell clearly in my mind and then began speaking it. Graythor began when I finished, and the way he pronounced every syllable and sound said he wasn't trying to understand it, only repeat it without the least, smallest change. When he

finished and I began to feel the draw on my strength
needed to sustain what the spoken spell had established, I used my left hand to wipe away the sweat on
my forehead.

"I think we got away with it, Uncle Graythor," I
said, hoping I was telling the truth. "Now all we have
to do is wait to see if it works."

"Laciel, what is that spell supposed to *do?*" he
demanded, as close to fretful as I'd ever heard him. "I
can't recall coming across anything like it before, and
most of the phrases went right past me. I can look at
them in memory, but they don't seem to make *sense.*"

"The spell is—reaching out to the edge of the universe, and—pulling away a nothingness cell," I explained in a stumble, wishing I didn't have to tell him.
"Once it gets here, it will appear around Morgiana.
It's *her* strength, after all, powering everything Triam
is doing, so she should be powering their link as well.
Once she's in the cell, her strength will be completely
drained—or it should be—and then the link will be
broken—"

The way his face paled told me he knew exactly how
dangerous it was to do what I'd tried, but he knew as
well that it was the only chance we had. Bringing a
nothingness cell to a world like that wasn't anything
like creating one in a place like the Realm of Dreams,
and how it would work out remained to be seen.

But not for long. There was suddenly a—shivering—in
the fabric of world-stuff around us, something to be
felt on the inside rather than experienced with any
outward senses, and then it happened. One instant
Morgiana was standing beside Triam, the attack still
going strong against us, and the next the attack was
over and Morgiana had been snuffed from view like a
pinched candle flame. Triam stood alone, and not only
just alone but the next thing to untalented.

"Now it's my turn," Togor growled from behind us,
and an instant later the hellhound was bounding toward
the man who had made him like that. For a moment I
thought Togor would attack his brother just as he was,
but apparently hellhound murder wasn't something

that would suit him. The hellhound shifted back to his man form just as he reached Triam, and then the two of them were on the ground, fighting for each other's lives. Triam was elegantly dressed and Togor was stark naked, but I didn't think that would make a difference.

"If Togor doesn't win, I'm taking my marbles and going home mad," Rik muttered from where he still stood behind us, but I hadn't the faintest idea what he was talking about. "And shouldn't someone see what happened to Morgiana?"

"Of course, of course," Graythor muttered in turn, coming out of looking shaken. "How unthinking of me. Laciel, we need to banish the wall *and* the cell."

I made the banishing gestures and Graythor copied them, and then we and Rik and InThig were able to hurry forward to where it was now possible to see Morgiana, lying unconscious on the ground. She was a little too close to the latest—and hopefully last—fight, so Graythor lifted her in his arms and carried her to one side and out of range of all the thrashing around. Guardsmen had appeared from somewhere and looked like they might try taking a hand, so we froze them in place to await the outcome of the fight.

Or final confrontation, which would be a better and more accurate description. Togor had been waiting to get back at the brother who had treated him so badly, and King Triam really seemed to hate the brother he'd pretended to scorn. They'd begun by beating at each other, but they ended with Togor's fingers wrapped around Triam's throat, and Triam unable to break the grip. The King tried very hard to free himself, but Togor must have learned quite a lot from his fight with Rik. When the former hellhound stood up, his brother was no longer moving, but he didn't seem as happy about that as he should have.

"You were my brother, so it was my place to do this," he told the unmoving form in a very soft voice, standing there and staring down at it. "I wish to the First Ancestor that it could have been different, that we could have been friends and brothers instead of enemies and strangers, but the choice was yours. No one was allowed to make that choice for you, so no one else could take the consequences. Good-bye, brother, and when you see our father give him my love."

Graythor and I released the guardsmen then to see what they would do, and what they did was follow the example of the only two courtiers still left in the place. They went down to one knee with their right hands fisted and the arm pressed diagonally across their chests, bowing to Togor as the new king. It seemed only fitting that the new king have the hellhound spell taken off him, so we saw to that first and then turned back to see to Morgiana.

It took some time for everything to get straightened out, but while Graythor and I looked after Morgiana, InThig and Rik helped Togor. InThig's presence especially cut down on a lot of nonsense, but demon or not it couldn't be in two places at once. While its back was turned with a chore involving checking the palace for any traps that might have been set by the late king's now out-of-favor favorites, a trap was sprung in Togor's vicinity. One of the exfavorites had made a deal with a surviving hellhound; as soon as InThig had left, the hellhound went after Togor. Imagine the hellhound's surprise when Rik shifted to his link-form, then took care of the matter. The hellhound didn't survive the encounter, so it wasn't possible to ask *him*.

Morgiana was vastly confused when she came to, and despite the help I'd given her to recover her strength more quickly, we could see she would need to rest before we could really talk to her. Graythor and I sat with her until she fell asleep, then we took care of some of the magical necessities that had been awaiting our attention.

We canceled as many of the general spells as we could—most especially that Chosen spell and the one covering hellhounds—brought ourselves back to our normal appearances, provided ourselves with the best meal we'd had in what seemed like months, and called up a wardrobe that was neither dusty, dirty, nor torn.

After we ate, Graythor went back to sit with Morgiana, and I went to get some sleep. I'd been tired when that day had first started, and I'd gone through a lot of strength since then. I barely made it to a wide lounge in the beautiful apartment I'd been given, and then I was out. Graythor and I had warded the rooms earlier, so I could sleep without a worry in that world.

It was dark when I finally woke up, but a single candle burned in a lamp on the wall and the tiny glow let me remember where I was. It also let me remember how dirty I was, but I couldn't have bathed before sleeping if the EverNameless themselves had demanded it. Right then was a different matter, though, so I dug out a large drying cloth and some soap, and headed for the room where the bathing pool was.

Servants are strange creatures in that the best of them—that is, the most efficient and caring—act as though they bought and paid for you. They own you, no two ways about it, and you'd better let them do what's best for you. One of that sort had lit the lamp in my apartment, and she and three of her co-owners insisted on helping me take my bath. I got the definite impression I couldn't be trusted to do it right on my own, and that despite the fact that I was one of those who had helped the new king defeat the old. The palace servants, at least, were glad there was a new king, and were eager to show exactly how glad.

After the long refreshing sleep I'd had, there was no danger of my losing my temper. I did, however, draw myself up to full height and tell the girls I would be happier bathing all by myself, and they suddenly discovered they had duties awaiting them elsewhere. Apparently they weren't used to females with my size and attitudes, and wisely decided not to see what I would do if they refused to leave. It was more than possible they'd heard about what I'd done to the former king, and were anxious to avoid an argument with me.

Whatever it was, I got to take my bath all alone. The lamps on the walls brought gleams from the gold and silver and jewels that decorated the walls and pillars of the bathing room, the costly yellow silks hanging everywhere, the yellow and while tiles on the floor. Everything including the yellow and white bathing pool was spotlessly clean or downright gleaming, and the water was fresh and pure and even warm. I used the soap on my body and hair, and when I climbed out of the pool and wrapped myself in the drying cloth, I felt wonderful. My very worn and dirty clothes could be left in the pile I'd thrown them into after taking them off, and I could go back to my apartment for clean, new—

"I'm sorry, Laciel, I didn't mean to startle you," Togor said quickly, holding one hand up. "Didn't you hear me coming in?"

"No," I said, wrapping the drying cloth more tightly around me. When I'd turned, it had seemed as though he'd materialized in front of me, and I'd almost gasped in surprise. It was a good thing for him I couldn't do magic on my own there, or I wouldn't have been the one who was *most* startled.

"I had a few moments free, so I thought I'd stop by to see how you were doing," he said, smiling at me as he stepped closer. "From here you seem to be doing beautifully, and I mean that in every sense there is. Your hair and eyes—is that the way they're supposed to look?"

"Yes, this is my natural coloring," I answered, for some reason feeling like stepping back from him. "Togor, I was about to go back to my apartment to dress, so . . ."

"No wonder it suits you so well, then," he said, reaching out one hand for a lock of my hair. "Even though it's wet it looks so light, and I can't decide exactly what color your eyes are. Are they violet?"

"Yes, violet," I said, beginning to feel very uncomfortable. He wore dark leather trousers and boots with a pinkish tunic that didn't look in the least feminine, and I would have enjoyed a full set of clothes of my own. "Look, why don't we postpone this talk until I can . . ."

"Pale hair and violet eyes, and the most beautiful face I've ever seen," he murmured, letting my hair go to put his arms around me. "Laciel, my brother was a man who was very much taken with his own importance, but I prefer a lesser amount of importance that can be shared with someone I have strong feelings for. Now that I'm King, I want you to be my queen."

I know my mouth opened so that I could say something, but none of the words in my mind seemed able to make it into my throat. Togor was *proposing* to me, and I was learning that the books never really tell you how *upsetting* a situation like that can be.

"Laciel, you aren't saying yes," he scolded gently with a mock scowl as he looked down at me. "Granted you aren't saying no either, but a yes is what I want to hear. We found a large number of female half-born quartered in a guarded section of the palace, and one of my father's old advisors made sure I knew I would have to choose one of them for my consort. But I don't want a consort, I want a wife, and since she has to be half-born, I have the perfect excuse for pressing you. Will you agree to becoming my wife?"

"Togor, I can't," I finally managed to get out, really wishing I could turn myself invisible and sneak away. "This world is yours, but it isn't mine, and I could never be really happy here. There are important things I need to do with my life, things you're much better off not knowing the details about . . ."

"But what could be more important than being my queen and giving me heirs?" he asked, back to that original murmur. "If my world doesn't suit you, then we'll change it until it does. Together we can do anything, and the first item on that list will be making *sure* you're happy. I can do it, Laciel, and you have to give me the chance."

I tried refusing again, wanting to be fair and let him know he was wasting his time, but he didn't give *me* the chance. Instead of keeping on with trying to talk me into it, he leaned down and kissed me. When I tried to struggle free, he simply tightened his hold. I was all wrapped up in a drying cloth as well as in his arms, and that left me a very limited number of things to do. I was about to choose one of them anyway, but suddenly something happened that made it unnecessary for me to do anything.

"What in the name of battle unending do you think you're doing?" a furious voice demanded from behind Togor, making the man raise his head fast to turn and look. "Let that woman go, and I mean *now*."

"This is none of your business, Rik," Togor answered, his arms still around me. "I'm grateful for all the help you've given me, but that doesn't mean you can tell me what to do. If I want to kiss Laciel, then I'm going to kiss her, and you have nothing to say about it."

"I've let enough times go by without saying anything," Rik ground out in answer, his hands curled to fists at his sides. "At first I thought it *was* none of my business, that Laciel should be free to kiss anyone she cared to, but I can't play reasonable any longer. I'm *making* it my business because I can't stand seeing her in the arms of another man, and if you don't let her go, you'll have to fight me."

"Do you think that because you won once, you're guaranteed to win again?" Togor blustered, finally letting me go to walk over and face Rik. "I'm the King now, and Kings aren't bested quite that easily. I dare you to start something, I just dare you."

"Okay," Rik answered agreeably, then hit Togor right in the face. I flinched a little even though the blow wasn't all that hard, and Togor went stumbling back to land abruptly on the floor. Once he was down he shook his head, then put a hand to his jaw.

"That was a slightly more vigorous response to my dare than I was expecting," he muttered, looking up at Rik with injured accusation. "I thought we were friends."

"We *are* friends, and that's why I didn't hit you very hard," Rik answered, coming forward to offer a hand to the man seated on the floor. "If anyone *but* a friend had taken advantage of a particular situation to ask my woman to marry him, he would have gotten a lot more than you did. But since you and I are definitely

friends, nothing like that will happen again, now will
it?"

"Fat lot of good it would do me even if it did,"
Togor grunted, then let Rik pull him to his feet. "Well,
my friend, once again you've proven yourself to be the
better man, so I'll just step aside to keep from having
to face your jealousy again. She's all yours, and I'll
leave you two alone."

He clapped Rik on the shoulder and grinned, winced
and ended the grin fast with a hand to his face, then
headed out of the bathing room without looking back.
I didn't have the faintest idea of what most of their
conversation had meant, but one point was very clear:
Rik was *jealous*, and had all but admitted it!

"I'd like to apologize for losing my temper like
that," Rik said as soon as Togor was gone, walking
closer to stop and look down at me. "My people teach
their children that showing jealousy isn't right, but
there's only so much a man of flesh and blood can
take. I'd like to say it won't happen again, but I'm
afraid I'd be lying. I'm much too jealous to overlook
anything like that again."

"You are?" I said, finding it impossible not to no-
tice that his eyes were that beautiful bronze again.
"And your people don't *believe* in showing jealousy?
You were taught not to?"

"That's right," he said very solemnly, looking down
into my eyes. "That's the way I was taught to behave,
but I couldn't take it any more. Do you forgive me for
making that scene?"

"Oh, Rik, of course I forgive you," I breathed,
feeling—ten feet tall and light as a wish, strangely
dizzy and ready to float away. It came to me then that
his arms were around me, holding me close to his
chest, and that was undoubtedly the only thing keeping me on the floor. He *did* care for me, he really
did—!

"So from now on if you want to kiss anyone, I guess
it'll have to be me," he murmured, touching my lips
very softly and gently with his own. "Do you by any
chance want to kiss somebody *now?*"

He must have seen the answer to his question in my face; I very much wanted to kiss somebody, but not just any somebody. When his lips came hungrily to mine, I met them with more than hunger, achingly aware of how much I'd missed him, how much he meant to me. I wanted him more than I wanted the breath of life, and it was killing me that it just wasn't meant to work out. If only he had never come back, if only I had died before reaching that point.

"Laciel, what's wrong?" he asked with great bewilderment, ending the kiss when he realized I was crying. "Please, my love, tell me what's wrong!"

Rather than answer him—which I couldn't do anyway—I simply pulled from his arms and ran to my apartment. It hurt so much I thought I would break, but I wasn't meant to *be* that lucky. All I could do was cry and hurt, and not even be ashamed of the tears I was shedding. There were a lot of things worse than crying—and even death—and I wished I'd never lived long enough to find that out.

CHAPTER 21

I lay sobbing on my bed for quite a long time, but eventually the tears stopped and I was able to pull myself together a little. I still lay on the bed, uninterested in moving, but at least I wasn't crying. I suppose I expected to be left alone for the rest of the night at least, but there were too many people around who'd had as uneven a day as I'd had.

"Laciel, are you there and awake?" Graythor's voice suddenly came, soft enough not to wake me if I happened to be asleep. I was tempted not to answer him, but if something was wrong and he needed me, I couldn't just turn my back.

"I'm here and I'm not asleep, Uncle Graythor," I answered with a sigh, not moving from where I lay on my right side. "Is anything wrong? Do you need me for something?"

"No, child, nothing is wrong," his voice answered, sounding perfectly neutral. "It so happens something is right, and I thought you would want to know. Morgiana is back to her old self again, we've exchanged embraces, and now we're hungry. Since you're awake, she'd like you to join us, even if you've already eaten. For some reason she'd like to see you and talk to you again."

"All right, Uncle Graythor, I'll get dressed and be right there," I said after the briefest hesitation. "I want to see Morgiana, too, but I don't think I'll be able to stay very long. After everything that happened today, I'm completely wiped out, and if I don't get a good night's sleep I'll be totally worthless tomorrow."

"Then we certainly won't keep you long," Graythor said. "We'll be expecting you in just a few minutes."

Since nothing but silence came after that, it was fairly clear the conversation was over. I let myself lie there for another minute or so, then went through the struggle of getting up, washing my face, and getting dressed. It wasn't until I was into dark blue trousers, light gold blouse and short, soft, light gold boots that I realized how chilled I'd felt being wrapped in nothing but a very damp drying cloth. Being dressed definitely felt better, but that didn't mean I felt good.

I trudged on over to Morgiana's apartment, and she certainly was back to being her old self. She and Graythor had put together a picnic spread in the middle of the sitting room, and the two of them were on the floor around the edge of the cloth, tasting one of the dishes by each dunking in a finger. Morgiana giggled at the very solemn way Graythor licked his finger before nodding very regal approval, and then she looked up.

"Laciel!" she exclaimed in delight, pushing her robe

aside to climb to small, bare feet. "Oh, my very dear! How wonderful it is to see you again, especially right now. If I'd known enough to hope for rescue, I also would have known enough to be sure my loved ones would accomplish it."

By then we had reached each other, and even though she was so small and I so big, she must have hugged me twice as hard as I hugged her. She had always had strength and enthusiasm and a sharing sense of love, this woman who had rescued and raised me, and as we held each other, I knew again I would never find it possible to fail her in anything I had the choice about.

"Come sit down with us, and share at least a taste of our picnic," she urged once the hugging was over, holding my arm to make me move back there with her. "Once I was able to understand what I'd been saved from, I felt like celebrating in an unconventional way. It was like being let out of a prison you'd had no idea *was* a prison."

"You weren't unhappy, then?" I asked, picking a piece of floor and sitting down on it. "He didn't hurt you or abuse you?"

"He went to great pains *not* to abuse me, and I thought I was the luckiest woman in the world," she answered, making a sour face as she sat down next to me. "If I'd understood what was happening, I wouldn't have been quite that contented, but he had me good and made certain I *couldn't* think clearly. If all of you hadn't come here to rescue me—"

"But we did come, my dear, and you certainly are rescued," Graythor said jovially when her words broke off, leaning across me to pat her hand. "And the one who deserves your thanks most, I believe, is InThig. If it hadn't come searching for you, we might never have found out where you'd gone."

"I already have thanked InThig," she said with a little laugh, brushing back her light brown hair. "It told me that thanks were entirely unnecessary; considering that no other being would have been *capable* of finding me, the accomplishment itself was more than

enough. It also spent quite a while lecturing me on the
follies of sticking my nose in places where it was
possible it might get snipped off. I think it's grown too
used to being around *you*, Laciel. That lecture came
out with the ease of long, ingrained habit."

"If InThig ever stopped lecturing me, I think I'd
faint," I said with as much of a smile as I could
manage. "I know demons really are superior to human
beings, but there's such a thing as getting tired of
hearing about it."

"Demons are superior only in some ways," she said
with a smile of her own, as assured and serene as ever.
"In other ways human beings are superior, and even a
demon will admit that if you get it drunk enough. The
trick, of course, is in getting it drunk enough."

"How do you get a demon drunk at all?" I asked,
intrigued in spite of myself. "I never knew anything
like that was possible."

"There are some bits of knowledge that come only
with the attainment of age and wisdom," Morgiana
intoned like an evil wizard in a play, and then she
laughed. "In other words I found out purely by
accident, but that doesn't mean I can share the
secret with you. InThig made me swear to keep silent
years ago, and as far as I know it hasn't changed
its mind."

"Speaking of things that are found out purely by
accident," Graythor said before I could question
Morgiana further, "I meant to ask if that was how you
found the answer to our puzzle. And please do remind
me to speak to you about proper timing in things.
The last possible moment is *not* the best time to
leave things for, most especially when our lives are
at stake."

"Now, Graythor, I'm sure she didn't do that on
purpose," Morgiana interrupted, only glancing up while
filling a plate with food. "And consider this, the next
time you think about the last possible moment: isn't
that better than not finding it at all? Here, Laciel, I
want to see you eat as much of this as you can. You're

looking almost as thin as you were when I brought you home as a child."

I suddenly found myself with a plateful of food in my hands, and Graythor looked as though he was working very hard not to laugh. That was also what Morgiana was like; unendingly determined to feed me until I burst.

"No, Uncle Graythor, I don't think my finding the answer was an accident," I said, falling back on a trick learned in childhood and simply picking up my fork. Someone who's holding a fork is *about* to eat, so anyone watching them closely doesn't have to keep prodding. "We both had all the information we needed to make the right guess, but we got bogged down in calling the outworld visitor 'he.' If we'd even gone so far as to say, 'he, she or it,' we would have had it right then."

"I still fail to see what you consider such conclusive information," he protested, no longer as amused as he'd been a moment earlier. "I grant you the use of 'she' might well have given us another avenue of investigation, but that's hardly the same as instant certainty."

"Look, Uncle Graythor, it works like this," I said with a sigh, using my fork to casually gesture with. "We discussed the fact that although women were kept closely in hand by the men, there was no physical abuse of them, no outrages. In a society where women have no rights at all, that isn't normal. Their very helplessness will goad certain men on, and others will come to think of it as their due. Even if whoever happens to be king dislikes the practice, it will still happen, because even men who would never dream of doing something like that themselves are still mostly incapable of understanding what it's really like. It takes a lot of insight for someone to see the difference between voluntary sex and rape—when they can't really suffer the treatment themselves."

"But it was always possible the King *did* have such insight, and passed it along to his heirs," Graythor maintained, taking a stalk of celery to help bolster his stubbornness. "If a king is firm enough about something and his successors continue in the same vein, a particular outlook could very well be stamped out."

"If you take the view that everything is possible, I suppose that's possible," I granted him. "The only problem is, it's also so unlikely that it's difficult to imagine. Kings do whatever they please, and you're telling me enough kings were pleased to worry about *every* woman in their kingdom? At a high enough priority level that every man in the kingdom was forced to do the same? *All* men, all the time, everywhere? And Triam was the first and only King to be self-centered and ambitious instead of dedicated and caring? And even he didn't dare abuse a woman, but that had no significance? Really, Uncle Graythor."

"She's right, my dear," Morgiana said, smiling gently at a very annoyed Graythor. "You can stretch coincidence only so far, and then it breaks and snaps back to hit you in the face. Most men would never consider harming a woman, but every world has its share of those who were hurt and therefore want to hurt back. If *no* one in a particular area acts like that, the reason can't possibly be ordinary determination by ordinary people."

"And that passing comment Triam made," I began, but was interrupted by the sound of footsteps. I started to turn to see who it was, but Morgiana had already seen and was smiling a greeting.

"Come in, come in and join our picnic," she called, waving toward the cloth we sat around. "There's enough here for an army, and since you're part of my army you're entitled to join in. But not you, InThig. Food like this will rust a demon's insides."

"Really, Morgiana, you know as well as I do that a demon's insides don't rust," InThig answered, padding over to sit down between Morgiana and me. "If you keep saying things like that, Rik and Togor will begin to believe them. I think you must be spending altogether too much time with Laciel."

The two men who had come in with InThig circled

to the far side of the cloth before sitting, which was something of a relief. When I left, it would not be necessary to pass either of them. And come to think of it, leaving wasn't such a bad idea. I'd said I wouldn't stay long, and now that there were others to help Morgiana celebrate, I could go back to my apartment. I was all ready to start making my excuses, but I'd forgotten about the argument I'd been in the middle of.

"What was that about a passing comment made by Triam, Laciel?" Graythor asked, his dark eyes looking as though he'd found a loophole in an airtight contract. "Since I didn't hear any such comment, it could well be a very significant point."

"Well, it was enough to make me start thinking about the problem from a new angle," I admitted, using my fork to toy with the food on my plate. "Triam said something about a First Spell, and it seemed to relate somehow to the way men behaved with women. Since it was called the First Spell, with clearly-heard capital letters, our assumed visitor *had* to be responsible for it. If it had been done by the first King to come after the visitor it could also have been called the First Spell, but then it wouldn't have done the job it obviously did. Other spells done by other kings, like the Chosen spell and the hellhound spell, *could* be resisted by a Sighted with enough willpower. If the First Spell was of the same quality, *some* men would be able to resist it, especially since there were men around who had cause to feel resentment and the urge to get even."

"The Sighted males of this kingdom, known as half-born," InThig put in, seeing the point immediately. "Most of them are indeed badly done by, but their tormentors would be other males. How could it follow that females would be involved?"

"As a means of getting even with those males you mentioned," I said, stirring around the potatoes on my plate. "If you haven't the strength—or the stomach—to strike back at those who hurt you, you sometimes take out your mad on those who are close to the ones you hate, but who are considerably weaker. Or you might resent the fact that no woman has been able to see your wonderful qualities, so none of them have mated with you. Being Sighted doesn't mean being without fault and poor judgment, it only gives you a potential for doing certain things that others can't. Sighted human beings are still human beings."

"So if the First Spell was done by our visitor," Graythor summed up, "and you do seem to have the evidence to support that, then it had to have been done almost as soon as the way to do magic was discovered. After all, why call it the First Spell if it wasn't? But you still can't prove . . ."

"Uncle Graythor, she was probably raped not long after coming here," I said, more than anxious to be done with the discussion. "If she wasn't, why would that be the *first* spell she cast? It couldn't have happened to a male visitor because even if it did, it wouldn't have produced a spell protecting *women*. If it happened to a woman a male visitor was fond of, he would have gone after the guilty rather than laying down a blanket spell. If he was bothered enough to consider all women and not just his own, he would have taken revenge first and *then* spoken the blanket spell. It wouldn't have been done first. Not long after that the male Sighted she worked with must have gotten the best of her, but he was never able to do anything about that spell."

"I'm afraid I have to agree with Laciel again," Morgiana said, now sounding disturbed. "Most women who go through that don't think about vengeance, they just want to be sure it can never happen again. I think we'd all be better off if they *were* a little more bloodthirsty, but you can't tell someone who's gone through that how to react. All you can do is give them whatever help they need."

"Yes, there's no feeling like helping someone, especially if you care about them," Graythor said, his voice just a little *too* hearty, stepping again on my intention to announce that I was leaving. "Even though Laciel found the answer because of the additional information she had, she *did* find it and we were able to help *you*. Although for a time there we were afraid the answer would do us very little good. Even though Triam was telling you what spells to speak it was *her* strength against yours, and we had no doubt about the outcome of such a match."

"But I did, and I even remember trying to warn Triam," she said, reaching in front of InThig to touch my arm. "I know Laciel a good deal better than you do, my dear, and I may have greater strength but she has something I don't—an original way of looking at things. Creativity has a habit of defeating strength, and since I was totally on Triam's side I tried to tell him that. He laughed off my advice because he thought I was jealous."

"I think it's time for me to be getting back to my apartment," I began, but even though I managed to get the words out that time, no one seemed to hear them.

"Yes, jealousy gets people accused of all sorts of things," Rik put in suddenly, just as though he'd been part of the discussion all along. "I can even see how it *isn't* considered the cause of certain actions, but maybe it ought to be. For instance, if a man tells a woman he doesn't want her to risk herself, it's fairly obvious he's too jealous at the idea of losing her to let her go off on her own, isn't it? Doesn't that sound like true jealousy?"

"I would have called it being concerned over her welfare," Togor said, obviously understanding whatever Rik had been trying to say. It had sounded just about unintelligible to *me*, but maybe that was because I was so tired. "After all, if you don't really care about someone," Togor added, "what difference can it make to you *what* they do?"

"I'm really very tired, so I think I'll . . ." I began again, but they still weren't hearing me.

"Well, see, that's why I have trouble with the concept of jealousy," Rik plowed on, sounding faintly confused but very determined. "I was taught that jealousy is a selfish urge, because it boxes in the person you claim to love. If you really love that person, you should want what *they* want, what will make *them* happy, and ideally they'll feel the same about you. If they don't, well, that's where the system breaks down and jealousy can't help. It can only make a bad situation worse."

"That sounds clear enough to me," Togor said, and now he was the one who seemed confused. "Jealousy can only hurt the one you care about, so you try not to be jealous. If it happens anyway, you apologize and try not to lose it again. Where does the trouble come in?"

"Really, it is getting very late, so . . ." I was speaking louder this time, but it didn't do any good at all.

"The trouble comes in when you try to keep your woman safe," Rik continued, speaking slowly and carefully in an effort to explain his thoughts. "You tell yourself you're not being jealous of her freedom, that you're only concerned about her welfare—as you put it—but is that the truth? I've learned there are times when you *should* show jealousy, mostly to reassure the one you love, but how far are you supposed to take it? Are you kidding yourself when you claim to be no more than concerned? Maybe not, but can loving someone really exclude wanting to protect them against all harm?"

"Wanting to protect someone you love is the most natural feeling in the universe," Graythor said, entering the discussion with quiet but full confidence. "As Togor pointed out, if you *don't* care about them, you couldn't care less what they do. Don't you agree, Laciel?"

Rather than answer I tried getting to my feet, desperate to be alone again, finally realizing they weren't ever going to hear me talk about leaving. I didn't know what they thought they were doing, but no matter what it was I couldn't handle it just then. The only problem was, I got no farther than putting my plate aside and shifting a little. By then Graythor's hands were on my arms from behind, and I was reminded that he hadn't banished that extra physical strength.

"It's not quite proper to leave a discussion before voicing the opinions you were asked for, child," Graythor said, having no trouble holding me still. "You may stare at nothing but InThig's side if you wish, but we still require an answer from you. Isn't it fairly obvious that when a woman tries to rush in to share the battle of a man, she has strong feelings for him? If that man is taken prisoner by their enemies and she all but drags her other companions along to rescue him, doesn't that show love? Especially when, at that point, she doesn't believe *he* loves *her?*"

"You agreed to let me leave when I wanted to," I said, aware of InThig's eyes on me but still staring at nothing but the demon's side. "If your word is worth anything, you'll let me go."

"If it pleases you, consider me a liar," he said at once, totally unbothered. "I would happily accept being called far worse than that if it allowed me to get to the bottom of your misery. Ever since I brought Rik to Morgiana's house, you've been trying to drive him away, but there can't possibly be anyone alive who isn't aware of how deeply you love him. You love him, he loves you—but still you refuse to accept him. Isn't it time you told us *why* you won't accept him?"

"I've given you reasons until they're coming out of my ears," I said, making no effort to keep the harshness out of my voice. "Since you don't like any of them, you can look for your own; I just don't care any longer. As far as I'm concerned, I don't even have to *have* a reason; if that's what I insist on, anyone around me has to accept it, otherwise they can find someone else to be around. Now, let me go."

"But, Laciel, my dear, you haven't told them the *real* reason," Morgiana said softly, the first words she'd spoken in a while. "Graythor and I went over everything that happened since you returned from the quest, using a visual-reconstruction-of-events spell. It took a little while for me to understand, but I think I have it straight now. It all has to do with your studying unSeen magic, doesn't it?"

All I could do right then was shut my eyes, but I wasn't the only one in the room. InThig, Graythor and Togor all began speaking at once, but Rik's voice rose above theirs.

"But we've already gone through that reason," he protested, seriously upset. "Laciel insisted I would be hurt if I was near her when and if something went wrong, and refused to understand that I was willing to take my chances. Are you saying that's still what's bothering her? The possibility that I might be hurt?"

"I'm sure she isn't *happy* with that possibility, but that's only part of what's troubling her," Morgiana answered with a sigh. "She may not even be fully aware herself— Graythor, do you remember the various times you discussed Laciel's future studies? You mentioned more than once that we both felt unSeen magic was what she was born to do."

"Certainly I did," Graythor agreed, taking his turn at sounding confused. "We did feel that way, and I still do. Have you found a reason to change your mind?"

"It isn't a matter of that . . ." she said, letting the words trail off, and then her voice strengthened again. "Rik, when you first discussed the problem with Laciel, one of your first suggestions was that she simply not involve herself in unSeen magic. You relented when she pointed out that it was part of her nature, but you still weren't happy with the situation. Would you say she knew you were as worried about *her* safety as she was worried about yours?"

"She couldn't have missed it," Rik answered with a snort. "I'm always worried about her safety, especially since she never seems worried about it herself. If she ever learned to take care of herself properly, I might be able to relax a little."

"But with unSeen magic it isn't always *possible* to take care of yourself properly," Morgiana pointed out gently. "There's no knowing when a spell you construct might decide to turn on you, and that no matter *how* careful you are. It's a risky undertaking any way you look at it, Rik. If Laciel married you, there might come a day when you seriously asked her to give it up. Isn't that true?"

"Morgiana, I'm not quite following you," Graythor said when Rik didn't answer, filling the awkward gap. "Are you saying Laciel won't have anything to do with Rik because he might, at some possible future time, ask her to stop working with unSeen magic? When even *she* wasn't totally enthusiastic over the idea at the time I first mentioned it? That would be too ridiculous for words."

"You're close, my dear Graythor, but you still haven't got it all," she replied. "Laciel loves Rik very much, but she knows he's bound to make an issue of her work at *some* time, and will no matter how careful she tries to be. She also knows you and I are very much *for* her studying unSeen magic, that we think she has a gift for it. Does Laciel love us, Graythor?"

"Why—I don't see how there can be any doubt," Graythor answered, his bewilderment clear. "Her love for us began when she was very young, and despite the disagreements we occasionally have I can't imagine that changing. She loves us as we love her."

"I believe it goes a little farther than that," Morgiana said, and suddenly her hand was on my arm again. "She loves us very much and would never do *anything* to really disappoint us, and we want her to work with unSeen magic. She also loves Rik very much and wants to make him happy, but he *doesn't* want her to work with unSeen magic. Even if he agreed to go along with her to begin with, he would almost certainly change his mind, and then she would have to choose between her love for Rik and her love for us. Would *you* want to make a choice like that? Wouldn't it be better not to allow the conflict to be established in the first place?"

"By the thirteen cardinal signs of life unending," Graythor whispered, his hands finally leaving my arms. "It never once occurred to me—! Do you see how badly I do with her without you, Morgiana? I'm just a thickheaded old fool who straps a burden to her shoulders, then turns away and leaves her to support it alone. You should never have allowed me anywhere near her."

"Now, now, my dear, it isn't quite as bad as all that," Morgiana soothed him with gentle compassion. "Looking back while already knowing there's a problem is a good deal easier than living forward through the time without a hint. If it had been me in your place, I undoubtedly would have done no differently. I *was* the one who first mentioned her creativity to *you*, if you'll recall."

"And I actually accused her of not caring about the feelings of those around her," Togor said, sounding painfully upset. "We've all done a lot of talking about caring, but the one who did the most acting also did the least talking. Action instead of words."

"Laciel—my love—I'm so sorry," Rik's voice suddenly came, but not from across the cloth. He was right there beside me to my left, and then he was down on the floor and holding me in his arms. "I didn't realize what a position I was trying to put you in, but you should have told me. I'd never have made you choose between me and your family!"

"I'd say she knew that," Morgiana offered while I simply leaned against Rik, floating in the feel of his arms around me. "You would willingly accept being unhappy for her sake, but she didn't want you to be unhappy. It would have been easier on you if you weren't there at all."

"The hell it would!" he answered vehemently, tightening his hold. "Just because you've walked away from someone you love, that doesn't mean you don't love them any more. It isn't something you can turn on and off like a wall lamp."

"Well, I think *I* can settle this whole problem, by saying something I should have said a long time ago,"

Morgiana announced, and something in her voice made me open my eyes to look at her. "It's the way Graythor and I both feel, but thinking back I realize we've never actually put it into words. Laciel, dear, the thing we want most for you in life is to do what *you* want to do, to do what will make you happy. There's no doubt you have a gift for unSeen magic, but others have had the gift before you and many of them never went anywhere near it. If you decide against involving yourself and take up something else, Graythor and I will still be delighted. Won't we, Graythor, dear?"

"Possibly more than you know, Morgiana," Graythor muttered, somehow suddenly sounding oddly relieved. "Rifts down to the very fabric of the universe, even *thinking* about trying to break out of a nothingness cell—! I'm beginning to believe some Sighteds are born *not* to involve themselves with unSeen magic."

"If she decides to choose something else, it'll probably be looking for the other side of the sky," Rik put in with a sigh while Morgiana laughed with her usual tinkle. "Or maybe she'll take up raising man-eating monsters and plants for pets. I have a feeling I'm going to wish she'd stayed with unSeen magic after all."

"Raising man-eating plants and monsters for pets," I repeated in a musing tone as I looked up at him, refusing to think about how so much had changed in so short a time. I didn't believe in those changes, not completely and not yet, but maybe in time . . . "That's a really good idea, Rik, and I also like the suggestion about the other side of the sky. I just may try them both along *with* unSeen magic."

"Okay, now comes the part where *I* lay down a few rules," he growled, looking at me very sternly. "I'm aware of the fact that you're entitled to do as you please with your life, and whatever your career choice turns out to be, I'll manage to live with it. *But*—! I cannot and will not live with you constantly flying around and doing as you please when not listening to me could put your life in danger. Taking risks for a career is one thing, but taking risks just for the hell of it is something else entirely. I simply won't allow it, so when there's the possibility of danger, you'll have to learn to listen to me."

"But Rik, what if I *can't* learn to listen to you?" I asked very innocently, not mentioning I'd asked a similar question not long ago with Triam. "You know how much trouble I have with that, and I'd hate seeing you unhappy . . ."

"Then let me set your mind at ease," he interrupted with a grin that would have looked more fitting on his link-shape. "I have a way to *help* you learn, and from now on I'll be applying it every time you show me you need the help. Do you remember that fight we had, and the way you almost broke my hand?"

"Oh, you wouldn't!" I sputtered, feeling my face go very red even though he hadn't mentioned the rest of that horrible incident. "Rik, you wouldn't dare!"

"He seems to dare a lot of things," Togor put in, for some reason vastly amused where he lounged on the other side of the picnic cloth. "Just to make sure you don't talk him out of whatever *that* daring is, though, I'll have to remember to tell him how we first met. That ought to keep him as hard after you as you need him to be. If somebody doesn't do it, you won't live long enough to become a nasty old lady."

I tried threatening Togor into keeping quiet while Rik tried demanding he tell his story that very minute, but all Togor did was grin at the two of us. Graythor and InThig chuckled with full amusement during that nonsense, and then Graythor held up his hand.

"My friends, no matter what small details still remain, our adventure is successfully over," he announced. "The five of us are or will be happy, and Togor will be happy once we teach him the language of spells. He's decided that the secret of magic should *not* be the exclusive property of the King, and intends seeing the Sighted in his kingdom trained as soon as he's far enough ahead of them to maintain his lead for a while. After that—"

"After that someone else can be King while I go traveling," Togor answered for himself, looking very comfortable. "Graythor has told me how magic works on other worlds, and I'm anxious to visit them and try it. Maybe I can even bring back a few ideas on how to make life easier for my people."

"And you must certainly not fail to visit us," Graythor said with another smile. "Now that all the necessary questions have been answered we'll be going home, and . . ."

"But there's one question we *don't* yet have an answer for," InThig put in, strangely sounding very— *determined*. "We've learned that Morgiana did indeed come through the gate here, got caught up in the Chosen spell, and ended being influenced by the late King Triam. The one thing Morgiana *hasn't* said was why she came here in the first place, as well as why she stayed long enough to be caught. Has no one else noticed that that's completely unlike her?"

"Why, InThig, I was just—distracted," Morgiana said, trying for a casualness none of us was suddenly able to believe. "I didn't notice anything when I first came through the gate, and when I finally did it was much too—"

Her words broke off under InThig's stare, and when she closed her eyes and covered her face with her hands, Graythor was suddenly at her side with his arm around her. She turned to him and let his patting hands and soothing murmur calm her, and then she took a deep breath.

"All right, the time has come to get it all out into the open," she said, looking at us again but not moving away from Graythor. "I came to this world specifically because it was so out-of-the-way, thinking I could hide here while I made up my mind. I had an important decision to make, and the distraction of that decision was what kept me from knowing the truth of this world until it was too late."

By then she was looking directly at *me,* and I felt a chill like few before it. If Rik hadn't still been holding

me I might have turned and run, not giving a damn
how much of a coward that made me.

"Laciel, my darling, you *must* understand how I feel
about you," she almost begged, all but putting out a
hand to me. "When I first took you in, it was because
I felt sorry for you, but it didn't take long to discover
there was nothing to feel sorry *about*. You were strong,
and courageous, and bright and loving, and I learned
how much I'd missed by never having children of my
own. You *became* my child, and I couldn't have loved
you more if you really had been mine.

"You were very happy being my daughter, but despite your happiness there was a cloud over your life.
You could never forget that your own people had
abandoned you, and I grew to hate those faceless,
thoughtless fools more than you ever could. They had
hurt *my* child, they had made her suffer, and if I could
have found out who they were they would have gone
up in a pillar of ravening blue fire!"

She was just about spitting the words rather than
talking, and Graythor was doing more to hold her still
than comfort her. I just sat there in shock, never
having dreamed Morgiana had been so—*wild!*—on the
subject. She'd never been anything but calmly disdain-
ing when the topic of my real people had come up,
and right then I couldn't think of a word to say.

"Yes, even though I never mentioned it, I spent all
of my spare time trying to trace your origins," she
went on, calming a little but still mostly scattered.
"The trail was years cold, the years you'd spent living
on the streets, but I refused to give up. I tried every
searching spell I knew and even had friends devise
new ones, but all I was able to discover was that you
weren't native to our world-dimension. Your original
resonance was faint and on the odd side, and I couldn't
seem to match it no matter where I went.

"And wouldn't you know it?" she asked with a
short, bitter laugh. "Not long after I gave up in total
disgust, the answer tumbled right into my hands. A
demon I met—a professional traveler who had worked

long enough to catalogue and list a full twentieth of one quarter-sector—it was telling me about worlds with odd resonances in their natives—actually we were exchanging information—and I threw in yours without stopping to think—and it knew where the world could be found—"

She stopped again to bite her lip, her eyes wide with misery, but now that she'd started there was no interrupting her.

"I suddenly didn't know what to do!" she said in an outburst, her beautiful dark eyes still staring at me. "The demon told me how to reach that world, and I just sat there not knowing what to do. If you'd still been a child, it would have been easy; I would have gone to that world and destroyed them for hurting my darling, but you *weren't* a child! You were a grown woman who deserved to be told, but how could I tell you? If you went there and found they'd had a good reason for abandoning you, or hadn't even done it themselves, you might have let yourself love them! I wouldn't have minded if I'd been sure it would have been 'love them, *too*,' but I couldn't bear the thought of your loving them *instead* of me. It's stupid and selfish, I know, but I couldn't help it. I just couldn't—"

This time the words ended in tears and sobbing, and Rik let me go as I rose to my feet, and Graythor moved aside to give me room to sit and hug her to me. She clung to me as though she were a small child, and no matter how disturbed I felt, I knew soothing her misery was the first and most important thing I had to do. She'd soothed *my* misery often enough, and it was time I returned the favor.

"Morgiana, listen to me," I said after a few minutes, still rocking her in my arms. "It's not selfish of you to not want me to stop loving you, it's downright stupid. Didn't you hear what Rik said? Love isn't something you turn on and off like a wall lamp, and I'll always love you."

"It *isn't* stupid," she muttered between sobs, needing to be comforted but at the same time wanting to refuse it. "I've seen things like that happen before, and no one's to blame. They'd become part of your life while you got to know each other, and I'd—fade into the past and distance as someone you *used* to know. But you're still entitled to meet them and know who they are, Laciel, so you have to go. I'll tell you how to find them . . ."

"Don't bother," I interrupted, using my best no-arguments voice, the one I'd learned from *her*. "I don't care who they are and I don't *want* to know them, just the way they didn't want to know me. If they'd been in the least interested, they could have come looking for me, but they didn't care to bother. Now I can't be bothered with *them*."

She tried to make a feeble kind of protest and everyone else had an opinion they wanted to mention, but I ignored it all. I didn't *want* to know about where I came from, and I wouldn't go anywhere near the place.

I wouldn't. I *wouldn't!*